CW01456697

A Prophecy of Chaos and Blood

A Prophecy of Chaos and Blood

Echoes of Darkness Book 2

Published by Skye Publishing

Copyright © 2025 Lucia Skye

No part of this publication may be reproduced, distributed, or transmitted in any form or by any means, including photocopying, recording, or other electronic or mechanical methods, without the prior written permission of the publisher, except in the case of brief quotations embodied in critical reviews and other non-commercial uses permitted by copyright law.

This book is a work of fiction. All names, characters, places, and incidents either are products of the author's imagination or are used fictitiously. Any resemblance to events, locales, or persons, living or dead, is coincidental.

The author acknowledges all song titles, song lyrics, film titles, film characters, trademarked statuses, brands mentioned in this book are the property of, and belong to their respective owners. The publication/use of these trademarks is not authorized/associated with, or sponsored by the trademark owners.

Lucia Skye is in no way affiliated with any of the brands, songs, musicians or artists mentioned in this book.

Editor: Ayden Rails

Proofreaders: Melina S (@mydadsaid_readabook), Roxana Coumans.

Art: Everything is painted digitally by the author.

Paperback ISBN: 978-1-0687616-5-2

E-book ISBN: *978-1-0687616-2-1*

All rights reserved ©

A Prophecy of Chaos and Blood

Lucia Skye

Content Warning

This book contains graphic violence and sexual content. It is not intended for anyone under the age of legal adulthood. All characters depicted herein are over 18 years of age.

Some contents within this book may be triggering or disturbing to some readers.

Reader discretion is strongly advised.

<u>Trigger warnings</u> include but are not limited to:

Alcohol consumption

Attempted suicide (not on page)

Anal Play

Blood

Death

Depression

Dubious Consent

Car accident

Fatphobia & body-shaming

(not by the MCs)

Gore

Gun violence

Grief & loss depiction

Kidnapping

Physical abuse

Raw sex

Restraint

Sexually explicit scenes

Strong language/profanity

Swallowing bodily fluids

Spanking/ impact play

Suicidal ideation

Talks of sexual assault

/attempted rape

Torture

Playlist

1. Brooke, Sam Tinnesz, Tommee Profitt - Forbidden Fruit
2. Sleep Token - Dangerous
3. Ari Abdul - Worship
4. Sleep Token – Provider
5. YUNGBLUD - I Was Made For Lovin' You
6. Aurora Olivas, Reed Wonder - The Machine
7. MIIA - Dynasty
8. Ari Abdul – Stay
9. Shaya Zamora – Cigarette
10. Billie Eilish – I Love You
11. Billie Eilish – No Time To Die
12. Sam Barber, Avery Anna – Indigo
13. Evanescence – Lithium
14. Sleep Token – Take Me Back to Eden
15. MVSSIE – Cold
16. Jared Benjamin – I'm The Sinner
17. Jutes – Vertigo
18. Jutes – Limerence
19. Jutes – Obsessed
20. Jacob Lee- Tragic Comedy
21. Jutes – Sleepyhead
22. Shaya Zamora – Sinner
23. Isabel Van Gelder – Die For You
24. Ari Abdul, Jutes – Red Velvet
25. VOILÀ - Figure You Out
26. Swedish House Mafia, The Weekend – Moth to a Flame
27. Jutes – Smut
28. Ari Abdul, Thomas LaRosa - Sinners
29. Sam Tinnesz, Shaya Zamora, Tommee Profitt – Lament
30. Halsey, Amy Lee - Hand That Feeds
31. Amber Run – I Found
32. Dove Cameron – Sand
33. Loreen – Tattoo Acoustic
34. Finneas- Break My Heart Again
35. Sleep Token – Blood Sport
36. Conan Grey – The Cut That Always Bleeds
37. Gracie Adams – I Love You, I'm Sorry
38. Lana del Rey- Love
39. Linkin Park – Two Faced
40. Ruelle – Game of survival

For those of you who choose to stay.
Another day. Another minute. Another second.
Even when the weight of the world presses too heavily on your shoulders. I hope you find that flicker of hope you lost to the shadows and the strength to smile again.
Because you are worthy.

And for those of you who are dying to
get Kaiden's POV, enjoy!
Now, spread these pages like a good girl.

1

Iris

Black cherries, rum, and fresh cloves — the heavenly scent envelops me like a cocoon. I don't want to leave this safe space, but a sharp throb in the back of my head makes me wince, and a pained moan tumbles out from deep within my chest before the Herculean effort to open my eyes is successful.

Warm orange light paints the walls of Kaiden's bedroom as I find myself in his bed again. Only this time, I don't feel healed. No. I'm on fire. On top of that, each jagged breath stabs me in the lungs. When I look down, I notice I'm dressed in an oversized tee, the lower half of my body covered by a black, silky sheet.

Sam is sleeping peacefully next to me. Resembling a crimson river, her hair is fanned out over the pillow while drool trickles down from her parted lips. She is wearing the same red dress from the club, holding my hand in slumber. Her grip is bruising—as if she's afraid I might disappear into thin air.

Untangling my fingers from hers, I try to push up, but the room starts twirling while an icepick pierces my brain. At the third attempt, I manage to shift upward a bit. A groan slips out. Sam jackknifes into a sitting position, blinking slowly, a disoriented look on her face. Her drowsy gaze jumps to me before she lets out a shrill cry that makes my teeth grind.

"Iris!" She throws her arms around my neck in a vise-like grip so fast I almost get whiplash. She starts sobbing, hiccups coming between each word. "You're a-awake! Th-a-ank the Goddess! And your eyes are back to n-normal."

"I can't breathe," I say. The words come out hoarse since my tongue weighs about a hundred pounds, and my throat is as dry as sandpaper.

"I thought you were dead when we found you."

"Sam—"

"I was worried sick."

"You're crushing my windpipe," I get out louder this time.

"I'm so happy you're not dead!"

"Sam!"

"What?" she asks through sniffles as she pulls back.

"It's a good thing I didn't die before because you almost choked me to death right now," I chuckle out, but the sound turns into a strangled whimper at the sharp stab of pain in my left side.

She wipes at her mascara-smeared cheeks and scowls at me. "Don't be a bitch; I thought I was going to lose my best friend. You don't know what that did to me." A look of utter sorrow passes over her features. "I'm so sorry for leaving you alone. I shouldn't have…I'm so stupid. This is all my fault—"

I cut her off. "It's not your fault."

2

"But—"

"But nothing. There's no way you could have known that motherfucker was going to drug and assault me in the back alley." I place my hand over hers on the bed and squeeze. "What did you mean by my eyes are back to normal?"

"Before you passed out, you looked at me, and your irises were a deep shade of violet, and the sclera was completely black. It was super freaky."

"Oh…"

"Do you remember what happened? Who did this to you? We found you beaten to a pulp next to a weird, decomposed body."

I white-knuckle the sheet. "I killed him," I whisper, my gaze burning a hole in the floor. The reality of what I've done comes crashing in at full speed.

I killed Erik.

Akin to lightning strikes, flashes of the attack invade my brain.

Fuckfuckfuckfuckfuckfuck.

Sam lifting my chin snaps me out of it. Wrath-filled emeralds spark with determination and a promise of vengeance. "Iris, look at me! You have nothing to feel guilty about."

"I…um…fuck—" Inhaling a few calming breaths, I drop my trembling fingers in my lap. "It was Erik. Grayson's grandson."

A muscle jumps in her taut jaw. "That fucking scumbag! His dead stare always creeped me out."

"Erik found me in the club and threatened to tell everyone in the Order that I was a demon-loving whore when I refused to kiss him." The tears blurring my vision spill over. "He had photos of me and Kaiden on his phone. He said Grayson put him up to it and he's been following me for a long time. That he knew it wouldn't be long before I showed my true nature and betrayed the Order." I sniffle. "I think he's been in my apartment, too. Someone stole some of my underwear, and things were slightly out of place. I chalked it up to me being tired and forgetful with all the crazy shit that's been happening since the umbra attack…but maybe it was him all along."

I shake my head. "Anyway, I think the motherfucker roofied me. Otherwise, he wouldn't have been able to overpower me. I was tipsy, clearly not that drunk. He must have slipped the drugs into my water when I got distracted by a ghost. Yeah, I saw another ghost to add to my crazy, and I know: stupid fucking decision to leave my glass unattended. I started feeling weird, and I desperately needed some fresh air, but I couldn't walk properly. It's all hazy; I kept blacking out. This guy took me outside and…and then Erik was there." Swallowing past the lump in my throat, I mumble, "He tried to, um…he tried to…rape me."

Sam resembles a tornado as she pushes off the bed to pace the length of the room in long strides. The undercurrent of Sam's magic electrifies the air before leafy vines spread up the walls. In two minutes flat, Kaiden's bedroom becomes a jungle.

"That sorry waste of oxygen! Motherfucking dickbag piece of shit!" she yells before she stomps back to the bed and plops down unceremoniously, the vines retreating until there's nothing left. "Sorry. You can continue now."

A soft smile tugs at the corners of my lips. "Feeling better?"

Her nostrils flare. "No. I wish I could strangle him right now. I would throw such vile hexes at him, Iris. He's lucky you killed him before I got my hands on that human version of period cramps."

I pull her into the tightest hug my battered body allows me. "I love you so fucking much, you know that?"

"I love you too, ho-bag. But I think I've aged at least thirty years these past months because of you. You owe me a lifetime of paying for my drinks when we go out."

"Deal." My smile dies when I remember Erik's words, and my eyebrows knit in a frown. "Do you remember those women found dead with 'demon whore' carved into their bodies?"

Sam inches backward, then gives me a confused look. "Huh? What women?"

"They found the last one in a back alley of a club in the Raven district the night before my birthday. You know, when the umbra came through the portal and attacked me in the forest. You were sipping wine on my bed when they announced it on the news."

"Oh yeah, I remember now. What about it?"

"Erik kept spewing some weird shit about how he needs to cleanse the demon from my body like he did to the other demon whores. His word choice was so specific. Because of the drugs, I couldn't grasp its significance at first. Then realization dawned…Sam, I think he killed those women. And I was supposed to be his next victim. Although, I also think he was the one behind the text Grayson sent me that night— the text that sent me into the trap. I mean, it would have been really easy for him to get ahold of Grayson's phone since he's his grandson. But it doesn't make sense why. Why send me into a trap if he planned on killing me all along?"

A knock comes from the open door. Fire and brimstone meet my gaze, and my pulse scatters. From under Kaiden's death grip on the doorframe, thick smoke wafts and the smell of burning wood fills the room. He surely heard our conversation because he looks downright murderous, the tendons in his hand threatening to snap from the pressure.

Sucking in a sharp inhale, he approaches the bed with measured steps. I don't miss the fury seeping out of his pores, akin to noxious fumes, or the charred imprint he left behind.

"How are you feeling?" Kaiden bends over me and gently traces my cheek with his knuckles before tucking a stray hair behind my ear. As always, his touch leaves a delicious wake of shivers behind.

Sam slaps her forehead. "Shit, I forgot to ask you that," she says guiltily from beside me.

"Like I got hit by a truck." I try to smile, but I'm sure it looks more like a grimace.

Kaiden's fingers curl into tight fists. "I'm going to run you a bath," he says in a raspy voice as he straightens and strides into the en suite bathroom, shoulders stiff.

"Sheesh. He's intense," Sam quips, throwing a side-eye my way.

"Yeah…"

"You should have seen him when we found you. He was feral. I had to fight him off you just so I could check if you still had a pulse. He also accidentally set the club on fire and somehow started an earthquake."

I gulp hard. I'm not ready to think about why he would be so affected by me getting hurt.

"Mmhm. I tried my best to heal you, but there was only so much I could do. Kaiden said his warlock friend, who healed you the last two times, had gone after that guy…what the fuck is his name?" She snaps her fingers a few times. "Adramelech! Lucifer's chancellor. He brought in his best doctor for you, though. You have a concussion and a few broken ribs. But, Iris, it's insane how fast you're healing. I mean, I'm not complaining, but it's weird because it surpasses your hellseeker abilities. At this rate, you should look good as new in a week."

"Well, that's not the only thing that's weird. I rotted Erik with my bare hands. How in the world was I able to do that? This…dark power electrified every cell in my body, and then it seemed to spill from me — like wisps of shadow. Don't get me wrong, I'm grateful this happened because otherwise…otherwise he would…he would have…" I gulp, unable to voice the words for a second time. "And as if this isn't crazy enough, I'm still seeing ghosts on top of everything. What is happening to me?" I whisper.

Sam's eyebrows shoot up almost to her hairline. "I'll start asking around.

But as far as I know, there's no being able to do what you did," she muses. "I know this is all insane, but we're not going to freak out, okay? You need to focus on getting better right now, and then we'll figure everything out."

"But—"

"Nu-uh. Healing first, freak out later." She stands and passes me a glass from the nightstand on her side. "Here. You should drink this; it will help speed up the recovery time."

Eyeing the suspicious brown liquid, I wrinkle my nose. "Do I even want to know what's in it?" My stomach clenches at the disgusting smell as I bring it to my lips.

"Nope. Now, drink up."

I gag at the first sip, but gulp it as fast as I can. "Fuck, it tastes worse than it smells. When did you even have the time to brew this atrocity and get the ingredients for it?"

"I told Kaiden what I needed. In less than half an hour, someone had already dropped off everything I asked for, even the rare bloodroot growing only at the highest peak in the Sacred Valley in Peru. I've been trying to find a supplier for this damn root for a fucking year, and he got it in twenty minutes."

Considering his cleaning obsession, I can't believe Kaiden allowed Sam to use his kitchen. She always leaves a disaster behind. I shudder in revulsion as I place the glass back on the nightstand before wiping my mouth with the back of my hand. "Where's the body?"

"I don't know…Kaiden took care of it."

"What day is it? Did I lose a lot of time?" Warmth pools in my belly as the disgusting potion starts working its magic. The headache immediately dulls while the white-hot pain pulsing in the side of my face becomes a distant throb.

"It's still Sunday."

I sigh in relief. "That's good. I'm working tomorrow night."

Sam sucks on her teeth. "Are you fucking kidding me right now? You need to heal. I'll strap you to this bed myself."

"Don't be ridiculous. You know this job is all I have," I huff.

She throws me an icy glare. "You also have me. And I don't appreciate you dying. You almost got killed three times in the span of two and a half months. That's beyond insane." She crosses her arms in front of her chest. "And how do you plan to go back to the Order and face Grayson? You killed his grandson."

I flinch. "I don't know, but I can't quit. You know how much this job means to me. Besides, don't you think it's going to look weird if Erik disappears and I take time off at the same time? Plus, if I quit, there's no going back. When you leave the Order, you leave for good."

She purses her lips in annoyance. "Maybe you're right, but I still don't like you being in danger. I swear my heart stopped for a full minute this morning."

I drop my gaze to the floor briefly, because I can't even imagine what she went through from the moment she found me, then take her hand in mine. "I understand you worry about me, but I could get killed in a demon fight every day. It comes with the job."

"Yeah, but this is different," she says, exasperated, before pulling back.

"I know." I fold my lower lip between my teeth to gnaw on it.

Kaiden clears his throat from the threshold. "The bath is ready," he says before turning around on his heel and stalking back into the bathroom.

"I think that's my cue to leave." Sam stands up from the bed to pick up her strappy, high-heeled sandals from the floor. "Do you want me to stay? Or maybe you want to go home? But I don't think you should move that much yet."

"No, it's fine. I'm okay here."

"That's what I figured." A wry grin tugs at her mouth. Then her eyebrows drop in a frown. "By the way, Noah's been blowing up your phone."

Pinching the bridge of my nose, I say, "Fuck. I texted him last night and told him he can take me out for dinner."

"You did that after you saw that Maeve bitch make herself at home in Kaiden's lap, right?"

I cringe hard and nod. My best friend knows me well. Now, I regret the hasty decision — not only because I was using Noah, and it wouldn't have been fair to do that to him, but also because Kaiden proved he only has eyes for me with those two earth-shattering orgasms in his office.

"I sent him a text pretending to be you, told him we went out, and that you got shit-faced and you're hungover as fuck. He called a few times, but I didn't answer; I sent him another text instead, saying you'll call him tomorrow. I also texted your aunt the same excuse since you were supposed to help her move those boxes from her basement this morning."

"Ah, shit. I completely forgot about that. I'll call her to reschedule. Thanks. You're a lifesaver."

She comes to my side of the bed, kisses my forehead. "I wouldn't leave, but I know you're in good hands." She winks at me. "There's some more of the healing potion in the fridge. Please drink it all."

I nod. "I'll call you."

"'Kay. Love you," Sam shoots back over her shoulder as she sashays out of the bedroom.

"Love you too," I say to her disappearing back.

2

Iris

Massaging my throbbing temples, I exhale a trembling breath. Sam is right. How am I going to face Grayson after killing his grandson? Just the thought of having to look him in the eye is a punch straight to the gut. He also clearly didn't buy my story of the umbra attack. Why else would he have assigned Erik to watch me?

"Ready for the bath?" Kaiden's smooth voice brings me back into the present. He's standing next to the bed, his big frame looming over me. The anger that shone in his gaze earlier dimmed down, only a glint of it still showing through. His hair is disheveled — as if he pulled at it in distress or ran his hands too many times through it. And he's still wearing the same black jeans and shirt from last night. Only, the shirt's all wrinkled and bloody. Dark circles paint his undereyes, but he's still as hot as sin and so beautiful it almost hurts to look at him.

"Yeah," I reply, and before I can make one move to get out of bed, Kaiden swoops me up in his arms and strides toward the bathroom. Fireworks go off at every point of contact between our bodies.

"I could have walked by myself," I mumble, heat scorching my cheeks.

"I don't want you to." He sets me down on the bathroom counter, the smooth marble cold under my naked thighs.

I clear my throat. "How much of my conversation with Sam did you overhear?"

"All of it."

"Oh," I breathe.

"I didn't mean to eavesdrop. I heard her screaming like a damn banshee, and I nearly had a heart attack thinking something had happened to you. Before I could pop into the room, I realized she was only reacting to you waking up. So, I waited outside until I couldn't anymore. I had to come in and make sure you were okay. Arms up."

"Why?"

He lifts an eyebrow as he looks down at me. "Do you usually take a bath with clothes on?"

"I think I can manage to undress myself," I scoff.

His nostrils flare. "Can you stop being so fucking stubborn just for one night? You almost died, and I thought I was going to lose my fucking mind when I saw you lying on the ground, beaten to within an inch of your life. Let me take care of you. This is more for *me* than it is for you," he blurts out the last part. The intensity of his gaze burns a fire trail straight to my soul. But more than that, it's the way his words poured out of him — like blood gushing out of a fresh wound — that steamrolls through my defenses.

And then guilt gnaws at my insides because he's right; I'm being difficult on purpose. Still, I'm a hellseeker, and he's an Elite demon.

Even us being in the same room together is forbidden. But every single moment shared with Kaiden blurs the lines of my reality a little more, making me question everything I know. If a demon is capable of so much compassion and a lightborn — a being blessed by the mighty archangels — could induce so much pain, then where do I stand in all of this?

He tugs at the hem of the oversized tee and pulls it over my head. Crooking his index fingers into the boxers I believe are his, he gently slides them over my hips. Eyes on me, Kaiden unbuttons his shirt. Then he takes off his jeans, followed by his underwear, leaving the clothes in a heap on the floor next to the ones he took off me. The need to memorize every inch of exposed bronzed skin with mine is all-consuming.

Kaiden's gaze travels the length of my body, which resembles a gruesome painting because of the caked blood splattered over bruises in various shades of purple, blue, and yellow. He steps closer and brings his fingers to the blemishes on my abdomen, his touch featherlight. Wrath stiffens his spine and shoulders.

"The violence burning in my veins, Iris. Fuck. You don't even know the lengths I would go to make that worthless piece of shit suffer. I want to revive him so I can skin him alive. I would use every ounce of power I have to kill him in the most torturous way I can think of. And then I would bring him back to life and resume the torture. I would continue doing so for all eternity."

Framing his stubbled cheek, I say, "It's okay. He can't hurt me anymore. Thank you…for saving me. For what must be the hundredth time."

Kaiden leans into my touch. "I didn't. You saved yourself." Something akin to pride shines in his gaze. "I just found you."

"Well, thank you anyway for taking care of me," I whisper while dragging my thumb along the shape of his perfect lips. A shudder passes through him. It's a heady feeling, Kaiden being affected by me. We are so close that the mesmerizing dance of gold and red in the obsidian sea of his eyes makes me dizzy. Drinking him in, I let my palms travel over the intricate tattoos on his torso. I gasp when the pads of my fingers sweep over numerous raised scars. "Whoa, Kaiden. What happened to you?"

Kaiden tenderly wraps his hands around my wrists and stops me from touching him further. A muscle jumps in his cheek. "My father."

I sweep over every inch of exposed skin on Kaiden's body with newfound scrutiny. He mentioned the dark room before but left out the part that gave him this many scars. I can't believe I haven't noticed them before. But I realize now that besides that day I woke up in his penthouse for the first time, I haven't seen him naked. The tattoos cover them so well, though. If you didn't know exactly where to look, you could easily miss the puckered skin and the faint white marks.

What kind of monster does this? I push down the smelted rage that overtakes me, threatening to spill over, before saying, "I'm sorry you had to go through that."

"It was a long time ago."

"Still…I'm sorry," I murmur and bend, brushing my lips over one of the marks on his chest. He sucks in an unsteady breath as I pepper kisses on all the visible scars.

"Angel," he rasps, letting go of my wrists to grab my chin softly between his fingers and tilt it upward. The emotion shining in the obsidian sea sends my pulse into overdrive.

I close my eyes as he bends, ready to feel his plush lips over mine. But bitter disappointment thickens in my veins like syrup when, instead, he slides his forearms under my thighs and picks me up again. Stepping over the rim of the bathtub, he sinks us both into the hot water with my back to his front in between his muscular thighs.

He washes me methodically, without lingering too much in one place. His touch isn't sexual by any means. Still, his growing erection digging in my back makes it clear how much he wants me. When his fingers whisper against the skin on my inner thighs, my lips part on a sharp inhale, and a slow burning fire pulses through me. He doesn't inch up, though.

Instead, he starts lathering my hair while his fingers massage my scalp. I've never felt more precious, more cared for than in this moment. A moan escapes me, and his cock twitches at the sound, followed by a rugged exhale. However, he still doesn't act on it and uses the detachable showerhead to rinse me.

When Kaiden finishes, he lifts me out of the tub, places me on my feet, and pats me dry. He then wraps me in a fluffy towel. Popping off, he lets me take care of my business. As I'm about to exit the bathroom, he appears out of thin air at the door, wearing only a pair of basketball shorts. My brain short circuits at how insanely gorgeous he is. The shorts hang low on his trim waist, accentuating the V lines on each side of his sculpted abs. He also has that happy trail of hair pointing south that I'm dying to follow down with my tongue.

I lift my arms for him to slide another one of his delicious-smelling T-shirts over my head. In a swift move, Kaiden picks me up in his arms again, brings me to the bed, and sits me on top of it. He vanishes and reappears a few seconds later, holding a hairbrush. I extend my hand to take it from him, but he shakes his head before sitting next to me. His movements are soft as he brushes my hair wordlessly from tips to roots.

"You should rest," he says before standing and laying down the hairbrush on the bedside table. "I'll be two doors down in my office if you need me."

I grab his wrist to stop him. "Stay."

Kaiden looks over his shoulder at me, a deep frown etched on his forehead. "I can't," he rasps, licking at his lower lip.

"I don't want you to go."

He avoids my gaze. "There's nothing else I want more in this world than to spend every second alongside you. And if it were up to me, I would chain you to my body and never leave this bed. But, after what you went through, I'm afraid I might hurt you. I just..." He swallows thickly. "I'm terrified that me touching you will bring back memories of what that piece of shit did to you...and I can't...I...Fuck."

"But—"

His eyes snap back to mine as he cuts me off. "I can't trust myself around you. I want you too much, Iris. You can't even comprehend the depth of what I feel for you. I crave you more than a heroin addict searching for his next fix. And that's not what you need. Not right now. I don't want to take advantage of your fragile state."

"Don't say I'm fragile. I'm not made of fucking glass," I clip out. "What if *I* want you to touch me? That bastard almost took something from me I could never get back. But he didn't break me." I swallow the vise that threatens to choke me. "I want you. Please!" I don't care if I sound desperate. I know that a man's hands on me is not something I should want in this moment, not after what that scumbag tried taking from me.

The sad reality is that we live in a world ruled by men, and society stigmatizes women who embrace their sexuality. Let's not even talk about seeking that sort of connection after being sexually assaulted. The accusing fingers somehow always turn on the victim.

What was she wearing? How short was her dress? What did she do to attract his attention?

She was asking for it.

She's a slut.

She wanted it.

These words kindle a spark inside me that picks up speed until it becomes a firestorm. Why should I let *them* dictate how I heal? Aren't women's bodies policed enough as is? Well, fuck everyone who thinks they can tell me what I can and cannot do with *my* body. They don't own me.

My body, my fucking choice.

I push away the shame and the dirty feeling that clings to me like a petrol stain. "I am choosing this. Your touch is what I need right now. Erase him from my skin, Kaiden."

His fingers twitch as if it's physically painful not to make a move toward me.

"Plea—"

Kaiden disappears and blinks into existence on top of me, settling between my thighs while caging me in, bracing his weight on his forearms. He slants his lips over mine in a scorching kiss that sets me ablaze. My head spins as his silken tongue dances expertly against mine, and I lose myself in this blissful moment. He flips us. The yelp of surprise I let out as he settles me on top of his hips turns into a pained grunt when my ribs scream in protest.

"Fuck. I'm so sor—"

"I'm fine."

"Okay. If we do this, Iris, you'll have to take everything you want from me. You're in the driver's seat, and I'm the luckiest son of a bitch in the world, riding along on the best journey of my life. I will not make a move unless you tell me to."

I sink my teeth into my lower lip, unsure what to do next, letting Kaiden's words wash over me. Determination soon settles in, and even though I'm insecure as fuck because of my limited experience, I won't let it ruin this moment for me.

I discard my tee on the floor. "I want your hands and mouth on my breasts. I love it when you suck my nipples."

His gaze smolders as it rakes over my curves. "You're pure perfection, angel. Nothing in this world compares to your beauty."

Kaiden props himself up against the pillow in a sitting position beneath me. His hands glide to my breasts, his thumbs circling my areolas. Dipping down, his breath ghosts against my skin before his lips latch onto my nipple. A desperate whimper tumbles free from my parted lips in response. He alternates between them, sucking, biting, and licking until I'm a dripping, soaking mess over his hard body.

"I can't take it anymore. Touch me. Please."

"Where do you want me to touch you, angel?"

"You know…"

"Say it!" he commands in a raspy voice.

"On my pussy." Anticipation for what's to come makes me feel like a string pulled too tight on a bow, ready to snap at any moment. "Please!" I cry out.

His fingers travel to the space between my legs, but he just holds them there.

I let out a frustrated huff. "Slide your thumb over my clit and use your fingers to fuck me."

He smirks as he sinks two thick fingers inside me. He draws them all the way back out and then pushes them back in, setting an unrelenting pace, curling them against my front wall, and reaching a spot that makes me see stars. I moan when his thumb starts tracing wet circles on my pulsing clit. But I need *more*.

"Stop," I tell him, and Kaiden obeys. Chest bouncing, I say, "I want your mouth on my pussy. Now!"

"Fuck me. You're spectacular when you're bossy." He gives me a roguish smile that steals the breath from my lungs, then he settles back on the pillow, knitting his fingers beneath his head.

"What are you doing?"

"You said you wanted my mouth. So come ride my face, love."

"Oh." He wasn't kidding when he said I'm in the driver's seat.

As I'm about to move, an idea pops into my head. I slide off Kaiden's basketball shorts before throwing them on the floor on top of my T-shirt. His massive cock juts out, and my mouth waters. I need to taste him. I'm so nervous my whole body is shaking, but what the hell…he told me to get what I want. So I do just that. I turn around, straddle Kaiden backwards, and sit on his face, my pussy directly over his mouth.

I put all my weight on my elbow while using my other hand to grip the base of his shaft, and I take him into my mouth to the back of my throat. Kaiden lets out a surprised hiss as a violent shudder wracks his body. This time, I don't gag. I would pat myself on the back if I could. Flattening my tongue, I run it along the underside of his cock before I stop at the crown and swirl it around the tip. Then, I suck it as if it's a lollipop, his piercing cold against my heated skin.

"Fuck, angel! You're going to be the death of me. That feels so good." His fingers bite into my ass cheeks as he inhales me deeply. "You're dripping all over my mouth. Is this all for me?"

I mumble a response around his length as I bob my head up and down.

My toes curl when his wicked tongue sneaks out and licks the length of my slit. "C'mon, angel, ride my face. I want to suffocate in your cum."

Gyrating my hips over his mouth, I suck Kaiden off like it's the last thing I'll do. He moves his tongue in mind-numbing circles around my clit and then brings it down to my entrance, spearing it before sliding it in and out of me. Pleasure obliterates my synapses. My back arches.

I cry out as the release burns through me with the power of a ravaging wildfire, leaving me in a pile of ashes. I'm sure the entire building can hear me. But I simply don't give a fuck. The groan Kaiden lets out as he follows me over the edge is sexy as fuck. I swallow greedily the jetting salty ropes of cum. He slows his pace but doesn't stop until he draws out the last aftershock and twitch from my body. I feel him move as I float a few inches above the bed before losing my grasp on reality.

When I come back to my senses, Kaiden is lying down next to me, his head propped on his bent arm. The glint in his eyes is electric as his knuckles caress the side of my face. "So beautiful. So responsive," he says, voice low, hypnotic. "Can I kiss you?"

"Yeah," I breathe, and he closes the gap between us. I can taste myself on his tongue. We kiss and kiss and kiss until we become a storm of battling tongues, writhing bodies, and tangled limbs. I don't know where I end and he begins. Soon enough, the fire that was quenched inside me a few moments ago is stoked anew. I let my fingers coast down before wrapping them around Kaiden's throbbing erection. He shudders in response as we continue kissing.

I pull back after a few moments. "I want you. All of you."

His Adam's apple bobs hard in his throat. "Are you sure?"

"I am."

A deep frown etches on his forehead. "I don't have condoms."

"I'm on the shot," I tell him. "They're mandatory for all members who date outside the Order. So, if you're clean…we don't have to use a condom." The Order only allows us to date humans if we don't marry or have children. Very few do, though. I was the only one in Ashville — yet another thing that makes me an outcast.

"I'm clean."

"Well, I've never had sex before, so I'm clean too," I blurt out, then cringe. I didn't intend to ever tell him that.

He sucks in a sharp breath. "What? You're a virgin? I mean…I felt how tight you were, but I never assumed…And you want me to be your first?" he rasps.

Sawing my lower lip between my teeth, I nod, not knowing what to say as the heat in my cheeks spreads all the way to the tips of my ears.

"Fuck, angel. You wreck me," he says, emotion threading his voice. Kaiden snaps his eyes shut. When he opens them again, the blazing crimson and gold in the obsidian void makes me melt into the mattress. "I don't deserve you, but I'm going to take everything you're willing to give me because you're everything I ever wanted. Everything I ever dreamed about."

He watches me through heavy lids as I straddle him and slide my clit over his length, rocking up and down, using my arousal as lubrication. Needing to feel his skin against mine, I lean forward. We're chest to chest. Hearts pounding at the same ardent rhythm. My hand trembles as I position the head of his fat cock to my entrance and try to slide down, but it doesn't work. I'm too tight, and he is too big. A cry rips out of me. Chancing a look down, I realize he's only halfway in. Frustrated tears spring to my eyes while my muscles tense up. "Fuck!"

Kaiden interlaces our fingers. "Relax, angel," he murmurs in the shell of my ear. "Can I touch you?"

I nod through a sharp inhale.

His hand glides down between us to the apex of my thighs. His taut muscles, and bulging veins show he's barely restraining himself, but he doesn't move. He just lets me adjust to his size as he circles my clit while his lips trace a fiery path on the column of my throat. Under the maddening assault on my nerve endings, my muscles relax. The pained whimpers are soon replaced by wanton moans. Craving more of him, I undulate my hips slowly. Pleasure entwines with pain.

"Fuck me, Kaiden," I pant. "I need you to move. Please!"

"Is my angel desperate for my cock?"

"Yes!"

Kaiden lets out a sharp curse as I begin riding him with abandon. "Your pussy was made for me, Iris." *Thrust.* "You're taking my cock so well." *Thrust* "You're so tight." *Thrust.* "So goddamn perfect!" *Thrust.* "You unravel me. I would do anything for you. Anything." Every roll of his hips has his piercing hitting my G-spot. Sparks fly between us while the sounds of pleasure echo off the walls.

"So good…aaah…Kaiden." I meet every thrust, chasing the high desperately, begging for more. And harder. And deeper. He is a sight to behold, jaw slack, pouty lips parted, and eyes at half-mast. A fine sheen of perspiration coats his glorious body as his muscles ripple under me. Kaiden drowning in our shared ecstasy will forever be etched onto my brain.

"Be a good girl and come all over my cock, angel!"

He pushes me to the brink of madness, and I lose myself in his rapture. The orgasm rips through me like a tsunami. His name tumbles from my lips as my walls pulse against his cock.

"Fuuuuuuuck," Kaiden growls while his body shudders, his cum filling me to the brink. Our gazes lock. Lips parting on a shaky inhale, something flashes in the confinement of his irises. It's equal parts awe and disbelief. There's also something more that I can't quite put my finger on, but it enthralls me as if I'm spellbound.

Our connection runs deeper than anything I have ever felt, like our souls are reaching for each other and grasping on for dear life. He frames my face and kisses me so slowly, so reverently, as if he's afraid I might disappear. One of his arms bands across my middle while the other caresses my nape.

If the first kiss we shared was transcendental, now I feel as though he's imprinted himself in the very fabric of my soul. And I know without a doubt that my fear has come true. Kaiden has ruined me for anyone else. I am forever altered by him.

"How are you feeling?" he asks after a few beats of silence.

"Sore, but it was worth it," I say on a giddy sigh before placing a soft kiss at the hollow of his throat.

"Do you want me to run you another bath?"

"Too tired," I mumble and burrow my nose in the crook of his neck, inhaling deeply. The heady scent of sex mingled with his cologne is the best kind of drug shooting up my veins. When he threads his fingers

through my hair, it only takes seconds for me to fall asleep in Kaiden's arms. At some point, his body heat is gone, and I feel a warm, wet cloth between my legs, but I'm too busy floating in a galaxy of pleasure to care.

3

Iris

I open my eyes to a dark room. A few streaks of silver light shine through the floor-to-ceiling windows, only a portion of the moon visible through the thick blanket of clouds. Sweat dots my hairline. I realize the reason I'm feeling as though I'm lying near a blissfully searing fire is Kaiden's body wrapped around mine, radiating heat.

Untangling myself from him, I pat my hand on the nightstand to search for my phone. The sudden burst of light when I find it burns my retinas. I blink a few times for my vision to adjust. I'm glad to see that, despite a crack down the middle, the screen still functions. As Sam said, I have numerous missed calls from Noah and a few texts, but I don't bother looking through them yet. She must have charged it, too, because the battery is full. The clock shows it's a little past midnight, and I'm dying of thirst.

I get up slowly, not wanting to wake Kaiden. He looks so peaceful in his sleep — eyebrows relaxed, lips parted, while the shadows dance with the streaks of moonlight along the hard planes of his body, accentuating his mesmerizing tattoos and sinewy muscles. He is breathtaking and entirely otherworldly. I could stand here forever watching him and not get bored in the slightest.

'Cause that's not creepy at all, Iris.

I use the screen light from my phone to search for the tee Kaiden dressed me up in earlier. I find it under the bed and slide it on. After taking care of my business in the bathroom, I tiptoe until I reach the door and shuffle out of the bedroom, making my way to the kitchen on the first floor. I stop at the bottom of the stairs to look through the floor-to-ceiling windows.

The glimmering city lights resemble tiny diamonds. Now that I can compare this view with the last time I woke up here, I can say I much prefer it at night. It's easy to understand the appeal of having the world sprawled at your feet. But then it hits me. The blinding sun reflects through these massive windows at daytime and bathes the entire penthouse. This is why Kaiden chose to live here — not to feel like a king, but to be as close to the sunlight as he could get. To somehow erase the years his father had kept him locked in the dark.

Every time I unwrap another layer of who Kaiden is, I inevitably fall harder. I wait for that crippling guilt of losing my virginity to an Elite demon to rear its ugly head…but it never does. Instead, I feel at peace, as though my soul has been forever searching for its missing half. Turns out, Kaiden had it all along.

However, the peace doesn't last long. In fact, it's the newfound serenity that reminds me I almost died the day before, and triggers the constant state of fight or flight I've been in for the last two months. *Fuck.* My lungs constrict while flashes of Erik's attack play behind my eyelids.

Pressing my hand to the center of my chest and leaning my forehead on the cold glass, I inhale and exhale slowly until the panic subsides.

On shaky legs, I stride to the fridge, take out a water bottle, and down its contents in three gulps. When my ears are working again, a constant *drip, drip, drip* makes me turn around. The sound is made by the greenish slimy goop trickling down the counter and onto the marble floor, where a disgusting puddle has already formed. A surprised laugh bubbles out of me at the destruction left behind by Hurricane Sam—splattered walls and stove; the blender turned on its side, which seems to be the source of the goop splatters; the breakfast bar buried under ingredients. This is worse than I imagined. I'm surprised Kaiden didn't suffer an aneurysm.

"NO!" Kaiden's blood-curdling scream breaks through the dead silence of the penthouse. I drop the bottle. A loud thud resounds when it smacks the floor. Luckily, it's plastic, so it doesn't shatter.

The penthouse must be under attack. I can't imagine any other reason for him to yell in that manner. I grab a knife from the magnetic strip mounted on the wall and ignore the way my ribs stab my lungs as I sprint toward the bedroom at warp speed. Squaring my shoulders to prepare for the incoming fight, I press the blunt edge of the blade to my forearm before barreling into the room. My eyes sweep the perimeter, taking stock of the situation. But there isn't anyone in here except Kaiden.

He is thrashing in his sleep. Incoherent grunts and sounds of agony tumble free from his lips while his fingers fist the silky sheets and sweat courses in rivulets on his exposed skin.

"Kaiden," I call out his name softly as I approach the bed, dropping the knife on top of the bedside table. He doesn't hear me. I know from personal experience that it would be better if I let the nightmare run its course and not wake him until the episode is over. But I can't stand anymore the weird feeling folding my lungs in two at seeing the anguish painted on his face. So, I lie next to him, trying not to get hit in the process, then frame his stubbled cheek with my hand. "Kaiden," I whisper again.

His eyes fly open, the abject terror of the nightmare lingering in his gaze as it slams into mine. In the next breath, I'm pulled under Kaiden's muscular frame. My ribs scream in protest at the jolt. He looks manic — gold and crimson crashing in the tumultuous obsidian sea.

"You're okay. You're alive. You're here," he repeats like a mantra as though he's trying to reassure himself that I'm not a figment of his imagination. His trembling fingers coast over every inch of my body, his eyes glistening through a curtain of unshed tears. Amidst whole body jitters, he envelops me in a hug like I'm the only thing tethering him to sanity.

A few seconds later, Kaiden's lips crash into mine. There's nothing soft about the way he kisses me. It's desperate. Bruising. Consuming. He sucks the soul right out of my body as his lips and tongue move against mine. Without preamble, he pops off. Only to appear standing at the foot of the bed, startling me. His chest heaves. "Fuck, fuck, fuck! I'm so sorry; I shouldn't have jumped you —"

"It's oka —"

I have never seen Kaiden so distraught. His next words pour out of him in an incoherent mess as he fists his hair, cutting me off. "No, it's not, not after what you went through. I just…I wasn't thinking. Please, Iris, forgive me."

Jumping out of the bed, I stride to him, ignoring the explosion of pain at the swift move. I place my hands on his jaw and lock our gazes. "I'm okay. And I love when you touch and kiss me as if it's your last time. I want *you* as much as you want me. You hear me?"

He rests his forehead against mine, his next words nothing more than a gravely rasp. "I need to hold you."

Wordlessly, I take his hand in mine and lead him back to the bed.

We lie down, and Kaiden drapes me across his chest. "Do you want to talk about it?" I ask as I trace imaginary circles over his chest tattoos.

"Not necessarily," Kaiden replies. He sighs, though, and after a while, his voice fills the air. "When I was a kid, I used to get nightmares about the times my father tortured me. I told you about my shattered hope that my mother would eventually come to rescue me from his clutches. She took the appearance of a mortal woman and seduced my father. Only for her to abandon me on the steps of the same facility where my father locked me up. He tortured me daily, calling me an abomination, telling me over and over again that I should have never been born because I ruined his life. Even when I escaped, he followed me into my nightmares." We sit in silence for a few seconds. "I used to think those nightmares were the worst thing my mind could torment me with—until tonight. Tonight, I dreamed about you." His voice is rough, anguished. "It was a replay of the moment I found you lying in the alley at the back of the club…only your heart was not beating anymore." His arms tighten around me as he expels the air in his lungs.

Why does he care so much about me?

Lifting my head, I take in his striking features—soot-black lashes fanning across angular cheekbones, full lips turned down, forehead scrunched in anguish. Unable to resist the impulse, I close the space between us. Kaiden's expression instantly softens when our lips meet.

It's the first time I have initiated a kiss between us. Kaiden groans in my mouth. He kisses me like he's drowning, and I'm the last breath of air left in the atmosphere. I return the sentiment, and we get lost in each other until the first rays of the sunrise trickle in through the windows.

4

Iris

The sky glows in a kaleidoscope of colors. It creates a bruised background for the dipping sun as I descend the stairs to the first floor of the penthouse.

I woke up half an hour ago, alone this time, and after I called my aunt, I shuffled to the bathroom, wincing at how tender the area between my legs still was. An array of brand-spanking-new women's toiletries greeted me from the counter—the packaging looked so luxurious I was afraid to touch anything. After making myself presentable, I made my way to the dressing room to grab another one of Kaiden's T-shirts. However, I stopped dead in my tracks when I saw that half of the room was now filled with women's clothes—rows upon rows of designer dresses, shirts, pants, jeans, athletic wear, and all types of shoes, from stilettos to sneakers and flip-flops. Let's not talk about the luxurious, color-organized, lacy lingerie. Flustered, I grabbed a pair of seamless panties and one of Kaiden's black button-downs and dashed out of there as if hellhounds were nipping at my heels.

My eyes land on Kaiden's spectacular back when I reach the last step. He's dressed in his usual classy black attire, his strong, tattooed forearms flexing as he fixes a plate at the kitchen counter. All the moments we shared in his bedroom—consumed by pleasure—replay in my mind, and I flush all over.

"Why did you get out of bed? I was going to bring these to you," he says as he turns to look at me, a taco in his hand. "How are you feeling?"

I lean my hip on the cold marble of the bar. "I'm good. My ribs still hurt like a motherfucker, but that thing Sam made me drink is amazing. I can't believe how well it worked despite the disgusting taste. The bruises are already fading."

From the bag on the counter, I notice he ordered tacos from *Tu Tía Loca*, my favorite Mexican restaurant in Ashville. It's a hole-in-the-wall type of joint, and the food is exquisite.

"Go sit on the couch; I'll bring these to you."

"I can eat at the bar," I say and pull out the bar stool closest to me. I'm always messy when eating tacos, and I don't want to ruin his cream couch, which I'm sure costs more than the GDP of a small country.

"The bar stool is too stiff for you to sit comfortably, given the state of your ribs. Couch, now," he commands in a gruff tone with no room for argument.

"Fine, but if any sauce gets on it, it's on you," I huff before striding to the couch, gingerly taking a seat.

Kaiden joins me a few minutes later, then hands me a few napkins and a shrimp taco-filled plate. He pops off, only to rematerialize a few seconds later with a glass of Sam's healing concoction in one hand and another taco-filled plate in the other.

His satisfied gaze roves over my body languidly as he places the glass on the coffee table, then his eyebrows furrow. "You didn't like the clothes I picked out for you? Don't get me wrong, you look sexy as fuck, and I only want to see you wearing my shirts when we're at home, but if you want, we can get other clothes," he says before lifting a taco to his mouth to take a huge bite.

When we're at home?

"The clothes are beautiful, but Kaiden, it's too much. All the skincare and makeup products. You shouldn't have spent so much money. I can't accept any of—"

"Don't tell me how to spend my money, Iris. I wanted to get the best for you, so I did. Plus, I'm richer than God; what I spent on the clothes and toiletries didn't even scratch the surface of my finances."

Warmth filters through me, but there's so much to unpack there. He's acting as if we're in a long-term relationship and we live together. His words imply that we have a future together, but that's impossible; I'm a hellseeker, and he's a demon. There's no future for us. However, too quickly I realize that's exactly what I want.

Fuckfuckfuckfuckfuck.

I know I have fallen for Kaiden over the past few weeks, but it suddenly feels much deeper than that—as if I've been in love with him for years. No, that's crazy! He's a demon. Plus, I've just met him. I should end things before one of us gets hurt, but I can't. Only the thought of being away from Kaiden sears like acid in my veins. He asks me something. However, it passes right over my head since I'm too busy freaking out on the inside. "Huh?" I mumble.

"I asked if you're not hungry."

"Yeah, I am...I um, I got lost in my thoughts for a second there." I bite into a taco. He got my order to a *T*, down to the extra avocado and Oaxaca cheese. It's delicious, but it's hard to swallow through the knot in my throat. Still, I finish it because I need my strength back, and I can't even remember the last time I ate something.

"Sam mentioned Malik went after Adramelech," I tell him.

Kaiden nods and swallows his bite. "Yeah, he did a location spell, but it was a dead end. By the time he and Dominic arrived, Adramelech was gone, and they weren't able to pick up his trail anymore. A dark witch probably helped him disappear. He owns a few houses all over the country. They're checking each one before coming back."

I scarf down the second taco before saying, "What if they don't find him, and Lucifer learns we kidnapped his chancellor? Have you thought about that?"

"It crossed my mind once or twice," he responds, as composed as ever.

"Well, what if he retaliates? What are we going to do?"

He lifts an eyebrow. "*We* will not do anything because *I'm* going to take care of it, and you're going to rest and heal."

I scoff. "How will you take care of it?"

"I'll go to Hell and search for him."

"Oh," I murmur. "But I don't understand how he got away. The basement in your building is safer than the freakin' Pentagon."

"He manipulated two of the wolf shifters working security— Adramelech's serpentine eyes have the magical ability to hypnotize people. I forgot to tell you about it because his influence doesn't work on lightborn or me, so I didn't deem it important at the time. But my head of security warned the wolf shifters before bringing in a…different prisoner not to engage with him or throw a look his way. However, the bastard lured them to his cell regardless of their precautions. All hell broke loose. He got his hands on a knife and sliced their throats. Not before compelling them to spill all the security codes to access the locks and the elevator."

"Fuck. Did Malik erase his memories, at least?"

Kaiden's jaw clenches. "No. We were afraid it would affect his long-term memory, so we wanted to wait until I was sure I couldn't get anything more from him."

I gulp. "So now, on top of everything, I have to look over my shoulder for that bastard, too. I imagine he's not too happy I gouged out one of his magical eyes."

"Iris, I would never let anything happen to you. Trust me."

There's a pause as I absorb his words because I do trust him, even if I shouldn't. Heaving out a weighted sigh, I say, "We need to find out what the prophecy says. We need an oracle."

Before Adramelech escaped, he gave up information about a prophecy and that the seraphim had put a secret clause in the Celestial Treaty that obligated Lucifer to banish the umbra into the farthest corner of Hell. He also implied my mother's death was not caused by a demon because her name was never written in some stupid ledger Lucifer keeps in his Hell palace. This reminds me that the first thing I need to do when going back to the compound is search for my mother's file.

"I agree," he muses, sliding his empty plate onto the coffee table. "But it's not going to be easy. Oracles are fae, and there hasn't been one in the human realm in hundreds of years—that we know of, at least. However, now that the war is driving the fae back here, maybe we'll get lucky. I already put feelers out."

Kaiden's right. The only oracles known to history were fae. Even hellseekers are aware of this fact. Because of their highly addictive blood, vampires hunted the fae almost to extinction. So, five hundred years ago, they fled back to Faerie. However, according to Ophelia—the fae woman I met when the vampires kidnapped me—a war started about fifty years ago between the Seelie and Unseelie courts. Trying to escape its harrowing consequences, some of the fae crossed back into the human realm. So, I guess the only thing we can do now is wait and see what Kaiden's contacts find.

After a few beats of silence, I'm not able to hold back my curiosity. "What is Hell like?" I ask. "The Order didn't teach us much about it aside from it being split into the Kingdom of Shades, the City of Ghosts, and the Desert of Despair."

"Well, first off, it's hot as fuck, but it's the kind of dry heat that seems to scorch your lungs from the inside out before coating them in tar. I fucking hate going there. The sulfurous smell still clings to you for weeks on end after you cross back to the human world. And it's like the topside's dark mirror, so you can also find cities and mountains, a sea, and a desert. But the buildings are ramshackle, and they're brimming with vermin and various demons. Also, the sky is a deep crimson — as if made of a river of blood." There's a pause as he gathers his words. "You already know that Lucifer is the ruler above everything and everyone, except the City of Ghosts. His gargantuan gothic castle sits right in the middle. Then, the lands expand from there like spokes on a wheel toward the nine citadels that form the Kingdom of Shades. Each of them belongs to a king of Hell. It's in the Kingdom of Shades I do my business."

"Have you ever been to the City of Ghost or the Desert of Despair?"

He flicks his gaze to the floor, then drags it back to me. "No. The City of Ghosts is off-limits since it's ruled by Azrael, the Angel of Death, and filled with fallen angels and infernal spirits condemned to eternal damnation. It's situated right at the border to the bridge over the river Acheron — where the fate of souls is decided. And the Desert of Despair is just that, a desert formed by wastelands. So there was no point in ever going there. No one even knows how far it expands."

"Where are you going to look for him? Are two days even enough?"

"A day here is a week in Hell, so that means I'll have two weeks at my disposal. It's not enough time to request audiences with the kings, but I will start in the citadels where I know Adramelech had contacts and work my way from there."

My eyebrows drop. "Aren't you going to be in danger, though?"

"Let's just say I'm not going to be well received. My position within the Conclave is coveted, and Lucifer hasn't shown his face to allow demons passage to the human realm in a long time, even though he was supposed to. But I don't believe I will be in immediate danger."

"Okay," I breathe. His words do nothing to reassure me, though, because I can't help but worry about him, and he hasn't even left. Using a napkin to dab my mouth, I change the subject. "Given the fact that you overheard me and Sam talking, I believe you also heard something about the text Grayson sent me?"

He grunts in response.

Ugh, he's such a man.

"I didn't tell you this before, but the night the umbra came through the portal, I received a text from Grayson with the mission to track and kill the fake covetorax demons. I don't think he sent it, though. I investigated it, but it was all a dead end until Erik found me at Sin, and I thought he had set me up. However, while he tried to kill me in the back alley…I let go of that idea. He wanted to kill me himself, not let demons do it." My fingers tighten around the plate while the tacos threaten to make a reappearance. "And you already know he was watching me — us. He was going to show Grayson the photos he took of us together." Panic sinks its sharp claws into me. "What if he already did?"

Kaiden scoots closer to me and untangles my fingers, discarding the plate on the table next to his. He pulls me gently onto his lap to face him. His big hand wraps around my jaw. "This okay?"

"Yeah," I mumble as his mesmerizing eyes capture mine.

His other hand travels to my chest to place his palm right over my heart. "C'mon, take a deep breath. We're going to take things in stride, and we're going to find a solution. Together."

"Okay," I say after swallowing a lungful of calming air.

Kaiden takes a moment to mull over what I told him. "As far as I'm aware, Grayson is as straitlaced as they come. But you never know what a person could hide. Did you mention the text to him?"

"Yeah. He looked confused, and then he said he couldn't have sent me a text because he'd misplaced his phone, only to find it the next morning." I swallow thickly. "He's already suspicious of me...and I'll look even worse in his eyes now that Erik is dead. It won't be long until he catches on," I say, sawing my lower lip between my teeth again.

Kaiden's burning gaze drops to my mouth as if he's hypnotized. "I need to kiss you. Is that okay?"

Electricity crackles in the air between us. I nod, all my worries about Grayson dissipating like smoke in the wind. Those can wait. His thumb frees my trapped lip before he dips, using the tip of his tongue to trace a fiery path on it. The hand he placed earlier on my chest glides to the curve of my hip as I sneak out my tongue to meet his. The kiss starts slow, but soon enough, we're devouring each other, and I melt into a pile of goo in his arms.

"Fuck, I could do this for hours," Kaiden rasps while he grabs my ass to glue my front to his. "Days." His hands sneak beneath my shirt to rub my taut nipples between his fingers. "Weeks." A breathy moan slips through my parted lips, which he swallows with undisguised hunger. "Years." I gyrate my hips over his massive hard-on, seeking friction, and my fingers thread through his silky, coal-black strands to pull at them. "Forever."

The sound of a phone ringing slices through the air. Kaiden lets out a disgruntled groan from deep within his chest as he inches back, eyes wild and lips puffy and red. "I have to take this, unfortunately."

"'Kay." I scowl, then slump to the side to allow him to get up. He stalks to the kitchen, where he left his phone. The choice to walk there instead of doing his Houdini thing has to be for the benefit of collecting himself before he takes the call.

Kaiden brings the phone to his ear. "You here?" He waits for an answer before saying, "I'll see you down." Striding back to the couch, he pockets the device. "It was Carter; he's here to guard the private elevator that goes straight to the penthouse. If there's anything you need, just text Carter, and he'll see that you get it. I had my cook make all your favorite meals. They're in the fridge, but you can also order in if you want something else."

"Where are you going?"

"I told you, I have to go to Hell and look for Adramelech."

"Oh, I didn't think you would leave now. Can Carter drive me to my apartment? I need to get ready for my shift."

He works his jaw. "You will not hunt demons until you heal properly. You need to rest, Iris. You'll stay here until I come back, and then we'll see."

I snort a derisive laugh and jump to my feet—a move I immediately regret because of the ripple of pain that follows. Gritting my teeth, I push it down. "Keep dreaming that you can tell me what to do. This is my job, Kaiden. And I can't just disappear after I killed Erik. It's going to look suspicious as hell, don't you think?" I fold my arms across my chest.

Kaiden's eyes narrow. "If you report to Grayson that you were on your shifts and nothing out of the ordinary happened, he's not going to know."

"I can't lie to him," I seethe.

He barks an incredulous laugh. "Oh yeah? And what do you call what you've been doing for over two months now? What happens when he notices the scum that was his grandson is missing? You're going to tell him the truth about that? Do you even know what will happen to you if the Aureal Council catches wind of this? They're going to torture you until you're nothing more than an empty shell and then throw you in a cell to rot. How the fuck do you even want to go back to being part of the Order after what that piece of shit did to you?"

"Being a hellseeker is all I know. It gave me a purpose. When I woke up in that hospital without memories and found out what happened, it broke me," I tell him, ire dripping from my tone.

Kaiden gulps, and something flashes in his eyes. An emotion that looks similar to guilt disappears so quickly I'm certain I must have read it wrong.

"The Order took me in and gave me a life, the chance to avenge my mother's death. This is not just a job for me. It never was. And I can't disappear; even if I don't go out on my shifts tonight and tomorrow night, I'll still have to show my face at the compound to train this week. If I don't, it'll be suspicious."

"All I'm asking is that you stay here until I return so you can recover from your injuries. Malik should be back by then, too, and he will heal you. Then we can discuss what to do next, and I can join you again on your shifts."

"We can't do that anymore. It's just a matter of time before someone else sees us, and then I'm fucked for good. It was reckless of me to accept it in the first place. So, there's no point in staying here until you return because you will not shadow me anymore," I say flippantly.

Kaiden levels me with a stony glare. "You're not going, Iris."

I throw him a saccharine smile. "Oh yeah, how are you going to stop me?"

His lips curve in an infuriating smirk as he takes out his phone, unlocks it, and taps the screen. He calls someone and puts it on speaker.

"Hello," Grayson's stern voice slices through the blistering silence. "Who is this?"

Kaiden raises his eyebrow at me—surely to give me a second to process what he's about to do. He lifts the phone to his mouth. Before he can say a word, I snatch it and jab the end-call button.

"Fine. You made your point." I slam the phone to his chest and then stomp to the other side of the kitchen, unable to be near Kaiden because white-hot fury blazes through every cell in my body. "But I'm not staying here; I'm going home."

"No, you're not. Malik put powerful wards on the entire building. This is the safest place for you right now."

"Sam put wards on my apartment when I moved—"

He cuts me off. "Light magic can only go so far, and you know it. Those wards will do jack shit against something that can present a real threat. Carter and another wolf shifter will guard the elevator while I'm gone. If you as much as step foot out of the penthouse, Carter will call Grayson for me, tell him all about the time we spent together."

"Un-fucking-believable," I mutter as I reach the bar and whirl around to face Kaiden, my hands balling at my sides. "I can't believe you're using this against me yet again. I hate you."

Kaiden disappears from his spot and reappears a hair's breadth away from me. He cages me in against the side of the bar. His spicy scent envelops me in silky waves that drug my senses. An infuriating smirk tugs at the corner of his lips before he bends, letting his hot breath fan against the shell of my ear. I shiver. "That so, angel? It sure didn't look like you hated me when you rode my face or when you came so hard your pussy strangled my cock."

Heat unfurls between my legs. I huff at his words, but it comes out weak. "Don't flatter yourself. I might have never been with a man before, but I had better orgasms using my vibrator," I snark.

Kaiden's hand comes up to collar my throat in that way that makes me weak in the knees. His thumb massages the fluttering vein on the side of my neck as the ghost of a smile dances on his lips. He pulls back slightly, his burning gaze capturing mine. "Ah, I see. Well, we'll have to rectify that, won't we? Be a good girl, and don't give Carter any trouble. I'll reward you when I'm back. Don't worry, I'll make it worth your while. I'm going to fuck you so hard, angel, you're going to forget your name," he says before he bends and claims my mouth. The kiss is filled with carnal need — a promise of what's to come.

I melt faster than butter on warm toast as I arch my body into his. His silky tongue glides against mine while my fingers burrow into his tee. When he pulls back, we're both struggling to catch our breath.

"Okay, I'll stay here, but I need to help my aunt move some boxes from her basement — "

"Absolutely fucking not. You can't carry anything until your ribs are healed."

I huff. "Well, I was supposed to do it on Sunday, but Sam blew her off with a text. Besides, I already called her earlier to tell her I'm going tomorrow. If I flake on her again, then she's going to get worried and start asking questions. Especially if I don't show my face at the compound either. And I can't have that. So, I need to do this to at least pretend some semblance of normalcy."

Kaiden sucks on his teeth. He snaps his eyes closed. Opens them. "Fine. Carter will take you, and you will have a security detail with you guarding the house. Then you'll come back here. Promise me."

"I promise," I grumble.

He heaves out a weighted breath, bending to place a soft kiss on my forehead. "I have to go; I'll be back as soon as I can. Make yourself at home. And, Iris? You still can't lie for shit." Kaiden winks before throwing me a roguish grin that makes my pulse hiccup. Then he disappears.

Ugh. Stupid fucking feelings and infuriating demon bastard.

5

Iris

"Hi dear," Aunt Josephine says before throwing her arms around me in a hug. "Are you feeling better today? You look a little green...and tired."

My reflection in the mirror earlier told me the same thing. I think I got like five minutes of sleep last night. Not only were my ribs stabbing my lungs, but my mind also kept torturing me with the gory replay of Erik's death. At least the bruises on my face have faded enough that I could easily cover them with a layer of that stupidly expensive foundation Kaiden got me. Of course, I can't tell her that, so I mumble instead, "I had nightmares, and my stomach is still pissed at me for doing tequila shots with Sam." I mean, what's another lie to add to the growing pile, right? I wonder when it will finally topple over and bury me under the debris.

Sympathy fills her kind brown eyes at my words when she inches back. "I'm sorry, dear. C'mon, I'll make you some chamomile tea, and we can start clearing the basement when you feel better. Did you have breakfast already? I can fix you something real quick." She takes my clammy hand in her warm one and leads me to the kitchen.

"I already ate. Thank you for offering, though." I pull out a chair from the table in the corner to drop down on it as Aunt Josephine busies herself, pouring water into the kettle that she settles on the stove. "Ezekiel came around the library to ask about you. He said you missed your weekend sparring session."

"I know, but I was too hungover to train. I swear I'm never drinking again," I lie, yet again, but hey, at least it's getting easier. Sparring with Ezekiel is out of the question until my ribs heal. One look at my weak stance would be all he needs to figure out something isn't right. And I can't tell him my injuries are the result of a demon fight since the streets were still empty the last time I checked. I might as well set myself on fire and say, *Here I am, the big fat liar.*

Last night was the second time I've missed a shift since I joined the Order—the first was when I attended the succubus party with Kaiden—and it's killing me. I'm lucky the demon numbers are so low; otherwise, someone from the Order would have figured it out by now. Or they already did, and Grayson is waiting to kick my ass to the proverbial curb as we speak.

That is, if he doesn't already suspect I was involved in his grandson's disappearance, and if he isn't already preparing my new home, a two-by-two meter cell at the Gomorrah Penitentiary—the prison where the Aureal Council sends all criminals against the Order to rot. My fingers clench and unclench in my lap.

That's what I deserve, right? After all, I killed a member of the Order. A *lightborn*. Being a half-blood on top of committing the worst crime known to the Order will only add insult to injury. I mean, they already view me as the stray Grayson picked up after my mother died. And even if I was only defending myself, I can't see the Council being too forgiving about what I did. Or *how* I did it.

Fuck.

The only good thing that came out of Erik attacking me in the dark alley behind Sin is that there were no witnesses. Which I think was his entire MO and the reason he was never caught. I need to find some sort of evidence against Erik to prove he killed those women and tried to kill me, too. If I present it to the Aureal Council, maybe I'll sway them in my favor.

Okay, Iris, you're getting ahead of yourself. As far as you know, you're not even a suspect yet, so stop freaking out!

The shrill cry of the water boiling snaps me out of my thoughts, and I realize Aunt Josephine was speaking to me, but her words completely flew over my head. "I didn't quite catch that. What did you say, Auntie?" I ask.

She flaps a hand in the air before pouring the hot water over the tea bag in the cup. I didn't even notice her taking it out of the cupboard. "Silly me, trying to talk over the boiling water. I said I also saw Noah, and he had that kicked-puppy look to him. He's been moping around the compound." A worried look passes over her features. "He told me he was expecting to hear from you, but you never called him back."

Shit. I've had time to call him since Kaiden left to look for Adramelech in Hell, but I didn't want to do it from the penthouse. It somehow feels like I'm betraying Kaiden. But if I'm being completely honest with myself…I forgot about Noah's existence, which is weird because he has been haunting my thoughts for the last five years. Still, I have to set things straight with him. I'm in love with Kaiden, and Noah doesn't have a place in my life anymore.

I flinch when Aunt Josephine slides the steaming mug of tea

before me. "Here, I hope you'll feel better soon." She pushes the sugar container closer and places a teaspoon next to the mug, giving me a toothless smile.

"Sorry, Auntie, I'm scatterbrained today. I didn't mean to be rude. I, um, I don't know what to do about Noah yet. I haven't decided. I texted him and told him he could take me out on a date, and then I flaked on him because I'm still not sure if I can forgive him for ghosting me for five years, and I just…" I drop my eyes to the floor, sighing. "I don't know."

She slides her hand on top of mine. I lift my gaze to meet hers. "That's why you *really* haven't been at the compound, right? Because of Noah?"

I swallow heavily, then decide to play into yet another lie because she's given me the perfect out. "Yeah…"

She tightens her hold on me. "I know heartbreak when I see it, Iris, and you wear it on your sleeve for the entire world to see. It's pretty clear you're both suffering. And if you can't find it within yourself to forgive Noah, maybe you should tell him and let him go once and for all. I think it's better this way. This uncertainty is not good — for any of you. It will eat at your insides, and it will fester."

Nodding, I push up from the chair to envelop her in a hug, grateful that she's perceiving my internal freakout over Erik's death as heartbreak. "You're right, Auntie. I'll make a decision, and then I'll let Noah know. Thank you for always being here for me."

She frames the side of my face lovingly, a soft look in her doe-like eyes. "Of course, dear. I will always be here for you, all right?" She steps back. "Okay, well, I'll let you drink your tea. Do you want to lie on the couch for a bit while I sort things out in the basement?"

"No, I'm fine. I was wondering if I could maybe take a look at Grandma's books in her office." I wait with bated breath for her answer.

The reason my question makes my insides twist is that Aunt Josephine took her parents' death badly. Both of my grandparents were scientists working for the Order. They died in a massive explosion at the lab they were working at. My mother left the Order and Ashville shortly after their funeral, so it must have felt as though she'd lost all her family in the span of a few days.

When my aunt first brought me into her house — the same one she and my mother grew up in — she strictly forbade me to go into my grandparents' bedroom or their office. Being a curious little shit, I, of course, found the keys she'd hidden from me and ignored her wish.

I instantly regretted my decision when I stepped into their bedroom, which was eerily the same as they'd left it the day they died: bed unmade, probably because they were in a hurry, curtains skewed a little too much to the right, a solitary blue tie thrown over the gilded mirror in the corner. Even my grandma's hairbrush on the dresser still held strands of her hair.

The image unsettled me so much I decided not to go into the office after all. I felt horrible for disrespecting my aunt's grieving process — or lack thereof. It can't be healthy to make shrines of a dead person's belongings. But who am I to judge? It's been eight years since my mother died, and I haven't visited her grave once…

One day, Aunt Josephine decided to dust the office, which shocked me, to say the least. I didn't enter the room until she called out for me to bring her the vacuum cleaner. While she busied herself cleaning with the utmost care to not disturb anything from its exact place, I stared in awe at the shelves stocked full of books. When my aunt took a break, I started rifling through them. I didn't recognize the language, but I knew they were mostly about fae because of the depiction of their elongated ears. I don't think I'm any more knowledgeable in languages today, but it doesn't hurt to take another look. Maybe there's some information in there that will help Kaiden find the fae quicker.

Her eyebrows furrow. "Why?" she asks, a strained edge to her voice.

I take a moment to think about the next words that come out of my mouth so I don't share too much. It's not that I don't trust my aunt, but I would make her an accomplice if the Order finds out everything I've been up to lately. She would be the first person they interrogate after me. One future imprisoned member of our family is one too many, thank you very much.

"Well, you know that a while back, I asked you to look up information about the umbra, right? I discovered a possible link between those demons and a prophecy. And the only oracles I know of were fae." I hike a shoulder. "I figured if I read about them, maybe I can get some answers. I know Grandma was really passionate about dark creatures. I saw her books that day you cleaned the office a few years back. Remember?"

Aunt Josephine sucks on her teeth while pondering her response. I think she's going to refuse, but she reluctantly says, "Fine. Just put everything back as you found it, okay? The spines need to be aligned. That's how she liked them. She would always scream at me when I took out a book and put it back in the wrong order."

Wow, I bet Grandma was a blast at dinner parties. I nod hastily and wait for my aunt to bring the key from the hiding place I shouldn't know about—her bedside table. Honestly, she could have hidden the keys in a better place if she didn't want me to find them.

From the grim set of her lips, I can tell she's not happy about my request as she slides the key into the lock and opens the door. But I need to find out what that prophecy says. So I only mumble a quiet "thank you" while stepping into the office, the steaming cup of tea in one hand.

"Drink your tea before you even touch anything, okay? And don't disturb the chair or the desk. My mother sat in it that morning before she—"

She clears her throat to find her voice. "Before she died, and I don't want anyone else sitting in it. Please bring whatever books you need to the living room. I'm gonna go put the rest of the things in boxes," she says through a weighted sigh before leaving me to it.

"Don't worry, I'll be careful. Holler if you need anything," I reply over my shoulder, then stride to the rich, cherry oak bookshelves on my right. The air is so stale and dusty, I sneeze five times in a row before I even get the chance to look at the spines. It's odd being inside here. Just like the bedroom, it's frozen in time—a sad window to the past.

A notebook, probably my grandmother's, remains open to the same page on the desk, a pen lying next to it. It reminds me of those post-mortem portraits the people in the Victorian era used to take of their deceased family members.

I immerse myself in one of the two books I can find in English about the fae folk.

"After the careful dissection of the tunica intima, we found unidentified cells present along the endothelial ones. They have a bioluminescence quality akin to the Arachnocampa luminosa. Aside from the luminescence, we believe that these cells are the reason why the *aether* is contained."

I am just getting curious about what this *aether* is when my aunt's shrill cry jolts me into the present. I drop the book on the coffee table in front of me and jump up from the couch. Tapping into my hellseeker speed, I zip to the basement door.

The second my fingers wrap around the handle, my aunt barrels out, slamming into my side and almost head-butting me. Luckily, I dodge right at the last second. I still suck in a serrated breath, though, at the pain rippling all over my body.

"Oh, snapdragons! I almost gave you a concussion. Sorry about that. Are you okay?" she inquires while pushing the curtain of wet hair out of her face.

Confusion pulls at my eyebrows. "I'm fine. But are you? Why are you wet?"

Aunt Josephine pushes past me in a hurry, half-yelling on her way to the entrance hall. "Because a pipe burst in the basement, and it's soaking all the boxes as we speak." She comes back, purse in hand. "Darn it, where is that phone?" she huffs as she rummages through it. "I'm going to call a plumber. Can you please start bringing the boxes up into the living room? Or whatever is left of them. And hurry. I'll be right with you once I find an available plumber." My aunt doesn't swear, so she mumbles a few euphemisms instead until she fishes the phone out of the bag.

The musty smell, enhanced by the water coming in rivulets from the burst pipe in the ceiling, coats my lungs as I descend the stairs. I blink a few times to adjust to the dim lighting. It's a good thing this happened now and not after she had already renovated or added any bookshelves and books. The water is pooling so fast it already reaches my ankles when I step onto the cement floor. I shudder in disgust. I hate it when my feet get wet.

Pushing the feeling aside, I grab the two boxes that are right under the spray. As much as I try to avoid it, my hair still gets soaked while I stack them on top of each other. The second my right foot touches the first step, the sopping bottom of the first box I'm holding gives out. Something passes in between my hands, falling right into the murky water with a *plop*.

Hastily, I balance the boxes on the steps and bend over to fish out whatever that was—maybe a notebook. It only takes a few seconds for me to find it, but it's so wet it's dripping. And it's not a notebook— it's a leather-bound book? Or maybe a journal? Shit. What if it was my grandmother's? My aunt is going to kill me. I untie it and thumb through it to see the damage. Hopefully, it's not too bad. The ink is smudged, and the writing is incomprehensible on most of the pages, but there are some that are still dry.

My eyes skitter over one of those pages.

Owen blindsided me today. He confessed his love to me, and I just stood there, not knowing what to say. He tried to kiss me and—

I look away. This has to be my aunt's journal—a journal I have no business reading, especially about her intimate moments with her dead fiancé. When I'm about to close it, though, the words a few rows further down catch my attention: *I should tell my sister, but how could I when they're getting married in only three months? And she has been radiating happiness ever since he proposed.*

Holy shit! Is this—did this belong to my mother?

"The plumber is coming in twenty minutes." Aunt Josephine's voice pulls me into the present.

Pulse hammering in my ears, I slam the notebook shut, then shove it into the waistband of my jean shorts at my back, under my tee, before she pops into the doorway.

Even if it's selfish, I don't want to show it to her. Besides, I don't think my aunt will be too happy to find out her dead fiancé was in love with my mother. When I used to live here, she often cried while looking at his photo, clutching the engagement ring—which she still wears on a gold chain around her neck—for dear life.

She gives me a weird look as she hurries down the steps. "Are you okay? You only moved two boxes? C'mon, they're all getting wet!" she shrieks, pushing past me.

"Yeah, sorry," I mumble and join her in stacking up the sopping boxes on the stairs before bringing them to the living room, the journal burning a hole in my back. I need to see if Sam can salvage at least some of the smudged pages.

We make quick work of clearing out the basement, but most of the boxes are ruined. I help my aunt take out everything she wants to keep so she can dry them, then throw out the rest. My fingers tremble as I open the one that held my mother's journal, hoping more of her belongings are inside. But I deflate like a balloon when I see it's filled with junk that wasn't hers. Someone must have misplaced the journal at some point and put it in there.

I hoped that I would at least find an old T-shirt, even something minuscule like a stray earring or a hair tie...anything really. Even though I just got a piece of my mother back, I can't help but want more. Heaving out a deep sigh, I grit my teeth and pick up the box. "I think this was the last one. I have to go, Auntie. I'll toss this on my way out."

She tilts her head up to look at me from her spot on the living room floor, her legs crisscrossed. "Oh, already? I'm making lasagna for lunch. Are you sure you don't want to stay?"

"I have plans with Sam. Sorry. Next time?" This is not a lie since I already texted Sam to let her know about the journal. She's meeting me at Kaiden's penthouse in thirty minutes.

"Okay, dear. I guess I'll see you at the compound."

I throw a hasty goodbye over my shoulder and stride to the door with urgency.

6

Iris

I'm sprawled on Kaiden's massive couch, watching a new season of *The Vampire Diaries*, but I can't concentrate because my eyes drop from the humongous screen to the coffee table—where my mother's journal is—for the umpteenth time. To be honest, I'm surprised I haven't burned holes in it yet. Since Sam left two hours ago, I've done nothing but stare at it. Unfortunately, she couldn't fix the water damage. Restoration magic is tricky, and it's not her specialty, but she managed to save some pages. I should find out what they say, right?

My lungs constrict when I pick it up, though, as if I'm on the verge of a panic attack. The trembling in my hands only gets worse as I open it. Blood drums in my ears. The blaring ringtone of my phone startles me, and I drop the journal in my lap. Shit. I pause the show to answer.

"Miss Harper, there's someone here for you," Carter tells me.

"Carter, for the hundredth time, call me Iris, please. I'm not expecting anyone—"

"It's Ava and Emily Dawson. Ava is Logan's wife, the alpha of our pack, and Emily is his sister. Should I let them come up?"

"Oh, um…s-sure," I stammer and hang up. Grunting, I stand, place the journal back on the coffee table, then brush away the wrinkles in my clothes. Thankfully, I changed out of Kaiden's shirt earlier after taking a bath in the beautiful Victorian claw-foot bathtub, and am now wearing jean shorts and a black tee that fits me like a glove. The fabric is so soft that if I didn't know better, I would think it's made of unicorn tears.

I shuffle on my feet as the elevator doors slide open. I'm curious why they're here and uncomfortable as fuck because I don't know what to do with myself, so I shove my hands into the back pockets of my shorts and wait.

The first to step out is a curvy woman—arrestingly beautiful. Natural caramel highlights thread through her wavy brunette hair, which she styled half-up. Her floor-length sundress swishes between her legs as she saunters toward me, a protective hand thrown over her swollen belly. "Hey, I hope you don't mind we're ambushing you," she tells me. A warm smile tilts her lips upward.

"Sheesh, you weren't kidding when you said this place is swanky," the other woman says after letting out a whistle, her mesmerizing citrine eyes sweeping over the first floor of the penthouse in awe. She follows close behind, and I recognize her as the gorgeous bartender from Sin. "I can't believe Kaiden never invited all of us over. The uptight, broody bastard was probably concerned we would soil his pristine marble floor."

I chuckle at that. If I wasn't sure when I first saw her in the club, the overhead lights make her relationship to Logan even clearer now. She has the same smooth amber skin—which is accentuated by the tangerine linen dress she's wearing—and bouncy ash-brown curls, though hers reach her shoulders. She strides to the kitchen, holding two paper bags.

The curvy brunette stops in front of me. "Logan mentioned you were alone in the penthouse, and we thought you might want some company. I'm Ava, by the way. Logan's wife."

"I'm Iris. Um, nice to meet you," I say, thrusting my right hand in her direction. She bypasses it to envelop me in a hug. After I pat her back awkwardly, she disentangles herself from me, and we both amble to the kitchen.

"I'm Emily," the other woman chimes in. "Maybe you remember me from Sin."

"Yeah, I do," I tell her, then offer a toothless smile.

Emily takes out a bottle of liquor from one of the bags. "We were dying to meet the woman Kaiden is crazy about. I swear Logan keeps his lips sealed tighter than the Pentagon's vault. He wouldn't give us any details, so we took the matter into our own hands."

"And we wanted to check up on you after what happened at Sin. How are you feeling?" Ava inquires, concern shining in her sea-foam green eyes as she sits down on a bar stool with the grace of a ballerina.

"My ribs still hurt, and I feel as though two giants used my head to play volleyball, but aside from that, I'm pretty much okay. My best friend made me a healing potion, and it's working better than expected." I clear my throat. "She's a light witch." Striding to where Emily is rummaging through the bag at the counter, I ask, "Do you need any help?"

She hands me two boxes that have the name Silver Moon Bakery written above a crescent moon in beautiful penmanship. "Just take these, and I'm going to start the cocktails," Emily instructs as she fishes out all the bottles, a few utensils, and a cocktail shaker. "Do you know where the glasses are?"

"Third cabinet to your right." I place the boxes on top of the bar in front of Ava.

"It sucks that Malik isn't here to heal you, but I heard he should be back soon. You look pretty good considering what you've been through," Ava tells me.

"Yeah…"

Emily turns, facing us. Her forehead crinkles as her eyebrows knit, and when her gaze flicks to mine, it's brimming with regret. "I'm sorry that piece of shit drugged you on my shift. I usually watch the bar like a hawk for creeps. But immediately after I gave you the water, I took my break, and when I came back, you weren't there anymore—"

"Don't worry about it. It's not your fault," I interrupt.

"At least he got what he deserved," Ava cuts in after a few beats of awkward silence.

As I take a seat next to her at the bar, I notice the faded scar on her right cheek that goes from the corner of her lips all the way to her earlobe. The scar doesn't deter from her beauty—it only makes it more striking.

Ava's eyebrows furrow as she nervously brings her fingers to the raised skin before trying to cover it with her hair. However, she realizes she has tied up the front pieces. Sighing, she places her hand on her lap.

Fuck. I'm such an asshole. "I'm so sorry. I didn't mean to stare," I blurt out. Heat crawls on the back of my neck. "I have a lot of scars too, from fighting demons, and I was just thinking it enhances your beauty and makes you look badass."

She flaps her hand in the air as if it's a non-issue, then beams at me. "S'okay, don't worry about it. For the first few months, it made me really self-conscious, and I would try everything to cover it, but eventually, I became used to it, and now it's part of me. It's proof that I survived," Ava says while opening the boxes.

I'm curious how she got it, but she would have shared that if she wanted to, so I don't ask. Two boxes overflow with mouth-watering pastries — mini round cakes and eclairs in a medley of flavors. If I were alone right now, I would stuff my face, but I've already shown how poor my people skills are, and I don't want them to think I'm a Neanderthal.

"C'mon, take something," Ava says, pushing the sweets-filled boxes toward me on the bar.

"I don't know what to pick. Everything looks delicious."

"Try this one. It's my favorite." She points to the biggest pastry in the box, roll-shaped and filled with white cream. She then takes one of her own and bites into it encouragingly.

I gingerly pick it up. As soon as my teeth sink into the buttery, flaky texture, my tastebuds start doing the *cha, cha, cha.* "Holy shit! This is the best thing I've ever tasted in my life."

Ava radiates happiness at my remark while she takes another bite of her roll.

"Ava made it. She owns the bakery. Actually, it's baker*ies*; she opened a second one a month ago," Emily chimes in as she strides to the fridge.

My eyebrows shoot up. "I know you're married to Logan, but I'm seriously thinking about proposing to you right now," I say through a mouthful. "I can't believe I've never heard of your bakery before. Prepare to get sick seeing my face almost every day from now on."

"I'm happy you like it," Ava says on a giggle at my enthusiasm.

"I love it. I'm already thinking about ways to make Logan disappear," I jest after taking my last bite and licking my fingers clean.

Emily carries ice, bottles of liquor, and everything else she brought over to the black marble bar. "So, Iris, how do you feel about coffee? I was thinking of making some espresso martinis for us. For Ava, I'll make an amaretto sour mocktail. I can make one for you, too, if you don't want alcohol."

"I love coffee, and I could use some alcohol; the espresso martini sounds like heaven." I wrinkle my nose. "But don't ask me how to use Kaiden's fancy-ass coffee machine because I might set it on fire."

Emily lets out a hearty laugh. "Don't worry, I think I can manage. My brother has the same one." She turns on her heel and presses a few buttons on the espresso machine.

"How far along are you?" I ask Ava.

She gives me a puzzled look. "What do you mean?"

My mouth opens and closes a few times. I probably look as red as a pickled beet. *Wow, Iris.* This must be a record, me putting my foot in my mouth twice in a few minutes. *You never ask a woman about being pregnant, you dumbass!* "Well, um…I, um — I think I've heard Logan and Malik talk about pregnancy cravings. How you wanted chocolate-mint ice cream, and I assumed — " I cringe, hands flapping at my sides.

Shoot. Me. Now.

Ava and Emily break into a fit of laughter. "Sorry, I was just messing with you, couldn't help it. Four months. We're having twins."

"Thank God," I sigh and wipe at my forehead dramatically. "Wow, twins. I'm sure you're excited. I would be terrified."

"Oh, I am terrified, but Logan is over the moon, and we have the entire pack to help us. We're a big family."

The bitter pang of jealousy blooms inside my chest because I've never felt that way about the Order — or, more precisely, them about me. Yeah, sure, the Order is my whole life. But I'm not theirs. They never fully accepted me, despite my efforts to prove myself. When I joined the Order at sixteen, my half-blood made me an outcast, and I faced relentless bullying. Now, everyone mostly pretends I don't exist.

Emily slides the three filled glasses toward us before taking a seat on the other side of Ava. "So, how did you and Kaiden meet?" she asks me.

"I was on hellseeker duty, and these demons I've never seen before attacked me near Shadow Lake in the national park. Kaiden saved me. I actually woke up here and spin-kicked him in the face when I realized he was an Elite demon," I chuckle out.

"You spin kicked Kaiden? IN THE FACE?" Ava squeaks in a high-pitched tone, her eyes bugging out of her head as she looks at me over the rim of her glass.

"You should have seen her at Sin Saturday night. She threw a whole bottle of water at him. I was laughing so hard, I thought my spleen would rupture," Emily says.

Ava's jaw is on the floor. "*No mames!* Are we talking about the same Kaiden? The one I know? But, he's so damn serious all the time and has that whole don't-fuck-with-me vibe." She shudders.

I shrug and take a sip from the martini glass. "Well, he deserved it. He was being an ass." I turn to Emily. "This is amazing."

She winks at me and raises the glass in the air in a salute before taking a sip. "Since you're a hellseeker, aren't you supposed to have light hair? Because of the blessed blood?"

"I'm a half-blood. The only one in the Order; that's why my hair is dark." My eyebrows knit. "And it's actually forbidden for us to interact in any way. You do know about that, right?"

Ava rolls her eyes mid-sip. "Pfft, it's a stupid, archaic rule. If Kaiden doesn't care about it, why should we? Soooo, what's up with you two? Don't skip any juicy details. We want them all."

I roll the slender glass stem between my fingers as I hike a shoulder. "It's complicated." I sigh. "I don't know what's between us. We've never discussed it, and there can't be a future for us anyway. He's only helping me while we figure out some things, and after that, we'll part ways." The words burn through me like acid, but they're the truth, even though I know I've fallen for him.

"I'm not so sure Kaiden thinks the same. I have never seen him look at anyone the way he looks at you." Emily throws me a pointed look.

I remember the way the bitch Maeve planted herself in his lap at Sin. I can't resist asking, "Not even Maeve?"

"Are you kidding?" Emily huffs. "Kaiden has never given her the time of day. She's always desperate for his attention, but he mostly ignores her. Besides, she's a raging cunt to everyone. She's lucky she's such a skilled dancer. Otherwise, Kaiden would have fired her already and sent her back to Hell."

"Well, I hope you guys figure it out," Ava chimes in. "We need more women in our group, and I would love it if you became a permanent fixture. You're nothing like I thought you would be."

The corners of my lips turn up. "Oh yeah, what did you think I would be like?"

"Um, you know, a shrew," she chuckles out. "Let's just say hellseekers don't have the best reputation among our kind."

"I can only imagine." Five hundred years ago, during the demonic plague, the fight against demons became too bloody. The archangels restored the balance of good and evil by closing all twelve Hell gates around the world and imposing the Celestial Treaty. Before Lucifer signed the Treaty and the Obsidian Conclave took jurisdiction, hellseekers also hunted dark creatures alongside demons. Now, even though a truce exists, there has always been mutual hatred between hellseekers and dark creatures. It's hard to admit, but the hellseekers' superiority complex is the main reason for the existing dissension.

The next two hours fly by. Emily tells us all about Hailey—the wolf shifter from the Iron Claw pack she's been dating—while Ava reminisces about the time she spent in Paris at the prestigious pastry school and all the places she and Logan visited in Europe. When it's time to go, both of them hug me and tell me they had a great time, and that they hope we'll see each other again.

What surprises me most is that I had a great time, too. I can't believe two dark creatures treated me better than the Order's members have since I first stepped foot at the compound seven years ago. These women — whom I barely know — acted as though we'd been friends for years.

NOT LONG AFTER Emily and Ava left, feeling restless and bored out of my mind, I decided to at least get a workout in. Carter joined me at Kaiden's private state-of-the-art gym two floors below. However, I could only do a basic stretching routine because my ribs kept sending jolts of fiery throbs throughout my body at the slightest effort. Frustrated, I stormed back to the penthouse, took a shower, and got ready for bed.

Nothing I tried to fall asleep has worked, though. I swear I even counted sheep. I keep tossing and turning, my body getting tangled in the silky black sheets. I bring them to my nose to inhale Kaiden's intoxicating scent, but it only intensifies the ache beneath my solar plexus that made its presence known the second he popped off.

Ugh, when the fuck did I become a simpering fool? Get a grip, Iris. It's been only two days.

Fuck this. Clearly, I'm not used to being in bed at this hour since my hellseeker shifts usually end right before sunrise. I don't even know why I tried. Heaving out a sigh, I push myself up and stride out of the bedroom — not before picking up my mother's journal, trying to open it, failing, and putting it back on the nightstand...again. Every single time I've tried to read even one sentence, guilt has shackled my lungs until I was on the verge of a full-blown panic attack. Guilt that I survived when she didn't, piled on top of the fact that, before a few weeks ago, I couldn't even remember her face. It's a tar-like stain, permanently marring my soul. Maybe it's time I finally visit my mother's grave after all these years and try to read it there.

I had intended to put a movie on, but now that I'm out in the hallway, curiosity gets the best of me, so I open the first door to my right. Blinking a few times, I take in the dark room. It's a library decorated in deep navy hues — vastly different from the modern décor of the rest of the penthouse. Silvery moonlight bathes the bookshelves, which are crammed full of books and cover the entirety of the walls. A vintage brass chandelier towers over the brown leather couch and the two armchairs that form a cozy reading nook in front of the fireplace in the center of the room. I don't know how I can tell that the huge canvas above the fireplace, depicting the same regretful angel bowing on one knee that Kaiden has tattooed on his back, is the real one — and the other in his office at Sin is only a copy — but I do. Like every other time I've seen the image, my heartstrings turn into knots. It somehow feels worse now. Ominous. So I shut the door and get out.

When I open the second door, I stumble into Kaiden's office. Here, the colors match the rest of the penthouse. The city lights sparkle through the floor-to-ceiling windows at the back of the room.

Prompted by my curiosity, I sit down in the executive chair behind the desk. There's a squeaky sound as my naked thighs stick to the cold leather. I spin the chair, trying to imagine Kaiden doing the same. A laugh bubbles out of me because he would never do something so childish. My elbow hits something, and as I whip my head around, the tower of files on the desk tumbles to the floor.

Shit.

I stand and kneel to gather the pages scattered across the hardwood floor. I don't mean to snoop more than I already have, but the photos of children and the word "missing" stamped above them in bold, red letters snag my attention. Kaiden never mentioned anything about missing children. Wait. Why would he have missing children reports? Unless they're dark creatures.

My suspicion is confirmed as I start reading through them: wolf shifters, light and dark witches, sirens, warlocks, fae, selkies. Even rare shifters like panthers and ravens. There are also some vampires among the kidnappings, but they're all adults. Maybe it's because vampires can't have children, and turning a child is strictly forbidden—not only because that's horrible but also because children lack impulse control when it comes to blood. It seems like the kidnappings have increased in number over the years, but in the last two and a half months, they're at an all-time high. That's weird. I wonder why that is…I need to ask Kaiden about this when he returns. There has to be something I can do to help.

I pile them in a neat stack before placing them back on the desk. Something catches my eye on the computer screen that is now turned on. I don't mean to keep snooping, I *really* don't, but Kaiden probably forgot to shut down his computer, and I must have moved the mouse when I hit the files, causing the display to wake and show Kaiden's email inbox.

What the?

The very first unopened email in his inbox is from the same chocolatier company that makes the chocolate-covered black cherries soaked in liquor—the ones I've received every year on my birthday since I woke up from the accident. With sweat-slicked fingers, I bend over the keyboard, grab hold of the mouse, and click on it. It's a promotional email showcasing the new flavors they added. I type the company's name into the search bar. A few emails containing receipts pop up. I open the first one. It's dated three days before my birthday. I open a second, dated the same but from the year before.

This can't be a coincidence.

Every time I got the feeling I knew Kaiden since waking here after the umbra attack flashes through my mind. I miss a few letters as I type the word "flowers" into the search bar. I have to delete them and start again several times. Sure enough, there's a receipt from a flower company for a bouquet of a hundred black irises dated a few days before my birthday. He ordered them all the way from Jordan.

My gut feeling wasn't wrong. Either Kaiden has been stalking me for years, or I somehow *know* him. We have to have met before the umbra attack.

A thousand scenarios bounce around in my head. The fact that it's been over two months since the attack and he hasn't mentioned he knew me once cuts me deep, like a serrated blade. I even blatantly asked him that night at the succubus party…and he avoided my question.

What if Kaiden was the one stalking me and not Erik?

I mean, he knew my name, my address, and my favorite foods. No, that can't be. The connection I feel to him, the chemistry charging the air whenever we're in the same room is too strong. Besides, Erik told me he was watching me. But what if they both were?

Determined to find out what else Kaiden has been keeping from me, I unleash the snooping. I rummage through the drawers but come up empty every time. When I tug on the last drawer, it's locked. My eyes skitter over the top of the desk as I nibble on my lower lip. *Bingo*. I jam the pointy tip of a letter opener through the keyhole and jiggle it until I hear the satisfying *click*. I slide the drawer open. My eyebrows furrow at the only item inside. It's an old sketch pad, slightly frayed at the edges, but as I pick it up, I can tell it's very well taken care of.

Relaxing back into the chair, I let the pads of my fingers run down the smooth texture of the cover. The gesture feels hauntingly familiar. The second I open it, all my blood rushes into my ears as I read the words on the first page: "Property of" right above a watercolor painting of an intricate iris.

Could this — is this mine?

Fingers shaking, I thumb through the pages. A weird feeling crawls beneath my skin when I recognize the drawings — they're all tattooed on Kaiden's glorious body — the skull and snake on his chest, the raven on his forearm, the Anubis on his abdomen. Even the jester on his left shin. My gaze meets Kaiden's on the next page. His features are softer, his teenage years still clinging to his bones. He doesn't have the bump in the middle of his nose, and his hair is shorter and pushed back. But it's him all right, complete with the infuriating, sexy smirk tugging at his lips.

Suddenly, the headache I had since waking up morphs into a fiery stab of pain that intensifies the throbbing in my temples by a hundredfold. I drop the sketchbook on the desk to press the heels of my palms into my eyes, but the ache only worsens. The office blurs as I'm transported to another room.

An easel sits before me, and charcoal-smeared fingers move fluidly over the drawing of an angel bowing on one knee as if in regret, its head hanging low and its wings spread wide at its back. Picking up an eraser pen, I add the finishing highlights to the drawing I've been slaving over for the last three weeks. I hope he's going to love it. I've poured my heart into it, and it's my favorite drawing I've done so far.

"Iris, honey, where are you?" a muffled voice comes through the door.

"In the studio," I holler back.

There's a knock on the door before it opens, and my mother appears in the doorway, her smile as bright as the sun as she rests her hip on the door frame. She folds her arms in front of her chest. "You pulled another all-nighter? You said you were going to sleep — "

"I wanted to finish the drawing before he gets here," I interrupt as I put down the eraser pen to stretch the kinks in my back and yawn.

Her cerulean eyes flick to the finished drawing. She shakes her head, saying, "It turned out beautiful. I can't believe someone so talented came out of me."

"Eww, Mom, gross." *I shudder and push back the chair to stand.*

"C'mon, go shower. Breakfast is ready," she tells me, then turns on her heel toward the stairs.

A bright flash, and I'm back in Kaiden's office. The excruciating pang between my eyes not only sears my brain but makes my stomach lurch. I stand abruptly, sending the chair sprawling at my back. It hits the floor-to-ceiling windows with a loud thud as I dash toward the en suite bathroom in Kaiden's bedroom at lightning speed. I barely make it in time to retch my last meal and all the cocktails I drank earlier into the toilet. When there's nothing left, I slump on the floor and wait for the tremors wracking my body to subside as tears flow freely, soaking my fanned hair.

I saw Mom again.

This was the first time I've gotten a memory flashback while awake, and that drawing…It's mine. I did it. Not only does he have something I drew hanging in his library and his office at the club, but he's got almost all the drawings from my sketchbook tattooed on his body. I know this should scare me because the gesture screams he's obsessed with me—that he's been obsessed for years because as far as I know, I haven't picked up a pencil since I woke up from the car accident at fifteen. Instead of being terrified, though, all I feel right now is warmth at the thought that he's carrying a part of me on his skin.

I'm so fucked in the head it's not even funny at this point.

Blowing out a shaky exhale, I close my eyes and replay the flashback on a loop until the chill of the tiles seeps into my bones. The weird dream I had before waking up in the cathedral crypt after the vampires kidnapped me pushes to the forefront of my mind, and now I know for sure it wasn't just a dream.

"Her nose is a little bigger in reality, don't you think?" Chester says as he pops out of thin air next to me. He's a cranky old man with a crooked nose and a shiny bald head. He looks like one of those desert vultures I saw in the animal documentary Mommy put on the TV for me to watch earlier today.

Amanda scowls at him. "You're one to talk." Her eyes soften as her gaze flicks to mine. "It's lovely. Thank you! You're very talented for being only five years old."

I smile brightly. "I know; Mommy tells me I'm going to be an artist."

When I finally feel in control of my body, I gingerly push myself up and trudge to the sink to splash water on my tear-streaked face. White-knuckling the sink, I let my head fall between my shoulders. Kaiden's got a lot of explaining to do. Hopefully, he'll be back soon.

I cast another glance at my disheveled reflection in the gilded mirror. My skin is so white it could very well be translucent at this point. I stride back to Kaiden's office and put everything the way it was, except for the sketchbook, which I take to bed and thumb through in the hopes it will spark another flashback.

7

Iris

Groggily, I open my eyes and rub the sleep cobwebs from my mind as muffled voices filter through the room. I must have fallen asleep. Wrestling out of the tangled sheet trapping my body, I pat my hand on the mattress in search of the sketchbook and finally find it under the pillow.

Magenta and lilac stretch on the indigo sky, casting the room in a faint, dusky glow. Holding the sketchbook in one hand, I push myself off the bed and shuffle toward Kaiden's voice. A sliver of light spills into the dark corridor through the crack in the library door. He's talking to someone on speakerphone — Malik. I halt, hug the sketchbook to my chest, and mentally prepare myself to confront Kaiden. When I'm about to open the door, I hear my name and pause.

"How's Iris?" Malik asks.

"She's sleeping. She's healing faster now because of the weakened barrier. Her bruises have almost faded entirely. That and her witch friend is really skilled; the healing potion she brewed helped a lot, but I still want you to come by and mend her ribs," Kaiden replies.

"We're on our way back. I'll be there by midnight. Did she remember anything else?"

"I don't think so. If she did…she hasn't mentioned it."

There's a long pause before Malik speaks again, his voice grim. "There's only a matter of time until she does, given the cracks in the barrier — if what happened at Sin didn't obliterate it completely. What are you going to do when she remembers you were the one who locked her powers away, alongside her memories?"

What the fuck.

I can't hear Kaiden's response because the singe of betrayal takes hold of my body one cell at a time as my heart breaks into a million jagged pieces that scatter all over the floor. I drop the sketchbook. The broken sob ripping from my lungs swallows the loud thump. Whirling around, I sprint toward the dressing room.

In the next second, I crash into a hard wall of muscle as Kaiden materializes out of thin air. The force of the impact makes my teeth grind as a stabbing ripple travels through the entirety of my torso. Still, the physical pain has nothing on the way I feel my chest crumbling within itself.

"Iris, what happened?" Kaiden asks, alarmed, his fingers wrapping around my shoulders.

I jerk out of his hold and take a stumbling step back. "Don't fucking touch me!" I scream.

Kaiden's eyebrows knit. He takes a tentative step toward me. "What's wrong?"

I shuffle backward again and almost step on the sketchbook I dropped earlier. "You lied to me! You fucking lied to me! I can't believe I trusted you." Glass shards impale the back of my throat. It takes everything I've got to stop the dam of emotions from bursting and sweeping me away in the devastating, murky torrent. I can't—*won't*—let him see me cry.

His expression is crestfallen as his gaze flits to the sketchbook on the floor, then back to me. "Whatever you think—"

"I know you're the one sending me flowers and chocolates every year for my birthday. I saw the receipts. I also heard Malik loud and clear. Don't even try to gaslight me."

His Adam's apple rolls on a hard swallow, regret brimming in his tormented eyes. "It's not what you think." God, even in this moment he's so damn beautiful it hurts to look at him. Like Icarus, I flew too close to the sun. No wonder I got burned.

Fuck, fuck, fuck, fuck, fuck.

I can't believe I let a demon touch me like no other man has before. The worst part is that I have not only given him my body, but I've served him my heart on a silver platter, and he crushed it to smithereens.

"You've got five minutes. I want the whole truth. Start by explaining how you have what I'm sure is my sketchbook and how we really know each other," I demand.

Kaiden works his jaw. "I can't."

I huff a derisive laugh. "How convenient."

"You don't understand—"

"Then explain!"

His fingers clench and unclench at his sides, and a bottomless pit forms at the bottom of my stomach that is filled by soul-crushing anxiety. All I want to do is curl into a ball on the floor, but the feeling is weird, foreign—as if it doesn't belong to me. But how could it not?

Kaiden's words snap me out of it. "There is a barrier on your powers. It resembles a mental shield or a wall. The memory loss was only a side effect. We knew it might happen, but I decided it was worth the risk at that moment. I wanted to tell you everything. You don't even know how much..." He lets out a trembling breath. "But any spell that tampers with the brain is of the most dangerous and damaging out there. If I had told you anything...if I *tell* you anything about your past, it might put you into a coma. That's why it's important that you remember everything yourself. I can't risk it."

I suck on my teeth. "Who's we? What powers are you talking about?"

Kaiden remains silent.

I expel a frustrated huff. "Is it the seeing ghosts and rotting people? Did I do this before? Are the shadows from the alley a part of it?" Again, I'm only met by a blistering silence that makes my skin itch, but I don't give up. "Why did you lock my powers?"

Our gazes engage in a silent war. "I can't tell you."

"You were there when my mother died, weren't you?"

Nothing.

"Did you kill her?" I seethe.

A flash of anger bounces in the confines of his irises. "How can you ask me that?" he spits.

"How? HOW? You refuse to tell me anything. It's a fucking valid question!"

"You know me, Iris. Do you think I would be capable of something like that?"

A manic laugh bubbles up my throat, but only a strangled whimper comes out. "That's the thing. I DON'T KNOW YOU. What I know is that you're a demon, and a demon killed my mother the day we fell into the canyon." A new wave of nausea hits me.

Fuck me. What if I fell in love with my mother's killer?

"You know what hurts the most, Kaiden?" I shake my head. "That I bared my soul to you, told you all about the accident—how much losing my memory hurt. And you didn't say a fucking word. You moved into my apartment, and we spent every second together for weeks, yet you chose to stay silent." I suck in a jagged breath. "Even if you're telling the truth about not being able to come clean...you could have at least tried to explain that we knew each other when I asked. Fuck. You could have said something. Anything."

"No, I couldn't, because I couldn't risk *you*. I will always put you first, Iris."

I will my legs, which feel heavier than two blocks of cement, to move. "This—whatever the fuck this thing between us is—*ends* now," I clip out before shouldering past him toward the dressing room.

Kaiden is hot on my heels. "You can't leave," he tells me, desperation coating every word and seeping out of his pores until I almost choke on it.

"Watch me," I snap and strip out of his T-shirt, which, like a fool, I slept in because I fucking missed him and his intoxicating scent, even after finding the hidden sketchbook and the receipts. I couldn't be more pathetic even if I tried. I throw it to the floor as if it's poisonous.

"It's not safe," he says at my back, so close his warmth seeps into my bones.

I bite the lining of my cheek until I taste blood to stop myself from leaning back into him, and I grab the first shirt on the shelf in front of me.

"My safety is no longer your concern." I slip on the random tee over the shorts and slide my feet into a pair of sneakers without socks on.

"I can't let you leave," Kaiden tells me, whirling me around and crowding me against the shelf. "I already let you go once, and it nearly fucking killed me, Iris. I can't do it again. I won't survive it this time."

"I said don't touch me!" I send my palm flying at his face.

There's a loud *crack* as it connects with Kaiden's stubbled cheek, catching him by surprise. His head snaps to the side. His nostrils flare as he whirls his head back, then he steps forward, caging me in. He slams one hand on the shelf at the side of my head, the other wrapping around my throat possessively. The silver rings adorning his fingers are cold against my heated skin.

"I don't care if you slap me. Fuck. I'll hand you the knife to stab me myself. Just. Don't. Leave. Me." The last word comes out in a broken whisper. "Please."

It almost shatters my resolve. *Almost.*

"Let me go!" I grit out through clenched teeth. My eyes throw angry daggers at Kaiden as I stare at him, face hot. The air sparks and sizzles between us, and fireworks crackle between my ribs.

He ignores me as his gaze darkens. "I'm sorry, angel...so fucking sorry for not being able to say a thing. I can't stand the idea of you hating me," he rasps, tone rougher than sandpaper.

My breath hitches when he inches forward, his lips hovering dangerously close, his eyes glimmering obsidian fire. "I can't let you leave because I love you, Iris. I've been in love with you since the first moment I saw you. You came into my life like a blazing sun and pulled me out of the pitch-black night I've been lost in for years. You're mine. Fucking mine, and I'm never letting you go."

Next thing I know, his lips bruise mine in a soul-searing kiss. Our tongues lash against each other in a fiery dance of destruction.

Then Malik's words start playing through my mind in a loop. They cut through me like a million razor blades, each slice drawing more blood. So, I let Kaiden incinerate me from the inside out, my fluttering pulse heavy against his fingers, for just a few seconds. Just a few seconds of indulgence to burn his touch and scent into memory because this is the last time I will ever allow Kaiden Black to kiss me.

With a muffled sob, I use my hellseeker strength to push at his chest. Kaiden stumbles back. A deep frown knits his eyebrows.

"That's funny, because you were nothing more than a mistake to me." The lie burns through my lead-filled tongue like battery acid. Still, I continue, "I don't want to see you ever again."

Kaiden's face falls. Akin to a hurricane, hurt ripples through his features. "You don't mean that. I know you feel something for me." Again, the foreign, jumbled emotions bounce in the confines of my ribcage, bruising my lungs and heart.

I force a brittle laugh from my lips. "Yeah, I feel something for you all right. It's called hate. Did you know that after the accident, I stayed in a mental facility owned by the Order for a fucking year? It should have been only a few months for me to adjust to the world without my memories, but losing them made me spiral into a depression so deep I tried to"—I swallow thickly—"to kill myself. I took an entire bottle of pills. If they had found me five minutes later…And you know what the worst part is? If they hadn't kept a close eye on me, I would have done it again."

Kaiden flinches as if I hit him. Slams his eyes shut. Then rakes a trembling hand through his hair as he lets out a sharp curse. When he opens his eyes, and his gaze finds mine again, shame and guilt flood his features. A silent tear rolls down his cheek. "I'm so sorry, angel. So fucking sorry." He crumbles to his knees, and I have to tear my gaze away because I can't look at him. "You're the only person I have ever loved in this world."

My hemorrhaging heart is urging me to go to him, but I can't. I fucking can't. "If you really did take my memories, then you took everything from me. I was nothing more than a shadow of a person for years. I blamed myself to the point where I didn't want to be alive anymore, and that's something I can never forgive you for." A trembling breath saws out of my lungs. "Goodbye, Kaiden. I wish I never met you. Stay away from me and forget I exist, because that's what I'll do."

He doesn't come after me as I storm out of the dressing room into the bedroom to snatch my phone and my mother's journal from the bedside table. I fly down the stairs and into the elevator. As I enter it and jab my finger into the button for the ground floor, Kaiden appears in the middle of the penthouse. His shoulders are slumped as if weighing a thousand pounds. He's only a few feet away, but it feels as though a chasm deeper than the Mariana Trench stands between us. I cast him one last glance. Our gazes hook and snare — mine resolute, his shining with defeat — and the sorrow on his face is almost too much to bear.

The doors slide closed, breaking our connection. I stagger backward, hitting the mirror wall. I can't break down right now. If I do, I'll never be able to leave this elevator. I square my shoulders and shove everything down, down, down — until I'm nothing more than a walking corpse. It's all a blur as I exit the elevator, stride outside, hail a cab, and find myself at Sam's door, banging on it as hard as I can.

A sleep-rumpled Sam opens the door. "What the...Holy Hecate! Iris, what happened? You look like shit. What are you doing here?"

I throw myself in her arms and finally lose it, sobbing my eyes and heart out.

8

Kaiden

I took an entire bottle of pills. If they had found me five minutes later…

"Fucking fuck!" I bellow and send my fist flying into the mirror perched above the sink. Knuckles split. Blood gushes out. A tornado of broken glass follows. Funny how the jagged pieces resemble the inside of my chest cavity. However, the punch does nothing to douse the crackle of *illum* she lit inside me with those words.

The overhead lights of the basement start flickering as blinding white overtakes my vision. I should despise the pure power flooding me because it's *his,* or better said, it belongs to the half I inherited from my father. But I don't. Because no matter how many times he brutalized me over the years to bring it to the surface, he failed—the scars riddling my body are testament to that. The *illum* came only after she barreled into my life. It answered to her.

My angel.

Expelling a trembling breath, I stop pacing and ground myself back to reality by slamming the door back on the thread of pure power before I turn this entire building to ashes. I strangle every emotion and bury it behind a titanium wall — the same one I erected when my father used his special whip on me for the first time. Once I'm under control, I march back to the sink next to the fortified door. The shards of glass, stained scarlet by my fury and regret, crunch under the soles of my motorcycle boots. I bend to pick up the trash can, then fill it with water before bringing it to the naked piece of shit slumped in the chair in the middle of the cavernous room.

He gasps when I throw the water at his face to wake him. Confusion blankets his gaze for a second. Then, in the next, he flicks his beady eyes to the table near him — where I keep all my torture instruments. A high-pitched whimper escapes him. "P-please. I have a f-family."

I raise a mocking eyebrow. "Oh, Gary boy, I know all about your family. You see, touching what's mine was more than enough to grant you a place in that chair. But I had a hunch you weren't just a drunk sleaze harassing women in my club, so I did a little digging. Well, I wasn't surprised to discover you raped and nearly beat your wife to death, and then did the same to your teenage daughter. But your uncle, the mighty judge, can't get you out of this one. When I finish with you, you're going to wish you were dead, you sick fuck."

The sinister smile spreading across my face prompts him to continue his useless begging as the smell of urine permeates the air. His cries don't play in his favor, though, because they only fuel my deviant half. I turn to my torture spread on the table. I brought every single weapon from Hell, then asked Malik to spell them so they would inflict a hundredfold the pain of their damage. Serrated knives, machetes, a knee splitter, thumbscrews, pliers, a tongue tearer — everything exactly two inches apart and polished to perfection. Just how I like it.

I finally settle on a sharp, medium-sized knife, curling my bloody fingers around its handle before striding back to the shit stain who dared put a hand on Iris. The second he bent over her while she was sitting on the barstool at Sin, I wanted to squeeze the life out of him. And then he tried to hoist her up.

You're nothing more than a monster.

An abomination.

You make me sick.

I let my father's words wash over me and dive back into the darkness — where I belong. Because my light is gone. I thought I was broken when I let Iris go eight years ago. But now. Now I can't fucking breathe. I can't think. I never knew this kind of pain existed. It's all-consuming. Like being swallowed by a black hole. So I embrace it. I inhale it and let it saturate every atom as I get to work.

The sound of the door closing reverberates in the cavernous space, snapping me out of the deep end I gladly threw myself into.

"Why is a human in the torture chair?" Malik asks as he advances toward me, letting out a whistle. "Is that his dick in his mouth?" He gags. "Well, this is new — skinning someone alive. How long did it take you?"

I'm sure the smell of charred human flesh is vile, but I'm immune to it by now. I've had years to get accustomed to it. When my father forced me to use my hellfire on one of the disobedient dark creatures they were experimenting on, I was only four years old. I was the same age when I killed someone for the first time. But the scariest part was the pleasure it brought me, my demon half. I welcomed it with open arms. I fed on the keening wails.

That hunger only grew over the years. I kept it satiated by finding the right dark creatures to torture — those who kill innocent humans. Being the head of the Obsidian Conclave has many advantages, but exerting punishment on the underworld beings who break the Celestial Treaty is what keeps it at bay.

"I don't know. I've been in here since early this morning." *Since Iris told me she's going to forget I exist.* I fist my right hand to hide the tremor in my fingers as I stop the gliding knife and drop the last strip of the asshole's skin on the cement floor. I injected Gary, when he passed out again, with an adrenaline serum Malik created a while back to keep victims awake through every single second of justice being served. He's now staring at me from a skinless, burnt face, eyes wide open and drenched in terror. After I cut out his tongue for how he spoke to Iris, I shoved his useless cock into his mouth.

"Well, it's almost midnight, so you've been here all day. What did he do anyway?"

"Touched Iris."

"Ah, that explains it. Wait. Is he the piece of shit Raul and Oliver brought in from Sin the night Adramelech escaped?"

I grunt in response as I stride to the table, drop the knife on top of the towel I laid out earlier, then trudge to the sink to wash my hands. The amount of blood mixing with water would make anyone else queasy. But I fixate on the red gurgling down the drain — painting the scattered pieces of glass in fresh streaks of violence — it's not nearly enough to satiate my thirst for revenge. It should have been *more*. It should have been Erik's.

"Wow. You're a real Chatty Cathy today." Even though I can't see him, I know he's rolling his eyes. "The last mansion we checked on our way back was also a bust. Dominic is grabbing a quick snack, but he said he'll join us in your library for the Conclave meeting after I heal Iris." He pauses. "Um, so are we letting the skinless human die? Judging by the way he looks, he doesn't have much time left. I'm talking hours… maybe less."

"Can you prevent his organs from shutting down, but not heal him further? I want him to live like this." I know Malik's question stems from the fact that the Celestial Treaty forbids us to kill humans. But that's not the reason I don't want Gary dead. Death is an easy way out. It would be too merciful. If Erik were still alive, they would make the perfect cell buddies.

"Um, maybe. I don't think I have enough juice left to heal Iris and attempt this, though. The multitude of tracking spells took a lot out of me while trailing Adramelech all over the country like a bloodhound."

"Just do it."

"But what about Ir —"

"She left." My voice is a deep, gravelly rasp as I white-knuckle the edges of the sink. While I had these poisoned-tipped words contained in my mind, I could pretend they weren't real. But now…

When I finally meet his cat-like eyes, his eyebrows draw together. "What happened?"

"She heard us talking on the phone this morning. Heard you… about the barrier."

Malik swears under his breath before closing the space between us to pull my shaking body into a hug. "I'm so sorry."

"I fucked up. Not only did I take away her memories, but I…Fuck. She tried to — tried to kill herself because of me. Because of what I did. I shouldn't have left her in her aunt's care. I should have been there for her."

Malik inches back, gripping my shoulders. He locks his kaleidoscope gaze with mine. "You *have* been there for her. You've watched over her for eight years. Protected her. She wasn't the only one who lost everything that day. You both did. You made what you could out of a shitty situation. She would've died if you hadn't activated that barrier. She was too far gone, Kaiden."

"But I should have been the one to take care of her after —"

He scoffs, cutting me off. "With Mammon watching your every move like a hawk? He would have killed Iris the second he found out about her, and you know it. He was already suspicious of you disappearing to visit her. Letting the Order take her in was the best solution at the time. And seeing you that soon could have compromised the barrier. Maybe even killed her."

I hang my head between my shoulders. "She'll never forgive me for this…"

"Yeah, she will. Because you're going to be your usual cocky, stubborn bastard self while groveling like your life depends on it. So snap out of it."

I clear my throat while stepping back. "I should go shower."

Showing this much vulnerability would normally embarrass me, but Malik and I…we go way back. He was one of the many dark creatures the Kabal had kidnapped. When he almost killed one of the scientists who experimented on him, they locked him up in a cell next to mine — in the pitch-black dungeon. For an entire year, he witnessed *everything*. Not only the torture my scumbag father inflicted on me, but also the horrible things he made me do. Things that still haunt me to this day. Things I equally despised and took pleasure from. Which, in turn, made me hate myself even more. Because they only proved he was right — I am a monster. The blood on my hands runs so deep it could turn an entire ocean crimson.

"Okay. I'll make sure the meat sack doesn't die, then put him back in his cell."

"I'm moving the Conclave meeting. I can't. Not tonight. Please let Dominic and Logan know," I tell him.

He nods. I lumber toward the door. Once I'm on the other side, where the wards Malik put in place don't hinder me, I tap into the angelic power that allows me to travel across space and distance, and teleport into my penthouse. I inhale a shuddering breath to fill my lungs with her lingering scent — sunshine, linden blossoms, and an undertone of something sensual, decadent. It only intensifies the hollow space beneath my ribcage where my beating organ used to be. Because she took it with her.

Her absence cleaves me in two. I can't even look at the couch as I make a beeline to the fridge for a water bottle. The memory of Iris straddling my lap and the way she melted into me as I devoured her mouth still flashes through my mind, though. It's bittersweet agony. Because for the first time in eight years, I held happiness in the palms of my hands, and like sand, it slipped right through my fingers.

Fuck. I sound like a limped dick motherfucker.

Malik is right. I need to put an end to this pity party. Because she is mine. To love. To possess. To give pleasure to. To break. To put back together. And I am hers in the same way. Every single broken, scarred piece of me belongs to Iris. After all, she was the one who stitched me back together with her light. I'll give her some space because she needs it. That doesn't mean I won't be watching. Waiting. And when the time comes, she will accept it because there's no way I'm letting Iris go again.

Not after holding her in my arms.

Not after tasting her lips.

Not after she gave herself so beautifully to me.

Even if I'm condemning both of our souls to an eternity of damnation. I can almost feel my demon half smiling and saying, *fucking finally*. If I thought I was obsessed with her before, it pales in comparison to how I crave her *now* – with an intensity that borders on insanity. Who the fuck am I kidding? I have not only skirted that line but flung myself over the edge of the jagged cliff at lightning speed. I'll gladly meet the bottom, impale myself on her hatred, and crawl for any crumb she throws my way if it means she will let me into her life again.

As I finish gulping the water, my phone starts ringing. I pull it out of my back pocket to check the screen. I know she wouldn't call, not this soon anyway. But I can't stop letting myself hope. That spark fizzles out in the next second.

It's Grayson.

"Where the fuck is my grandson?" he seethes, venom dripping from his tone.

I take my sweet time as I twist the cap back on, then chuck the empty bottle in the bin beneath the sink. "Who is this?" I pretend not to know, partly because I'm beyond tired of arrogant lightborn who believe their blessed blood grants them license to treat dark creatures however they please, and partly because I enjoy toying with him. "I think you have the wrong number."

"This is Grayson. The head of the Ashville Order. Now answer me. Where. Is. My. Grandson?" he spews.

"How should I know a lightborn's whereabouts? Ah. My apologies. I haven't taken into consideration that at your advanced age, things can get a little…murky. Maybe you have forgotten that I am, after all, the leader of the Obsidian Conclave and such matters do not concern me," I drawl.

My bored tone only serves to grate on his nerves further. "I tracked his phone. I know he was in your filthy club Saturday night. He vanished right after."

"Which club are you exactly referring to? I own several across the world."

"Don't pretend you don't know what I'm talking about. It's the one in the Raven district — Sin."

"Sin can hold up to a thousand people, and since opening, partygoers have filled it to capacity. My responsibilities within the Conclave don't involve babysitting the club's clientele."

"Stop pussyfooting around and tell me where the fuck is he before I destroy your entire organization."

"Hmm. So, your grandson broke the lightborn's number one rule by entering an establishment not only owned by an Elite demon but also filled to the brim with dark creatures, and somehow I am to blame for it?" I let out a dry laugh. Then my tone turns deadly serious. I don't know if Grayson is aware his piece of shit grandson was a lowlife rapist and possibly a serial killer, but I can't stop myself. "Tell me, Grayson, does the Aureal Council know about your grandson's nighttime activities? I imagine they wouldn't be too happy if they did."

He ignores my question, swearing sharply under his breath. "You have by noon tomorrow to hand over the security footage from Saturday night and surrender your employees to interrogation."

Power is a curious, fickle thing. An addictive mirage. Grant it to a weak-willed man, and they will get drunk on the first drop. While it's a heady feeling, it can be more treacherous than a siren who lures a sailor to their death. After all, Grayson is no more than a cog in a wheel. Even if he is the head of the Order in Ashville, he can't lift a finger without all the Aureal Council members' approval. I thoroughly enjoy bringing him down a peg as I say, "I think I missed the Council's letter about an official investigation. Maybe it was lost in the mail. Or maybe you are trying to strong-arm me. As low as you think dark creatures are, we don't answer to you—I don't answer to you."

"Mark my words, demon. This is not over." He ends the call.

I shake my head as I ascend the stairs to the second floor. As convenient as it is to pop around at whim, I like to walk when I need to think. Grayson's call was only a desperate bluff; he doesn't want the Council to know his grandson broke the rules. A head of the Order trying to push me around with an inflated ego is nothing short of laughable. Not only do I have years of experience dealing with the Council and their crooked ways, but I have built an entire empire on cutthroat deals and intimidation tactics. And his was weak as fuck.

He didn't mention anything about Iris, which tells me he doesn't know she was at Sin—I saw to that by having my hackers pin her phone's location at Samantha's house for the entirety of that night. I also don't think Erik showed him the photos he took of us. Grayson would have surely used those as leverage, if that were the case. My steps falter when I cross my bedroom's threshold. Her scent is more concentrated here. I inhale sharply to trap it into my lungs and teleport inside the bathroom before my mind decides to torture me with the passionate moments we spent in my bed. The best day of my life — not because she gave her body entirely to me, but her soul. I've never felt more at peace. More complete. It was utter bliss. A rapturous dance of frenzied heartbeats and future promises.

However, in the next second, I'm met with the array of makeup products Iris haphazardly spread on the black marble counter. Fuck. The compulsion I usually feel to clean the mess is absent, though. I want her to mark every single millimeter of this penthouse like she branded my heart — with a finality that transcends space and time.

Before I peel off the blood-soaked clothes from my body, I text Carter, the wolf shifter from Logan's pack and my head of security. He is in charge of keeping Iris safe whenever I'm not available. The instant Iris left my building, he and his team of five wolf shifters followed her.

> **Me: I need an update.**

> **Carter: She's still at her friend's house. We're doing patrols at half-hour intervals. So far, we haven't detected any threats.**

Heaving out a weighted sigh, I step into the hot spray and close my eyes. I was so lost in the bloodlust that I hadn't even noticed the hours trickle by. But I do feel them now. My muscles are sore as fuck. I wish the water would also wash away the blistering guilt for being the one who hurt Iris. Who made her cry. Because her happiness is more vital to me than the air I breathe. What kills me most is that I lost her trust. But what was I to do? I feel as though I'm trapped between a rock and a hard place. As much as I want to tell her everything, I can't. I would rather set myself on fire than risk anything happening to her.

Iris might not want me in her life anymore. But I'll do whatever it takes for her to forgive me. And right now, I'm just waiting for her to fall asleep so I can teleport into her friend's house and watch over her — just like I've been doing for the past eight years. No, eighteen years — from the moment I first saw her.

9

Iris

"Rise and shine," Sam chirps, pulling the blackout drapes from the window.

I squeeze my eyes shut at the sudden burst of blinding light searing my retinas. Styx, Sam's hairless cat, startles me as she nimbly jumps on my chest. She looks down at me as if she's a queen, casting a glance at an undeserving peasant. "Go away," I grumble and pull the blanket I've been rotting under for the last three days in Sam's guest bedroom—trying to forget all about the demon who stomped all over my heart—above my head. Styx lets out a fierce meow to scold my insolence.

"C'mon, Iris. Get up already. I made breakfast, French toast slathered in hazelnut cream, your second favorite," Sam says, exasperated as she swipes the blanket off my body.

I snort. "You made breakfast? Are you trying to poison me?" Sam is a fire hazard in the kitchen. It's beyond me how the heck she is so good at brewing healing potions.

She rolls her eyes. "Fine. I got breakfast from that brunch place two streets over that you love. Same thing." Her nose wrinkles. "For the love of Hecate, please take a shower before you come into the greenhouse. My plants are going to wilt under your hobo aroma."

"I'm not hungry." I turn my back to her, hide my head under the pillow, and crush the third black iris I've found on my bedside table in a tight fist. *He's* been here, every night since I left, and he wants me to know. *Fuck.* I haven't told Sam about it, though; I don't want to freak her out. I'd been holding the iris and sobbing into the pillow for hours before Sam came into the room. She must have had enough.

She wrestles the pillow from me and hits me over the head with it before throwing it on top of the blanket on the floor. Planting her hands on her hips, she pins me with a stony glare. "Iris, I swear to Hecate, if you don't get up in the next five minutes, I'm going to throw a bucket of ice-cold water on you and use a wire brush to scrub you down. You stink, and I could probably fry an egg on your hair. You've barely eaten anything these past three days. I'm getting worried..." her voice trails off. "C'mon, you said you wanted to go to the cemetery today."

"I changed my mind. Stop hounding me."

Sam mutters under her breath at the ceiling, "Hecate, help me," then flicks those burning emeralds my way. "I did you a solid when I told Ezekiel you're not training today, so you owe me. Get the fuck up if you don't want poisonous mushrooms growing on every available inch of your skin. Don't think I won't hex you if that's what it takes to force you out of bed."

I ponder her words, then huff, "Fine." I refuse to acknowledge how much I resemble a petulant child.

"Shower first." She gives me a poignant look before stalking out of the room, Styx hot on her heels.

Pushing myself off the bed, I trudge into the walk-in shower in the en suite. Staring blankly at the water swirling down the drain by my feet. If only it were as easy to get rid of your feelings as it is to cleanse your body of dirt. It doesn't count as crying if the tears get mixed with the water raining down on my face, right? I feel weirdly detached from my body as I take care of my business and finish getting ready, slipping into the clothes Sam brought over from my apartment yesterday. Then I lumber down the curved staircase to the first floor.

Sam lives in a gorgeous two-story, restored Victorian house near my aunt in the residential area of Ashville. It's decorated in an eclectic mix of colors and patterns, matching the personality of my spitfire best friend. The best part of the house is the massive greenhouse that offers a view of the sprawling garden outside. Sam transformed it into a dining area. Thriving plants of different sizes and colors cover every inch of available space, and I blink slowly as I enter the sunlit jungle, its walls and ceiling made entirely of glass. However, since I arrived three days ago, everything has seemed muted, as if I'm crawling through shades of gray. The happy trill of bird songs spilling from the open door grates on my brain like sandpaper.

Sam steps into the room through the kitchen archway, holding two mugs of steaming coffee. She heaves out a relieved breath the moment her eyes land on me.

"Shouldn't you already be at the flower shop?" I ask, plopping down on the scalloped, hot pink chair at the massive glass table. Even though I'm not hungry, I cut the French toast into tiny pieces and chew on a small bite. It tastes like the ashes of what is left of my heart and settles at the bottom of my stomach like a thick layer of cement.

"I didn't want to go in case you needed me," she tells me as she slides the steaming mug of java on the table next to my plate and sits down on the chair opposite mine with feline grace.

My eyebrows knit in a deep frown. "Sam, I...you shouldn't upend your life because of m—"

She cuts me off. "Have you looked in the mirror? Fuck, Iris. I've never seen you like this. Not even when Noah ghosted you. How could I just leave you here? You know who you remind me of? Me, a few years back, after Ian betrayed me and erased all traces we had ever met."

Her words plow through the paper-thin barrier I erected over my hemorrhaging heart. Apparently, bricks are too expensive these days. You need mental fortitude and a spine of steel to afford them. Both of which I clearly lack because how the fuck did I allow myself to fall head over heels for a demon?

I didn't want to acknowledge this before, but now that Sam spilled it in front of me like spoiled milk, I can't deny the truth—Kaiden's betrayal cut me deeper than Noah's ever could. I put on a mask of what I hope resembles my usual self. "I'm fine. I'm already feeling better," I say as I reach for Sam's hand and intertwine our fingers. "Thank you for taking care of me. You know I love you, right?"

She nods, but the deep lines etched at the corners of her eyes and between her eyebrows tell me she doesn't buy a word. "I love you too. Finish your toast. I'll drop you off before going to the boutique. I need to pluck some fresh delphiniums and snapdragons from my garden first." She clears her throat, visibly uncomfortable. "Um, there's another truck full of flowers outside. I gave the delivery guy twenty bucks and told him to wait in the driveway. I don't know what to do with them..."

Since I arrived at Sam's, Kaiden has sent two trucks full of the same rare, wild black irises from Jordan that he secretly gifted me every year on my birthday. I didn't want to accept them, but the delivery guy said he would lose his job and possibly his life if he took them back. Reluctantly, I instructed him to unload the flowers in Sam's garden, where I planned to set them on fire. But just as I was about to light the match, Sam came back from work and balked at the blasphemy. Apparently, these irises are so rare they cost more than a lung on the black market, per piece. So, I told her she could resell them if she wanted.

Massaging my throbbing temples, I say to Sam now, "Can't you tell him to deliver them to your shop, like the last two days?"

"Iris, the shop is so full right now you can't even drop a pin on the floor. There are too many flowers to sell before they die. My magic keeps them alive, but not forever. I thought maybe we could find a women's shelter and drop them there. Hecate knows their abusive, dickbag husbands never gifted them anything nice."

"That's a good idea," I mumble through another bite of ashy French toast.

Thirty minutes later, I'm staring at the wrought-iron gate of the cemetery, my mother's journal in a tight grip. Even though I've repeated every encouraging mantra I could think of…my legs seem to have grown roots thicker than a mangrove's, planting me in place. The guilt of surviving when she hadn't is still too heavy. Not only that, but it's entwined with the feeling of shame that I had years to find the demon who killed her. And failed. But most of all is not knowing how my mother would feel about everything. If she would be disappointed.

I've only been past this wrought-iron gate once — at the funeral. That day is forever seared into my memory, even though I was high as a kite on pain meds. Grayson pulled some strings and got me out of the hospital for a few hours. There is no honor for a hellseeker who leaves the Order, so it was only me, my aunt, and him watching the casket being lowered into the ground. Of course, it was out of the question for my mother to be buried in the Order's cemetery at the edge of the compound's property. My aunt chose the one closest to her house since I was going to move there in a month or two anyway. But then I swallowed a bottle full of pills.

I remember how out of touch I felt, not only with the world, but with my body, too. As if I was missing important parts of myself. As if someone had taken all the shattered pieces and glued me back together all wrong. I didn't even cry. I stared at the scene unfolding in front of my eyes as if watching a movie. I kept thinking to myself, *This is your mother. Aren't you going to at least shed one tear? Just one. They're going to think you're a fucking robot.* Even the sun radiating warm rays from the cloudless azure sky mocked me. Because if I didn't care that my mother was dead, why should the weather?

The fury came one week later. At the world. At the injustice of it all. At my stupid body for healing faster than humanly possible, but not being able to mend my broken brain so I could get my memories back. All that apathy was the ocean drying one drop at a time to expose the bare bones before the wall came. You know that wall of water right before the tsunami hits? It reached a hundred feet before it smashed into me with a deadly force. I couldn't escape it. It flooded my airways until it reached every single cell in my body to the nucleus. So, I did the only thing I could: I trashed my hospital room.

The bill was astronomical. My aunt was beyond livid, but she understood I was only a teenager. I think she was relieved that I wasn't a zombie anymore. Luckily, the inheritance my mother left covered the cost because Aunt Josephine couldn't afford it. The aftermath of that tsunami wasn't pretty; the flooding waves continued to slam into me for weeks on end. However, the rage turned inward until I was choking on guilt. I just wanted to disappear. To fade away into nothingness… So, judge me all you want for trying to kill myself, but at the time, it was my only way out.

When two hours pass—and I haven't moved an inch—I let out a sigh of defeat before trudging back toward Sam's house.

Maybe next time…

10

Iris

"This is it," Sam says, glancing at the wooden Apothecary sign perched above the door.

The bell chimes when we enter the shop. Vintage dusty blue cabinets and shelves filled with ornate jars line the walls. It's quaint and cozy—like one would expect when entering an apothecary on the main street in Salem. We're the only ones here since it opened ten minutes ago. The earthy smell of dried plants and spices tingles my nose as we weave through the shelves. The scent reminds me of Sam's kitchen when she prepares a new potion.

Sam picks up one of the brass-lidded jars to inspect its contents. "I've been looking for this brahmi root for a few weeks now."

"What can I help you—You! OUT!"

I whirl around to look at the white man behind the counter. His shiny bald head is beet red, and bulbous veins pulse along it as if they're going to explode any second now. He has one angry finger pointed at Sam, practically foaming at the mouth.

I throw her a confused look. "What's happening?"

"Eh, you remember that warlock that made Grammie mad, and she practically spurted a tree out of his ass? This is the guy," she whispers before turning to the old man. "C'mon, Mr. Havirsham, Grammie did apologize."

"Then why did you poison me?" he bellows. "Out. Of. My. Shop. NOW!" His hands glow as his power electrifies the air.

Sam huffs. "Stop acting like a baby. It was just a little hemlock sprinkled into your food. I only let you suffer for half an hour before giving you the antidote anyway. You know you deserved it since you called Grammie a bitch. We all heard you."

He lifts his right hand as if he's going to blast Sam. Before he gets the chance, I swipe the dagger at my belt and send it flying. It pierces the old man's shirt sleeve, pinning it to the wall above his head.

"If you value any of your body parts, I suggest you retract your power," I clip out.

As if seeing me for the first time, his ruddy complexion loses all color, turning ghastly white. Confusion shines in his eyes as they flick between my onyx choker and hair. Back to my choker. "Y-you—you're a-a h-hellseeker."

"Yup, and she's my best friend," Sam chimes in, throwing him a saccharine smile. "We don't want any trouble, okay? We came here to see your wife, that's it."

His demeanor does a one-eighty for the second time. "I'm not letting a hellseeker see my wife. She's innocent. She didn't do—"

"What's all this ruckus?" A gorgeous woman with warm copper skin and Middle Eastern features spills into the shop from a back door, wiping her hands on the apron tied to her plump middle.

"Iman, she's a hellseeker. Run!" the man shouts in abject fear.

"It's okay, Harold." Her gaze cuts to Sam and I. "I'm under the protection of the Obsidian Conclave." She turns her forearm so we can see the Baphomet sign—the head of a goat inside a pentagram—inked on the inside of her wrist.

I lift my hands in a show of surrender. "We don't want to cause you any trouble, Mrs. Havirsham. We're here because I need your help. It's not related in any way to the Order. It just happens that I'm also a hellseeker."

Iman's head tilts. "A hellseeker and an Ambrose witch. Interesting pair—"

"They might be lying, Iman. Don't help her," Harold intervenes, an edge of desperation added to the fear seeping out of his pores.

Sam's eyebrows furrow. "Mrs. Havirsham, you know my Grammie. I would never bring trouble to your door, even though your husband is an asshole."

Harold looks flabbergasted. "Me?!? Your hellseeker friend attacked me!"

"You were about to blast Samantha," I remind him dryly. Harold cusses under his breath. "Listen, I understand why you might distrust hellseekers, but as long as you are under the Conclave's protection and you don't harm humans, I don't care if you're a dark witch. This is something personal I'm seeking help for."

"Distrust? You lightborn think you're above any other creature out there. Our vampire friend disappeared a month ago, and she was last seen in a dark alley alongside a hellseeker," Harold spews. "No one did anything."

"Okay, Harold dear, calm down. That's only speculation. We don't know anything for sure," Iman soothes before inquiring, "Can I unpin my husband from the wall now?"

I flap a hand in the air. "As long as he doesn't intend to fry us anymore, sure."

"I'll make sure of that." Iman strides behind the counter. She takes out my dagger and uses magic to make it float back to me. Snatching it from the air, I slide it back into its holster. She plants her hands on her hips. "Now, what can I do for you?"

"Well, this is a delicate matter. Before we can tell you anything, we will need an oath of secrecy from both of you," Sam answers.

Iman and Harold share a look. Iman drums her fingers on her arm, the lines around her eyes and mouth where the passing years have left their mark deepening in thought. "It's going to cost you."

"Name your price," I chime in.

"Word has it you're the only light witch able to grow rafflesia arnoldii. I want ten," she tells Sam.

Sam nods. "That can be done. I need a week for the plants to reach maturity, though."

"Okay, then. Please follow me. This does not seem to be a discussion we should have here, where customers might walk in. Harold, dear, can you please lock up and then join us in the office?"

He sucks on his teeth, clearly displeased that his wife didn't heed his warnings. "Sure."

Iman leads the way through the door she came out earlier. We pass a kitchen where two pots of fragrant plants are boiling on the stove. When we reach another wooden door, Iman opens it, waiting for us to file inside the office. Harold strides in after a few minutes. He's huffing and puffing as we gather in a circle, holding hands while Sam chants something in a language I don't understand. We each seal the secrecy oath with blood by cutting a crescent line into our palms using a special ceremonial dagger Sam brought specifically for this purpose. A breeze coming from nowhere hits the circle and flutters my hair before this weird feeling seizes me — like an invisible ribbon tying around my tongue.

"It's done," Sam announces, and we step away.

Iman tilts her chin toward me. "Okay, let's hear it. Why are you here?"

"Well, since the age of fifteen, I've had amnesia. I thought it was because of the trauma I suffered during a severe car accident, but I recently found out that's not true. Apparently, someone put a kind of barrier in my head."

"Grammie said you were the only witch she knew who dabbles in mind-altering magic."

A shadow passes over Iman's features at Sam's words — the kind that speaks of sorrow and regret. "Yes, that was before I joined the Obsidian Conclave and left my coven. Many years have passed since I've touched that kind of magic. It's very taxing. Let's just say I'll never recover the pieces of my soul I lost in the process of accessing that type of power." She blows out a breath as if trying to cleanse herself of the past before gesturing toward the chair in front of the mahogany desk. "Take a seat."

I sit down while Sam strides to stand next to me. Harold leans back on the wall, watching us like a hawk, a sour look pinching the planes of his face. Iman bends and places her warm palms on the sides of my head, right at my temples. When she starts chanting, a thick, inky fog envelops the room. "I am going to examine the barrier. Close your eyes," she whispers.

I do. At first, nothing happens. Then, without preamble, my back bows as white-hot pain burns through me and blisters my insides. The migraine I've had since waking up at Kaiden's penthouse after Erik's assault intensifies to the point of madness. Someone screams. I think it's me, but I can't be sure because the pain is all-consuming. As fast as it sank its claws into me, though, it dissipates.

"Iris?" Sam's worried voice brings me back into the present. Something wet tickles my top lip. I wipe at it with a trembling hand. It's blood.

Sam passes me a tissue. "Here."

"Thanks," I mumble, using it to wipe off the blood as best as I can.

"You shouldn't have agreed to this," Harold chastises his wife acidly as he helps her to her feet. She must have collapsed.

"I'm okay," Iman says, but her voice is strained, and her knees wobbly. "Whoever put that wall in your head is extremely powerful. Only direct descendants of Hecate can perform such intricate mind-altering spells. There's only one warlock I know of, but he's almost a myth amongst our kind."

Does that mean K—*he* had a warlock put the wall there? But who? Malik? And why? Jesus, I thought that by coming here, I would get answers. Instead, I have more questions than before. "Is there any way to break it?"

"Not unless you want to become a vegetable. The risks are too high, especially now that the wall has already been breached. There's this *darkness* inside you. I can feel it seeping through those cracks. If I try to take the wall down, you might succumb to it and never be yourself again. Or you could go into an eternal coma. Mind spells are unpredictable, and one should never tamper with them. You'll have to regain your memories gradually and on your own. Even so, there's still a high risk that all those things will happen."

Great. Just great.

"You got what you came for. My wife needs rest. Now leave," Harold grits out through clenched teeth as he supports Iman's weight on his side.

She gives him a withering glare. "Don't be rude. They have done nothing wrong."

"It's okay. We'll go. Thank you for your help!" My knees almost give out when I stand, but I regain my balance.

"You all right?" Sam asks. I offer a nod. "I'll come by next week to bring your payment," she adds over her shoulder as we make our way outside.

"Well, that didn't go the way I thought it would," I mutter, climbing into the passenger seat of Sam's red Mini Cooper. I press the heels of my palms into my eyes in a failed attempt to still my quivering stomach. Despite Sam's protests, I haven't had breakfast, but I still feel as if I'm going to throw up any second now. And not just because I'm in a car.

Sam closes the door on her side. "At least we know that K—he," she corrects herself quickly. She knows the rule: no pronouncing *his* name in my presence. "Wasn't lying."

I huff. "About that, he wasn't. What if I never remember everything on my own? It took me eight years to get only some of my memories back."

The sound of Sam rummaging through her designer bag fills the cabin. "Here, drink this. I don't know, Iris, but you heard Iman. It's too dangerous to even try tearing it down. Your scream earlier—I've never heard anything like that. My heart literally stopped."

"Yeah, it was painful as fuck. Thanks," I say, opening my eyes to take the vial from her outstretched hand. I uncap it and down its contents in one go.

"The other thing Iman said about the darkness inside you…have you considered your father might not have been human?"

"I have, yeah. Since Erik's attack. What I did to him, and seeing ghosts on top of it. But I've never heard about a lightborn falling for a dark creature or having children with one."

"Do you really think that in all history, since the initiation of the Order hundreds of years ago, it hasn't happened? It not being in your history books at the compound doesn't mean it can't be true."

She's right. Of course, I've already considered it. But that would mean, again, that the Order lies and hides things from us, and that's a bitter pill to swallow. A lightborn and a dark creature being in love would be sacrilegious for the Order. One of the worst sins, next to falling for a demon. They would do anything to bury it.

Still, I wouldn't even know where to begin looking for my father. His name is not on my birth certificate. Unless…my mother wrote something about it in her journal. However, I still can't imagine how combining the blood from a lightborn and a dark creature would allow me to have all these enhanced abilities.

"Maybe your Mom wrote something in her journal about your father."

"That's what I was thinking just now."

"Have you started reading it?"

A boulder lodges in my throat. "No…I can't. Not yet. I—" I suck in a jagged breath. "It's too hard, Sam. I've tried so many times. It doesn't feel right to do it unless I visit her, and I couldn't even get past the cemetery's gate when you dropped me off." I blow out a trembling breath. "What if I'll never be able to go inside?"

Her perfectly manicured hand squeezes mine. "It's okay, Iris. Don't rush into it. Grief doesn't have a timeline. You'll get in when it feels right. I'll call Grammie and tell her we're on our way."

The drive to Sam's grandmother's house only takes fifteen minutes. She moved from Ashville to Salem to be closer to her friends—all light witches—when Sam turned twenty, leaving her the Victorian house. She now lives in a charming two-story Colonial, white with blue shutters. As soon as we get out of the car, Beau, her Bernese Mountain Dog, runs from the porch to greet us. I bend and scratch the cuddly giant behind the ears while Sam takes out the Himalayan cheese treat from her tote. As soon as Beau sees it, he lets out an excited *woof*.

"Don't tell Grammie, okay?" she whispers conspiratorially before giving it to him.

As if understanding his assignment, he runs off with it toward the back garden, tail wagging and ears fluttering.

"I saw that," Grammie drawls from the open door, a hand perched on her hip.

"I don't know what you're talking about," Sam retorts in a nonchalant tone.

"The reason I don't give him snacks anymore is because the vet said he needs to lose weight. You're not helping by bringing him treats every time you visit."

Sam gasps. "Don't you dare call Beau fat. He's perfectly chunky."

Grammie shakes her head. "C'mon, you two. I made muffins and they're getting cold," she says as she waves us in. "Iris, my dear, it's so good to see you." She pulls me into a warm, motherly hug. "Oh, my. Your bones are stabbing me, child. Did you lose weight?" Concern flashes in her mossy green eyes—the same hue as Sam's—when she pulls back. Wild auburn curls frame her heart-shaped face. Light magic helps her keep the color alive. It's the only indulgence she allows herself because even if she could decrease the signs of passing time, she always says that aging is a privilege. Every etched line is a new year she got to live when her son—Sam's father—couldn't. In fact, looking at her is like looking at Sam's aged reflection in a mirror. Not only is Sam the spitting image of her grandmother, but she also inherited her feistiness and quick wit.

I clear my throat. "I don't know. I don't think so."

"Well, she's not eating," Sam says.

I scowl at my best friend.

"What? It's true. And it's killing me watch you do this to yourself."

Grammie takes my hands in hers. "Heartbreak is a horrible thing to go through, my dear. I know it's hard right now, but trust me when I say this: time heals all wounds. Also, fuck him for making you cry. No man is worth your tears."

A surprised laugh bubbles out of me. After Sam and her grandmother share a long hug, we all shuffle into the living room, which smells divine, like a mixture of herbs and freshly baked pastries.

"So? Did Iman help you?" Grammie asks, sitting in the quilted armchair next to the arched window.

"Yeah, she asked for ten rafflesia arnoldii in return," Sam answers as we both sit down—me gingerly because of my aching ribs, and her with feline grace—on the couch facing Grammie.

"I hope Harold didn't cause any problems."

"Oh, he was his usual asshole self. But Iris pinned him to the wall when he tried to blast me. He about pissed himself when he realized she's a hellseeker," Sam tells her.

Grammie chuckles. "I wish I were there to see it."

"Iman is a doll, though," Sam adds.

"She confirmed that the barrier is real, but she didn't explain exactly what that means. Or how it works. She also said there's this darkness inside me spilling through cracks that apparently have formed in it," I chime in.

"There aren't many texts about mind-altering magic since it's not only rare and dangerous, but forbidden. Most books about it were burned centuries ago. You could use it to bend anyone to your will— transform them into mere puppets. Imagine having that amount of power at your fingertips. It's the kind that could destroy worlds. But it also comes at a high price. It can poison your soul." She pauses. "However, I did some digging these past few days and found a few things in a history book. Hecate's daughters used magical barriers in the first war against the dark warlocks to render them powerless. Think of it exactly like that—a wall built brick by brick, and the magic the mortar keeping it together. That wall serves as a barrier on someone's power. It blocks it from manifesting. Locks it away. The side effects are always unpredictable, though, as are all matters of the mind. It is said that Hecate's daughters cast the magical barrier on triplets. One of them went insane, the second couldn't remember anything about his life—just like you, Iris, dear—and the third remained catatonic until he died."

"And the cracks?" Sam inquires.

"Hm, the cracks are exactly that, fissures in the mortar of dark magic. I can only assume what happened at that nightclub flared your power, Iris. Akin to a tumultuous, overflowing river swelling and breaching a dam. Or perhaps the umbra demons gave you those cracks during their attack, and the darkness used them to slip through. The problem is, you can only chip it so many times until that barrier bursts."

"So if something like that happens again, it might obliterate the barrier? And then I could go into a coma or get my memories back?" I ask.

"Or go insane…or die. There are endless possibilities," Grammie retorts, her lips setting in a thin line.

A heavy silence falls over the room.

Sam's worried gaze finds mine before she leans forward. "What if we fix those cracks somehow?"

"You already know that each witch or warlock has a unique weaving pattern they use to sew their threads of magic—light or dark. Because of that, the original dark magic wielder who cast the spell might be the only one who can repair those fissures. Even then, we can't be sure it would work. Another dark wielder can try, but it's only like slapping Band-Aids on them. It wouldn't be good as new."

"And besides Iman, you don't know of anyone else who dabbles in mind-altering magic?" Sam asks.

"Sadly, no."

"Well, we have to search—"

"We're not searching for anyone else," I interrupt Sam. Even though I'm aware Malik can access that kind of magic because he was supposed to erase Adramelech's memory after we tortured him for information. But at the same time, I assume that K—*he* thought of that already and probably came to the same conclusion as me: the consequences far outweigh the benefits. Regardless, I can't ask for his help. Not anymore.

She recoils as if I slapped her. "What? How can you say that?"

"I don't want to repair the barrier. I want my memories back. And if this is the only way I can get them, then so be it. Plus, you heard Grammie. Even if we find the dark magic wielder who erected the barrier, it's uncertain they can repair those cracks."

Her nostrils flare. "But—"

"I'm tired, Sam. Of this void inside me. Of feeling lost. You know how hard it's been for me…what happened in that Order mental institution. What if repairing those cracks erases the last eight years of my life, too? Erases *you*. We don't know what might happen. And I can't go through that again. I just can't."

She sucks on her teeth, then jumps to a stand. "Who wants muffins?" She asks before she storms off into the kitchen. I don't miss the tears brimming in her eyes, though.

Grammie offers a smile, but it's tinged with sadness. "Give her some time, Iris. She loves you and she's worried."

"I know. I love her just as fiercely, but the risks are not worth it."

"I agree." She pushes up. "I'll put the kettle on for some tea and check on her."

"Okay," I sigh.

11

Iris

Nervousness carves a scorching path in my stomach's lining as I step into the compound's foyer. Almost all hellseekers of the Order in our city are standing under the grand cupola, which is a replica of the Vatican's Sistine Chapel fresco, waiting for the meeting Grayson called for to start. I square my shoulders and let my cold mask slip into place.

As per usual, they all pretend I don't exist. Not even a chin tilt or a "hello" is thrown my way—as if they're afraid they'll catch the half-blood from me. I'm used to it by now, but every time this happens, it still stings a little. Mostly in my pride because even though I have dedicated all my years since the accident to the Order, it still isn't enough. And I think it will never be. Well, at least this time, it plays into my favor since I'm too rattled to speak to anyone anyway.

Grayson hasn't called a general meeting in a long time. The last time he did, there was a hoard of ghouls wreaking havoc on the outskirts of Ashville, and we all had to work together to kill them that night. Today, he's going to announce either another mission or Erik's disappearance. My money's on the second option. I mean, it's been a week. He surely knows his grandson is missing by now. Honestly, I'm surprised he waited this long.

Fingers drumming an erratic rhythm on my thigh, I cast a glance over my shoulder toward the entrance. I can't help but wonder if the Aureal Knights are going to burst any second now through the massive double door and handcuff me, then bring me before the Council to confess my crimes.

Stop being a drama queen!

If that were the case, it would have happened by now. Well, even if slim, there's still a chance Grayson wants to make a spectacle out of my arrest. The stifling silence that shrouds the room as Grayson descends from the massive staircase on my right, accompanied by Noah, interrupts my racing thoughts.

Even if Grayson's shoulders are slumped as if he's bearing the weight of the world on them, his gait is as determined as ever. While I study him, a set of mercurial eyes settle on me. So I look toward Noah. Hurt flashes in them like lightning before he rips his stormy gaze away to follow Grayson into the boardroom we use for our debriefs. I expect the usual warm tingles to take over my body at Noah's presence, but there's…nothing.

I trudge forward, my feet heavier than two blocks of cement, and file into the room with the other hellseekers. Veronica and Tessa are already inside, huddled together over a distraught Britney.

"Half-blood freak," Veronica spews under her breath while Tessa narrows her venomous eyes in my direction.

I throw them a fake-sweet smile but say nothing as I make a beeline for my usual seat at the enormous table, which accommodates over twenty people. Instead of Raquelle dropping unceremoniously in her chair next to mine, though, the crisp scent of sandalwood and cedar fills my nostrils before Noah occupies her seat.

He heaves out a weighted sigh. "Feeling better?" The minty gum he's chewing does nothing to hide the pungent smell of alcohol lacing his breath. Has he been on a bender?

He avoids my gaze to look at his steepled hands on top of the table. He's as gorgeous as ever — sun-streaked hair, pouty lips, and a jaw that could cut diamonds. All topped off with a body that would make angels weep. What is shocking is that this is the first time I can appreciate his beauty almost from a distance — as if he's merely an acquaintance. A painting I admire in a museum briefly before moving on to new sights. "Yeah. I've been meaning to call. I just — "

He cuts me off. "Not here."

"'Kay," I mumble.

The only response I get from him is a nod as he sucks on his teeth. But he still doesn't spare me one glance. I can feel Veronica's eyes drilling holes in the back of my head as she whispers something snarky to Tessa behind my back. They resemble two hyenas as they cackle.

"If you could all please take a seat. The meeting is about to start," Grayson's deep, gravelly voice bounces off the walls.

The chatter quickly dies down while everyone obeys his request. I haven't had the courage to look at Grayson since entering the room, but the moment I do, the pit in my stomach transforms into a cavernous hole. For the first time, he's showing his real age. Judging by his gaunt features, he has lost weight since I last saw him. The circles under his eyes are a deep purple, so it's pretty clear he hasn't been sleeping either. Erik was the only family member Grayson had left.

"Some of you might wonder why I called a general meeting. And some of you might already know." There's a long pause that makes my skin itch. "Erik, my grandson, is missing. Saturday evening was the last time Britney, his fiancée, heard from him. We don't know yet what happened, but we are investigating his disappearance."

Britney hyperventilates at Grayson's words. More than half of the hellseekers swivel their heads in her direction. Her sobs wash over me like acid-riddled guilt. *Fuck.* As much as I hate Britney because, let's be real, she was one of my biggest bullies, she doesn't deserve this. Still, she would have married a rapist and a possible serial killer if I hadn't killed Erik.

As if sensing the war waging inside me, Grayson's unyielding gaze rakes over my face. Its intensity blisters my skin. Sweat pools in the center of my palms. It takes everything in me not to look away. Luckily, he turns his attention to the rest of the hellseekers in the room, and my lungs expand on my next breath. At least until his next words efficiently knock the air out of them.

"Unidentified demons attacked Iris a little over two months ago. Though slim, it's a possibility Erik might have fallen victim to the same demons."

All eyes turn on me. My cheeks blaze under the weight of their scrutiny. I suppressed the urge to wipe my sweaty palms on the insides of my thighs, where my nails dig deep grooves.

"Over two months ago!" Dana's eyes almost bulge out of her head as she flaps her hands in indignation from my far left. "Why haven't we been made aware of this information sooner? Or better yet, right after it happened?" She is so enraged that spittle flies out of her mouth with every word. The buzz of displeased exclamations fills the room.

Grayson slams a palm on top of the table. "Enough!" The effect is instantaneous. Quiet settles over the room akin to a suffocating blanket. The look he throws Dana could level a city to mere ashes as he grits out, "Have you forgotten who you're speaking to, Dana? Have you all forgotten *I* am your leader and make decisions according to our covenants? The Council decided it's best to keep it under wraps until we know more."

I don't miss the way his and Noah's gaze lock briefly before cutting back to Dana. Interesting. So he also needed the Kabal's permission to let everyone know about the umbra attack. That's probably the reason Noah's here—to supervise Grayson. I bet he doesn't like that one bit.

"Or do you disagree with the decision of the Aureal Council?" Grayson clips out, raising a mocking eyebrow.

Dana flinches, eyes downcast to her wringing hands. "No, sir," she almost whispers.

"Well, now that that's settled, I want you all to be careful when you go out on your hunts. Be vigilant; anything that seems out of the ordinary, you will report directly to me. Starting tonight, you will hunt in pairs and not only look out for demons but for my grandson as well. The teams will rotate every week. After the meeting, Timothy will send you the new schedules and team assignments for this month. Questions?"

Where were these measures when I got attacked by the umbra? I want to ask, but don't. I wonder if he would have done the same if any other hellseeker disappeared or if he would have even cared if *I* did. Deep down, I know the answer; it's kind of staring me in the face. I just don't want to acknowledge it right now. I don't know if I can handle another emotional beating.

Paula, Raquelle's wife, is the first one to break the silence. "For how long is this going to last?"

"It's indefinite, until the Aureal Council decides it's time to go back to normal."

"What did the demons that attacked Iris look like?" Hank, Dr. Corey's son, asks in a gravelly voice across from Noah. He has the same deep, umber complexion as his father, but his hair is longer, touching the middle of his back, styled in dreadlocks. The blond is so ashy it almost looks silver.

"Iris?" Grayson gestures to me, shrewd eyes fixated on my face. "Can you please let everyone know what they should look out for?"

Heat burns the back of my neck as I become the center of attention again. I clear my throat. "The demons consisted entirely of shadows. They had bat wings and resembled decaying corpses with mostly bones showing through the rotting flesh."

"The situation on the streets hasn't changed, though. Aside from a few lesser demons and zombies, we almost haven't encountered any demonic presence for over two months. I mean, I'm not complaining... but it's weird," Raquelle intervenes.

Collective sounds of approval come from almost everyone in the room.

"I know. All your reports are the same. The Aureal Council is working hard on this matter. Any other questions or observations?" After a few beats of silence, Grayson says, "The meeting is adjourned." Spine rod straight, he pushes up from the chair at the head of the table and strides out of the room.

I'm relieved; I was expecting him to ask me to stay behind again so he could ask me questions. Before I can move from my chair, Noah's warm hand wraps around my elbow. There's not even a tiny spark at the touch, an absence which makes my eyebrows knit. Apparently, Kaiden's betrayal has made me immune to all men, even to Noah. I can't say I'm not relieved, though. I've had enough drama these past few months to last me a lifetime.

"I guess we should talk," I say before he opens his mouth.

He drops his hold on me to rake a hand through his sandy-blond hair. "I would prefer you meet me in the training room so we could spar instead."

I tilt my head to the side. "Why?"

Determination is etched in the lines around his mouth as he responds, "Because I don't think you've changed that much, Iris. And before I left, we were always able to settle our differences in combat."

"Fine. I have to pass by my locker to change, and then I'll join you." I wasn't planning on training today because of my ribs, but I can't refuse Noah's request. I actually think it's a good idea. It's not the first time I'll train while injured, and to be honest, I desperately need to blow off some steam. I've been moping these past few days like a simpering fool—a shadow of my old self. I need badass Iris to show her face again so I can finally move on with my life.

"I'll go warm up," Noah says, standing.

I offer a toothless smile. "'Kay. See you in a bit."

12

Iris

After I change into my training clothes, I make my way toward the library. Noah can wait. I wanted to do this the second I entered through the massive doors of the compound. However, Grayson's meeting and my nerves held me back. I can't shake Adramelech's words off anymore, though, like I've been doing all week. They sink their hooks in me with every second that passes.

There's a ledger Lucifer likes to keep with every single hellseeker death caused by a demon since the initiation of the Order. Your mother's name is not there. I would know; I'm the one writing in it.

My footsteps reverberate loudly in the vast space as I stride toward my aunt. She's perched on a ladder, sliding books back into their place on the intricate white shelves. The sun's rays filtering through the stained-glass windows illuminate her form, and I have to blink a few times to adjust to the bright light when I look up.

She casts me a glance. "Iris, dear. I've missed you. I haven't seen you all week."

"Hey, Auntie. I've been busy." Busy wallowing in my self-pity. The thing I'm most ashamed of—on top of not even trying to stretch or train these past few days—is that I didn't have it in me to go on my shifts. I would have continued rotting in bed if it weren't for Sam. Thank God I have her. I can't believe I've missed six shifts in a row. I guess my truancy is ending now, though. I'll have an assigned partner to keep me accountable.

"Can you pass me those two books at the top of the pile?"

"Sure," I say and approach the cart, then stretch to hand her the books she asked for.

"Thanks! It shouldn't take me more than an hour to put all these away if you want to grab lunch."

"Um...that's not why I'm here. I need to check something on one of the computers."

She offers a smile, but it's tinged with disappointment. "Oh, I see. 'Kay, then. Holler if you need anything."

"I will," I say over my shoulder, passing the six grand cupolas, which depict the imperial court of Elysium and its riches. It's the first time I don't take a few seconds to marvel at the artistry behind each brush stroke. It must be the result of feeling like my organs are wilting slowly one by one. When you're dead inside, the outside world loses its importance.

I stop at the computer near the windows and sit down on the chair, then turn it on. Just like human law enforcement agencies, the Order has its own software to manage demon reports and all types of files about hellseekers and the other lightborn. After Grayson questions us about our shifts, his job is to write up a summary and file each one. Tim scans them to later introduce the data or appropriate files into the system. We usually go over them in debriefs in our weekly meetings. I don't envy Grayson's job as the head of the Order. I mean, sure, it gives him a lot of power and influence, but it's boring as fuck.

I type my unique username and password into the portal to which only hellseekers have access. When it loads, I search for my mother's name. Her file appears on the screen. I click on it. I suck in a shaky breath as I pass her photo and all the standard data from the date of birth to when she left the Order. However, when I reach the last page where the report of her death should be, there's only a big red stamp that says "CLASSIFIED."

In all these years, I haven't looked at the file. I had no reason to, really—I trusted Grayson and the Order with every fiber of my being. And he had shown it to me in the hospital after the accident. Granted, I was just a kid and still high as fuck on pain meds. He took out the photos for obvious reasons, but even with the state of my addled brain back then, I can still remember the words written under the cause of death: inflicted wounds by an unknown demon.

Now that I think about it, to my knowledge, a hellseeker's death is described in detail. I once saw Grayson write a three-page summary. It was after one of our rare group missions had gone to shit, and Dave—Tessa's boyfriend at the time—was killed by a ghoul. My mother's was one sentence.

Just to make sure, I search the system for Dave's file, then two others. Not only was I right, but there's also a thorough autopsy report to accompany each of Grayson's. My mother was not a hellseeker anymore or part of the Order, but still. I feel like I'm the biggest fool on planet Earth.

Was her file always confidential? If that's the case, then how come Grayson was allowed to show it to me at the hospital? Or did they restrict it after? All of these questions ricochet around my skull at the speed of light, intensifying the usual pounding behind my eyes to the point where I feel on the verge of throwing up. And the most important question of all: Why classify it at all?

The need to know the truth is like fire ants crawling beneath my skin. As much as I avoided Grayson until now, he's the only one who can provide answers. Everything is a blur as I shut down the computer and make my way to his office.

I knock three times.

"Come in."

When I enter, Grayson looks at me over the rim of his large cup of coffee. He takes a sip before saying. "Iris, to what do I owe this pleasure?" His tone is distant. He's always been stern, but ever since the umbra attack, his demeanor toward me has only gotten colder. I imagine his suspicion hasn't lessened one bit, especially after Erik's disappearance. He doesn't even invite me to sit.

I clear my throat. "I was looking into my mother's file in the hellseeker portal, but her death is deemed top secret. Why?"

His shrewd eyes examine me for a few seconds. "You know I can't answer that. It's way above your pay grade."

"But, when did the Council restrict it?" I huff. "I remember you showing it to me at the hospital when you first visited."

He sets the coffee down. "Iris, I showed it to you as a courtesy before it got filed because I wanted you to know the truth. Your mother's death was closed to anyone but higher-ups from the very beginning." Steepling his hands on the cherry wood desk, he asks, "Why look at it now, after so much time has passed?"

Fuck.

In my desperation to get here, I didn't prepare a reply, even if him asking this was a given. I resist the urge to wipe my sweat-slicked palms on my leggings.

Think, Iris, *think*!

"Well, I had a flashback of the accident for the first time in eight years. It was short, though. We were rolling into the canyon, and then I woke up. I wanted to see if maybe looking at the file would help me remember more."

"I see. That's not possible, unfortunately."

I know I'm stepping on his toes, but I have to at least try. "Can't I have a quick look? I mean, I've already seen it—"

"You've got some nerve asking me to bend the rules. Rules are for everybody. And as much as you think they don't apply to *you*, our covenants are sacred to me."

I almost get frostbite from the iciness in his tone. "I'm sorry. I shouldn't have asked. Thank you for your time." I scamper out of there, my insides turned to a block of ice because even though I don't have enough proof right now, I can't escape the feeling that Adramelech was telling the truth.

The Order is hiding something…but I don't know how I can get my hands on my mother's file. If it were in Grayson's office, I would break in to get it. However, the Aureal Council keeps all classified documents at a secret location. The heads of the Orders in each city have to make a special request to get access to them.

This only strengthens my resolve that my top priority is finding evidence against Erik. Not to present it to the Aureal Council but to the human police. If they can bury my mother's death, they can bury his crimes. Which is not fair to his victims or their families. This would also be my first line of defense if they ever find out I killed him.

However, as I scroll through the new schedule Tim just sent, I realize that for the next three weeks, I don't have even one free day. Shit. And the first place I need to search is Erik and Britney's apartment. But the only time I know for certain she won't be home for several hours is when she's on a shift. Which, of course, coincides with mine. I'm also paired with Tessa for the first week, then with Veronica, and to top it all off, Britney is next. It's like Grayson did it on purpose.

I can't wait that long. There's no other way…I have to ask Noah for help.

ENTERING THE FIRST training room, I look around for Noah. I spot him in the far-left side corner, the muscles in between his shoulder blades dancing with each speedy jab he sends flying at the punching bag. The sound of him pummeling the shit out of it echoes in waves, covering the noise made by the hellseekers occupying the training mats. He looks as if he's trying to exorcise some inner demons. The smell of fresh sweat and the lavender of the cleaning products mingle as I make my way to him, spine rod-straight.

"Hey, Iris. Haven't seen you in a while," Ezekiel says while tilting his chin mid-stretch, making me flinch. I was so focused on Noah I didn't even notice him.

I stop in my tracks. "Hey, Zeke. Yeah…I um…"

He raises an eyebrow as he pushes up from the mat on the floor, his taut tawny skin on display since he is shirtless. "You were trying to avoid a certain someone?" He's not subtle at all when he flicks his gaze toward Noah.

I play into it. I've never been so grateful for being a love-sick fool for years than in this moment. "Something like that. So what, is all the Order privy to my personal life now?" I offer a brittle smile as I fold my arms over my chest.

"No, but Noah has looked fucking miserable because you ghosted him these past few days. He got a taste of his medicine, huh?"

I scoff bitterly — for this, I don't have to pretend. "Yeah, like one percent of it. Maybe even less."

There's a pause as if he's pondering his words before he continues, "I took him out to a bar last night. We talked. A lot. Then we got smashed." He places a hand on my shoulder. "Listen, I'm not going to sit here and tell you to forgive him because if I were you, and Christina pulled something like that on me...fuck, I don't know if I could ever move past it. What I'm saying is maybe let him show you how sorry he is. He really is suffering, Iris."

I look to the ceiling, suck on my teeth, then back at him. "I'll think about it."

He drops the hand. "I've got to go." Ezekiel gives me a warm smile, his dark eyes wrinkling at the corners before he turns on his heel. "And don't you dare flake on me again! I miss the challenge. No one spars as ruthlessly as you," he half-yells over his shoulder.

I stride toward Noah. The smell of last night's alcohol seeping from his pores is so potent that I feel the urge to breathe through my mouth. He turns before I get the chance to make my presence known, his T-shirt plastered to his body, accentuating every ridge of sinewy muscle and his trim waist. Droplets of sweat rain down from his forehead onto the rubber floor as he bends for the water bottle. He gulps down half of it.

Angry music blasts from his headphones, so he bends again to pick up his phone, then taps on the screen to pause it. "I didn't think you would show up, so I started without you," he grits out, equal parts anger and hurt thick in his tone.

"Sorry it took me so long. I had something I needed to take care of first." I force my fingers to relax when they restart their nervous dance against my thigh, then clear my throat. "Actually, I need your help."

His eyebrows furrow. "With what?"

"You're staying here at the compound, right?"

117

Pushing a wet lock of hair out of his eyes, he says. "Yeah, I have a room on the second floor."

"Can we go talk there?" I ask.

"Why? What about—"

"Please, Noah. We can do the sparring or the hand-to-hand some other time."

A muscle jumps in his cheek before he mutters, "Fine. Let's go."

We don't talk on the way to his room. I'm too busy running through different scenarios in my head. Noah opening the door snaps me out of my racing thoughts. He lets me pass first before closing it at his back. Sunlight filters through the stained-glass windows, painting the floor in an array of vivid colors. Tiny flecks of dust whirl in them.

The room is spacious but almost spartan. A double bed sits in the middle, flanked by two white oak bedside tables and a matching dresser pushed against the wall on my left. The only sign that Noah has been living in it is his phone charger in the outlet next to the bed.

"Can it wait until I take a shower?" Noah asks as he bypasses me.

I saw my lower lip between my teeth. "Sure."

He nods and disappears through the semi-open door at my left. I plop down on the bed, the pristine white sheets crinkling on my sides. Ten minutes pass before Noah gets out of the bathroom. He's wearing only a towel wrapped around his waist, his damp hair pushed to the side. Again, I expect that ember of heat to rekindle at the expanse of rippling muscles in front of me, but there's zip. Zilch. Nada. Old Iris would have had a heart attack if she saw Noah almost naked. New Iris is blissfully apathetic.

He smirks when he catches me staring, though, then strides to the dresser. Heat does crawl on the back of my neck the moment he drops the towel at his feet. However, it's not the good kind. It only makes me uncomfortable.

"What are you doing?" I croak, averting my gaze, my eyes drilling a hole through the wall in front of me.

"What does it look like? I'm getting dressed," he replies, chuckling. His right thigh grazes mine when he takes a seat next to me. He's the first to break the awkward silence. "So, what do you want to talk about?"

"As I said, I need your help."

He tilts his head, waiting for me to speak again.

The proximity to Noah is blistering through every layer of my skin, so I stand up to pace the room. "I need you to trade places with Tessa on our shifts for the first half of next week."

"Why?"

"Because I have to do something, and I can't attend one of the shifts. I need you to cover for me. No one from the Order can know."

His eyebrows knit. "What is so important that warrants missing a shift? The Iris I know would crawl through the fiery pits of Hell before that happened."

Yeah, well, the Iris you knew is so far gone it would make your head spin. "I can't tell you. It's a secret."

Noah drops his gaze to the floor as he ponders his answer. When he finally drags his eyes back at me, it feels like an eternity has passed. "I'll ask Grayson to switch up the schedules under two conditions. I know you've been keeping things from me, Iris, and this proves it. I'm not a fool. I recognize this is because of all I've put you through. You don't trust me yet. Don't worry...I know I have to earn it, and I will. But no more lies or secrets, okay? I'll let you have this secret, but I want you to tell me the truth from now on. This is the first condition."

I fold my arms in front of my chest. "And the other?"

"You will let me take you out on a proper date. I'll pick you up; we'll go to a nice restaurant. Not Ciprianni's. Let's leave the past behind. We need a fresh start."

"Deal," I say reluctantly, because he's basically forcing me, "but we'll go only as friends." If I have to go, I might as well be clear about it. But at the end of the day, how is this any different from Kaiden strong-arming me into our first date?

13

Iris

"Hi, Mom! Wow, this didn't sound so lame when I rehearsed it on the way here. B-but what else can I say after not coming to see you for ei-eight years straight? I just—" Fuck. A sharp hiccup slips out. The sobs wracking my body are so violent I'm surprised my ribs don't shatter to smithereens. My knees buckle as I read for what feels like the umpteenth time since I arrived here: "Eliana Harper. Beloved mother and sister."

Tipping my head back, I take a moment to suck in a lungful of air. The dreary clouds rolling in on the gunmetal sky match the storm brewing inside me. I don't know what pushed me past the wrought-iron gate today. Maybe it was the passing of time that washed some of that bone-crushing guilt. Or maybe it was the urge to find out the truth after seeing that the Order classified my mother's death.

But if I look deep down, I can acknowledge it's more than that. I think I'm finally coming to terms that it wasn't my fault for not being able to remember her. That my brain isn't broken—that *I'm* not broken. Took me long enough…trust me, I know. But when something is ingrained in the very essence of your soul, you can't just move past it because the cuts and bruises are still there. And when you least expect it, fresh blood seeps out. For the first time in eight years, though, I'm allowing them to heal, and it feels as though I'm breaking the bars of the cell I've locked myself into when my mother's casket touched the ground.

I wipe the tears with the back of my trembling hand before shrugging. It's stupid, of course, because she can't see me. She can't even hear me. I'm aware.

Still, I continue, even if my words are not intelligible, "I'm so-sorry. S-so sorry. I couldn't, you know. I thought that I would be able to—to r-remember y-you. And when I got my memories back, then I could come see you. Th-then this guilt that slashes my insides to ribbons would eventually fade away. I was such a fool because it's only gotten worse over the years. And I—I miss you so damn much. T-there were s-so many times I needed you to just hug me and be there. Every s-single birthday. When I graduated from the Order, I wanted you to tell me how proud you were because, against all odds, I made it—I became a h-hellseeker just like you. When I went out on my first date…

"Not o-only that. I might n-not remember you aside from those two flashbacks or our relationship before you—before you…" I can't finish it. Instead, I say, "I wish we could have lunch and dinner or simply shoot the shit over coffee. But most of all, I needed you to tell me it's going to be o-o-okay. Especially now, Mom, because I fell in love. Please don't be mad. I know this sounds bad, but he's an Elite demon. Yeah… You're probably not surprised he stomped all over my heart, huh? I shouldn't have been blindsided by it, either. Trust me, the irony of a demon hunter falling for a demon is not l-lost on me."

I let out a mirthless chuckle. "A-and I thought I knew what heartbreak felt like before, you know...when Noah left and then ghosted me. But what I'm feeling right now surpasses every pain I have ever known. I'm drowning in a sea of black. Every time I gasp for air, this sludge-like tar fills my lungs. And I'm at the bottom of the ocean." Taking a moment to fully absorb the words, I let them out on a trembling whisper, "I don't kn-know if it's worth swimming anymore, trying to break the surface."

Another hiccup slips out. "I'm so tired, Mom. Of being strong. Of pretending I'm not falling apart at the seams when my insides are so threadbare you can see right through me. I wish you could give me some advice...tell me what to do."

My fingers white-knuckle my mother's journal, now sitting in my lap. "I mean, sure, I have Sam and Aunt Josephine, but it's not the same. There's this gaping hole inside of me, and it's in your shape. If that wasn't enough, everything I believed in, my world...has been tilted on its axis. The Order is not what it seems. They're lying. Keeping secrets. I can't help but wonder if this was also the reason you left, not only because you fell in love. God, Mom, it would be so simple if this wasn't a one-sided conversation. Silly me to think that maybe I would come here and see your ghost, right? I mean, it's for the best. With how many years have passed since—since you've—since the accident, you wouldn't be sane right now. You would probably be a poltergeist. So, yeah, what I'm saying is that I'm glad you passed on to the light. But I'm not gonna lie, there was this part of me that wished you were a ghost...

"Anyway, the reason why I'm really here is because I found your journal. And I've been making myself sick, wondering if I should read it or not. Most of it got ruined anyway because it fell into water. This pipe burst...Ah, you don't need all the details. Sam used magic to restore it, but she couldn't save more than half of the ruined pages. Oh yeah, she's a witch; I haven't told you that yet, have I?" I blow out a breath, then mumble, "There are so many things I haven't told you."

I swallow past the heavy knot in my throat. "I'm still torn because I want to respect your privacy. But this feels like I have a tiny part of you in my hands. And I'm so desperate to know you. More than that, I need to find out why you left Ashville, because I can't shake the feeling that the Order is lying about your death. They classified your file, which has never happened before with a hellseeker who left the Order. I know because I checked."

Gnawing on my bottom lip, I ponder my decision while ignoring the new, messed-up sonar in my head that's been counting the bodies buried beneath my feet since I entered the cemetery. Don't ask me how I can tell, but there are exactly two hundred seventy-five. It's creepy as fuck, but if I count all the memories of the last eight years I haven't shared with my mother, or the questions I haven't asked her, the number is so much more overwhelming, so I brush the weird sensation off my shoulders. I cram it into a box, put the lid on it, and label it "later" before shoving it into a dusty corner of my mind.

The smell of rain hangs heavy in the air, so if I'm going to read from the journal, I better make it soon because the storm is approaching.

"Okay, Mom. Please don't be mad, but I'm going to start reading a few pages. And if it feels wrong, then…I'll stop."

I untie the leather strings and thumb through the pages until I find the first entry where the ink isn't terribly smudged.

Owen blindsided me today. He confessed his love to me, and I just stood there, not knowing what to say. He tried to kiss me, and I froze. Luckily, I snapped out of it at the last second and turned my head to the side. He only missed my lips by a few millimeters, his whiskey-laden breath brushing against my cheek. The worst part is that tonight was their engagement party.

My parents wanted to celebrate big, so they rented Ciprianni's for the night and invited the whole Order. It struck me as weird that instead of looking like a man living his best life, Owen was pushing his food around the plate and drinking as though he were a soldier about to go off to war. Each glass transformed the stolen glances toward me into outright staring. He made me uncomfortable as fuck, so I excused myself to take some fresh air. What I wasn't expecting was for him to follow me to the outdoor terrace at the back of the restaurant.

He accused me of distancing myself since the moment he and Josephine got together. He said he thought our friendship weighed more than that. But I explained to him that my sister asked me to, and yeah, while it hurt because Owen has been my best friend my whole life, I didn't want to make my already strenuous relationship with Josephine worse. Then he blurted out the three dreaded words: "I love you." I stood there like a deer in headlights. Which, in turn, gave him the chance to ambush me with the kiss. He told me he'd been in love with me since we were kids and I punched him for calling my sister ugly. But I never responded to any of his advances over the years, so he thought if I saw them together, I would finally wake up and, out of jealousy, break them up.

His logic stumped me. I mean, I knew he had a crush on me — it was hard not to notice — but surely he had moved on since he'd been in a relationship with my sister for two years. TWO YEARS. And while I do love him, it's only as a friend. Nothing more. How couldn't he see how wrong it was to use her like that? He didn't wait for me to finish chastising him, though. He stormed off.

When I went back into the restaurant, he and Josephine were already gone. I asked what happened, expecting them to tell me Owen had broken off the engagement because it was the right thing to do. But my mother only muttered that he was feeling under the weather, and they left early. My parents were upset Owen got smashed, but their joy that Josephine was going to get married to one of the best hellseekers in the Order overshadowed that.

And here lies my conundrum…I should tell my sister, but how can I when *they're getting married in only three months? And she has been radiating happiness ever since he proposed. At the same time, though, I think she already knows. Why else would she ask me to step away from my friendship with Owen?*

Unrequited love is a burden no one wants to carry. I wonder if that's why Josephine has always been distant with me, or if at least this is one of the reasons. Ever since we were kids, when she looked at me, I caught glimpses of searing anger, but they dimmed in the next second...as if I imagined them.

Oh, wow. I had no idea my mother and Owen were best friends. My aunt never mentioned anything on the subject. Well, to be honest, she had little to say about my mother either, and I didn't want to push her. Even if I was starved for every little scrap she would throw my way.

Talk about a complicated love life. I wonder what Mom meant when she wrote that she and Aunt Josephine already had a strenuous relationship. I don't get to find out because the drizzle that started a few seconds ago is already taking the shape of big, fat drops, and I don't want to risk the journal getting even more damaged.

"I'll be back soon, Mom. I promise," I murmur and push up, hurrying my steps through the tombstones toward the exit.

14

Iris

These past few days have been interesting, to say the least. Working alongside Noah to patrol Ashville is the equivalent of walking a tightrope while doing a clumsy dance to avoid landmines at the same time. Because there are so many things I can't tell him—even if I promised I wouldn't lie anymore. At least our conversations haven't veered toward the umbra attack and everything that happened after, but toward the past, reminiscing. And for that, I'm grateful.

But what I'm most grateful for is that tonight I get a break from Noah. If old Iris could hear my thoughts right now, she would have a conniption. The summer air is stifling, and a fine sheen of perspiration coats my hairline while I cross the street in the southern part of Ashville—where Britney and Erik's apartment is located. This part of the city is filled with skyscrapers, posh cafes, Michelin-star restaurants, and high-end boutiques, most of which a certain Elite demon owns—ugh, here I go again, thinking about *him*.

I take out my phone to look over the address I have in the notes app. Then check the time before flattening myself against the side of the building, blending into the shadows. Five minutes later, Britney's blond ponytail swishes in the opposite direction. I wait until she disappears from my field of vision to step out of the darkness. In the next second, though, I'm pulled back by strong fingers shackling my wrist. I swiftly unsheathe one of my daggers and whirl to press it against the man's throat, drawing blood. My eyes slam into quicksilver.

"Noah?" I ask in disbelief, while dropping my hand at the side of my body and stepping back. "What the fuck? What are you doing here?"

His jaw ticks. "I should be the one asking you that, don't you think? So tell me, Iris, what are *you* doing outside Erik and Britney's apartment building? I saw you waiting for Britney to leave, so you better think twice before spewing a lie."

"I can't believe you followed me. We had a deal," I seethe.

He cocks an eyebrow. "Our deal was only regarding the schedule. You never said I can't follow you. Now, start talking."

Shit. This looks bad. So bad in fact, that if I don't tell him about Erik, and the Order finds out about my nighttime activities, my ass will land in Gomorrah faster than I can blink.

Here goes all or nothing.

"I killed Erik."

Noah gapes at me for a few blistering seconds. Tilts his head. Then places his hands on my shoulders. "I don't think I've heard you right. You did what?"

I can barely hear myself over the war drum in my ears. "Erik is dead. I killed him."

"What the fuck?" Noah lets go of me as if I've burnt him. "How?

What happened?"

I prepared myself for the possibility that I might have to confess I killed Erik at some point, so I tell him the story I've rehearsed in my head, sprinkled here and there with lies and omissions—a mirror, really, of all our interactions since he came back. "Sam and I were at a club Saturday night. When she went to the bathroom, Erik found me at the bar. He wanted me to kiss him...I said no." I sigh and squeeze my eyes shut before snapping my gaze back to his.

"He told me that Grayson put him up to watch me after the umbra attack. But he was already lurking in the shadows. I think he was stalking me." I sniff. "Long story short, he roofied my drink when I wasn't paying attention. Next thing I knew, I was outside, drugged out of my mind, and he came for me." I blurt out the last words, "He tried to rape and kill me."

It takes a few seconds for Noah to process my last sentence. When it finally lands, his entire body starts shaking. "FUCK!" he yells as he punches the wall at his back so hard, it leaves a dent in the bricks.

I flinch at the unexpected sound. Noah is still shaking as he turns, pulls me into an embrace, and cradles my head against his chest. "Why didn't you tell me before, Iris?" he demands, indignation lacing his words.

"How could I tell anyone I killed a lightborn?" His embrace is supposed to be calming, but it only suffocates me. The realization that my body's reaction to Noah might be the effect of Erik's sexual assault makes my lungs fold in two. I can't stand his touch anymore, so I push out of his hold to step back. "I'm sorry. I—I can't do this."

Confusion knits his eyebrows. Then, something flashes in his eyes before they turn all hail and thunder. "Is it because of him? Of what he did to you?"

"I think so."

"Did he...did he..." he grits out through clenched teeth.

"No, he was about to. Somehow, I found a sliver of strength and stabbed him with the dagger I had hidden in my boot. You know I never leave my house without a weapon. He beat the shit out of me, though. That's why I haven't been at the compound all week. If it weren't for Sam…"

His upper lip curls. "Good. He's lucky you got him first. But where's the body?"

"It's best you don't know. All I can tell you is that Sam took care of it when she found me."

"And no one saw you?"

"No, it all happened in the back alley of the club." I swallow. "There's more. I don't know if you've heard anything about the women being murdered over the years in Ashville. The ones who had the words 'demon whore' carved into their bodies. I believe Erik was the serial killer because he said some implicating shit while he was attacking me. So that's why I'm here—to search his apartment for evidence." I don't think Noah would approve of me getting the human police involved, so I serve him another half-lie, "To have something to sway the Council in my favor if they ever find out I had something to do with Erik's death."

Noah takes a few moments to absorb my words. "Okay. Let's go."

"Um, where?"

"To search his apartment. I'll help you."

"Are you sure? You would become an accomplice."

"I don't give a fuck. C'mon. I'll drop you off when we finish."

"Okay," I mumble as he pulls me toward the entrance. "I think we should wait for a tenant to come in or out, though." I tilt my chin to the front door of the building. It's locked, and we could pick it, but there's a security camera.

As soon as I finish saying that, someone strides toward us, holding a ridiculous number of designer shopping bags. It's a woman who looks to be in her late fifties. I can't help but wonder what store is still open at eleven at night. Well, I guess if you have enough money, the schedule doesn't apply to you. And by the looks of it, she bought half the store. She huffs as she unsuccessfully tries to fish something out of her designer bag. Her keys, I presume.

Noah throws her a smile that could blind the sun. "Do you need any help with the bags, ma'am?"

"Oh — um — I, um," she stammers, and I bite my lower lip to stifle a laugh. I think I had the same dazed expression when I first saw Noah. Actually, I vividly remember tripping over my own legs like an idiot. It's refreshing not to be the one bearing the brunt of his charm.

She shakes her head, then smiles back at Noah after she schools her features. However, the reddish tint in her cheeks betrays she is still flustered. "Sure. If it's not too much trouble. My shopping spree got a little out of hand, and my driver had to go pick up my husband from a late meeting, so I thought I should walk," she prattles on as Noah bends to take the bags from her. "I haven't seen you before. Did you just move in or…?"

"No, we're waiting for a friend," I chime in before following them into the foyer. I stop near the plush emerald couch, plopping down with what I hope is the air of someone who's been here before. "Noah, I'll wait for you here. Melissa should be down any minute now."

He nods.

"Noah. That's a lovely name. I'm Charlotte. Oh my, look at those bulging muscles. You work out, don't you?" the woman gushes all over Noah while they enter the elevator.

He throws me a panicked look when Charlotte starts feeling him up. This time, I can't stop the chuckle from springing free when the elevator doors slide closed.

Thirty minutes pass before Noah finally makes a reappearance.

"Did that lady try to kidnap you or what? I was about to call the police," I say, tone full of mirth while I stride toward the elevator, where he's waiting.

Noah lifts his hand to show me the white card tucked between his fingers. "Apparently, you weren't prepared enough. We also needed one of these." He swipes it over the access reader when I step next to him, pushes the button for the twenty-fifth floor, then visibly shudders. "That woman is batshit crazy. I only accepted a drink from her because I was trying to get this damn card out of her purse. She excused herself to go to the bathroom, and when she came back to the living room, she was fucking naked."

I whistle. "Whoa. You really unleashed the Kraken with that smile, didn't you? Jeez. I bet my neighbor, Ms. Robbins, would be so jealous if she knew she didn't get to pull that move on you first. If you ever want to change jobs, I think you would make a good living as a sugar baby. Not like you need the money, but you know."

He shakes his head at my antics but still smiles.

The elevator dings. "C'mon, Casanova. Let's get you inside before Charlotte comes looking." When we reach the apartment's front door, I unlock it with Britney's extra key—which I swiped from her locker at the compound earlier today. What's a minor break-in next to killing someone? Am I right?

Looking at the spacious living room with its walls full of cute pictures of Britney and Erik from their vacations all over the world, you wouldn't think he was a psychopath and, most likely, a serial killer. I was afraid that entering the place where Erik used to live would bring forth that blistering guilt. However, it doesn't come. It seems to be attached only to the people close to him, those who suffer from his absence.

I don't get the chance to take anything else in because the moment Noah closes the door at our back, a high-pitched shrill reverberates in my eardrums as something sharp latches onto my right ankle.

I shriek back and try to shake the...rat? off.

Nope, not a rat—a dog.

Of course Britney has a Chihuahua.

"Do something!" I fire at Noah, who, instead of helping me, is shaking with laughter while recording everything on his phone. "Do you really think you should film this? It's evidence we broke in," I mutter as I bend to dislodge the vicious creature from my leg. The little fucker is stronger than one would think. Luckily, I'm wearing hellseeker gear; otherwise, it would have done some real damage to my ankle.

I grab the dog from the back of its head to immobilize it, careful not to hurt him because I would never injure an animal on purpose—even one that looks like a rat. Letting Styx, Sam's Sphynx, sleep next to me every night is a testament to that. He's shaking as though he's rabid and practically foams at the mouth as I push his small body into the bathroom at my left, then shut the door. Muffled, high-pitched barks travel through the wood.

Facing Noah, I shoot daggers at him with my eyes. "Seriously? I can't believe you just stood there. And filmed everything no less." I extend my hand toward him. "Give me your phone."

"Nope. Not gonna happen. That video's going straight to the vault. C'mon, Iris, you have to see the irony. You don't bat an eye at fighting three ghouls at once, but you get ambushed by a two-pound Chihuahua. Fucking gold," he chuckles out and shakes his head before sliding his phone back into the front pocket of his pants.

"Vault? What vault?"

All the levity in the air evaporates as Noah's expression turns serious. "Well, I have all these videos of us, of you...from before I left." He pauses, lines forming at the corners of his mouth, a haunted look in his eyes. "There were some moments when watching those was the only thing that got me through the day. It cost me a fortune to get them back when my phone broke. But it was all worth it to have a little piece of you with me. Of what we had."

"Oh," I mumble and look down to escape the intensity in Noah's mercurial gaze. Maybe his words would have meant more if I hadn't fallen for a certain Elite demon. Instead, they only make my skin itch because I now have something to compare our past relationship to. And what we shared doesn't even hold a candle to what I feel — *felt Iris, felt* — for Kaiden.

I clear my throat, unable to withstand the awkwardness blanketing the air anymore. "'Mkay, well, we better get to it. Where would you hide something if, say, you were a serial killer?" Turning on my heel, I traverse the corridor to my right, where the portion of a bed covered by a pink polka dot comforter is visible through the crack in the door. "I'll take the bedroom. Will you look through the living room?" We could search together, but I need some space.

Noah heaves a weighted sigh. "Sure."

15

Iris

How many shoes does one person need? No, seriously. I've been in this damn dressing room for over an hour, and I still haven't gotten through all the shoe boxes, ninety-nine percent of them filled with sky-high stilettoes. When does Britney even wear these? I haven't seen her wear anything other than her sneakers at the compound. Maybe she collects them as a hobby. What the fuck do I know?

Not like I imagine Erik would hide his murder trophies in Britney's shoe boxes, but I have to check, just in case. Besides, I've already looked everywhere I could think of: under the mattress and bed, in the air vents, under the picture frames, in his socks and underwear drawers. Not only that, but I also dug through the soil in their potted plants. Hell, I even checked the floorboards to see if one would move. And I still came out empty. Looking from the outside, you would think Erik's life was picture-perfect. However, I know it was only a façade. I just need to find the cracks.

"Anything?" Noah asks as he props his hip in the door frame.

"Other than Britney's unhealthy shoe obsession?" I shake my head and blow out a frustrated breath, making the tendrils of hair that escaped my braid dance. Then I flick my gaze to him after closing the last shoe box. "You?"

"Nope. But there's still the office. I figured we could look there together. I've already checked the kitchen and the living room."

"Even under the smoke alarm?"

"Yeah."

Damn it.

When we're done ensuring everything looks how we found it, hours have passed. Good thing Noah is here. We then make our way to the office. Like the rest of the apartment, this room doesn't say serial killer in the slightest — light gray painted walls, minimalist desk, black leather executive chair, a walnut bookshelf, and a love seat next to it in the corner. Judging by the lack of pink, I don't think Britney spends much time in here.

The only things that stand out are the three paintings perched on the wall behind the desk, which seem to tell a story. The first depicts a scantily clad woman riding a red beast that has seven heads with horns. She's surrounded by a hoard of demons as though she commands them. The story changes in the second — seven men wearing crowns appear amongst the demons. They're kneeling before her. The third is the most gruesome: an archangel holds the head of the now dead woman, her blood gushing in a crimson river over the slain beast, while the demons run for their lives. Tendrils of light touch the foreheads of the seven kings, who are standing with their heads tilted skyward as if thanking divinity.

It's an allegory told through the strokes of a brush. The message is loud and clear: good conquers evil. However, it leaves me with an oily feeling because it is one portrait of millions that only serve to perpetuate the patriarchal society we live in. That if a woman is not the perfect Stepford wife and dares to embrace her sexuality, she's the portrayal of evil — the whore who commits spiritual adultery with the beast/demon and uses her body to manipulate. To bring men to their knees. And there is nothing worse than that. After all, lust is a cardinal sin.

I know others wouldn't catch the subtle meaning, but to *me*, these images scream of Erik's deep hate of women. I wonder if, in his fucked-up head of his, he was excusing every murder by doing God's work. His words ring inside my head, *"Stay still! I need to cleanse that demon from your body."* Surely, his lightborn blood made him some sort of righteous savior in his mind — like the archangel in the painting. But who knows? It's too late to ask him now, anyway.

Ripping my gaze away, I stride toward the desk to sit down on the chair. The leather creaks softly under my weight. "Do you think Timothy already went through Erik's computer?"

"Knowing Grayson, it's a pretty big possibility. I don't think he would leave any stone unturned."

I ponder his words before powering the PC. "Yeah, you're right, but if Timothy did look, it surely was for signs of someone having the intention to hurt Erik, not the other way around."

But any hope I had fizzles out when I see that the computer isn't even password protected. You would think it's a good thing, but why would someone with something to hide leave his computer unprotected? If Erik was a serial killer, we won't find anything incriminatory in there, that's for sure. So, I don't even bother looking. It's a waste of time, and we have little left of that anyway because Britney should be back from her hellseeker shift soon.

"I'll take the drawers. Will you look through the bookshelf?"

Noah nods before rifling through the dusty books in the corner. *Not much of a reader, eh, Erik?*

"So, how come you're staying at the compound? I imagined you would be more comfortable living in your old house." I'm not proud to admit how I know Noah held on to his parents' house: I frequently checked online real estate property records over the five years he was gone to see if he'd sold it or not. If he still held on to it, it meant he had a reason to come back. Yeah, trust me, I'm aware of how lame I sound.

He could have made a lot of money from it since his parents were filthy rich. Though, you couldn't tell by looking at Noah because he always dressed off the rack, and he was never a snob or made me feel inferior. Moreover, he could have had any car he wanted, but he chose to save his hellseeker salary for over a year to buy Betsy—his beat-up Kia. That's one of the many reasons I fell so easily for him.

"When I landed in Ashville, I took a cab straight to the house. You remember Robert, our butler?"

"Yeah."

"He and his wife Maria still live there, and they take care of everything. I've been paying their salaries over the years, but I never kept in contact. I told you about the no-attachments-to-the-past rule the Kabal imposes on us." He chuckles softly. "Maria almost had a heart attack when she saw me. She was tending to the azaleas on the front lawn. The ones my mother loved so much." There's a pause as he sighs, a forlorn expression on his face. "Anyway, I couldn't get inside. My feet stopped working when I reached the front door. Maria and Robert were upset I didn't stay, but I couldn't bring myself to get past the threshold. All these memories of my parents flashed before my eyes. I got Betsy out of the garage and bolted out of there. Maybe someday…"

I know the feeling. I haven't been back to my apartment since I left Kaiden's penthouse. I can't. It's too damn hard. I know I have to eventually. But my safe haven — the place I was so proud to call home — became infinitesimally better when Kaiden lived with me. The short time we spent together between those walls made me realize a home is not made out of bricks and mortar, but of flesh and bones, a beating heart, and a warm chest to lay your head on.

Not a place but *a person*.

Kaiden was my home.

Now, the rooms are haunted by the ghosts of us laughing in the kitchen while he whipped up something quick for dinner, watching movies together on the couch, and him holding me every night to chase my nightmares away. And I know I'm not strong enough to face them yet.

I blink back to reality and continue rummaging through the drawers.

"Fuck," I let out under my breath when both Noah and I come up empty. Again. Frustration has me gnashing my teeth as I plonk down on the loveseat unceremoniously. Short of slashing through the furniture and pillows, we searched in every single nook and cranny we could think of.

Noah takes a seat next to me. He heaves out a defeated sigh. "Maybe we should go through his computer after all."

"There's not much time left." I purse my lips, eyes fixated on the three paintings. Then it hits me — the freakin' paintings. Huffing in disbelief at my stupidity, I jump up, startling Noah.

"What are you doing?"

I don't answer. My legs eat up the space to the back of the room in three long strides. I lift the first canvas to look behind it. Nothing. Then the second. Again, nothing. But when I look behind the third.

Bingo.

Taped to its back are a flash drive and a key. I unstick them with careful movements, then beam at Noah when I turn around to show him what I've found.

"Finally! You're a genius," he says as he pushes up from the loveseat and strides toward me, pulling me into his arms to twirl me in a circle. A surprised squeak leaves me. My whole body stiffens, but he doesn't seem to notice. When he stops spinning and settles me down, happiness dances in his eyes, turning them to burnished steel. "You're so beautiful," he murmurs as he brushes my hair behind my ear. His hungry gaze drops to my lips.

The caress is soft, but it grates on my skin like sandpaper. Alarm bells go off in my head. It's *wrong, wrong, wrong,* every cell in my body shrieks. Is he really trying to kiss me after our earlier discussion about Erik's assault? I push back, but he dips at the same time. His lips seal over mine, his arms still bands around me like steel. He takes advantage of my surprised gasp to force his tongue in my mouth with a guttural groan.

What the fuck?

In a flash, I'm thrown back into the dark alley with Erik on top of me and blinding panic sinks its talon-tipped claws into my lungs. I shove him back. Noah's back hits the wall with a loud *thud.*

"Are you out of your fucking mind?" I bellow. My hands ball into tight fists at my side.

There's a glint of anger in his gaze, but it dissipates like smoke in the wind as if I imagined it, because he's crestfallen in the next second. "Fuck, Iris. I thought you wanted this. I—"

My tone is glacial. "What part of my body language were you reading, huh? The part where I was as stiff as a board in your arms or the one where I was inching away from you?"

"I'm so sorry." He rakes a shaking hand through his sun-streaked hair. "I want you so much that I didn't think—I didn't think at all. I—fuck—punch me."

His words confuse me enough to douse a bit of my rage. "What?"

He takes a tentative step forward. "Punch me. That's what I

deserve, so do it."

"Yeah, you deserve it, but I'm not going to." I suck on my teeth, then shake my head. "Just—just don't ambush me again. I'm not ready for anything like this, okay? I don't want a relationship, Noah. And even if I was ready for one, it wouldn't be with you. Friendship is the only thing I can offer you. Nothing more than that."

"I completely understand, and I'm so sorry."

I suck in a lungful of calming air.

"What do you think the key is for?" Noah says after a few moments, to break the tense silence, which is louder than a raging storm in the confined space of the small office.

"I'm not sure," I mumble, but something tickles my memory. Earlier, while scouring through the drawers, I saw a sealed envelope from a company that seemed familiar. However, I didn't think much of it because I couldn't remember where I'd heard of it before. "Actually, I think I know."

I spin on my heel and sift through envelopes in the second desk drawer again in a frenzy. I find it quickly—it's the same company I hired to move my stuff from my aunt's house to my apartment. I received an email from them a few months later announcing that they also added storage box units to their services. My fingers tremble in anticipation as I rip it open, then rake my eyes over the monthly bill for the storage unit and its address.

Fuck, yeah!

I pass it to Noah to take a look while I insert the flash drive into the computer's slot. A window pops open. It's password protected. On instinct, I type in the first thing I think Erik would use: "demon whore." *Shit.* I've got two more tries. Maybe "demon-loving whore." It's wrong. Drumming an erratic rhythm with my nails on the desk, I ponder if I should try again and risk never seeing what's on it. I sense Noah approaching to look over my shoulder. Thankfully, he doesn't invade my space.

C'mon, Iris, *think*! What would a psychopath who hated women use as his password?

I think back to the significance of the paintings, which Erik must have felt a deep connection to. Why else hide these under the one with the strongest message? A scantily clad woman, riding a beast, commanding demons while bringing men to their knees...I can't believe I didn't think of it first! The New Testament, Book of Revelation 17:5. Fingers trembling, I type in "whore of Babylon."

This time, I can't contain the excited scream from slipping free when another window pops open. Twenty-five folders stare back at me, each titled "demon whore," followed by an assigned number. I open the first one. There have to be over a hundred videos here, so I choose a random one. It's footage from inside someone's bathroom. A brunette woman is taking a shower. It's not clear at first what's happening, but then a moan reverberates over the running water as she moves — a man is eating her out, on his knees.

I close the video, uncomfortable as fuck. This is nothing like the time I attended the succubus party with *him*. Those were willing participants; they wanted to be watched. This woman wasn't aware that Erik had put cameras all over her apartment and was stalking her.

Holy shit! What if —

I scroll to the last folder in a panicked daze. When I finally open it, I choose another random video. The room is dark, shrouded in shadows, but even so, it takes me about a second to recognize *my* bedroom. And lying on the bed — fingers sliding in and out of my pussy — is me. I feel so violated, more so when I realize this is one of the moments etched on my brain forever because sitting in the armchair in the corner, watching me, is Kaiden. And that sick fuck has tarnished it.

The sound of the front door being unlocked slices through the silence. "We have to go," Noah whispers, tone steady, but his body trembles with undisguised anger.

Fuck, fuck, fuck, fuck, fuck.

I'm so stupid. In my earlier frenzy, I completely forgot he was watching over my shoulder. Did he see Kaiden? Did he recognize him? Does he know what the Elite demon running the Obsidian Conclave looks like?

Calm the fuck down, Iris! The room was dark, and the camera was behind Kaiden. He only saw his back, that's all. Fuck, at least I hope so. As Noah zips through the room to close the door, I safely remove the flash drive, shut down the computer, and pocket it along with the key and the envelope I found earlier.

"Brutus! Mommy's home." At hearing Britney's voice, the dog lets out a series of sounds so awful they seem to come straight out of the pits of Hell rather than the body of a two-pound Chihuahua.

"What do we do?" I mouth at Noah while we both press our ears to the door.

He shrugs.

"Brutus? Why are you in the bathroom? Oh no, did Mommy close you in there by mistake? Bad, bad, dog! Look at what you've done. You made Mommy step in poo-poo. No! You're not going anywhere. Mommy has to bathe you. You stink. Oh God, there's shit and piss everywhere. Why are you acting like this? Brutus, calm down!"

I crack the door and peek through the gap just as Britney disappears into the bathroom; her gagging sounds now muffled by the closed door. Throwing one more cursory glance at my back to make sure everything is in place, I tilt my head to Noah to signal him it's time to go. We tiptoe through the corridor until we're in the building's hallway. Luckily, Brutus made such a ruckus there's no way Britney could have heard us. We bolt into the elevator.

"Phew! That was a close one," I let out on a relieved exhale.

Noah doesn't even look at me, his eyes drilling holes in the elevator doors while we descend. His fists are so tight I'm surprised his tendons don't fracture under the pressure. "Who was that? Watching you?" he snarls acidly.

I huff in disbelief. "First, that's none of your fucking business. And second, don't you think it's kind of fucked up that you weren't even concerned that Erik — who almost raped and murdered me — was stalking me like a creep? He probably put cameras all over my apartment. Who knows for how long he had been watching me? In all of my vulnerable moments…I feel so fucking violated, and you're concerned about *that*? Frankly, you can take your jealousy, Noah, and shove it up your ass." Folding my arms over my chest, I mutter, "Un-fucking-believable."

Noah snaps his eyes shut, and after a few moments, he murmurs, "I'm sorry."

A brittle laugh escapes my lips. *Men and their fragile little egos.* "Yeah, you've said that a lot today. I don't want you to drop me off anymore. I would rather walk." Without sparing Noah another glance, I stalk out of the building and into the empty streets of Ashville.

16

Kaiden

The *tap, tap, tap,* of the inquisitor's cane—which is not only solid gold but also adorned by garish angel wings—reverberates over the low sensual music as he enters my club, spine rod-straight. His upper lip curls in blatant disgust when he passes the two wolf shifters guarding the inside door. My teeth grind as I shove down the urge to incinerate him on the spot for that disrespect alone. Alec and Zayn are loyal to a fault, and ten times the man he is.

He swivels his head to take in his surroundings, crinkling his nose like he's smelling something foul. The suit he's wearing is ivory, embellished by thick golden embroidery at the lapels and sleeves. A shiny bow decorates his long, dirty-blond hair, which is tied at the nape. But the worst part of the entire ensemble are the shoes: suede loafers that match the suit. I'm surprised my eyes haven't started bleeding at the sight.

"Is this guy for real?" Malik snickers at my back, where he's standing beside Emily at the bar.

"Right? I swear all he's missing is a minion," Emily whispers back on a low chuckle.

Before he reaches us, the inquisitor snaps his fingers. A gangly young man with a large briefcase spills through the open door. His short, white-ish blond hair is sticking every which way, and sweat dots his forehead.

"Never mind," Emily adds on a muffled laugh.

I have to bite the inside lining of my cheek to stop the one bubbling its way up my throat. However, despite the levity my friends bring, I wish I didn't have to bear the presence of this pompous snake. Hell, I would even take the *Narnia* marathons Malik has forced me into countless times over being here. He always says my TV is better than his before he parks his ass on my couch. Which is a lie. Not only did I gift them—Malik, Dominic, and Logan—the three apartments on the level beneath my penthouse, but I also made sure they got the same electronics, too. The real reason he does this is because they were his little sister's favorite, and there are days when his grief is suffocating. So even though I would rather stab myself in the eyeballs with a ballpoint pen than go through six and a half hours of that torture again, I would never refuse him. Not after he lost her so tragically.

The inquisitor doesn't even spare a glance at the teenager who looks as if he's about to piss himself any second now. "Has the witch arrived?"

"N-no, sir. She sent a text, letting me know she's going to be here in five minutes."

"Tardiness is unacceptable, Sebastian. I'm cutting her pay in half for the insolence. Write it down."

"Yes, sir." He swallows thickly, then murmurs barely above a whisper, "My name is Simon," before scribbling on a notepad from his pocket.

Simon's remark falls on deaf ears as the inquisitor regards me over the bridge of his aquiline nose. "Black." Pure hatred flashes in the confines of his irises. His attempt at intimidation is pathetic because not only is he two heads shorter than me, and dressed like a damn peacock, but I can tell he practiced it in the mirror.

"Barnabas," I say. My smile is all teeth and sharp edges. "Welcome to Sin. May I offer you a drink?"

Malik coughs to cover his snort at hearing the inquisitor's name, and Emily wheezes, "This keeps getting better and better."

Barnabas cuts them a searing glare, then says, "I am here because you are under investigation by the Aureal Council, demon. Not to debase myself with debauchery."

I lift a nonchalant shoulder. "Suit yourself. Simon?" He doesn't hear me because he's busy staring at the succubi and incubi dancers finishing up their practice in the gilded cages above our heads, slack-jawed. Maeve is not among them. After the shit she pulled when she dropped into my lap to make Iris jealous, I offered her two options: to work at a new club that's opening in Tokyo or a trip back to Hell. She chose the first.

When I repeat the question, Simon whirls his head toward me and turns beet red. "Y-yes. Wat—"

Barnabas interrupts him. "He's not having anything. Now, let's get down to business. I don't want to spend all day *here*."

As soon as he finishes saying that, a petite middle-aged woman hurtles through the door. Her sandals slap against the onyx dance floor in her hurry to reach us.

Barnabas twists his thin lips. "Ms. Jones. Finally."

"I'm so sorry. Traffic was crazy."

"Hm." He turns his beady eyes on me. "You said there was a fire here last Saturday. Quite convenient for a fire to damage the server holding your security footage on the same night a lightborn disappeared in your establishment. You wield hellfire, don't you?"

"Yes, but I didn't use hellfire to start it, if that's what you're implying." This is not a lie. That night, I sensed Iris's abject terror. My inability to teleport long distances forced me to make two stops before reaching the club's back alley.

I couldn't get there fast enough.

The second I saw Iris lying in a pool of blood, I snapped and lost control of my *illum*.

Icy flames engulfed the outer wall faster than I could take my next breath. Only the fear that it could spread and hurt her broke through the white-hot fury. I drew it back just in time. The wall didn't collapse, but the server, the computers in the surveillance room, and two high-top tables melted. Luckily, nobody was harmed. However, the acrid smoke overtaking the club and the sprinklers activating produced a mass hysteria. Which played in our favor because the madness that ensued is the perfect excuse for not knowing what happened to Erik—everyone was too busy running for their lives. Also, by the time the firefighters arrived, we were gone from the back alley, and I had already smashed Erik's phone.

"That remains to be seen. Ms. Jones, do your job," Barnabas orders. A smug smirk lifts the corner of his lips.

The witch huffs at his rudeness but nods before making her way to the wall covered in soot at the back of the club. She places her palms on it and starts chanting. Waves of light magic spread from her touch. When she strolls back to us, she says, "Hellfire wasn't the catalyst. I don't know what it was, though. I have encountered nothing like it."

Barnabas's face falls. "I assume you prepared a room where I can question your employees," he grits out through clenched teeth. He was banking on the witch, declaring me the culprit to make a quick arrest. That's why he brought four Aureal Knights, who are waiting outside the club.

Well, tough luck, motherfucker, 'cause you're not making any arrests today. Barnabas already interrogated me yesterday in a more official setting where all the Aureal Council members could watch. I could feel Grayson's venomous gaze drilling holes in my head through the two-way mirror for the entire three hours. Adramelech's escape gave me the perfect alibi, though, because aside from those closest to me, no one knows I am only half demon and can teleport. That's how I joined the Obsidian Conclave when it was still under Mammon and climbed to the top — by hiding my real heritage. Surveillance footage from my residence showed me entering my basement before the fire started and Erik vanished, and not exiting until much later. Grayson insisted I must have had something to do with it because everything that had happened was too convenient.

I'm sure it also rubs him the wrong way that not only did I push back on the Council's decision to hold the questioning for my dark creature employees somewhere else, but also for Grayson to attend. My argument was simple: Erik's family members shouldn't be involved because they lack the ability to be objective. Lightborn already treat dark creatures like second-class citizens, and I will not allow them to bully my employees. Besides, they don't have any evidence aside from the camera footage of the ATM Erik passed on this street and his phone location. They're grasping at straws.

"Follow me," I retort before striding to the bathroom hallway where the rooms the vampires in the Conclave use to feed are, alongside my office. I punch in the security code, then open the door for Barnabas, Simon, and the witch to enter. They wait for me to lead the way through the corridors until we reach the conference room next to my office. I flick the lights on before they file inside.

Barnabas snaps his fingers. "Steven, set up the camera." He turns his pinched face toward me. "The bartenders and bodyguards are first, followed by the dancers."

"Very well," I say and take a seat at the head of the table.

"What do you think you're doing?" he snaps with vitriol.

"What does it look like? Settling in for the questioning," I drawl as I lean back in the black leather chair and raise a mocking eyebrow. "The Celestial's Treaty annex contains no law forbidding my presence during these interrogations, as long as my employees face no accusations. I know my rights."

He white-knuckles his cane. "I told you to set up the camera, boy," he barks at Simon, who has been watching our exchange wide-eyed. This must be the first time he's seen someone defy the inquisitor.

Simon flinches and almost drops the briefcase as he struggles to open it. The witch mutters a whispered "asshole" under her breath. I take out my phone and shoot a text to Malik while Simon is busy arranging the tripod.

> **Me: Send Emily in, please. And then tell Leo he's next. Can you also let the dancers know they have time to eat before they come in? They can order whatever they want. It's on me.**

> **Malik: Sure. Should I also fix the wall?**

> **Me: No. That can wait until Captain Dickbag is gone.**

> **Malik: 'Kay.**

Emily strides in after a few minutes, plopping down on the chair to my right. The witch sits next to her while Simon starts the camera.

"State your name and species," Barnabas tells Emily.

"Emily Dawson. I am a wolf shifter pertaining to the Silverfang pack."

The inquisitor's lips turn down in contempt. My fingers curl into tight, eager fists beneath the table in response. It would be so simple to teleport to where he's leaning against the wall and snap his neck. *Do it*, my demon side urges. But I can't. So I bury the alluring violence beneath that titanium wall.

"Are you under a magical oath of secrecy?" he asks.

"No," Emily replies, tucking a stray ash-brown curl behind her ear.

"Ms. Jones. Verify the statement."

"I will need to touch you," the witch tells Emily.

When Emily nods, the witch closes her eyes, then her fingers circle the wolf shifter's wrist. She opens them. "She's telling the truth."

17

Kaiden

"What now?" Dominic asks while raking a hand through his raven hair. He's standing next to the floor-to-ceiling windows in my library, the night sky and city lights glimmering at his back.

"We just have to wait and see how the Council reacts," I reply, massaging my pounding temples as I sink further into the soft leather of the armchair. "But they have nothing on us." Barnabas dragged the interrogation until I could barely contain the urge to shove that ridiculous cane down his throat. His blatant show of repugnance almost pushed me over the edge.

Between this never-ending day and the countless board meetings I had to attend this week, I feel like I can't catch a fucking break. But I ignored the legitimate side of the Obsidian Conclave's business for far too long while I was Iris's shadow. And now I have to deal with the consequences. I don't regret it, though. Hell, if it meant we could be together again, I would relinquish my position within the Conclave and give away every cent I possess in the blink of an eye.

Logan's amber gaze flicks to Malik. They're both seated on the brown leather couch on my right. "Did you erase Erik from everyone's memory?"

Ava's absence is notable. Since becoming Luna of the Silverfang pack, Ava has been a permanent fixture at our Conclave meetings. She and Logan make all decisions for the wolf shifters together. But because it's past midnight, and she had a tiring day running her bakeries, she decided not to attend.

Malik shakes his head before replying, his septum ring catching the light cast by the chandelier. "That would have been too suspicious. Only of those who saw that shit stain with Iris."

"We couldn't deny he was at Sin because of his phone's location," I chime in. "As long as the Order thinks Erik fled the club in a panic when the fire broke out alongside the other patrons, we're good."

"I wish I was there to see that inquisitor's dipshit face when he left empty-handed," Dominic says.

"It was fucking priceless," Malik chuckles out, then takes a long pull from his beer. "Smoke was coming out of his ears all the way to the exit."

"What about the Kabal? Did you find anything?" Logan inquires. Malik and Dominic were investigating a lead on the Kabal the night Adramelech escaped and Iris killed Erik.

"No. They burned down the building before we got there," Malik answers.

Logan swears sharply under his breath. He jumps up to pace the room. Frustration is pouring out of him in thick, noxious waves. And for good reason—he's worried about his wife.

The Kabal, my father's organization, operates in the shadows, kidnapping and experimenting on dark creatures. This is why I endured years under Mammon's thumb to become the leader of the Obsidian Conclave—to finally obtain enough power to undo the gruesome crimes committed by my father. To atone for my part in them. After we blew up their secret lab in the Vatican five years ago, we thought we had eradicated them. Or at least hindered them enough not to present a problem anymore. But like a damn hydra, when we least expect it, the Kabal grows two more heads.

Before Logan met Ava, she was just a human who had a miraculous heart transplant. Turns out, this was another one of the Kabal's sick experiments. Ava received the heart of a wolf shifter whom they kidnapped when she was only a teenager. Somehow, by receiving Hope's heart, Ava became a wolf shifter and Logan's new fated mate.

We know the Kabal has been watching her. Not only because Ava felt like someone had been following her ever since the surgery, but also because Tony warned Iris about them. The friend he was so worried about is Ava. Before a rogue wolf shifter murdered Tony, he and Ava became close while working together at the Shabby Shotglass.

Logan flew off the handle when I told him about Tony and doubled the wolf shifters and vampires guarding Ava twenty-four-seven. If we thought he was overprotective before, it doesn't even compare to how feral he has become—understandably so. However, despite everything we've done over these past two years to find them, the Kabal have somehow managed to stay under the radar. The most vexing part is that for the last three months, the dark creature kidnappings around Ashville have increased at an alarming rate, and we don't know why.

"What about that vampire who disappeared in Salem?" Logan clips out, his fingers flexing at his sides.

"Another dead end," Dominic replies. "But we don't know if it was the Kabal because the only witness vanished without a trace.

Before disappearing, though, they told an old warlock who owns an apothecary that they last saw the vampire in a dark alley alongside a hellseeker. So maybe it was just a hellseeker showing their true colors. We can't be sure…"

"And I can't file a complaint to the Aureal Council on hearsay alone," I add.

A stifling silence falls over the room. The only sound is that of Logan wearing down the Turkish rug.

"Are you ready to go back in?" I ask Dominic. For the past year and a half, we have been working tirelessly to infiltrate Dominic into the vampires that took over Mammon's dark creature and human trafficking ring when we dismantled it. They mostly sell fae at auctions to other vampires because of their highly addictive blood that also allows them to walk in daylight. Dominic has saved three fae so far by pretending to be a buyer. We're hoping to gather enough intel to find the vampire den behind it and dismantle their organization from the inside.

He swirls the amber liquid in the crystal lowball glass before downing it. Exhales through his nose. Then locks his blue-green eyes with mine. "Not really, no. Every time I step back into that world, it strips another layer of the little humanity I have left."

"No one would blame you if you want to get out, Dom. You know that, right? We will use whatever you've gathered and go after them," I say.

He scoffs. "It's not nearly enough. This is bigger than anything we could have ever imagined. And I can't back down now. Not after we worked so hard. Besides, I want to help the fae. Someone needs to. Fuck. The things I've seen. How they're treated…"

"Fine. It's up to you. Can you speak to the fae you rescued and ask them about an oracle? I wasn't able to find out anything through my connections so far."

Dominic tilts his head. "I can try, but it's difficult to earn their trust.

And for good reason." He pauses. "What about you? Did you find out anything about the bounty on Iris while in Hell?"

"Nothing of substance. Only contradicting rumors. Whoever is behind it, though, must be powerful because secrets in Hell have a steep price," I reply.

Malik leans forward, resting his elbows on top of his knees. "Do you think Mammon targeted Iris to get to you?"

Even though our plan to banish Mammon to Hell a few years back was successful, he is still one of the nine kings—the King of Greed. That same boundless greed was his downfall. So when we presented Lucifer with the evidence of not only the atrocities he was committing behind his back, he had no choice but to strip Mammon of almost all his powers. However, he still holds his title and the reverence of demons in the citadel he lords over.

"I can't be sure. But why would he need her alive? If he wanted revenge for our little uprising, he would have tried to kill her by now. I still think it's linked to the prophecy."

"We all know there are far worse things you can do to someone than kill them."

Akin to barbed wire, Logan's grim words wrap around my lungs, pulling blood. Because he's right. Just the thought of Iris being in danger is enough to push me over the edge straight into a bloodlust frenzy.

"For fuck's sake, Lo. He's fucked enough in the head about Iris without your cantankerous ass saying things like that." Malik places his beer bottle on the side table before pushing up and striding to Logan. He opens his arms. "Now stop pacing and bring it in." He whirls his head to Dominic, then to me. "You too, asswipes. Come here."

Dominic snorts. "What are we, five?"

Malik gives us a sinister smile. "Shut the fuck up and do as I say before I hex you all."

Logan rolls his eyes but halts and folds his six-foot-nine frame around Malik's smaller one. Dominic shrugs, then ambles to them. I shake my head as I stand to join them in a group hug. Weirdly, it's exactly what I needed.

Logan's heavy exhale says the same about him. "Cantankerous, really?" he chuckles out after a few seconds. "Have you been reading the dictionary?"

"What, like I don't know big words?" Malik counters as we all pull back.

"Did you want to discuss anything more tonight? I haven't had time to eat today, and you fuckers smell like a Thanksgiving feast," Dominic says. Now that he's closer, I notice that his normally tan-olive complexion is paler, his eyes glassy—which are clear signs he needs blood.

I hike a shoulder. "I have nothing else."

When Logan and Malik say nothing, Dominic brings two fingers at his temple in a salute. "Sayonara, fuckers. I'm off to find a pretty lady."

Malik makes a kissy noise and winks devilishly before they both shuffle out the door. "You can bite me if you want."

"No thanks, dipshit. I like to fuck when I eat."

"Pfft, please. I would rock your world, and you know it."

The corners of Logan's lips pull up at their banter. "Ava's waiting for me in bed."

"You're staying here tonight?" I ask.

"Yeah. We're heading back to the pack tomorrow."

I wrap my fingers around his shoulder. "Don't despair, okay? We'll protect Ava at all costs."

He nods, face stoic, and strides out.

The silence that follows is oppressive because it only serves as a reminder that *she* left me. So, I spin on my heel and let my eyes sail over the charcoal drawing of the angel bowing on one knee, perched atop the fireplace—my only source of comfort in the eight years I have watched her from afar. Cursed to remain in the shadows while she moved on with her life. Drinking in her smiles while dying inside because I wasn't the one who put them there. So close but always too far.

Iris's talent never ceases to amaze me. Even though I've found myself in this exact spot countless times before. She knew how I felt about my scars. How every time I looked in a mirror, all I could see was *him* — his hatred not only carved into my mangled flesh, but into every fold of my brain…into my goddamn soul. So she drew it for me. Specifically for my back, which carried the worst of the abuse. Iris healed every part of me. With her glow. With her friendship. With her love. Accepting the guardian bond was the easiest decision I have ever made.

I shuffle down the stairs, avoiding the creaky step in the middle, and flatten myself against the hallway's wall to listen. Iris's parents have been fighting for the last twenty minutes in the living room. They probably think we're both sleeping. And while Iris is curled up in my bed since she snuck into my room an hour ago — just like she always does when I visit — I couldn't close my eyes. Even blinking is torture because, in the darkness, today's events keep coming back in terrifying flashes. What sucks most, though, is the lingering dread. Because I couldn't find her.

So much for my promise to always protect her. I thought I sounded so heroic, like in the movies. But at the end of the day, my actions only demonstrated I'm just a dumb fucking kid. Today was close — too close. And it's all my fault. I swear I only turned my back on her for two minutes while buying her cotton candy, and she was gone. I should have never taken Iris to that fair. But she begged me with those iridescent sea-glass eyes. And I'm so weak for her. If the fact that I stole her away wasn't enough, we also rode on my new bike. Stupid fucking decision because if her dad doesn't bite my head off, Eliana sure will. I cringe just thinking about the three-hour lecture awaiting me tomorrow. Eliana is scary as hell when she's mad.

"You can't force a guardian bond on him. If Iris" — Eliana's voice breaks —

"d-dies, Kaiden will suffer the same fate. It's not fair. Iris would never want that. He's already sacrificed so much by joining the Conclave and doing Mammon's bidding. Plus, we don't even know if it's going to work, since he's a hybrid."

"Then we're not going to tell her," Iris's dad says.

She huffs. "I already agreed on that damn barrier you want to put in her head. And Kaiden's just a kid. You can't blame Iris for wanting to experience the real world for one day, and you can't blame him for giving that to her. What happened today is our fault because we've transformed every house we ever lived in into her prison. A cage is still a cage, no matter how you paint its bars."

Iris's father swears sharply under his breath. "Do you think I don't know that, El? Kaiden's fifteen, and wise beyond his years. As much as it hurts to say this because I love him like a son, he was never a kid. Not when I broke him out of his cell at only nine years old, and not now. What that motherfucker Raphael did to him altered him forever. But with a guardian bond, he would be able to feel any time Iris is in danger and track her anywhere. We almost lost her today, and at the hands of scumbag humans of all creatures," he spits out the last words as though they're venomous.

He heaves out an exhale, then his tone softens. "We have to face the truth, my love. We will not be here forever. Not with all the lightborn we've killed so far. There will come a time when Kaiden might be everything she has left. I'll explain what a guardian bond means, and he will be the one to make that decision."

"I still think it's a bad idea. Especially since we're still not sure if they're already empyreal soul-bonds. I mean, have you seen how they look at each other? Iris has been saying they're soulmates since the first moment they met, and she was only five. I thought it was a childish crush or she was repeating our bedtime stories, but she stayed steadfast in her belief to this day. If we put a guardian bond on top of that, what will happen?" Eliana takes a deep breath in. Blows it out. "I've made my decision. The barrier is where I draw the line. We're not getting Kaiden — "

"I'll do it."

159

I step into the room and meet both of their surprised gazes with a determination made of steel. Not only is tying my life to hers an honor, but a world where Iris is no more is a world I refuse to live in.

Eliana was right, after all. We are soul-bonds. Though I shouldn't have been surprised when it snapped into place, because deep down I knew it from the second I saw Iris for the first time. I close my eyes and look inward to the two woven threads—one violet, one gold—residing beneath my solar plexus and connecting me to Iris. The gold one is new, still fragile in a way, but stronger than anything I have ever felt. While the guardian bond alerts me any time Iris is in danger and allows me to reach her anywhere, the soul-bond is different. It entwined our hearts and paths for all eternity. It's the sole reason I haven't fallen into a pit of despair at Iris's cold shoulder; our destinies will never be far apart.

I follow the violet thread, teleporting into my kitchen to grab something from the cupboard before popping into Samantha's spare bedroom. In stark contrast to the first time I teleported here, when the damn Sphynx jumped on my head in a vicious attack, she's now stretching from her curled position at Iris's legs and leaps onto the floor to receive her payment.

She regards me through slitted eyes as if saying, "I'm watching you. Dare to hurt her, and I'll have your balls." She resembles her petite but fierce owner on that front. I dread the moment I'll come face to face with that five-foot-two spitfire. However, I'll take anything she throws at me because she's only having Iris's back, and I respect the hell out of her for that.

Following our truce, I take out the tissue from my pants pocket and unfold it on the floor. The Sphynx starts nibbling at the salmon treats while I turn the chair in front of the vanity dressing table in the corner, then sit.

I forget how to breathe the moment my ravenous gaze finds Iris. The gold bond sings in her presence, and I revel in the peace flooding me. She is sleeping on her back, pouty lips—that I'm dying to taste—slightly parted. Never thought I would ever be jealous of moonlight. But I wish it were my fingers caressing the side of her face instead. Her beauty is as deadly and untamed as the sea. A contradiction. Tempestuous and serene. Sharpness and wit wrapped in soft curves and skin as pure as freshly fallen snow. A siren song luring me into the abyss. The thing is...I've never been more eager to drown.

Her fingers twitch slightly before a frown etches in between her eyebrows. Her breath comes out in a staccato rhythm. After years of watching her sleep, I recognize the early signs of an impending night terror. So, I try something new because, as much as I wish I could wrap Iris in my arms to chase it away, I can't. Snapping my eyes shut, I tell her through our bond, *"You're safe, angel. I'm here."* Then I send her my memory of the day I picked her up for our first date in the meadow where fireflies danced all around us. How her perfect body pressed into my back while we rode on my Harley. How the fire-kissed sky reflected into her mesmerizing eyes. How my heart punched its way out of my ribcage when I held her. How the desire to kiss her burned through me, obliterating every thought. Her breathing slows down. It worked.

Oh, this could be fun.

18

Iris

"What are you planning to wear?" Sam asks as we pass storage box after storage box.

I pop a shoulder. "I haven't decided yet."

"Well, you need a nice dress. This restaurant is going to be the hottest place in all of Ashville. I don't know who Noah had to sell his soul to in order to snag a reservation on opening night, but I went there yesterday to discuss the final details for the flower arrangements, and I'm telling you, my jaw was on the floor. I don't want to spoil it cause you need to see it for yourself. But it's swanky as fuck."

"You do remember Noah's parents were loaded, right? He probably pulled some strings. Now I'm panicking because I don't have anything *that* fancy." My mind immediately goes to the custom dress Kaiden gifted me before the succubus party. It's still the most ethereal piece of clothing I own, though I don't think I can wear it ever again. Even if I fixed the straps Kaiden ripped in the car when he — *Nope. Not going there.*

"Don't worry, I ordered some new dresses anyway. They should arrive by the end of next week. There's this black number that shifts an electric blue when the light hits it. It's understated but will mold to your every curve. Noah's going to lose his shit. Are you sure you want to go on a date with him, though? After he kissed you like that?"

Knowing Sam, she ordered the dresses specifically because she knew I have a date. Probably some new shoes, too. "We made a deal, and I won't back down on it. Besides, he apologized…profusely. And it's not a real date; we're only going as friends. But I don't know, Sam. Every time he gets too close, I suffocate. I get this sudden urge to push him away. And I hate that piece of shit, Erik, for transforming every interaction I'll ever have with men."

Sam is quiet for a few moments as she ponders my words. "Did you feel the same in Kaiden's presence?"

"Don't mention his name," I hiss.

"I'm sorry, okay? I know the rule is to treat him as if he's Voldemort, but it's a valid question. If Erik had such a lasting effect on you, shouldn't it also extend to him? Plus, you had sex with him right after what happened at Sin."

I gnaw on my bottom lip pensively. As hard as it is to admit, Sam's right. Whenever Kaiden was near, it took every ounce of self-restraint I possessed not to pull him *closer*. I crave him so much it's borderline unhealthy. It's paradoxical, I know, not only because he is a demon but also because of his lies. Of what he did to me.

And despite all of those things, he still is my haven. I've never felt more protected than in his arms. But that's the thing about love — two things can be true at the same time. You can still be deeply hurt by that person, but love them all the same. You can't just snap your fingers and unlove someone like in *The Vampire Diaries* when they turn off their humanity. If only it were that simple…Hell, I've been hung up on Noah for years, and what I felt for him isn't even a blip on the map of my feelings compared to Kaiden.

"You're right. I don't." I keep my answer short because I don't want to talk or think about him anymore. It hurts too much.

"That son of a bitch really had to pick the last storage unit, huh?" Sam grumbles as she dabs at the perspiration beads coating her hairline. "Ugh. It's hotter than Hades's ass, and I'm betting that storage box is going to be worse than an oven. We're going to look like two overcooked chicken legs when we're done."

I appreciate how smoothly she changed the subject. She might push my buttons from time to time, but only good intentions are behind it. God knows I'm far from perfect and she sometimes wants to smack the shit out of me, but I wouldn't change our friendship for the world. If Kaiden is my haven, then Sam is my anchor because every single time I feel unmoored, she is always there to ground me.

We finally enter the last row of storage units. We've been walking forever under the blazing sun since this place is huge — perfect for staying under the radar.

When Noah asked if he could accompany me to check out the address, I refused. Not only because of how we left things, but also because I didn't know what I would find — didn't know if Erik had more evidence of the time I spent with Kaiden. He was upset, but I played it off as needing space. While that flash drive contained stalking videos of twenty-four women aside from me, they weren't a smoking gun. I know deep in my bones that Erik murdered those women. However, I need more than that footage to prove it.

Fishing out the envelope along with the key from my jean shorts, I unfold the piece of paper to double-check the number. This is it. Before I unlock and lift the garage-style door, I roll on a pair of nitrile gloves, then pass Sam hers.

"Holy shit!" Sam lets out sharply under her breath because what greets us are hundreds of pictures covering the entirety of the three available walls. Erik, in typical serial-killer fashion, had captured his assaults and mutilations in minute detail, from the bloody "demon whore" letters carved into the innocent flesh to himself, violating his victims' cadavers.

Blinking lamppost, cold, rough concrete against my back, copper in my mouth, sluggish thoughts, a scrap of fabric, air between my legs, despair spreading like black ink.

Nononononononono.

I don't realize I've taken a few steps back and am heaving my breakfast until Sam's hand rubbing circles on my back jolts me back to reality. "I don't think it was a good idea for you to come here. Let's go home, and then I'll come alone tomorrow and look through everything, all right?"

I straighten while I wipe my mouth with the back of my hand. "No. It's fine. I'm fine." Swallowing a lungful of calming air, I mumble, "I can do this."

"Here." Worry pinches the planes of Sam's gorgeous face as she passes me a water bottle from her bag. "Are you sure?"

"Yeah. Besides, you might not know what to look for. I don't want anything to be traced back to me." While I do want to show the human police and the Aureal Council that Erik was a perverted killer, I don't want them to possibly find out about my involvement with Kaiden. So, everything has to go.

She purses her lips. "Fine. But at the first sign you're not okay you'll let me know?"

I nod. Squaring my shoulders as if preparing for a demon fight, I enter the storage unit. Luckily, it's one of the fancy ones, powered by electricity from a solar panel, and it has air-con. We get to work. It takes us hours to go through every single one of the file cabinets, but I find all the lingerie that sick fuck stole from me—even the lacy, soft pink one I got from Kaiden. I'm sad I won't ever get to wear it again. But how could I when that dipshit touched it? He probably did some other things with it that I don't even want to think about. There are also various items he took from the women he stalked and murdered: sex toys, jewelry, other pieces of clothing, and IDs.

The sheer amount of evidence here would make any homicide detective do the lambada. There's no way the Order can bury a case of this magnitude, especially since I'm also planning to send anonymous tips to the news outlets in Ashville. Removing all pieces of evidence that link to me turns out to be trickier than we expected, since we have to sift through everything, including hair strands.

The shrill sound of my alarm startles us both.

"Shit. It's already eight thirty? No wonder I feel like my stomach is sticking to my spine," Sam says while shoving a pair of panties back into one of the plastic bags.

I offer a hand to pull her up with me. "We can come back this week and do a final sweep. Just to be sure we didn't miss anything." Once I have everything, it's off to the human police.

"'Kay. I would die for a burger right now. Wanna go to Jane's Diner?"

"I'm not hungry—"

"C'mon, Iris. You only took one bite of that wrap at lunch," she scoffs. "You can't keep going like this."

Guilt twists my insides into knots because behind the wrath in her blazing emeralds is a deep-seated worry. "Can we order something instead? I'm not sure if I have enough time to eat and then change for my shift. Especially with the traffic at this hour." I only say this because I know that if we go to the restaurant, I will have to finish at least half the burger to appease her, and if we order in, I can just take it to my room under the guise that I have to get ready.

"Fine," she grumbles as we walk out into the stifling night air.

19

Iris

Apparently, hell has a basement. And I just fell through it because working alongside Veronica is torture times infinity. We're only an hour into our shift, and I already feel the urge to drive a rusty fork through my eyeballs. This is going to be the longest week of my life. If everything that has happened before with Erik didn't rattle me enough, this might be what pushes me over the edge straight into a boring human life.

"Yeah. Have you seen how much weight she put on? I don't know what Liam sees in her, I swear. She looks like a cow. And Liam's soooo hot. Why do all the uglies snatch the most gorgeous, mouth-watering men?" She throws me a dirty look, courtesy of Noah, I'm sure.

I roll my eyes so far that I can almost see the back of my head. Aside from having the emotional intelligence of a pet rock, her brain is frozen at fifteen, too, because who the fuck talks like that? She clearly hasn't outgrown her bully phase. Liam is a hellseeker who is married to one of the accountants at the compound. She is gaining weight because she's pregnant. And aside from being drop-dead gorgeous, the woman is glowing. Veronica is a bitch.

And don't worry, she's not speaking to me. This is how she and her pack of hyenas work—they talk on the phone for the duration of their shifts. At least she's wearing headphones. When I asked how the hell she stays under the radar to follow demons, she snarked that I would know if I had any friends or a social life. "But how could a troglodyte like you ever understand that?"

Not throttling her is proving to be the feat of my life.

"Maybe he's going to finally realize she's a whale and ask you out, Tess. I can lend you that lilac dress I just bought. But you need to drop a few pounds to fit into it. Don't think I haven't noticed your thigh gap is not as big anymore. And you started to get some cellulite on your ass. You can even see it through your leggings."

Holy fuck! She even bullies her presumed besties. I have the sudden urge to buy a bottle of bleach on the way home so I can marinate my brain in it. I didn't think I would be so grateful for demons to be back on the streets of Ashville, but it gives me something to do aside from listening to their mean chatter. And it keeps my mind off *him*. It finally feels as though I got a semblance of my old self back. At the end of last week, we caught two lesser demons, and then on Sunday, we sent back to Hell two ghouls cornering a couple in a back alley. Even though Tessa's a catty bitch, she's a ruthless fighter. I can respect that.

I guess it's been long enough since the incident at Shadow Lake that the demons aren't afraid of getting blasted by *illum* or coming face to face with an archangel anymore, and that's why've they started to crawl back out of their hiding spots. That's the only theory I have so far for their reappearance. I never did get the chance to ask Kaiden about the state of the forest, about the *illum,* in the national park after the night he saved me…

Ugh. I would kill for a little bit of wind right now. Hell, even a slight breeze. The worst heatwave in years hit Ashville, and despite it being the middle of the night, I feel like I'm breathing air coming out of a hot oven. I'm sweating in places I don't even want to talk about as we patrol our assigned area. The soles of our boots falling against the pavement and Veronica's annoying voice are the only sounds in the creepy silence.

It's one of those cookie-cutter neighborhoods situated right at the edge of Ashville's residential area—the border before you enter the slums. The people living here are middle class, most of them working in the factories at the edge of town. We rarely encounter demons on these streets since demon activity is mostly concentrated where lust, gluttony, and greed engage in a promiscuous dance of carnal urgency and illicit substances to dull or heighten your senses. That's why the Raven district is their favorite playground. Demons are attracted to people who live fast and dangerous, not nine-to-fivers who go to sleep before ten p.m.

However, there have been some strange disappearances in the last two weeks. According to the police, ten children have vanished without a trace. And they were all living in this neighborhood. When cases become inexplicable to law enforcement, they usually pass them along to the Order to check if they're demon related. So, this week, Grayson also assigned us the mission of finding the missing children to see if a demon is responsible. You can never know for sure until you find the demon.

I'm trying my best to tune out Veronica when something catches the corner of my eye—a little body and blond hair vanishing in a blur on the next street to the right. What the hell is a child doing past midnight on these abandoned streets where a possible serial killer or demon might be on the hunt? Without a second thought, I tap into the hellseeker speed to zip after the kid.

"What are you doing, you weirdo?" Veronica hisses from my back, but I don't pay her any attention.

Soles pounding fast on the asphalt, I finally reach the road juncture and turn to the right, where I saw the child disappear. There's nothing here—just more houses. I slow my run to a swift walking pace while I swivel my head. But again...nothing.

Veronica reaches me in a jog. "What happened?"

My eyebrows knit as I answer. "I thought I saw something."

She huffs. "Of course you did. I can't believe I hung up on Brit and Tess for this." Then she mutters under her breath, "That dirty blood must be rotting her brain."

As soon as she finishes saying that, the swing set on the front lawn to my right starts swinging by itself, making a low, creaky sound. All the hair on my body stands on end as phantom fingers brush across the nape of my neck, followed by a child's laughter. It resembles an echo—as if coming from a dream. The street lampposts flicker to the rhythm of the giggles.

Veronica throws a nervous sidelong glance at the swing set, which is still swaying forward and backward in the absence of wind. "That's kinda creepy, right?"

I don't get to answer because a blond girl wearing overalls and holding a teddy bear blinks into existence in the middle of the road. Her form ripples like the sun's rays reflecting off the water's surface. She beckons me with a finger.

Without preamble, the ghost girl turns on her heel and breaks into a run. There's a second of hesitation as my gut screams in warning that something isn't right about this. But what if the little girl knows where all the children are, and that's why she's trying to get my attention? Ignoring my gut, I follow in a sprint.

Veronica mutters something snarky again, but she jogs right behind me. "Are you going to tell me what the fuck we're doing?"

"I want to check something."

"Are you freakin' kidding me?" she snaps, but she still hasn't stopped. I guess the moving swing set creeped her out since demons can sometimes make lights flicker. I don't think she heard the laughter, though.

The houses pass in a blur as we dash on the ghost's heels, the cadence of our footfalls mingling with our heavy breathing. We pass street after street until we almost reach the slums. Here, the lampposts have stopped working altogether. Trash is scattered all over the street, and the houses are ramshackle.

The blond girl halts and flickers out of existence, only to reappear to my left, where the last house in the neighborhood is. She throws me a poignant look over her shoulder before disappearing through the front door. As if on cue, my onyx choker warms up.

"I think that's where the missing children are," I tell Veronica, who has been weirdly quiet.

She throws me a confused look. Surely, her onyx choker is also alerting her of a demon presence. "But how—how did you know?"

I shrug because telling her the ghost of a little girl led me here is out of the question. "Just a hunch."

Snorting, she says, "You don't say." She purses her lips. "Well, how are we going to do this?"

"We'll each take a floor? I'll take the second."

"Fine. But you'll go in first. If I'm lucky enough, the demon will eat your ugly face, and then I won't have to stare at it all week."

I almost laugh at that because I can only hope the same thing happens to her.

Even though the whip is my preferred weapon, it's not as efficient in confined spaces. So, I take out the sword from its holster at my back before striding to the house. Veronica follows close behind.

The smell of sulfur hangs heavy in the air, and the ground on the front lawn is cracked, the grass long dead as if something sucked all the vital force out of it. These are clear signs that a demon — a powerful one — has been here a while. Lesser demons don't affect the environment. In fact, there are only a few that can do this. The onyx stone becomes hotter with every step.

Light on my feet, I climb the decaying stairs, careful not to make them groan. It's futile looking through the windows since it's pitch black inside. When Veronica joins me on the front porch, I square my shoulders and try the door handle. It's unlocked, so I push it open with the sole of my boot. The hinges screech ominously.

"Well, if the demon didn't know we were coming, it sure does now," she mutters.

I brush her jab off my shoulders. Adrenaline buzzes beneath my skin as I enter the house with measured steps. The first thing that hits me is the unmistakable putrid odor of death: a combination of rotting flesh, sulfur, and something sickeningly sweet. Lungs freezing up, I fight to death my gag reflex. That fucked up sonar in my head? It makes its presence known again, telling me there are fourteen dead bodies in this house. I pass the stairs while I let it guide me through the cramped hallway toward the back of the house.

"You said you were taking the second floor," Veronica whisper-yells at my back.

I ignore her as I forge on and enter what seems to be the kitchen. The empty, decomposing husks of what I assume were once a man and a woman sit at the table. Blowflies buzz in the air above their heads while roaches scamper all over the table to get a bite of the spoiled food in front of them. The couple look as if something drained the life out of them — which is weird because when a demon consumes the soul completely, the bodies still have some vitality. It's what transforms them into zombies.

Veronica gags. "Fuck, that's vile. Weren't they supposed to turn into zombies?" she muses, coming to the same conclusion as I did.

I can't help but compare these bodies to the way Erik looked when I rotted him to death. Only, they don't have the black vines. And he resembled a shriveled prune — as if he was being mummified. Shaking my head to rid myself of the memory, I finally say, "Yeah." The death radar is telling me there are a few bodies on the second floor, while the rest are in the basement. We still need to check the entire house, though. "I'll go search upstairs."

Veronica nods, and I leave her in the kitchen so she can do the rounds here. The inside of the house doesn't look as bad as the outside. Sure, the furniture is old, but judging by the photos I pass as I ascend, a family used to live here. Two boys, not older than seven, smile at me from one of the framed pictures. I already know what awaits me once I reach the second landing. But I still hold a tiny spark of hope that maybe those kids grew up from when that photo was taken or weren't home when the demon murdered their family.

Please.

Taking a deep breath — which I quickly regret because of the foul stench — I push open the door of the first bedroom to my right.

Fuck.

A small body is lying on the bed in the same condition as the man and woman in the kitchen, hugging a Batman toy to his chest.

Over the years, I've seen some really bad shit. Still, nothing affects you like the death of a child. And dying at the hands of a demon is a horrible way to go. Gritting my teeth, I turn on my heel and enter the second bedroom, only to find the same macabre image. Tears stab at the back of my eyes, but I shove them down. There's no place for sadness right now. I focus instead on the rage crackling like lightning beneath my skin. I hone it. Let it burn through me until the thirst for vengeance is my only drive.

A terrified scream slices through the eerie silence. *Veronica.*

I zip down the stairs but don't make it far because a clawed, monstrous hand shoots from below, shattering the wood and wrapping around my ankle. My fingers clutch the railing in a death grip, but it's no use. Something pulls me down in an explosion of splinters right through the stairs.

Shitshitshitshitshitshit.

20

Iris

Pain detonates in every single one of my nerve endings as I collide with the basement's cement floor. Something hard pokes me in the back. The sword, which I dropped on my way down, clatters behind me. Warm, sticky liquid coats my nape. Blinking rapidly, I try to clear the dancing red and white dots in my vision. As I'm about to swipe one of the daggers strapped to my thigh, I'm pinned down by a heavy body.

The image finally clears. Two reptilian eyes stare back at me from a face made of leathery skin covered in dragon-like scales. It takes me a while to come to the conclusion that it's the Lamia, an ancient demon no one's seen in ages. What stumps me is that it's just lying still on top of me. I don't have time to dwell on it, though. I thrash my body, but the damn demon is too heavy. So, I do the only thing I can think of—

headbutt it. Hard. So hard, in fact, that I lose consciousness.

Its shrill cry quickly snaps me back to reality and almost makes my eardrums shatter. However, I've shocked the creature enough for it to slacken its hold. I put all the strength I have into my legs and bend my knees to kick the demon square in its chest, making it skid across the floor — which is covered in a gory blanket of blood, scattered limbs, and tiny skulls — a few feet away.

I jump up, but I'm not prepared for the blast of power that smashes into me. It sends me sailing through the air straight into the exposed brick wall at my back. Fuck. My lungs rattle hard with the sensation of a semi-truck crashing into my body at full speed. Blood floods my mouth while fireworks go off behind my eyelids. Hello, concussion, dear old friend. Can't say I missed you...

It takes a while for the haziness blurring my vision to dissipate, but I try to fixate on the power source. The blob turns into a middle-aged woman, who, aside from clearly being a dark witch, looks pretty unremarkable: ratty brown hair, checkered slacks, and thick-rimmed glasses. Heck, she could pass as your neighborhood librarian if it weren't for the black vines shifting beneath her skin. She's leaning casually on the wall opposite the one I'm being immobilized on by her magic. Veronica lies unconscious in the center of the basement, over the death blanket, a pool of fresh blood beneath her. At least her chest is still moving.

The dark witch smirks before whistling, as if calling a dog. The Lamia glares at her through slitted eyes, then reluctantly trudges to kneel at her feet. "Do you like my pet?"

I can't believe I haven't noticed until now the thick leather strap decorated with engravings and sigils adorning the Lamia's neck. It is said that the Lamia was once a beautiful woman. However, the fact that she couldn't bring children into the world drove her mad, and she started snatching babies out of their cribs, consuming their flesh so she could feel the life of a child in her womb. She once stole a powerful witch's baby. Some Order historians say it was Hecate herself who cast a horrible curse upon the woman, transforming her into a four-legged beastly creature — that looks like a cross between a Komodo dragon and a furless bear — before banishing her to Hell for all eternity. No one has seen the Lamia above ground in a hundred years or more.

This witch collared an ancient demon and made it her lapdog. I can only imagine the Lamia is not too happy about that. Its nostrils flare as the witch pats its scaly head before saying: "Good pet. You can go eat now." It lets out a disgruntled huff but listens to the command, crawling to the scattered human remains and diving right in.

Trying my best to ignore the horrible *chomp, chomp, chomp,* of razor-sharp teeth gnawing on little bones, I snap, "Why are you doing this?"

The witch tilts her head. "You don't know by now? You've got Hell in a tizzy. The bounty on you keeps growing by the day. And everyone wants to cash in." She has a lazy gait as she strolls toward me, stopping near Veronica. "With Black watching you like a dragon would its most prized possession, I had to get smart about it. Illusions are my specialty. And you fell right into my trap. I created the little ghost girl especially for you. I even tricked the two wolf shifters he has following your every move. Now that your boyfriend is out of town, I had to shoot my shot."

The unexpected mention of Kaiden's name is a punch straight to the gut. He's still watching over me.

She flicks her hand, and like a log, I drop to the floor on my side. The impact knocks the air out of my lungs. Copper coats my tongue yet again while the white and red dots from earlier make a reappearance. As if I'm merely a puppet on the witch's strings, my body bends until my feet and hands are brought together. At the snap of her fingers, rope materializes out of thin air, binding my limbs in a hogtie. The magic releases me, but there's no way I can reach any of the weapons strapped to my body.

"Was killing all those innocent kids necessary?" I grit out as I start working on the rope. It's tight as fuck. But I only need a little give.

She hikes a nonchalant shoulder. "Well, you can't summon a demon just like that. You need sacrifices. And nothing is purer than a child's soul. Besides, my pet had to eat."

"What's the demon's name? Who put the bounty on me?"

She waves a hand in the air, but this time, it's to push the remains on the cement floor to the side. The Lamia growls because the move interfered with its feeding. It crawls close to me and resumes the sickening, grating sounds that make my stomach lurch in my throat.

"Ah, I'm in a good mood, so I'll indulge you with an answer. No one knows. It's a big secret. But there are rumors that the demon is powerful. Some say it's a king of Hell. I just have the spell I need to perform so one of his cronies can come collect."

Shit. I always imagined the demon who put the bounty on me to be powerful, but never in my wildest dreams did I think it might be a king of Hell. But which one of the nine is it? And most importantly, what would he need me alive for?

The witch strides to the stairs to pick up a copper bowl that looks ancient before ambling back to where she cleared the floor. She turns her back to me while crouching to trace a circle with blood-soaked fingers. I really do not want to think about where the blood came from.

If she completes that circle, I'm fucked.

I swing my limbs and slam my left hand to the floor. Three of my fingers snap. I swallow the whimper, fighting to get free. Thankfully, the cracks were muffled by the Lamia's chomping.

I'm so close to freeing my hands, now that I'm no longer hindered by the bone structure of my fingers, but the witch has finished the circle. *Dammit.* She stands to appraise it briefly. After a content nod, she strides to Veronica and bends to place the copper bowl she's holding on the floor.

Veronica is still out of it until her eyes fly open when the witch grabs her by the hair to angle her head backward. "No hard feelings, but I need to make a call," she tells Veronica as she snatches one of her daggers before pressing the blade to her throat.

Fuck. They're too far away, and I still haven't untied my legs. On instinct, I grab one of the daggers strapped to my belt. I have to make a split decision: send the dagger flying at the witch's head or release her beast. Because there's a chance the witch could stop the dagger in mid-air, I lurch my body to where the Lamia is still eating. With a clean swipe, I slice through the spelled collar. The demon roars. It launches like a feral rocket before barreling into the witch's body.

That allows me enough time to unbind my ankles. A bit clumsily, I jump to stand. The sudden move makes me dizzy, and my limbs are full of pins and needles as the blood starts circulating again, but I regain my balance. I cast a look at the opposite side of the basement, where the Lamia is unloading all of its pent-up rage on the witch.

I can't say I'm too sad about it. Actually, I'm pissed I didn't get to kill her myself. I wanted my pound of flesh for what she had done to the poor children. But unleashing a demon on her seems much more poetic. And efficient.

"You missed all the fun," I tell Veronica, who's on all fours, heaving her stomach contents on the blood-soaked floor. I can't tell if it's because of a concussion or the gory scene unfolding before us. Probably a bit of both. She's been out of it a long time, and the back of her head is caked with blood. "I had to break some of my fingers on my left hand to get free. It's useless now. I'm gonna need your help. You up to it?"

Veronica heaves one last time before pushing to stand. She wipes at her mouth and lets out a, "Mhm." However, right away, she sways as if she's on a boat navigating treacherous waters.

"You sure?"

"Do it already before I pass out," she fires back, tone full of venom.

"'Kay, then take out your sword." I uncoil my whip in a swift motion. I circle it a few times above my head before flicking my wrist. It slices through the air toward the Lamia. The moment it snares around its neck, I use my core muscles to pull the demon toward us. It thrashes and claws at the whip to no avail as I drag it across the floor. "Now!"

Veronica's sword slashes through the Lamia's neck. A spray of ichor follows as the decapitated head smacks the floor with a wet *thwack*. Veronica doesn't dodge in time. I snort-laugh at the way her full face of makeup gets showered in it. Been there, done that. I can only hope a little got in her mouth, too.

What? I saved her life. I've earned the right to be a petty bitch.

She mutters a warped "fuck you" through the violent heaves.

That triggers my own gag reflex, and I have to step away. "You okay?" I ask when the heaving finally stops.

She huffs. "Define okay."

"Do you think you can walk back to the compound?"

"Not a chance."

"Okay. I'll call this in so Grayson can notify the authorities, and then I'll tell him to send a car and a medic, too." I fish the phone out of my back pocket. Thankfully, only the screen protection is cracked.

"Iris?"

I flick my gaze to Veronica, who looks greener by the second. She purses her lips, all of her features pinching in a way that has me worried she's about to have a stroke. She spews the words as if they make her physically ill, "Thank you...for saving my life." Then she hastily adds, "Repeat that to anyone at the compound, and I'm going to fucking destroy you. Also, I still wish the Lamia ate your stupid face."

A small smile tugs at my lips. I offer a nod before calling Grayson.

THE SKY IS the color of a bruised peach as I get out of the cab, freshly showered and feeling like I belong in a retirement home because every single muscle in my body screams at the slightest effort. Luckily, the drive here was so short that it didn't throw me into the clutches of a panic attack.

After I gave my report to a haggard-looking Grayson — sprinkled, of course, with half-truths and some lies — Doctor Corey and his team tended to my injuries. Aside from having a nasty concussion, three broken fingers on my left hand, and two bruised ribs, I also have to wear a splint. Dr. Corey insisted I would heal faster wearing a cast, but I refused. At least I didn't break any ribs. Thank you, God and baby Jesus, for small miracles. Plus, I'm counting on my healing at lightning speed, now that slivers of some supposed power are slipping through the barrier's cracks. Hopefully, I'll regain my hand's mobility in no time.

Suddenly, a familiar weird sensation has me pressing my uninjured palm to the center of my sternum, as if —

"Angel."

I'm so immersed in my thoughts as I lumber down the front lawn of Sam's house that I almost jump out of my skin at hearing Kaiden's gravelly voice. I halt, legs turning to jelly. My head snaps to the six-foot-four demon sitting on the steps. At first, I think I'm hallucinating because I vividly remember that dark witch saying he was out of town.

So what is he doing here?

Kaiden stands. Fuck me. I don't understand how this is even possible, but he's somehow more beautiful than the last time I saw him. "I felt —" He shakes his head as if changing his mind on what he is about to say. As if answering the question I thought, he says, "Carter called me in a panic. He told me something happened to you when he and Dean were trailing you tonight. When they realized they actually couldn't scent you or the other hellseeker, your bodies dissipated like smoke. Then they couldn't find you. I was so worried—"

"Weren't you out of town?" I interrupt.

He runs a hand over the back of his neck, which causes the black T-shirt he's wearing to ride up. My mouth waters at the way his sculpted vee disappears into the waistband of his jeans. "I rushed back after Carter's call. I shouldn't have left. I didn't want to, but I had to close an important deal." His eyebrows knit. "Wait, how do you know that?"

I flap my hand in the air. "A witch might have mentioned something."

His eyes snap to my splint. In the next second, he pops off to appear in front of me. He takes my injured hand in his. The simple touch sends a shock wave through the entirety of my body.

Jaw ticking, his thumb brushes softly over the giant bruise I have above my right eyebrow from headbutting the Lamia. He trails it down the side of my face before framing my cheek with his big hand. "Tell me who I need to kill." The gentle touch is at odds with the violence—so potent I can almost taste it—dancing in the tumultuous obsidian sea of his irises. Still, it rips right through those thinly scabbed welts all the same.

I allow myself a few seconds of weakness as I lean into it, even if the love-sick organ in my chest is bleeding all over the ground. Closing my eyes briefly, I swallow a lungful of the scent that is uniquely Kaiden. It envelops me like a warm blanket.

Gritting my teeth because my legs are putting up a hell of a fight, I finally manage to take a step back. The second I do, the frost sinks its claws back in. It will turn into a goddamn glacier the moment he's gone. "The dark witch is dead. I took care of it. Well, more like the demon she was using as her pet to do her bidding took care of it." I let out a brittle laugh. "I had a rude awakening tonight. Apparently, the bounty on me is growing by the day." I recount the night's events before saying, "I naively thought that maybe it wasn't so bad anymore since nothing happened in the last few weeks. Turns out, it was only because of you. Thank you. I wasn't aware you were still watching over me."

Kaiden shoves his hands in the front pockets of his jeans. "You don't have to thank me, Iris. You are and always will be my top priority, no matter what happens between us," he rasps.

"Well, if that's all…" I say and brush past him.

"I miss you," he whispers when I almost reach the stairs.

My steps falter. There's so much pain in his tone that I almost crumble to my knees. Still, I let his words roll off my back as if they didn't eviscerate me and forge forward.

When I enter Sam's house, he's already gone.

21

Iris

"I did it, Mom. Erik's face is all over the news. He's a wanted serial killer. Of course, they don't know he's already dead. The case is so big, even the FBI got involved. Apparently, he killed more than those twenty-four women I found videos of. The news reporter said this morning that the police suspect the victim count is over thirty because the DNA they found in the storage unit matched missing cases from neighboring towns as well. There's no way the Order can spin or bury this. Even with Grayson's connections," I say as I arrange the peonies near the tombstone.

My next exhale is liberating, as if the bricks of guilt pressing down on my lungs since that night at Sin have finally vanished. If someone asked me if I would go through everything again—even the assault—to get the chance to kill Erik and expose his crimes, I would say yes with a hundred percent certainty. That motherfucker deserved to die. I wish it was slower, though. More painful. I would take weeks to carve vengeance into his body like he carved into the innocent flesh of his victims.

"Anyway, I brought the journal again. I thought maybe I could read some more pages today."

Steeling my spine, I try to ignore the fucked-up sonar in my head that's alerting me it has found new bodies to add to the count. Apparently, a few more people have died since I've last been here. Great. Love that I know that. There's more, though—I also have the sudden urge to lay my palms flat on the ground and call out to them.

And here I was, thinking my life couldn't get any weirder.

I flip through the pages filled with smudged ink until I find a later entry. It stands out because the letters are wobbly and crooked, not caused by the water damage, but as if she wrote them in a frenzy.

I don't even know where to start. Today changed everything. Everything. I am beyond livid. MY WHOLE LIFE IS A LIE. They lied to me from the day I was born. I can't believe it. But at the same time, I can because it explains why I've always felt as though I don't belong. Turns out, every single day I mourned something I couldn't quite grasp wasn't a delusion, but my soul longing for a different existence.

Still, I've let my mother control every aspect of my life. She pushed me into becoming a hellseeker even though I never wanted to. I feel so cheated, so betrayed.

How could they do this?

They're not even my real parents.

My mind can't comprehend the lengths they went to sustain this vile lie. I've seen the photos of "my mother" when she was presumably pregnant with me. Was she wearing a fake baby bump? She had to be, right?

Jesus.

At least my father feels guilty about it. That's how I found out; I overheard them fighting earlier — about me. My father thought it's time they told me the truth: that my rare blood condition isn't even real, but something she made up so she could treat me like her own personal lab rat.

Then my mother shouted, "Are you going to tell her she isn't our daughter, too? Huh? If you're so keen on sharing, Frank, then why don't you spill the whole fucking truth? That she's nothing more than the fae we experimented on since she was an embryo — our Eve. Make sure to also add that we mutated her genes to transform her into the perfect warrior. Is your precious little Ellie still going to love you when you tell her all this?!?"

My mother stormed out of the house, and my father followed her. While I...I was nothing more than a statue facing my bedroom door. They didn't know I was home and could overhear everything. I had a bridesmaid dress appointment today, but the seamstress had called earlier to cancel because she couldn't find a nanny.

My brain can't even compute what I've just read. What in the? How? The rest of that day's entry is all smudged, incomprehensible. So, I flip quickly with trembling fingers to the next portion of legible text, because I might have gotten the explanation for everything — my mother was never a lightborn, but a mutated fae. I can't stop wondering what experiments they could have done on her so she could pass as a lightborn. But most importantly, why would they do something like this?

Owen died today.

There...I said it.

I hoped that writing it down would lessen the blow. That it would somehow help ease this suffocating guilt I've been choking on since his blood slipped between my fingers — because it's my fault.

Mine.

That same day I discovered my whole life was nothing more than a lie, a hoard of draconic ravengers attacked Ashville. All available hellseekers were called to fight them off. We lured them into the old beer factory at the edge of town, but I was still shell-shocked, reeling in the aftermath of the bomb my mother dropped on my life only a few hours earlier.

Too distracted to be of any use in a demon fight, I didn't even notice the ravenger that came at me with startling speed. Owen pushed me out of the way at the last second. It all happened so fast. The ravenger slashed his entire torso to ribbons right in front of my eyes. Luckily, I came to my senses and cut off the demon's head.

I tried to staunch the bleeding. I really did. But there was so much of it... His last words were "I love you" not addressed to my sister — who was out of her mind, her wails ripping me to shreds as she knelt beside me — but to me.

Tomorrow is the funeral, and Josephine won't even cast a glance my way. Any hope I had at a reconciliation between us is shot to pieces. Just like my life. I'll always be the person who took away the love of her life.

I can't blame her, though, because I don't know what I would do if I were in her shoes. I wished that after she married Owen and finally had him, as she always wanted, we could move past our differences. She always said that I'm the golden child, "perfect little Ellie" who could do no wrong in our parents' eyes.

I can't help but wonder if she knew about the experiments, or if we're even real sisters. And if that, coupled with Owen's crush on me, has led to the rift between us.

I guess it doesn't matter now anyway, since I'll be leaving soon. When rummaging through my mother's safe — the one she thinks no one knows about — hidden under the painting in her office, I found an address. I think it's the secret lab they use to conduct their experiments. Tomorrow, I'm going to sneak in. After I discover who I really am, I'm never looking back.

There's nothing for me here anymore.

I flip the pages with an edge of desperation. However, this was the last legible entry. Fuck. Blood pounding in my ears, I push up and run at lightning speed toward the exit, jumping in the cab idling at the curb. I need to talk to my aunt. She's got to have answers.

22

Iris

In the past, the compound's foyer and its grandeur always instilled a feeling of adulation—something to aspire to. Now, as I stride forward in a daze, every polished surface and ostentatious decoration makes my skin itch because I only see them as the glorified façade that hides the rot beneath. The thing about rot is that it doesn't matter how many times you paint over it because it will fester and spread until the foundation crumbles.

I round the corner to the library, and as I'm about to enter through the double doors, the image before me makes me stop in my tracks: Grayson is embracing my aunt near her desk, one hand wrapped around her middle, the other cradling her face. He bends to kiss her passionately.

WHOA!

Cringing in awkwardness, I put my back to the wall. I know Grayson is good looking, but I never imagined my aunt going for someone almost twice her age. Well, if she's happy, who am I to judge? I never in a million years thought I would fall in love with a demon, either. Besides, my aunt's love life is none of my business. To be honest, I was worried about her. In all the years since she took me in, I've never seen her go on a date or talk about a man other than her long-lost fiancé, Owen.

This is awkward as hell, so I peel myself off the wall. I'll hide in one of the rooms on the second floor and then come back in twenty minutes. However, when I take a step back, I hear my aunt mentioning Erik's name. I freeze. Then drop into a crouch, pretending to tie my shoelaces.

"I can't believe they're saying Erik did all of those horrible things. Do you think he —"

"He didn't," Grayson snaps. "They're all lies. Timothy tracked Erik's phone to a club in the Raven district called Sin. He also hacked an ATM camera on that street that recorded him passing by around one a.m. That's his last known location. He didn't pass the ATM again, and there aren't any other cameras on that street that we know of. The club is owned by the Obsidian Conclave."

"Did Britney know about this?"

"No, Erik told her he was going to have a quiet night in and go to sleep while she was on her shift. When she came back, he wasn't there, so she assumed he was training at the compound. He often trains at that time; he likes to have the place to himself. Britney only started to worry after a few hours when he wouldn't respond to her messages."

"Why in the world would he go to a club owned by the Conclave? All Order members know the rules," Aunt Josephine muses.

"I don't know, but I will find out. That fucking Elite demon, Kaiden Black, must have had something to do with it. I feel it deep in my bones. He's lying, but we can't prove it. Everyone knows he has the chief of police

cornering its next meal while circling her chair. A cruel smile curves his lips upward as though this is one of the best days of his life. *Sick fuck.* The deep scar running down from his hairline through his missing right eye and stopping at the base of his neck makes him look all the more demented. He got it when a ghoul clawed at his face. His lean figure only adds to that image because despite him not being as muscular as the other hellseekers, he somehow looks deadlier—like a double-edged sword meant to cut through skin and bones.

With a sardonic *tsk, tsk, tsk,* Cain stops in front of Emily, fists her hair, then pulls on it hard while bending to be at the same eye level as her. "I'm going to ask again. Where is Erik?"

She spits in his face. "I don't know!"

Cain backhands her, sending her head flying to the side. Emily doesn't make a sound, but my hands still ball into eager fists. This motherfucker needs a lesson from someone who isn't tied to a chair, defenseless. He straightens, using the sleeve of his Henley to wipe the gobble of spit and blood. "Ah, mutt. You will learn it's not a good idea to provoke me," he says as he strolls to the table in the corner of the room to take something. I can't see what it is since his back is facing me.

When he turns, he's holding a syringe filled with a strange, black glowing liquid. "You see, this is a concoction I made especially for you." He smirks before he impales the needle into the side of her neck. "Maybe this will help you remember."

Emily's eyes roll to the back of her head. She foams at the mouth. Horrifying wails fill the air, followed by the sickening *crack!, crack!, crack!* of her bones breaking one by one. Fur pierces her skin. However, the transformation looks all wrong because she's now stuck somewhere in between. I almost storm into the room, the urge to wring Cain's neck all-consuming, but I stop myself at the last second. I can't do anything rash. I have to think this through. Blood pools from the deep grooves my nails are digging into my palms.

"Fuck you!" she clips out through a sob that morphs into another blood-curdling scream, because the transformation starts again. Then stops. Starts again. It goes on and on and on in an endless loop of broken bones and wails of suffering.

Silence blankets the vast space when Emily faints mid-transformation. The stillness is eerie—akin to a flash of lightning before an impending storm. Cain strides toward the exit of the interrogation room, prompting me to flatten myself against the wall before sprinting on the balls of my feet toward the armory. The sound of the door to the interrogation room closing echoes in the quiet. So, I hurry my steps. In the pitch-black darkness of the armory, I close the metal door after me as silently as I can. The *click* reverberates against my eardrums like a thousand rusty nails. I expect Cain to burst into the room any second now.

I heave out a relieved exhale when his disappearing footsteps travel through the door. However, it doesn't last long because frustration has me biting my knuckles as I let out a muffled scream, then swear under my breath.

Every second that trickles as I wait for Cain to leave the basement is a grenade bouncing in the confines of my ribcage.

Tik. Tok.

Tik. Tok.

Tik. Tok.

There's no doubt in my mind that I have to save Emily. She can't suffer more for something I've done. She shouldn't be suffering at the hands of a hellseeker, period. This is a direct violation of the Celestial Treaty, and I know how this is going to end if Cain doesn't get what he wants from her—he's going to kill Emily. Bit by bit, a plan forms in my mind. I just hope it won't go to shit.

If it does, I'll do everything in my power to get Emily out.

No matter the consequences.

23

Iris

I press my finger on the light switch to my right. The burst of fluorescence sears my retinas, so I blink a few times to adjust while I stride to the shelf in front of me and swipe a dagger — my excuse if someone saw me coming down here, or if I encounter anyone on my way up.

Even though it kills me to stay five more minutes in the armory without helping Emily, I have to make sure I won't bump into Cain. When the time is up, I get out and climb the stairs. My muscles twitch with the need to tap into my hellseeker speed. But I don't. I can't appear anything but oblivious to the hate crime happening in the basement. As my feet touch the first floor, I make a beeline for the back of the mansion, exiting through the door and taking the pebbled mosaic garden path.

The sun is high in the sky. It flickers a dizzying dance through the shrubs and the luxuriant branches of the hawthorn trees. Even though the radiating heat is beating down on me, I can't shake the iciness that sunk its claws deep beneath my skin — akin to permafrost — the moment I left Kaiden's penthouse. Today, though, it somehow seems worse. Ominous. It sends shivers down my spine.

Aside from the two men attending to the flower beds, the garden is empty, so my shoulders sag a bit in relief. It's short-lived, though, because the second I reach the gargantuan oak tree and take my phone out of the back pocket of my jean shorts with trembling fingers, all my muscles lock up.

Biting my lower lip, I tap on the screen to unblock *his* number before calling. All the stoicism I gained from my mental prep on my walk here is shot to pieces when he answers on the first ring. "Angel."

Kaiden's pet name for me lands like a sucker punch to my solar plexus. My legs can't withstand my weight, so I slide down the tree until I'm seated on the grass. The bark prickles my skin through the thin fabric of my T-shirt, as I say, barely above a whisper, "Don't—" *Fuck. Why is it so hard to speak?* "Don't call me that," I repeat, white-knuckling the phone. Somehow, I find it within myself to clip out, "Something happened—"

"What's wrong?" he interrupts, alerted by the urgency in my tone.

The velvety timbre of his voice cleaves my bleeding chest wide open again. I inhale sharply through the debilitating pain. "I um…fuck, I don't even know how to tell you this. Grayson has gone mad over the news of Erik being a serial killer. It's my fault…I gathered all the evidence, called the police, and also alerted the media because I didn't want to risk the Council burying it. And now Grayson thinks you fabricated the evidence to hide Erik's disappearance." My next breath stops short in my lungs. "Kaiden, they kidnapped Emily. She's being interrogated."

The sound of something smashing to pieces pierces my ear. "Motherfucking FUCK! That self-righteous scum. Logan and the pack

196

have been going crazy looking for her; she disappeared last night."

"He's torturing her. Cain. The enforcer," I mumble. A string of sharp curses follow from his end. "This is all my fault."

"None of this is your fault, Iris," he snaps.

"Yeah, it is—"

"Stop blaming yourself for killing that piece of shit and letting the world know what a sick fuck he was."

"Listen, I will try everything I can to get her out, okay?"

"No, Iris. I'll come deal with it. I'll burn the building down if I have to. This is a blatant breach of the Celestial Treaty; Emily is under the Conclave's protection. They have no fucking right."

"I know, but Kaiden, please think before you do something stupid. This could start a full-on war between the Order and the Conclave."

"Grayson should have thought about that before kidnapping and torturing one of us."

"Let me at least try. If I don't succeed, you can come, but you must know there are wards in place to protect the house against demons."

"The basement isn't warded. They can't bring demons in there otherwise."

I scoff. "That might be the case, but you can't even set foot on the grounds. How will you get into the basement?"

"Let me worry about that. I'll let Logan know. The Order better be prepared to face the wrath of the pack because they will come swinging—"

"Kaiden, your way will result in a bloodbath. I don't know how many wolves are in Logan's pack, but I don't want to risk any of their lives. Trust me, *my* way is better."

He takes a long moment to sit with my words. "Fine. There are secret tunnels under the compound. You can use them to get Emily out."

My eyebrows pinch in confusion. "What are you talking about? What tunnels?"

"Trust me, bootleggers built hidden tunnels all over the city during Prohibition. Beneath the Order's house are tunnels much older than that—since the initiation of the Templar Knights. How do you think the Order brings demons into the cells?"

"They told us they drop the wards momentarily, but we never know when it happens, so there are very few chances for a security breach."

Kaiden lets out a mirthless chuckle. "That's a big, fat lie. They use the tunnels, Iris."

"How do you know all this?"

"Does it matter?"

"No, I just…fine. How can I get to them?"

"I'll send you a blueprint of the house and instructions on how to get to it. One entrance is right next to the cells."

"Okay." This plan is much better than hiding Emily in one of the rooms and waiting until the opportunity to escape presented itself, which, in hindsight, wasn't the best idea. "Just don't do anything rash."

"You have until midnight. I won't be able to hold Logan or Ava back longer than that. They're worried sick. And, angel? If anyone touches you, I'll burn that fucking house down, along with everyone in it." He hangs up.

His words shouldn't warm up my insides, right?

There's something seriously wrong with me because I should at least be a little unsettled by them.

24

Iris

I shoot a message to Noah.

> **Me: Are you at the compound?**

> **Noah: Yeah. Why?**

> **Me: Can you meet me in your room?**

> **Noah: I'm already there. I wanted to talk to you anyway.**

Fiery ants are crawling beneath my skin; that's how hard I'm itching to get going. However, I have to appear normal, so I slow my pace toward Noah's room. A thousand scenarios bounce in my head at the speed of light.

What if he tells Grayson? Or worse, the Kabal? I have no idea what they actually do aside from being above the Order. I would have asked my aunt for help if I hadn't seen her in the library with Grayson. I don't think she would rat me out, but given their relationship, I don't want her to unintentionally say something that would throw me right under the bus. Plus, she knows about Emily being tortured. And she isn't doing anything about it.

I knock on Noah's door, then tap my foot as I count the agonizing seconds until he tells me to get in.

"I saw the news. That storage box unit...it was the same company as the one on the envelope we found in Erik's apartment. You were the one who gave the anonymous tip, weren't you? What the fuck were you thinking involving the human police in the Order's business?" Noah snaps from his standing position near the bed as I close the door at my back. "You lied to me after you promised you wouldn't anymore."

I raise an eyebrow, muttering, "Hello to you, too." Then I shake my head in disbelief. "I had to because I knew you wouldn't approve. And since when is a serial killer the Order's business, huh? You didn't see that storage unit, Noah. I spent hours in there, combing through evidence and what he did to those poor women...Jesus. I will never be able to get those images out of my head. I wanted his victims and their families to at least get a semblance of peace."

"You already killed him," he seethes. "Wasn't that enough?"

"No."

His nostrils flare. "You should have let the Aureal Council deal with it, Iris."

I huff. "And have them bury everything? Yeah, no, thank you."

"They would never do that."

"Oh, trust me, they would."

His eyebrows scrunch in confusion. "What are you talking about?"

"I don't have time for this right now, dammit. I need to tell you something. It's urgent—"

"Did you at least take care of the evidence tying you to Erik?" he inquires.

"I did, yeah. I spent two days in that fucking storage unit."

"And what did you do with it?"

"It's still at my apartment."

"Good," he sighs, plopping down on the bed and resting his elbows on top of his knees. "What's so urgent?"

Nerves strung high, I start to pace the length of the room. "You're going to think I'm crazy for saying this." A manic laugh bubbles out of me as if trying to convince Noah that I, indeed, am losing my marbles. I halt in the middle of the room before spilling the words, "I need your help to break someone out of the compound."

His eyes widen. "What?"

I suck in a lungful of calming air. *C'mon, Iris, just get it over with! Emily needs you.* "Okay…so, um, you know how Erik went missing because he followed me to a club in the Raven district?"

"Yeah."

"That club is owned by the Obsidian Conclave. Before you chastise me for it, I wasn't aware of that, okay? Anyway, Tim tracked Erik's phone there."

He interlocks his fingers while narrowing his eyes at me. "How do you know all of this?"

"I overheard Grayson talking about it earlier. But that doesn't matter. What matters is that they kidnapped a woman working at the club. She's a dark creature."

"And?"

My eyebrows furrow at his question. "They are torturing her. They brought in Cain to interrogate her, and he is doing all these horrible things to her—"

"So? Why do you care what happens to a lesser being?" he says flippantly.

I recoil. He sounds exactly like Grayson. "What do you mean, why do I care? Why don't you? Being a wolf shifter doesn't grant her this kind of treatment; she's still a person, Noah. How can you even say that? And it's a fucking violation of the Celestial Treaty. She's under the protection of the Obsidian Conclave," I snap.

He raises a nonchalant shoulder. "Just use her as a scapegoat, then. Maybe they think she has something to do with his disappearance."

The iciness in his tone only adds fuel to my fire. I don't know what the fuck happened with Noah in the past five years because I don't recognize him in this moment. Balling my hands at my sides, I throw him a withering glare. "But she did nothing wrong! And what if she saw me with Erik? If she did and tells Cain, I'm next in the torture chair."

"Fuck," Noah mutters under his breath.

"So, are you willing to help me get"—shit, I almost said Emily—"that dark creature out?"

He works his jaw. I wait with bated breath for his response. He finally nods after a few moments of blistering silence. "There's this charity gala. It's an event my parents used to attend every year. They were big donors. They extended the invitation to me over the years, but of course, I couldn't attend until this year. If I do this for you, I want you to come with me. And no more fucking lies. I mean it."

"Fine," I clip out, and tell him my plan.

TWENTY MINUTES LATER, I'm plastered against the concrete basement wall, adrenaline surging through my veins. It's different, though, from the times I've mentally prepared myself for a demon fight. It makes me feel off-kilter. It's probably the old Iris—who thought the sun rises and sets with her duty to the Order—screaming in my head that this is all wrong.

My hands have already been stained by lightborn blood, so what's another minor transgression? If Grayson finds out about everything I've done, he'll send me to rot away anyway. Also, I can't let them do this to an innocent person—dark creature or not. Before, I couldn't understand the disdain Kaiden showed every time I mentioned the Order. Now, it's slowly filtering through the cracks in my beliefs like black ink.

I don't know where Cain went since he hasn't shown his face in the last hour, but I'm grateful, because he left an opening for me. I take out my phone to send Noah a text.

> **Me: Ready to go in.**

He's supposed to distract Tim from the wall of security footage in his office. Luckily, I've avoided all the cameras around the compound so far. At least, I hope so. I send a text to Kaiden, too.

> **Me: I'm getting her out. Meet me at the end of the tunnel.**

> **Kaiden: Be careful, angel. I'll see you both there.**

Every second that passes spreads over my skin like a poison ivy rash as I wait for Noah's reply. It's an itch I can't scratch. A bead of sweat falls from my hairline, gets stuck in my eyelashes, then rolls down my corset. I changed into the spare hellseeker gear I kept in my locker for surprise demon attacks, just in case. But I'm sweating worse than a pregnant nun at confession, even if the sanctifiber is breathable and the basement is chilly.

The phone buzzes.

Noah: Done. You have 15 min.

Even though I know I'm alone, I still scan the perimeter before tiptoeing to the interrogation room. I snap my eyes closed. Inhale. Exhale. Open them. Then tap into the hellseeker speed to push open the door. I flick my wrist, sending a dagger flying into the air at light speed. It impales the security camera perched in the right corner of the room right in the middle. The sound of the glass shattering, followed by the dagger clattering to the floor, fills the air. I pick it up, sliding it back into the sheath strapped to my leg. If I thought the smell of burnt human flesh was terrible before, it's ten times worse in the small space.

Emily is still passed out, her legs caught in the middle of changing into her wolf form, clothes hanging in tatters from her body. I bend to place the sneakers I brought with me next to the chair. I don't want her to walk barefoot in the tunnel. Who knows what's down there? I need something to break through the chains holding her to the chair, since Cain must have taken the key. So, I make a beeline for the table in the corner of the room. The torture instrument spread reminds me of the one in Kaiden's basement. Swiping the pliers, I hurry back to Emily.

I crouch, then begin working on the chains around her ankles. It's not easy because my still-bruised ribs keep sending jolts of pain throughout my body when I put my whole strength into it. However, I push past it, teeth grinding, and finally manage to cut them off after a few moments.

Her skin is so bloody and raw under them it turns my stomach upside down. She stirs as I cut through the chains shackling her wrists. They rattle when I drop them to the floor next to the others.

A pained whimper leaves Emily's lips. She opens her eyes, confusion blanketing them before her amber gaze meets mine. "I-Iris. Wh—" she rasps.

"I'm here to help you, okay?"

"But...are you...aren't you going to get into trouble?"

"Probably, but I don't care," I shoot back. "Do you think you can change back your legs now that the chains are off?"

She sucks in a serrated breath. "I don't know. That bastard injected me with something really strong. It did a number on me."

"Can you try, please? It'll be faster if you can walk. That motherfucker Cain has been gone a while and I don't know how much time we have left."

"He said something about a gun earlier. That he was sad it wasn't delivered on time. Maybe he went to get it...I don't know." She bites back a few sharp curses while her body trembles violently. "Okay, Em, you can do this. One, two, th-th-ree," she mutters to herself. "Fuuuuuuuuck!" *Crack! Crack! Crack!* Her bones crunch and shift. Pained groans that make my hair stand on end follow. Sweat streams down in rivulets on her face and torso, plastering the semi-torn shirt to her body as fur recedes into the skin of her legs.

She loses consciousness.

I let her rest for a moment as I slide my sneakers on her feet and tie them. They're a little snug, but it's better than nothing. "Em, you need to wake up," I say as I straighten, then tap her cheek lightly. She groans again, but this time when she opens her eyes, they're more alert. I bend to place her arm around my shoulders. Propping her body against my side, I lift her up from the chair, taking her weight.

"Shit. Fuck. Motherfucker," she half blurts–half whimpers as she takes her first step. "My legs are on fire. Actually, my whole fucking body is."

"I'm sorry, but you're going to have to push past it because I can't walk for you even though I wish I could. C'mon, Logan is waiting for us. We can't disappoint him, all right?" I encourage, dragging her with me.

We're hobbling a little too slowly for my liking, but there's nothing I can do. Again, I ignore my screaming ribs, concentrating instead on each step. A little huff of relief leaves my lungs when we finally reach the hallway where the detainment cells are located. If the blueprints Kaiden sent me are correct, there should be a door at the end that opens to a room with a fake wall.

"Can you stand by yourself for a minute?" I ask Emily. She nods, so I leave her leaning on the wall. I round the corner to throw another flying dagger at the camera surveilling the cells. It drops to the ground, shattering.

I stride back to Emily and take her weight on my side again. As we shuffle down the corridor, a hissing ghoul interrupts the eerie silence when it smashes into the bars of its cell. Sharp claws swipe in the air toward Emily. She lets out a surprised yelp, but I pull her out of the demon's reach just in time.

The enchanted bars of the cell activate, turning bright gold. They burn through the ghoul's sickly white skin. Its three pairs of eyes roll to the back of its bald head as it shrieks and the smell of burnt flesh mixed with sulfur and rot coats the back of my throat.

Emily gags. "Ugly, stinky fucker."

I only huff in response because I'm getting too tired to speak. We almost topple over when I bend to collect my dagger from the broken camera on the floor. "Fucking finally," I say as we reach the old wooden door. The elation is short-lived, though, because heavy steps echo in the vast space behind us.

"Where do you think you're going, mutt?" Cain's menacing voice booms before a shot rings in the air.

I throw us both to the floor. Emily grunts, then hisses in pain when

I land on top of her. The bullet flies right over our heads and impales the wall, leaving spiderweb cracks in its wake. I jump up, pulling Emily with me. She doesn't complain that I'm being rough because if we stay here for one more second, we might die.

Fingers wrapping around the knob, I turn. *Fuck.* It's locked. I chance a look over my shoulder to see how long we have. Cain is running toward us at lightning speed while pointing the gun at Emily again. I push her out of the way when he pulls the trigger. An explosion of pain blurs my vision as the bullet grazes my shoulder.

I shake my head to gain some clarity before throwing out my leg in a punishing blow. The door creaks loudly, but it opens. Taking Emily's hand, we spill into the room. A rat scurries on the dirty floor between our feet to get outside. Judging by the musty air, the thick layer of grime covering the brick walls, and the rickety wooden table pushed against the wall, it's pretty clear no one has been here in decades.

I dash to the table, ignoring the white-hot pain from my shoulder that blinds me for an instant when I push it against the door, and plunge the room into pitch-black darkness. It's not much of a barrier, but it might buy us a few minutes.

"What now? We're trapped here, and that psycho is coming," Emily says, her voice laced with panic.

"There's a tunnel underneath us; one of the bricks opens a fake wall. Help me find it!" I take out my phone, tap on the flashlight, then slide it into my front pocket, the light pointing forward. I need both of my hands. I let my palms roam in a frenzy over the wall next to me. Emily copies me on the opposite wall.

A loud bang echoes through the door as Cain manages to push back the table slightly. Through the thick layers of grime, the pads of my fingers stumble upon some sort of engraving on one of the lower bricks. *Bingo.* I push my palm against it. At first, nothing happens. But after a few seconds, the wall at the back of the room opens slowly as the bricks drag on the cement floor with a loud grind.

I bite hard the inside of my cheek when I hook Emily's arm over the back of my neck. We hobble-run through the opening. The problem is that I have to search again for the mechanism to close the wall, so I use the pads of my fingers once more to feel the brick texture.

"Where the fuck is it?!" I mumble to myself. Cain finally pushes through the door, the table smashing and sending wood shards flying into the air.

The sound startles Emily back to reality. "Here!" she exclaims, slapping her palm against the brick above my head.

The fake wall starts closing. We don't spare a second, hurrying through the corridor. Emily looks back and swears loudly. "That fucker slid through the opening. He's gaining on us."

Turning us around, I pull out one of the daggers strapped to my thigh and flick my wrist to send it flying at Cain's forehead. He dodges at the last second, but it still impales his shoulder.

"You fucking half-blood filth!"

Before we can enter the ancient elevator that doesn't even have a door, Cain fires the gun again. The sound is deafening in the cramped corridor. I try to duck and shield Emily in one motion.

But it's too late.

She screams.

We collapse to the ground, the cement scraping my knees and forearms, my phone flying into the elevator. I scramble to Emily, then lift her by the armpits to prop her back against the wall to check her injury. The bastard got her in the left shoulder. If I hadn't ducked, it would have pierced her heart.

Her honey-colored eyes lock with mine as her face scrunches in a grimace. "It's silver," she grits out through clenched teeth.

Nonononononononononono.

Black vines spread slowly from the gunshot wound. *Fuck.* Not only is the bullet silver, but it was also dipped in aconite. In the spur of the moment, I push my finger inside the hole.

"What the fuck?!" she screams in agony as I search for the bullet, blood leaking from the wound in rivulets.

"I'm sorry, but I have to get it out." I can't be worried about sepsis at this moment. A silver bullet dipped in aconite is a death sentence for a wolf shifter. But only if the poison gets to her heart. By some divine luck, I find it and pry it out. The bullet clatters to the floor. Emily blacks out from the pain. Fuck! I need to stop her bleeding.

As I'm about to turn around, the cold barrel of a gun is pressed to the back of my head.

"You scum! I knew you would turn on us. I told Grayson it was a bad idea to allow filth into the Order, but he didn't fucking listen, and look where we are now," Cain spews.

"Fuck you!" I shoot back.

"Get up slowly and don't try anything. Let me see your hands. A silver bullet is still a bullet; it'll pierce through your skull regardless of what it's made of. But then, I wouldn't have the pleasure of torturing you." His maniacal laugh bounces off the walls.

I put my hands in the air and inch up slowly. He uses the gun to push me back toward the way we came. When Emily sputters a pained moan, I hear the second of hesitation in Cain's next step. I take it as my cue. Using my unearthly hellseeker speed, I twirl around, grab the barrel with my left hand, then lean my body out of the direct line of fire to karate chop Cain's wrist. The gun drops to the ground, so I kick it back toward Emily.

Fisting my fingers, I swing my arm in an arc at Cain's head. He blocks my punch with ease before tackling me into the wall. Hard. I don't get a chance to catch my breath because his fingers wrap around my throat in a punishing grip. Then he smashes the back of my head against the brick wall. The pain lends itself to little white dots swarming my vision. Sticky, warm liquid coats my hair as I gasp for air. Whatever reprieve that gives me is short-lived because my head meets the bricks for a second time. Blackness envelops me. I lose my grip on reality for a second. Then come back to in the next.

Somehow, in the middle of all this, I regain that equilibrium that accompanies me whenever I hunt demons. Letting out a feral scream, I palm the dagger closest to me on my thigh, take it out of its holster, and slash the side of Cain's neck. It goes through skin and muscle like a hot knife through butter, severing his carotid artery. Blood shoots out. It sprays my face and torso.

Disbelief flashes in Cain's eyes. He lets go of me to cover his wound—a last-ditch attempt to stop the bleeding. It's futile, though. He mumbles something that resembles "You cunt!" but I can't be sure because, in the next second, his head bends at an unnatural angle. He falls first on his knees, then on his side with a loud thump.

I don't know how, but I can feel his soul slipping away. It's like a ball of pure energy calling out to me. But it's tainted...corrupt and as black as pitch. I don't dwell on it, though. Ignoring the red-hot pain bursting from my every nerve ending, I hop over his lifeless body and scramble to get to Emily. When I reach her, her chest isn't moving. At all. So, I drop into a crouch and place two fingers under her nose. I heave out a relieved sigh when her exhale whispers against my skin. Thank fuck!

"Emily," I call out her name as I take off my belt to make a tourniquet.

Her fingers twitch. She opens her eyes slowly. It takes a few seconds for her to fully come back to reality, and when she does, she lets out a string of curses when I tighten the belt above the gunshot wound. "Did you get it out?"

"Yeah," I reply, inspecting her chest. The black vines stopped spreading, which gives me hope that we might make it out before the poison gets to her heart.

A manic laugh belts out of her. "You look like Carrie."

I shudder in revulsion. "Oh, I wish it was pig blood."

Emily flicks her gaze over my shoulder, where Cain is lying in a puddle of blood on the cement floor. "You killed him," she states the obvious. "Don't get me wrong, I'm happy the psycho is dead, but aren't you going to suffer the consequences?"

"I didn't have much of a choice. It was either kill or be killed." I sigh. "Let's hope no one knows about this tunnel."

I push up and stride toward the elevator to take my phone. The screen is cracked and useless, but at least the flashlight is still on. So I slide it back into its place in the front pocket of my pants. Then I help Emily get up, crooking her uninjured arm around my shoulders again. We get into the elevator. I press my hand on the button for it to go down, but nothing happens.

"This is old as fuck. Kind of funny we managed to escape that dipshit just to possibly die in a stuck elevator," she says with a bitter laugh. The sound gets swallowed by a loud screech as the elevator starts descending. It's shaking so badly that my teeth chatter. I throw another look at the corridor.

And find myself staring right into Cain's open eyes.

25

Iris

On instinct, I swipe a dagger and flick it at his head. Cain's form ripples and it flies right through him. A relieved chuckle bubbles up my throat. He's a fucking ghost.

"What the hell is happening?" Emily shrieks.

I can't answer her because Cain's spirit rushes at us, clearly not realizing he's dead yet. Believe it or not, I now have tiny packets of salt on me at all times. So, I take one out of the back pocket of my pants, rip it open with my teeth, and throw the salt in the air at him. His eyes bulge out of his head when static takes over. There's a bright light, followed by a pop as he disappears.

I hope you never find peace, motherfucker, I tell him in my mind.

"What the? Was that salt?" Emily inquires.

"Yeah."

She throws me a suspicious sidelong glance. "Um, why'd you do all that?"

"It's a long story," I mumble. "Basically, I can see ghosts. And Cain suddenly appeared in front of us. I didn't realize he was a spirit at first because it's pretty new—the seeing ghosts. Hence me throwing the dagger at him. And yeah, now I have to keep salt on me at all times because spirits are kinda crazy."

"Well, that's um...I don't know what to say to that."

"Trust me, I've been there more times than I would like to admit," I agree.

The elevator finally stops to a screeching halt that jostles our balance. Grunting, I support both of our weights so we don't topple over. Now that the adrenaline crash is starting to settle in, my body feels like one giant bruise.

"How are you feeling? Are you cold?" I ask while shuffling out with Emily attached to me. Dusty, cold air and the musty smell of mildew enhance the creepiness of the narrow corridor in front of us.

"Wolf shifters have a higher body temperature. Besides, whatever the fuck that piece of shit injected me with made my insides burn, so the air in here actually feels nice. Aside from the fetid smell." She gags. "What the fuck died in here?"

We get our answer when a multitude of rats and roaches scurry to get out of our way, their clicking reverberating in the vast space. We shudder at the same time. "I hate rats. But I despise roaches," I mutter as I take in the fist-size insects scampering on the grimy walls. I can't wait to get out of this fucking tunnel.

We continue hobbling through the pitch-black darkness. My phone's flashlight doesn't provide much light, but at least we can see in front of our feet. The only sounds are the *click, click, clicks*, our heavy breaths, and the occasional *splash* as we trek through portions with puddles.

Emily breaks the strained silence after about fifteen minutes. "Why did you save me?"

I shrug and instantly regret it because of the white-hot stab in my shoulder. Tearing a hole in my cheek, I ponder my answer, then finally say, "Because you're innocent, and you didn't deserve what that bastard did to you. I don't give a flying fuck that you're a dark creature." I let out a mirthless chuckle. "I'm ashamed to admit that if I had been faced with the same decision three months ago — before my life started to go downhill — I'm not sure I would have given you a hand. But too many things have happened, and now I see the world in various shades of gray."

"Well, thank you for saving me."

"You don't have to thank me," I murmur. "It's my fault this happened to you."

"No, Iris. This is most definitely not your fault. You have to get that out of your head. You just defended yourself at Sin. It's pretty clear what that scum's intentions were when he spiked your water." She wheezes a breath. "Because the moment you give men power, they will take advantage of it and use it for their own benefit. And tell people that a god blessed their blood, and it will get to their heads. They will justify every atrocity as bringing down the divine hammer on so-called lesser beings."

Her hollow laugh morphs into a grunt, but she continues anyway, "If it's not the color of your skin making you inferior, then it's your blood. Lightborn are supposed to be the good guys, right? Where's the light in what they did to *me*?" she spits out the words like they're venomous.

They bulldoze through those cracks in my already shattered beliefs. While I can't fully comprehend Emily's life experience from my privileged position, how many times have I bitten my tongue against being called a dirty half-blood either to my face or behind my back? Too many to count. I always thought that if I trained enough, if I gave a little more each day, then surely everyone at the compound would look at me in a different light. That I could at least gain their respect if I became one of the best hellseekers in the Order. Well, that didn't happen. Ultimately, all lightborn will ever see me as is a half-measure, a freak...just *different*. And now, after everything that's happened, I have to ask myself: do I even want to be one of them anymore? It's surprising how easily I find the answer within me. I no longer want to take part in an organization that not only lies but also uses its power to hurt the innocent.

In the silence stretching between us, I'm waiting for that debilitating guilt to take over — to fold my lungs in two and suffocate me because I have killed another lightborn. Which is beyond crazy. But strangely, I feel numb this time.

We've been in the tunnel for about an hour. Or possibly more; I can't tell for sure. It feels like days, because Emily's weight presses heavily on my side. Even with hellseeker strength, my muscles are screaming while fatigue seeps deep into my bones. She's burning up, so at least I can't even feel the chill in the air anymore.

"I don't think I can go on," Emily lets out in a strained whisper. Her knees buckle.

I halt and pull her closer to my side, stopping us from face-planting. My fingers brush momentarily over a cockroach as I use the wall for support. At this point, I'm so tired I don't even care. Emily disentangles herself from me to slouch on the wall. She slides into a crouch.

"The end of the tunnel shouldn't be too far," I say to encourage her, but her beautiful face, normally the color of rich amber, is ashen. I chance a look at the black, spindly branches that spread from the gunshot wound to her chest. *Fuck.* They weren't as dispersed twenty minutes ago when I last checked. This can only mean one thing: the aconite is festering deeper into her bloodstream. If the paleness of her features doesn't give it away, her glazed eyes and the sweat covering every inch of her body sure do.

Emily sways to the side before closing her eyes. "I just want to sleep. I'm so tired," she whines. "Tell my brother Logan I love him. And—and tell him to let Hailey know I love her too. I never got the chance to say it...I wanted to make it special, you know? Take her to a nice restaurant, buy her a big bouquet of lilies, that sort of thing."

Fuck that. I drop to my haunches and slap her cheek. Hard.

Her eyes snap open, throwing daggers at me through the hazy fog. "What the fuck?" she screeches.

"I'm not letting you die on my watch, dammit! You're never going to wake up if you fall asleep. C'mon, we're going to power through this, and you can tell Logan and Hailey you love them yourself." I pull her from the wall back to my side and hurry our steps, even if Emily calls me a ruthless bitch more times than I can count.

Shortly after, my phone battery dies and we're plunged into darkness, but I've never been one to let a little darkness stop me. Soon enough, though, a dim orange glow seems to take shape in the distance. I don't know if I'm seeing things or if it really is the end of the tunnel until the tiny fleck of light takes the shape of a circle, getting bigger as we approach it.

"Fucking finally," I mutter.

A wrought-iron gate comes into view at the end of the tunnel, with a staircase visible through its bars. A few more minutes and we are standing in front of it. I wrap my fingers around one bar to pull at it. It doesn't budge, so I take two steps backward before I throw my leg in a powerful kick.

Nothing happens.

"Let me try something," Emily says, a pained groan slipping through her lips as fur pierces the skin on her pointer finger, which now has a long, sharp claw instead of a nail. She lodges the claw into the keyhole, turns it. A *click* breaks through the silence, followed by a rusty screech when the gate opens slightly.

I grin at her. "Nice trick. Do you do parties?"

"You can't afford me." She smiles, but it's more of a grimace. "I don't have the strength to shift it back."

We climb the stairs, or better said, I ascend while hauling Emily after me like a sack of potatoes. She's not out of it completely, but she's close to passing out. If it weren't for the hope that we are so close to getting out, I would collapse. However, I keep repeating in my head: *just a little more.* We probably resemble two girls who had too much to drink at a wild Halloween party. If only the blood and the gunshot wounds were fake.

I almost burst into relieved tears when we reach the top of the never-ending stairs. I cram as much air as I can into my lungs. It isn't fresh, but it's much better than the musty draft in the tunnel. Once the dizzy spell subsides, I cast a glance over the space we're in. Thick cobwebs hang from the marble angel statue on my right. A dusty bench sits in the middle of the floor with tombs sealed into the grimy marble walls on its sides, illuminated by the orange streaks of light that shine through the small window on the wooden door on my left. It's pretty obvious no one has been here in a very long time. I think we're in a crypt.

There's a weird pang right below my breastbone — like a tug. I'm unsure how to explain it otherwise, but something deep within me feels Kaiden's presence. Cain must have smacked my head real good.

As I'm about to drag Emily toward the exit, a muffled, angry voice travels through the wooden door. "I'm fucking going in, Kaiden. I can't wait anymore."

It's Logan.

"Let's give them a few more minutes. We don't even know which crypt it is."

217

My hellseeker hearing must have picked up their voices, and my addled brain couldn't compute it yet. Surely, that's what that weird sensation was.

"I don't give a fuck! I'll search each one if I have to. Emily is hurt. I can feel it. It's a twin thing. They should have been here by now," Logan huffs.

"Just let him do it. He's like a dog with a bone," Malik replies, amused.

"Shut the fuck up, Malik!" Logan snaps at him.

"Seriously? This is not the time for jokes, Malik," a feminine voice intervenes—Ava, I think.

"Yeah, you're right. Sorry," Malik sounds sheepish now.

"Do you hear that? We made it," I tell Emily. She doesn't reply because, in the next second, she's out cold. Not ready to withstand her entire weight, my knees buckle. "Logan!" I scream.

Logan barrels through the door, throwing it off its hinges. Angry, fiery amber eyes immediately find Emily. When he takes in her injuries, he bellows, "I'm going to fucking kill them!" He stabilizes me, then bends to take Emily in his arms protectively.

Her eyes crack open a smidge. A lone tear teeters on her eyelashes before it rolls down her cheek. "I never thought I would be so happy to see your dumb face, little bro," she whispers.

Logan smiles softly at her. "We're twins, Em. We kinda share the same face."

"I don't care, your face is still du—" She loses consciousness again.

Fuck.

Her chest is not moving.

"Malik!" Logan roars, voice drenched in panic as he flies outside.

26

Iris

I descend the three marble stairs after him. But I'm not prepared to collide with a wall of muscle as Kaiden blinks into existence in front of me. I'm ashamed to admit that I lose my balance. He stops my fall by wrapping a hand on my waist. "You okay, angel?" His touch is a live wire that electrifies my skin and knocks the air out of my lungs for a few seconds. It feels so good to be near him again that I almost throw myself into his arms.

I don't.

However, I indulge in a few moments of basking in the delicious heat rolling from his body. Only a few seconds in his presence and the frostbite that burrowed to the marrow of my bones is gone. Damn him and his intoxicating scent that I can't stop inhaling like a heroin addict. It takes everything I have in me to shake his hold as though he's radioactive—mainly because it feels like my very soul is purring in his presence.

Shit. I'm more concussed than I thought.

Or I'm just pathetic.

Probably both.

"Don't touch me," I sputter, refusing to look into his mesmerizing eyes. Or at his annoyingly perfect face. I'm afraid if I do, my resolve will shatter like fragile glass. Of course, he looks like sin wrapped in a deadly package, wearing his usual black attire: straight jeans, a simple tee, and worn motorcycle boots. And those tattoos that are a constant reminder that he carries a part of me with him forever, etched on his skin. "And how many times do I have to repeat myself? Don't. Call. Me. *That.*"

Kaiden ignores my barbed words. "Fuck, you're bleeding. Who did this to you?" he seethes. I might not be looking at his face to see his expression, but I almost choke on the fury emanating from his pores. It's so potent that I feel it bubbling beneath my skin. Weird. He reaches a tattooed hand toward my throat, where I probably have a big fat imprint from when Cain grabbed me. It stops mid-air when I flinch away. Heaving a weighted sigh, he closes the hand in a tight fist, which he drops to his side.

"Cain, the enforcer," I retort flippantly. "The blood is not all mine. Actually, maybe only ten percent is mine. The spray hit me when I sliced his carotid."

"Good."

Like every time he is near, everything fades away. Being this close to him is equal parts heaven and hell—my insides are being torn to pieces while my soul sings. I need to escape this bubble we have immersed ourselves into to check on Emily. "Yeah, I killed another lightborn. Yay me. They'll probably burn me at the stake," I mutter mostly to myself as I push past Kaiden, careful not to brush against him.

There's also the fact that I'm covered in blood and sweat. Not only mine but Emily's, too. I probably smell worse than a sewage pipe in Victorian London during a cholera outbreak.

Ugh.

"I don't know how he got his hands on a gun with silver bullets dipped in aconite since they're so rare, but I did my best to shield Emily. He still got her in the shoulder, though. The bullet almost pierced her heart." My voice wavers. "I'm afraid the infection has spread too much."

"She's going to be all right. Malik will heal her," Kaiden reassures me from my back.

In front of me, Malik is kneeling on the ground over Emily, who lies on a raised marble tomb, a blood-drawn pentagram beneath her. Dark magic flows in the air at the rhythm of Malik's incantation while his fingers are wrapped around her injured arm.

Silent tears carve a path down Ava's cheeks. Her voice cracks when she grits out, "You have to fight, Em, you hear me?!? My babies need their aunt. And I need my best friend." She's hanging to her other hand like to a lifeline, kneeling opposite Malik on the grass.

A blistering silence stretches between us as we all wait on pins and needles for a sign that Emily is going to make it. The only sound is that of Logan's frantic steps. He resembles a wolf locked in a cage, pacing at the head of the tombstone amidst whole body shakes.

C'mon, Em. Don't give up!

A few more torturous minutes pass. Then, the spindly black vines on her chest retreat as if vanishing into thin air. There's a collective sigh when Emily sucks in a serrated breath. She hasn't opened her eyes yet, but she's safe. Malik got the infection out of her bloodstream.

The toll the dark magic took on his body is evident, though, in the lines at the corners of his cat-like eyes and sunken cheekbones when he stands with sagged shoulders. Even his hair, normally the color of lively silver, is now limp and lackluster. Malik flicks his gaze to Logan. "She's going to be okay, but she needs to rest. She won't wake up for a few days."

Logan tips his head skyward. Relieved tears stream down his face. He murmurs something, then blows out a heavy exhale while raking a hand through his ash-brown curls. "Thank you," he rasps. He bends to place a kiss atop his sister's forehead. "You're lucky Mom is on a beach in Bermuda sipping on cocktails right now; otherwise, she would have killed us both."

Completely absorbed by the emotional scene in front of me, I'm taken by surprise when Ava flings herself at me. I let out an *oomf* that transforms into a pained groan when she squeezes the bejesus out of me, pregnant belly and all. She's much stronger than she looks. "Words are not enough to express our gratitude for what you did. *Eres familia.* You're family now. You will always be welcome in our pack no matter what."

"Ava, you're hurting her," Kaiden warns under his breath.

Her cheeks take a pink hue when she pulls back. "Sorry about that."

Needles stab the back of my eyes. Aside from Sam, no one has ever said anything like this to me before. It means more than she knows — more than she can ever imagine. My voice trembles when I tell her, "I — um, yeah. You don't have to thank me."

Topaz green eyes lock with mine. "I do." Then she wrinkles her nose. "Man, you stink. You really need a shower."

We all break out in laughter at the startling levity. "Yeah. I know. I'm a walking dumpster fire. Thanks for reminding me, though."

"That's what friends are for. I'll see you around." She beams at me before turning on her heel to follow Logan on the winding path through the marble tombstones.

Malik ambles toward me. His gaze rakes over my body as if cataloging each one of my injuries. "Hey, sweets. You look like shit."

I snort a laugh. "Thanks. I'll add that to the dumpster fire."

"You know, I've never met someone so prone to dying before.

You're a magnet for bad luck."

"Yeah, tell me about it," I mutter.

"Are you ready?" he asks. "Kaiden, I need to pull some juice from you, man."

Kaiden appears next to Malik.

"What are you doing?" I ask when he places a taupe hand to the center of my chest.

He raises an amused eyebrow. "What does it look like? I'm healing you."

"No offense, but you also look like shit, Malik. I can't possibly ask you to do more. I'll be fine."

"Well, tough luck because you're one of us, and we take care of our own." He drops his head in between his shoulders and starts chanting when Kaiden's hand wraps around his upper arm.

Dark magic engulfs me completely while the physical pain seeps out of my shoulder, my head, and my sore muscles in small increments. I revel in its absence as I swallow a lungful of air. If only his abilities would go further — to the emotional welts that bleed akin to an overflowing river in the presence of a certain Elite demon. My vision clears when Malik steps back, breaking our connection. He sways slightly on his feet.

Kaiden catches him by the elbow. "Pull more from me."

I don't know how, but in the span of a few minutes, Malik has become so haggard that I swear his leather duster hangs on him two sizes too big. A hunted shadow passes over his eyes before he says, resolute, "You know I can't."

"You can barely stand. Take more."

Malik only glares at him, but that look conveys so much more. "I'm fine. I'll go. Logan and Ava are waiting for me."

A muscle jumps in Kaiden's cheek, but he drops the hold on Malik's elbow. I wonder at that bizarre exchange, but I don't ask. It's pretty clear it's personal.

"Bye, sweets. Try not to get into mortal danger for another week. Or at least until my power is back fully," Malik says, his lips curving in a rakish smile. The bravado he's trying to hide under is so thin we can see right through it. Though, neither I nor Kaiden say anything about it.

I smile back. "I'll try. Thank you so much, Malik."

He winks. "My pleasure. Besides, you're a badass. You've made me a lot of money." Malik chuckles at the confused look on my face. "I placed a bet with Dominic on how long it would take you to get Emily out."

"And, who won?"

"I did, of course."

My eyebrows knit. "Where is he, by the way?"

"Did you forget he's a vampire? The sun's still up."

"Oh yeah," I say and shake my head at my stupidity.

"Also, he's undercover, working to find the vampire den responsible for the fae kidnappings. But we're keeping him informed."

"I'll meet you at Ava and Logan's. We'll have the Conclave meeting there," Kaiden chimes in.

Malik nods in response and trudges down the same path Ava and Logan disappeared down earlier.

To prolong the moment before having to meet Kaiden's gaze, I take in my surroundings. Cottony clouds float in the azure sky while the sun casts streaks of golden light that glitter through weathered tombstones and overgrown blades of grass. Even the bird songs are uplifting. It seems wrong on so many levels to be shot at and covered in blood during the day. Let's not even mention killing someone. If I dare say, the atmosphere is creepily idyllic.

If only there wasn't the same strange feeling crawling beneath my skin every time I'm in a cemetery — a foreign energy that calls to me from below.

Kaiden's voice snaps me out of it.

"Iris, I'm dying here. Would you look at me?" He sucks in a

sharp breath. "Please."

I pretend I didn't hear him. "Since my work here is done, I'm gonna go." I take a step before a strong hand wraps around my wrist and whirls me around. Kaiden's touch singes me.

"Please come back home," he rasps.

Home.

These four letters slice through me like a serrated blade. I meet his gaze. There's so much pain etched on his beautiful face that it makes my hands tremble. I swallow past the knot lodged in my throat to clip out, "What home? You got this idea in your head that we were somehow living together, but you and I were on borrowed time anyway. It was never meant to happen, so it's better it ended sooner than later." I hike a nonchalant shoulder. "You should move on because I already have."

"You're lying." His jaw is an iron bar of tension, his eyes fire and brimstone as they bore into mine. "You and I are meant for forever, angel. There's no one else. Only you. It's always been you."

His words start a riot beneath my ribcage. I grasp that mask of indifference with broken fingers and bloody nails to force it on my face. It's too tight and uncomfortable, but I need it because I'm on the edge of folding like a cheap suit. I blow out a heavy exhale. "I understand, okay? Why you can't tell me about my past. I went with Sam to see a dark witch and—"

Panic ripples through his features. "What did you do?"

"Calm down. She just inspected the barrier. And told me the same things you did. But while you see a future for us, I can't—because you can't build one on top of lies. That's not the kind of relationship I want. I can't be with someone I can't trust...I'm tired, and I desperately need a shower. Goodbye, Kaiden. Have a nice life." I turn on my heel and traipse down the path toward the exit. "And stop sending me flowers. I'm running out of women's shelters to drop them at."

27

Iris

My shoulders tense when a set of footsteps follow close behind. "What are you doing?" I grit out through clenched teeth while my gaze drills a hole through the tree in front of me.

"My car is parked this way. You do know you look as though you've been resurrected from a gory crime scene, right?"

"Well, I haven't looked in a mirror yet, but I assume, yeah."

"And how do you think you're getting home like this? If someone sees you, they will not only call an ambulance but the police too."

My steps falter. He's right. If someone calls the police, I will have to explain how I ended up covered in someone else's blood. I could tell them I'm from the Order and fought a demon, but then the report would get to Grayson. Plus, demon blood is the color of tar, not ruby-red. They wouldn't know the difference, but Grayson sure would. *Shit.* It's not as easy to disguise blood in the middle of the day. "I'll manage." Somehow.

"I'm taking you."

I huff. "I would rather let a souldrake burn me to a crisp then chomp on me like overcooked bacon than get into a car with you, thank you very much."

"That's your only solution if you don't want Grayson to catch wind of this."

Gnawing on my bottom lip, I try to devise a different option. Anything to not be in an enclosed space near Kaiden. There's a pond to my right, but the water is so murky I can smell it from here. Given my luck, I would probably catch ten different skin diseases. A few minutes of blistering silence pass before I reluctantly mutter, "Fine." The only pleasure I take from this is that I'll most likely ruin his ostentatiously expensive Italian leather seat.

The weird buzz beneath my skin only seems to intensify the longer I'm in the cemetery. As does the cadaver count and the inexplicable urge to slam my palms on the ground. A group of about seven ghosts catches the corner of my eye, momentarily distracting me. They float chaotically over the pond. Are they...racing? Nope, I can't do crazy right now.

This is the oldest cemetery in Ashville, and since the people buried in this section are over two hundred years old, mourning relatives rarely visit. Which is good because we don't encounter anyone on our way to the parking lot. I roll my eyes when Kaiden opens the passenger door of his Escalade for me. On the inside, though, I melt like butter on warm toast at the gesture.

The moment I sink into the soft leather of the chair, my nose wrinkles. Not even Kaiden's heavenly cologne can mask the horrid stench of the car. I wonder what it is, but I don't dwell on it too long. He then slides behind the wheel, holding a towel and a T-shirt from the trunk. "Here, I keep these with me in my gym bag. They're clean. You can use the towel to wipe off the blood, and I thought you might want to change."

"Thanks. Can you wait before driving off so I don't give anyone a heart attack through the windshield?" I say as I take them from his outstretched hand. Sparks fly when I accidentally brush my fingers against his.

He gives a curt nod in response.

Hand still tingling, I use the water bottle resting in the center console to soak the towel. My reflection in the sun visor is something else entirely. Emily was right. I do resemble Carrie. I wipe off the dried blood on my face and neck as best as I can, but unfortunately, I can't do anything about my braid, which is caked with it. *Ugh.* Heat scorches the tips of my ears when I tell Kaiden, "Turn around, please."

His eyebrows knit in confusion. "Why?"

"So I can change. Duh."

"Should I remind you that you were riding my cock like a goddess only three weeks ago, angel? Stripped to your skin while moaning my name. I think we're past the point of me turning around when you change your top, don't you think?" He challenges me with a mocking eyebrow, followed by that infuriating smirk of his.

This demon is going to be the end of me. The air in the cabin thickens dangerously. Because my devious mind hates me—and the images of me losing my virginity to Kaiden aren't enough—it also sends me flashes of him feasting on my pussy and sinking his fingers into me in this very car. I damn nearly combust.

What are you going to do when she remembers you were the one who locked her powers away alongside her memories?

The recollection of that sordid morning efficiently douses the flames of desire. Teeth gnashing, I wrap my fingers around the handle to open the door. "Fine, then I'll go change behind a tree," I snap.

Kaiden wraps a hand around my forearm to stop me. "I'll go," he grits out before closing the door at his back. His muscles are coiled like tight springs while he takes a few steps away from the car.

I make quick work of peeling off the corset, followed by the long-sleeved blouse underneath. Gagging, I throw them to the floorboard along with the dirty towel, then slip Kaiden's tee over my head. Holy fuck! I have to bite my lower lip to stop the moan from tumbling free at being engulfed in his scent. I'm glad the sour ammonia smell inside the car didn't permeate the fabric. I'm about to bring it to my nose and sniff it like a creep, but luckily, I spot Kaiden just in time, striding back to the car.

"What's that smell? Did you eat fish in here?" I blurt out when Kaiden slides back behind the wheel.

His lips twitch. That little movement is maddening. All I can think about is how good it would feel to have him devour me whole with a scorching kiss.

Earth to Iris!

We're not going to fantasize about six-foot-four sexy demons that betrayed us anymore.

"Funny you ask," he responds, shifting the car into drive and effortlessly gliding into the evening traffic. "Someone thought it would be a good idea to leave rancid seafood in all twenty-five of my cars. I can only assume a fiery redhead took revenge because, quote, 'You make my bestie cry, I fuck up your stuff.' was written in red lipstick on all the smashed windshields."

My eyes widen. "What? Sam did this?"

"Oh yeah. I don't know how the fuck she pulled it off because the cameras didn't catch anything suspicious. I got the Escalade from the shop today. They tried everything to get the smell out, but clearly, it didn't work."

I can't stop the chuckle that bubbles up my throat. It morphs into a hearty laugh—the type that makes my head tip back on the rest and my eyes water. It dies when I feel Kaiden's burning gaze on me. He's drinking me in as though I'm the last drop of water in the desert, and he's dying of thirst. The fact that he's not paying attention to the road would normally send me directly into the arms of a panic attack, but the evening traffic is brutal. We're moving at a snail's pace.

"Fuck me. You're the most beautiful thing I have ever seen. But nothing—nothing in this world compares to your laugh, Iris. It steals my goddamn breath away."

Kaiden's words are like a match thrown over a gasoline-soaked floor, setting me ablaze. Fuck. I knew getting into a car with him was the worst idea ever. Now he's looking at me as if I'm the sun, the moon, and everything in between, even though I'm a mess. Not able to withstand the brunt of his gaze anymore, I turn to glance through the window, feigning indifference.

The silence is deafening. I break it after a few minutes when I turn on the radio, then ask, "Um, can you drop me off at Sam's?"

"Sure."

"Good thing you already know where she lives," I drawl dryly, my eyes still glued to the window. "I know you've been in my room… You weren't exactly subtle when leaving those irises on my pillow. It's creepy, so stop doing that. If I didn't make it clear enough before, let me spell it out for you again: I don't want you in my life, Kaiden."

Why do my insides twist into painful knots when saying this?

Even though I'm not looking at him to see his reaction, his hurt is palpable. It coats my lungs like the soot left in the wake of a chemical fire. "I will never stop looking after you. Not until you're safe. And beyond that, because I meant what I said. There's only *you*," he rasps.

I huff and snap my mouth shut because what else can I do? This man has a response to everything I say. I wish someone would have warned me that being stuck amid a bloody war between your heart and mind crushes you. He will eventually grow tired of watching me if I ignore him, right? I can't take this push and pull that saws through my bones like a knife with a dull blade anymore.

It doesn't take long for the usual panic that accompanies me in a moving vehicle to force my fingers to clench and unclench involuntarily while I struggle for air. Even though I desperately need to distract myself somehow, I pretend Kaiden doesn't exist. It's okay…I'll r-ride it o-out. Shit. I think Kaiden said something, but all I hear is the *whoosh, whoosh, whoosh* of the blood rushing into my ears.

"W-what?" I mumble.

Worry shines in the obsidian void as our gazes lock. "Do you want me to stop?"

"No, I'll be fine. I j-just—" I snap my eyes shut. "What were you saying before?"

Kaiden's big hand engulfs mine in my lap. The visceral reaction to his touch anchors me to reality. I take the opportunity to cram as much air as I can into my useless lungs.

His eyebrows knit, but he indulges me. "How did you get Emily out? I need to be prepared in case Grayson confronts me, since you killed one of the Order's best assets. Cain was known worldwide for his skills."

I sniff. "Well, I had someone distract the guy who watches the security cameras while I broke her out of the interrogation ro—"

"Who helped you?"

"Someone I can only hope I can trust."

"What's the name of the person, Iris? That's what I want to know."

I roll my eyes. "Noah Pierce. He's been gone for a few years, but we were close once. I didn't want to involve anybody else, okay? But I couldn't have done it by myself."

Kaiden's eye twitches. "I know how *close* you once were," he spits out the words as warm as a glacier.

"Oh yeah, I forgot you've been stalking me for years," I fire back while pushing his hand away as if it's venomous.

He white-knuckles the wheel. "Are you a hundred percent sure you can trust him?"

"I don't know, Kaiden. Can you be a hundred percent sure about anyone these days?" I can't resist adding, "I've trusted *you*...and look where it's gotten me." I let him stew in my words for a few moments to make sure I got my point across before continuing, "We've made a deal, and I think he will respect his end of the bargain."

The vein on the side of his forehead is pulsing so violently, I'm afraid it's going to burst any second now. "What. Deal?"

"That concerns me and me alone." I suck on my teeth. "For what it's worth, I don't think anyone saw me. I was careful to take back all the daggers I used to disable the cameras. We were also already in the secret tunnel when Cain caught up to us and shot Emily. That's where I killed him. So, as long as they don't go into that tunnel...I think we're good. But I'm not sure what the situation is at the compound. The screen on my phone got smashed in the struggle with Cain, and my battery is dead anyway, so I can't call Noah to ask." Now that my hands are free, I push back the bloody strands that escaped my braid. "On that note, how secret was that tunnel? Because if Grayson knows about it and finds Cain's body, we're fucked...well, actually, I am fucked." Not that I didn't take that risk into consideration when I decided to get Emily out. But if I can avoid rotting away in a cell for the rest of my life, of course, I'm going to take that chance.

Kaiden reads me like an open book. "Iris, I will level this entire city to mere ashes before the Aureal Council gets to you. Fuck that, I'll burn down the entire world."

And there it goes again: my heart is doing the *cha-cha-cha* while my mind screams at the love-sick organ.

There's a little pause as he switches lanes. "The tunnel is a secret. Mammon traded a lot of favors to get those original blueprints for leverage in case a war started between the Order and the Conclave. That tunnel was the first built when the Order arrived in America near the end of the sixteenth century. Since then, they've remodeled and updated the house many times, and when they built the new tunnel for transporting demons, they shut down the old one. It's not even on the Order's blueprints anymore."

"Well, it did look deserted, so I hope you're right. What about what the Order did? Directly violating the Treaty. What are you going to do about it?"

Kaiden huffs. A muscle pops in his cheek. "The only thing dark creatures can do in a situation like this is file an official complaint with the Aureal Council. They are supposed to open an investigation and then hold trial if there is enough evidence."

I go from zero to one hundred in a second. "WHAT? But that's crazy! They will never blame Grayson because he is one of them."

"Exactly my point. Do you even know how many innocent dark creatures have been severely injured or killed at the hands of hellseekers since I took over as head of the Conclave? A hundred and fifty-seven—eight, if you count Emily too. And do you know what the Council has done, Iris? Jack shit. Because a lightborn can never be at fault, even if there were witnesses to attest to the crimes. I personally filed all the complaints and fought tooth and nail for each case, only for them to be dismissed or for the witnesses to disappear under mysterious circumstances. That's why I wanted to storm the compound. Because I knew if I didn't, Emily would end up dead, and Grayson wouldn't even be reprimanded for it."

Emily was right—the system is rigged in the Order's favor. This is all new information for me and, if I had to guess...for everyone who's not in a leadership position within the Order.

How the fuck did they keep so much from us?

I can't believe I've been so blind. I'm ashamed to admit that I've never even questioned this before. Dark creatures are briefly covered in the lessons at the compound before graduation, but we are only taught that we are not allowed to harm those under the Conclave's protection because the Celestial Treaty forbids it. I always imagined that the repercussions would be equally as harsh as when dark creatures injure lightborn: a death sentence or life at Gomorrah. But now that I think about it...they were never stated.

And *this* is why.

Sighing deeply, I ask, "Did you find Adramelech?" I have to change the subject before the unraveling of all I've ever known destroys my sanity.

Kaiden's hands tighten on the wheel, making the thick ropes of muscles in his forearms flex in a way that sends my pulse spiking through the roof. And with the tattoos and those damn silver rings adorning his fingers? Straight arm porn. I don't catch the first words he says. *Fuck, Iris. Concentrate!*

" —bastard is as slippery as an eel. Being Lucifer's right-hand demon for hundreds of years has allowed him to build strong connections. Someone's hiding him for sure. With the hatred toward the Conclave blooming in Hell, let's just say that I'm far from welcome. So even though I tried my best, no one would give away his hideout. You would think it would be easier to bribe demons."

Tapping my foot against the floorboard, I shift to yet another topic. Might as well get as much information as I can out of him since I don't plan to be this close to Kaiden ever again. I ignore the annoying voice that screams *liar* inside my head. "Any luck with the prophecy?"

"Since the rogue vampires took over the trafficking rings, we saved a few of the enslaved fae, but they know nothing about an oracle. They're scared. The rescued women mentioned fae meeting places, but because their magic is not from this world, we can't track them down."

"I tried to do some research into the fae folk, too," I say. "My grandmother had all of these books on dark creatures, but the majority were in a strange language, and the only two books in English were some sort of medical journals. Honestly, I didn't even understand half of the notes, so I gave up." But maybe I shouldn't have because they might contain information about what they did to my mother. I don't tell Kaiden about my mother's journal. If I want him out of my life, I can't keep pulling him back in. I need to figure things out myself.

We don't talk for the rest of the ride. I sense multiple times that Kaiden wants to initiate a conversation, but I pretend he doesn't exist as I try not to freak out at the thought that my life keeps going downhill at breakneck speed. The sigh of relief leaving my lungs when I spot Sam's house fills the cabin.

Gaze fixated on the front door, I say, "Thanks for the ride. I'll give you an update after I talk to Noah. But don't get any ideas; I'm blocking your number immediately after that." Not waiting for a response, I get out with my dirty gear in hand, and trudge toward the front door.

28

Iris

"We have a reservation under Noah Pierce."

The maître d' doesn't register the words. She's too busy ogling him. I'm two seconds away from asking her if she needs a tissue to wipe the metaphorical drool at the corner of her parted lips. It's not out of jealousy but because I'm tiptoeing that line of becoming hangry.

Okay, I might already be there. It's mostly because I can't remember the last time I ate something. Even if I get hungry nowadays, I can't take more than a few bites because everything still tastes like ash. But if I'm being completely honest with myself, I've actually been on edge since Kaiden dropped me off at Sam's yesterday. According to Noah, Grayson hasn't announced Cain's disappearance yet, but I'm sure it will come out any day now. I'm using these two free days as an excuse to not show my face at the compound and calm the fuck down before I hand in my resignation. I'll also talk to my aunt about my mother's journal then.

To give it to the maître d', Noah does look as if he stepped off a runway in a casual gray suit and a crisp white shirt, his sun-streaked bedroom hair styled to perfection. In comparison to our first date, though, there was no excitement or trepidation when he arrived to pick me up in a flashy Mercedes. More than that, I would have preferred a quiet night in, rotting on the couch.

However, that would have ruined Sam's hard work. She was right, the dress she ordered for me clings to my every curve. Its open back is not something I would have ever chosen for myself, but it's not at all indecent because of the high, turtleneck-style neckline and knee length. She also put my hair in a high ponytail and did soft smokey makeup to enhance the blue and violet of my irises.

When Noah repeats his name after a few seconds, the maître's cheeks turn cherry red before throwing a cursory glance at the clipboard atop the luxurious glass station. She clears her throat. "If you could please follow me, Mr. and Mrs. Pierce."

"We're not married," I blurt out.

"Sorry, my bad," she replies. Judging by the hopeful glint in her eyes before she turns around to sashay down the corridor in front of us, her remark was intentional.

"Not yet," Noah chimes in, tone full of mirth, but the heated look he throws me tells me he's not entirely joking.

Dafuq?

Now I feel the urge to tell her we're only friends and this is not even a real date. Maybe she would shoot her shot if I did. Even though I made things clear when he tried to kiss me, he still doesn't seem to grasp the notion because he guides me after the hostess by placing a hand at the small of my naked back — as low as the dress allows him. My spine is so stiff it's going to snap in two any second now. When his palm moves to the side and his fingers slip inside the dress to brush against my belly, I have to bite the inside of my cheek until I taste copper to stop myself from forcefully removing it. I don't want to cause a scene.

Maybe I'm still reeling after Erik's assault. But why does it feel like he's staking a claim?

That aside, Sam wasn't kidding when she said this restaurant was something else. *Holy shit.* It reminds me of Kaiden's penthouse because it's also on the last floor of a skyscraper, giving the perfect view — through floor-to-ceiling windows — of Ashville bathed in the dusk's lavender light. And the artwork on the walls alone must have cost millions. There's even a large white piano at my left, where a pianist is deftly playing a harmonious tune. The interior is a perfect synergy of modern and old with the charm of a speakeasy brought into the twenty-first century, if the speakeasy was also in a magical yet sophisticated jungle, with lush greenery and intricate flower decorations. My bestie is so freakin' talented. I have to send her a text and let her know she kicked ass as soon as we get seated.

We finally arrive at our table, right next to the window, and Noah drops his hand to pull out my chair. My shoulders sag in relief as I emulate Sam's feline grace to sit down. Immediately, the waiter makes an appearance, but I can't concentrate as he prattles on about the special tasting menu they have for tonight because I get that weird feeling again, right below my breastbone, that is somehow tied to Kaiden. I dismiss it as wishful thinking. I would give anything for him to be here right now instead of Noah. For him to take me to his penthouse after dinner and strip me to my skin.

"What do you think, Iris?"

"What was that?"

Noah's jaw ticks in annoyance. "I asked what you think about the bottle of wine I chose."

"Sorry, I was admiring the décor. This place is incredible." He seems to soften at that. I glance at the menu, pretending I know what he's talking about. "The wine you chose is perfect," I reply, even though I have no idea what he picked. I only hope it's white. I hate red wine.

As soon as I finish saying that, a shiver works its way down my spine. I lift my eyes from the menu.

They collide with obsidian fire.

Behind Noah, at the ritzy bar situated in the middle of the restaurant, is Kaiden. The five people he's talking to have an air of importance. I think I recognize one of them from the news, he's a senator or something. Kaiden's not paying much attention, though, because even from here, I can feel the fury radiating from him like plumes of fog from dry ice. The lights above us flicker for a few seconds as he white-knuckles his glass. No one else seems to notice, though.

He looks devastatingly beautiful in a black suit. Deadly so. Like a sharp blade honed to perfection. I know I should look away, but I can't. The attractive, long-legged blond next to him throws her head back and laughs exaggeratedly before she paws at his chest as though he just said the funniest thing in the world.

I see red. Before I realize what I'm doing, I'm already standing. Noah throws me a concerned look.

"I'll be back in a few minutes," I mumble while forcing my fisted fingers to relax enough so I can grab my clutch. "I need to…powder my nose."

Spine rod straight, I weave through tables and waiters who resemble busy bees until I reach the hallway where the bathrooms are located. I need a few moments to compose myself in private. Luckily, the bathroom is empty. Locking the door, I step up to the sink. I have the urge to splash cold water on my face, but I will surely ruin the beautiful makeup Sam did. So, I settle on washing my hands instead, hoping it will help douse some of the inferno blazing through me.

Then my eyes clash with Kaiden's in the mirror's reflection. My heart slams to a stop, and a sharp curse leaves me. He's livid. If I thought his fury was palpable before, now I'm choking on it in the confined space as if it's the mushroom cloud forming in the wake of an atomic bomb explosion.

I spin on my heel. "Kaiden, wh—"

"Tell me to leave," he says in a deep, gravely voice as if it was dragged through shards of glass.

Dumbstruck, I stare back. I should say something, right? Then why can't I move my lips?

"Tell me to leave, Iris. Because if you don't, I'm going to fuck you so hard you're going to forget your name and that you're here with *him* on my restaurant's opening night. You should be on my arm. Not his," he seethes, gold and crimson dancing dangerously in the obsidian void.

My throat rolls on a hard swallow. I open my mouth. However, nothing comes out. His crude words have already ignited my blood to the point of insanity. It only took him a few seconds to render my panties useless, and he's not even touching me.

His ravenous gaze drops to my diamond-hard nipples. I'm not wearing a bra because of the dress's open back, so he can see the evidence of my arousal. His nostrils flare. "What's your safe word?"

"Cherries," I squeak.

"If you want me to stop, say it, and I will." That's the only warning I get before I'm twirled around and bent over the counter. There's a metal *clang* as he slides off his belt. At first, I think he's going to use it like in his office at Sin, but am surprised when he brings my hands together at my back and tightens the leather around my wrists. He doesn't stop there; he takes off his tie to gag me. "That's only because I know you can't be silent. You're killing me. Looking like my wet dream come to life in this dress. Since the moment you walked in, all eyes were on you.

And I've never before wanted to kill so many people at once for daring to glance at what's *mine*."

Kaiden pushes up my dress, bunching it around my hips before he kneels to inhale my pussy from behind. "Fuck, you smell divine." My hips buck the moment his fingers graze my clit as he moves my panties to the side. "Look at you. Your pretty pussy is drenched. Weeping for my cock." A strangled whimper tumbles free when he flattens his tongue and licks me from clit to back hole.

He hums deep in his throat, the vibration against my heated flesh making me moan, which comes out muffled because of the silky tie. "Nothing compares to your taste." I watch him through the mirror as he stands. There's a crazy glint in his eyes. In the next second, he rips my panties clean off my body. He brings the lacy scrap of fabric to his nose and breathes it in before shoving it into his pocket.

The wicked grin he gives me makes me melt straight into a puddle. It dies in the next second, though. His eyes turn all hail and thunder as he rasps, "Now, Iris, I'm going to remind you what happens when you make me so mad the heat of a thousand suns blisters my skin. You can't possibly fathom what I felt when I saw you walk in at the side of another man. You ripped me to shreds."

His palm comes crashing down in rapid-fire succession on my right ass cheek. The pain makes me see stars. But it's oh so, so deliciously good. Every single slap is a bolt of lightning going straight to my clit. He switches to the other ass cheek, using the same punishing blows.

Smack!

Smack!

Smack!

"Open your eyes," he commands. I do. "Watch us. I want you to see my cock stretch that perfect pussy."

I flick my gaze to the full-length gilded mirror to my right. I was so lost in the delicious agony as he spanked me I didn't even realize he'd taken out his hard-as-steel cock. He wraps my ponytail around his fist, pulling on it as he slams into me to the hilt—skin on skin. My lungs freeze, and my eyes well up because I'm still too tight to take him. However, I'm wet enough, and the sting only makes it better.

He lets out a hiss as he allows me a few seconds to adjust to his size. "So tight. So goddamn perfect. So. Fucking. Mine," he growls. He starts nailing me to the counter like a man possessed. Our reflections are lost in carnal urgency. I can't stop staring at Kaiden—lips parted, pupils blown, and eyes glazed over in bliss.

The orgasm takes me by surprise. It slams into me like an avalanche. My pussy spasms around his length, and Kaiden lets out a sharp curse as he slows his rhythm. It's a good thing he gagged me because otherwise, every single patron in the restaurant would know what's happening inside this bathroom.

I'm floating somewhere on cloud nine when I'm rudely interrupted by Kaiden, who slides a hand beneath me to lift my torso. A muffled sound of irritation leaves me, which makes him chuckle. "I'm not done with you, angel," he says in the shell of my ear as he glues my back to his front before lifting my right foot on the counter. "Eyes on the mirror."

A hand wraps around my throat while the other finds my clit to stroke it. Then he enters me again, but this time it's slow. Agonizingly so. Inch by inch. Holy fuck! From this angle, I can feel him *everywhere*. It's so deep. When he pumps his hips, my eyes roll into the back of my head at the way his piercing hits my G-spot. Using his thumb, Kaiden angles my jaw before sliding the tie down.

He swallows my cries by slanting his lips over mine. There's a stark contrast between his kisses—languid, sensual, consuming—and the way he wages war on my body with his cock.

A loud knock slices through the air. "Iris?" It's Noah. "Are you okay? You've been in there for a long time."

"Does it turn you on even more that I'm fucking you while he's on the other side of the door? Showing you who you belong to," Kaiden rasps in my ear. *"Now be a good girl and fucking take it."* He pumps his hips faster while his fingers move furiously over my clit.

"I'm coming!" I half moan, half cry. It's the only thing I manage to get out because Kaiden cuts off my air.

I detonate.

Synapses snap. Fireworks go off. The explosion of bliss blinds me for a few seconds. My pussy clamps down on him and continues to pulsate for what feels like an eternity. Kaiden follows me over the edge with a rough groan. He swiftly takes off the belt and tie before tucking his now semi-soft dick inside his slacks. He's gentle as he uses tissues to wipe our mess and pulls down my dress. Luckily, it's made of a ruched, stretchy fabric that doesn't get wrinkles.

The reality of what I've done is the equivalent of a bucket of ice-cold water being dumped on my head. Fuck.

"This means nothing. It was only sex," I blurt out in a whisper, facing Kaiden.

That infuriating smirk of his makes an appearance. He dips. Goosebumps bloom across my skin as his breath fans over my neck. "Keep telling yourself lies, angel. While you have dinner alongside that dipshit in my restaurant, it will be *my* cum leaking down the inside of your thighs, and you won't be able to think about anything else because you are mine. Until the end of eternity. Whether you like it or not."

He vanishes.

Another knock.

"Just a second," I mutter as I spin to look in the mirror. Thank you, Sam, for being a makeup god. Not even an eyelash is out of place. That magic-infused setting spray of hers could sell for millions. I only have to smooth down my ponytail and reapply my lipstick. Inhaling deeply, I open the door.

I'm met head-on by Noah's stormy gray eyes. His tone is filled with equal parts annoyance and concern. "What happened? Are you okay? You've been gone for over twenty minutes." He pushes me out of the way to look inside the bathroom. "Were you in here alone? I heard you talking to someone."

Okay, so we might not have been as quiet as I thought. I serve him the first excuse I can think of. "I was talking to Sam on the phone. Something happened, and she needed my help."

"Seriously, Iris? You've left me alone at the table for almost half an hour while the food is getting cold because your friend needed someone to talk to?" His nostrils flare. "Do you even know how hard it was to get a table at this place? How expensive the food is? Just that bottle of wine runs for two thousand dollars. And you act as though you don't even want to be here. I thought you would be more grateful than this."

Who the fuck even is this person? It's like he deliberately hides this whole new personality from me, and it only comes out in glimpses. Although, to be fair, I would be mad too if he left me alone at the table for so long. But that doesn't mean he has to throw in my face how expensive everything is. I never asked to be brought to such a fancy place.

"You're kidding me, right? Have you considered that I'm here not because I want to but because you forced my hand? Your help came with terms and conditions, so sue me if I'm bitter about that. That's not what a genuine friend or someone who claims to love you does. Not really." I can't resist adding, "You know who's been there to pick up the pieces after you left and ghosted me for five fucking years? Sam. So yeah, if she calls, I'm going to spend however long on the phone talking to her."

His fingers clench and unclench. "Fine. Whatever. Can we go to the table now? People were staring."

I roll my eyes and hurry down the corridor before he gets the idea to put his hand on me again. On my way to the table, my head swivels as I look for Kaiden. However, I can't see him anywhere. Also, that new feeling that makes itself known whenever he's near is gone. So, I can only assume he left. Sitting down on the chair, my eyes zero in on the wine glass.

It's red.

29

Iris

Even though I always do the shopping for Ms. Robbins in the first part of the day, it's almost ten p.m. as I ascend the stairs to the fourth floor of my apartment building, carrying five grocery bags. I moved back to my place yesterday. Somehow, it feels as if this is the first real step to moving on from Kaiden. Living at Sam's trapped me in limbo—a space where I didn't have to make decisions…just feel. But it was time. Even if Sam would have been happy if I moved in with her permanently—she offered it every day—I couldn't impose on her anymore.

But my fears became true the moment I stepped over the threshold—Kaiden not only imprinted himself in every single cell of my being, but in the walls, too. In the goddamn dust particles. In every nook and cranny. In every breath. In every thought.

It's suffocating.

So, today I did everything in my power to stay out of my apartment. After searching for hours and removing the cameras that son of a bitch, Erik, installed, I went for a jog. I really hope I've found them all. The one pointed at my small walk-in shower filled me with equal parts rage and disgust. Then, Sam and I rifled through all her grandmother's books on premonitions in hopes we would find something about an oracle or prophecies. Unfortunately, we came up empty. Her Grammie also made a list of people she thinks could help us find one of the fae meeting grounds in the human realm. Next week, we're tackling that. Once I resign from the Order.

However, no matter what I do, I can't escape *him* because I dream about us. Not only spending time together, but also having sex. Most of the time, I end up orgasming so hard I wake up screaming. I haven't had a night terror since the day I left his penthouse, so I'm not complaining.

If I had known it was Kaiden's restaurant, and opening night, I would have asked Noah to make a reservation elsewhere. But not even Sam was aware. I can't believe he hired her after she trashed all his cars. When she found out, she said she wouldn't accept the pay because of what he did to me, not because she damaged his property. This was one of her best paying gigs this summer, so I told her she would be a fool not to. Besides, she did such a spectacular job that she is booked until the end of the year for all kinds of events, not only weddings, which are her bread and butter.

I move all the bags into one hand to knock on Ms. Robbins's door.

There's a shuffling sound, followed by steps that stop on the other side of the door. The visor darkens. "What do you want?" she asks acidly.

"I have your groceries."

"It's late. I was sleeping."

Seriously, this woman is something else. "C'mon, Ms. Robbins, I know you watch soap operas until midnight daily. I can hear your TV from here."

"Fine," she grumbles. It takes a few moments before she unlocks the deadbolt. The chain is still on, though. She narrows her eyes through the crack. "Did you get my hazelnut milk?"

"Yup."

"I had to drink my coffee without it today. Don't be late next time." Huffing, Ms. Robbins slides the chain, opening the door to let me in.

Sheesh, you would think she was doing me a favor, not the other way around. My eyes widen at the short, lacy nightie she's wearing. Where has she been hiding that body? In the absence of her stern clothes and tight bun, she looks at least ten years younger. While she disappears into the bedroom, I stride to the kitchen to put the groceries away. I'm almost finished stocking the fridge when my phone buzzes.

> **Noah: There's a movie premiere next weekend. It's**
>
> **supposed to be really good. Wanna go?**

I purse my lips and drop the phone on the counter to my right. I'll make up an excuse later. Sitting next to Noah in a dark movie theater where he can get handsy is not my idea of fun. If the conversation over dinner last night wasn't strained enough, I also had to remove his hand from inching up my inner thigh while he was driving several times. And he tried to kiss me when he dropped me off.

He made me so uncomfortable I've decided to officially kick him to the curb. Fuck him and that fundraiser gala. Clearly, he doesn't care how I feel. Every time I reject him, he doubles down, only to serve me what seems like a heartfelt apology after. Well, words are meaningless without the actions to back them up. What's concerning is how good he is at lying, because I believed he was sorry the first time. But you know what they say: fool me once, shame on you, fool me twice...

"You haven't been at home much," Ms. Robbins says as she ambles toward me, fastening a robe that matches her nightie.

"Yeah, I've been busy." When I close the fridge, my onyx stone warms up. Brows furrowing, I bring my fingers to it.

"Where's that dark-haired, broody young man? The one who was attached at your hip?"

"Oh, well, um—"

I don't get to finish my sentence because the glass door of Ms. Robbins's balcony explodes into a million pieces. A flying souldrake just used a voidstalker as a cannonball.

What. The. Fuck.

The voidstalker, resembling a creature from your worst nightmare with its giant, muscly rat-like body and scorpion tail, smacks the middle of the living room floor, rattling the wood planks. Shattered glass flies everywhere when it pushes to all fours and shakes its heads—made only of two gaping maws lined with razor-sharp teeth. It sniffs the air through the two slits where its eyes should have been.

Shock pins me in place a second too long. The voidstalker dashes at me.

"Ms. Robbins, RUN!" I bellow, pushing the old woman toward the front door.

I uncoil my whip, which I now carry on me at all times. I swing it in a figure-eight pattern in the air before I lash it at the demon's neck. Ichor sprays everywhere as the leathery skin splits. The smell of rot and sulfur permeates the air. It lets out a high-pitched screech when one of its two beastly heads slaps the floor. However, it doesn't stop its momentum.

I wait until the very last moment to crouch and roll, avoiding its poisonous tail. The demon slams headfirst into the counters where I was standing. Wood groans and splinters while plates fall, smashing on top of its remaining head. I jump to my feet, flick my wrist to crack the whip, and slice the voidstalker's remaining head. My eardrums almost bleed at the howl of pain it lets out. I don't dwell on it, though. I tap into my hellseeker—

or whatever the fuck I am—speed and start pumping my arms.

Ms. Robbins watches everything from the front door in eerie calm. "What are you still doing here?" I ask in disbelief. She must be in shock.

Before I can reach her, something slams into me with the force of a freight train. Too late, I realize the souldrake—which looks like a humanoid vulture, with deep, spiky crimson skin—flapping its wings outside has used another demon as a missile. My lungs rattle as I hit the wall. Hard. And drop my whip. I expect to be crushed by this second voidstalker, but instead, a gigantic sphere of glowing water sends it back where it came from. The two-headed demon punches through the wall next to the smashed balcony door. It leaves a gaping hole behind, then it starts freefalling.

"Ms. Robbins?" My jaw drops as the swirling colorful dots in my vision finally dissipate to reveal a young woman—beautiful beyond reason—standing where Ms. Robbins was a few seconds ago.

"It's Adrianna. My real name is Adrianna," she replies. "C'mon, let's go."

Peeling myself off the wall, I only take two steps toward her when four more voidstalkers are thrown in the living room. Two come at me while the others corner Ms. Rob—Adrianna. I cast a quick glance at my whip, which slid under the couch. It's not far. However, the demons keep advancing, forcing me to walk backward toward the balcony. I feign to the right, but they don't take the bait. Instead, they snap their teeth in warning. What's weird is that they don't pounce or attack. As if they want me alive. Unfortunately, the only other weapon I have on me is a dagger. I swipe it from its holster at my belt.

The two voidstalkers cornering Adrianna soar through the gaping hole behind me one by one. Wet squelches resound as they hit the asphalt outside. But when she lifts her hands in the air to send another one of those powerful water spheres, nothing comes out. Her eyes widen as they fixate somewhere behind me. "Watch out!"

In the next second, sharp talons sink into my shoulders before I'm being lifted into the air. The souldrake, which I'm surprised hasn't burned us to a crisp since it can breathe fire through its grotesque beak, had dived through the hole and grabbed me like a hawk. I use the dagger to stab at its talons. However, I don't get the chance to take it out because the demon drops me as it lets out an ear-splitting shriek. Teeth gnashing, I hit the floor. What I'm not prepared for is another souldrake to take its place. White-hot pain ripples through me when it sinks its talons in the same spot.

Motherfucker! Where are all these demons coming from?!?

I thrash with all my strength, but it's futile—I'm being dragged outside. When I'm almost halfway through the gaping hole, Adrianna bolts and grabs my ankles, using all her strength to pull me back into the apartment. Being the rope in a tug of war is much more painful than one would think. Especially when a demon uses its talons as hooks. It takes everything I've got not to pass out.

The two remaining voidstalkers slam into the water barrier Adrianna created at her back. Again and again. Relentlessly. Sweat drips down her forehead as she holds onto me, her grip unyielding. "Listen to me, Iris. Your mother saved my life. She asked me to watch over you and continue her search for an oracle if something ever happened to her," she grits out, voice strained.

"What?"

"I found an oracle. Go to the Drunken Owl. There's a tarot card in my nightstand. Give it to Rhett at the bar."

Her knees buckle. The barrier drops. But she keeps holding on.

"Let go, Ms. Robbins!"

She gives me a sad smile as the voidstalkers start clawing at her back viciously. "It's okay." Still, her grip remains strong.

"Let go! Please! Adrianna!"

"Find the ora—" Blood gushes from her mouth as one of the clawed limbs punches right through the center of her chest. I can feel her soul slipping away before the light in her eyes dims bit by bit.

Nonononononononono.

The winged demon jostles me as it puts more force into its next tug. I snap. My vision darkens at the edges. All I see is black. It spreads through my veins like ink—until I become the void. There's this insatiable hunger. A gaping hole cracked open inside me.

It only wants to *take, take, take.*

And I let it.

I give it everything it wants.

30

Iris

"Any news, Adrianna?" Mommy asks her pretty friend. She's got silky blond hair and ocean-blue eyes, but she looks different when she steps outside our house — all wrinkly — as if she's an old lady. Mommy said it's magic; she glamours her appearance because she is in danger. She also doesn't like kids or people. That's why Mommy asks me to stay in my room whenever she visits. I don't want to make her mad, but I was playing hide and seek with my new transparent friend before she arrived and I got stuck in the cupboard.

"Yeah. Though, you're not gonna like it. Rhett brought another group from Faerie. He said there are rumors that King Orion had the last oracle executed. She apparently had a vision he would lose the war, and let's just say he wasn't thrilled about that. He probably thinks if the oracle is dead, the prophecy won't come true. Too bad prophecies don't work that way."

"Fuck. She was our last hope. What are we going to do?"

I inhale sharply at the bad word. Mommy never uses those around me. Well, she said it once when she stubbed her toe on the coffee table. But it was only because she was in pain.

"We have to wait for another one to be born, I guess."

Mommy lets out a hollow laugh. "What if that never happens? Iris's powers are growing by the day, and it's hard keeping her hidden as is."

"What did that seraph tell you? I don't get why he can't tell you the prophecy."

"Because he's bound by divine oath. They all are. He only paid us a visit to warn us of its existence."

"C'mon, angel, snap out of it."

Kaiden?

The fogginess finally dissipates. However, the feeling that my brain is being pierced by an icepick doesn't. I grind my teeth hard to stop my dinner from making a reappearance as everything comes back in horrible flashes. A boom. Smashed glass. Voidstalkers. Ichor painting the walls. Talons sinking into me like a hot knife through butter. Red-hot pain. And Ms. Robbins. Oh God, Ms. Robbins. When the room comes into focus, I realize I'm holding Adrianna's lifeless body to my chest, rocking back and forth while tears stream mercilessly down my face. The demons are nothing more than dried-up husks lying on the floor.

There's so much *blood*. I'm covered in it. It not only stains my skin, but it digs deep through every layer until it reaches the very essence of my soul.

Ms. Robbins is gone.

My mother's friend is *dead*.

And it's all my fault.

Sobbing, I try to wipe the crimson guilt off, but I only make it worse. "Take it off! Take it off! TAKE IT OFF!" There's not enough air left in the atmosphere as my lungs fold in two, battling for tiny scraps.

Strong arms lift my trembling body. "Shh, I got you." It's all a blur as I'm carried inside my apartment. "You have to breathe. In and out. Good. That's my girl." When he enters the bathroom, he maneuvers me with my legs wrapped around his middle. It's a tight fit in the small walk-in shower, but he somehow manages to turn us around so I'm facing the pounding water. When it hits my shoulders and trickles down my back, I realize why: my back is shredded. At least, that's how it feels — as if someone took a cheese grater to it. I bite the inside of my cheek hard to stop the scream bubbling up my throat from getting out.

"I'm so sorry," he murmurs in the shell of my ear as he strokes my hair. "I already called Malik. He's on his way."

I don't know how much time passes while Kaiden holds me to his chest, but his intoxicating scent wraps around me like a warm blanket. We are immersed once again in our little bubble where nothing and no one can touch us. *Thump. Thump. Thump.* My breathing finally slows down as I concentrate on Kaiden's steady heartbeat. His presence equally tethers me to reality and soothes something deep within me.

There's a knock on the door. "Kaiden?"

"Just a second," he replies to Malik. "We'll get out, and then Malik's going to heal you, okay?" he says softly.

My grip on Kaiden's neck tightens in panic. "No! I—I can't—no. P-please. I can still feel the blood. It's everywhere."

His gentle hand wraps around my jaw, and fresh tears blur my vision. "Okay, we'll stay in here. Malik?"

"Yeah?"

"Come in."

"I hope you're not naked because seeing your dick wasn't in my plans for the day." All the mirth in his tone vanishes the moment he opens the door, and his feline hazel eyes land on my back. He lets out a sharp curse before his legs eat up the small space in two long strides. "Hey, sweets! I see you've got yourself in some more trouble. I'm surprised it took you this long. You know, women are usually happy to see me, but they're not quite as wet as you. At least, not with their clothes on."

The joke helps, and I let out a small snort.

"Shut the fuck up and heal her. She's in pain," Kaiden growls.

Malik purses his lips as his palm settles on top of my chest. "Jeez. It's not my fault your bedside manner is nonexistent. I'm just trying to lighten the mood." His magic envelops me like a thick fog. Skin tissue pieces itself together until there's no more pain—at least physically. Now that my back is no longer screaming, I can draw my first breath without it catching fire.

"Thanks," I say when the inky fog dissipates.

He winks at me. "Anytime. Well, if you guys don't need me anymore, I'm going to help Logan clean up in the other apartment."

"Wait!"

Malik looks back over his shoulder.

"Ms. Rob—the fae woman is—was my neighbor. We need to have a proper burial for her."

He only nods in understanding before leaving the bathroom and closing the door at his back.

"How are you feeling?" Kaiden asks after a few moments.

"My back doesn't hurt anymore..." *But my heart does.* The unspoken words hang heavy in the air. However, I don't have to voice them for him to understand.

Obsidian eyes search mine. They bulldoze through all the barriers I erected around myself as if they're made of nothing more than papier mâché. "Now that the lacerations are healed, I can wash you properly. Or I can let you do it yourself. Just tell me what you need."

I'll surely regret this tomorrow, but I'm not strong enough to push him away. Somehow, it feels as if I've lost my mother all over again. Or, at least, a part of her. And I can't face that on my own. "No. Don't leave me alone. I need *you*."

"I'll have to let you down and undress you. Is that okay?"

"Yeah," I whisper.

Kaiden peels the blood-soaked clothes off my body before he starts washing me slowly, as if I'm the most precious thing in the world. And even if the usual electricity charges in the air between us, there's no sexual tension—only tenderness. I've never felt more cherished than when Kaiden takes care of me. It blurs the stark line I have drawn between us. Because as hard as it is to admit, my feelings for him only grow instead of wilt. And that mask of indifference I so desperately cling to whenever he's near? It's nowhere in sight tonight.

Twenty minutes later, Kaiden carries me to my bedroom and sits me on top of my bed. I clear my throat. "The clothes you left here are still in my closet if you want to change."

The corner of his full lips lifts in that sexy, infuriating way that makes my blood pressure go through the roof. "I'm surprised you didn't burn them."

"Not gonna lie, I did think about it more than once," I mutter.

"Will you be okay if I leave you for a few minutes so I can take a shower, too?"

I nod, and he strides to the closet to rifle through the drawer I gave him when he was still my shadow. Picking up a pair of his usual black jeans and tee, he disappears through the bathroom door, his sopping clothes leaving a trail of water behind. As much as I try not to think about tonight's events, they replay in gory details the moment I close my eyes. I don't even realize I'm crying again until the bed dips under Kaiden's weight. He thumbs the tears gently as he frames the side of my face.

"Did you know Ms. Robbins was fae?" I ask. "Please don't lie."

"I had no idea."

The glint in his eyes tells me he's being honest, though given everything that happened between us, I don't know if I'll ever be able to trust what he says entirely. "I can't believe she's dead. I was bringing her groceries. I was supposed to do that this morning, but I spent all day at Sam's." I shake my head in disbelief. "I've never seen anything like that before. It was fucking crazy. Souldrakes threw voidstalkers through the balcony door. They cornered me until the souldrakes could snatch me through the gaping hole in the wall. If I had just come home first and waited until the next day to bring her the groceries, they would have attacked me in my apartment. I had all my weapons here—"

"Stop blaming yourself, Iris. It's not your fault."

I suck in a serrated breath. "Don't say that. Those demons were there for me."

"They couldn't have attacked you in your apartment. That's why they came for you there."

My eyebrows furrow. "What? Why?"

"I asked Malik to put the same wards I have on my building on your place. He finished the night you and Sam were at Sin. Unfortunately, he couldn't do every apartment in the building because it takes a lot of time, and he would have needed access to all of them. It took him over a year to finish placing the wards on my building."

The fact that he didn't share this information before, when I told him I wanted to go home while he searched Hell for Adramelech doesn't escape me. However, he was right, it was safer for me there. Of course, I would never admit that. "So, um, why are you here? How did you know I was in danger again?"

He tilts his head. "Seriously? Carter was patrolling the perimeter; it's hard not to notice demons flying out of your neighbor's window. I'm sorry it took me so long to get to you."

"It's okay. It all happened in under ten minutes…I think. I kind of blacked out, and I don't remember what happened until I woke up with um," I sniff, "Ms. Robbi—Adrianna in, um, in my arms. Her real name was Adrianna."

He takes my shaky hands in his warm ones. I don't pull away. In fact, I'm barely restraining myself from crawling into his lap. Nibbling on my lower lip, I deliberate if I should tell him the rest, too.

"So, um, I guess I can also rot demons, now. Too bad I don't remember how I did it. Was I going ballistic when you popped into the room?"

"No, you were already on the floor, but you were out of it."

Pulling back, I make my decision. Maybe he can help me find Rhett. And when we know what the prophecy says, we'll finally part ways because every time he swoops in to save or take care of me, I feel my resolve chipping away as though it's nothing more than cheap paint. As hard as I try to be the granite rock that stops the crashing waves, I'm afraid I'm nothing more than soapstone. And I don't know if I can ever forgive myself if I sweep all Kaiden has done under a rug. There will surely come a time when, eventually, I'll trip over it. And the fall will break more than my bones.

"Right before she...died, Adrianna told me my mother saved her life. She has been watching over me and searching for an oracle at my mother's request. She said she found one. She also mentioned a place — the Drunken Owl — and a guy named Rhett. I think it's a bar." I don't tell him about the flashback, though.

Kaiden runs a hand on the back of his neck. "Okay. I'll see what I can find about the Drunken Owl —" The sound of his phone ringing interrupts him. "Sorry," he murmurs as he takes it out of his front pocket to respond. Even though I don't want to listen in, I can't help my enhanced hearing.

"We're done. I used magic to restore everything as it was. I also had Carter transport the fae woman's body to our guy at the morgue. But what do I tell him to do with it?" Malik inquires.

"Wait a second." He turns to me. "They transported Adrianna's body —"

"I heard. Um, well...I don't..." Something hard lodges in my throat.

A fresh wave of sadness hits me because I don't know what she would have wanted…if there are fae customs to honor her. Everything I knew about her — which wasn't much anyway — was a lie. It's starting to feel like a recurring theme in my life.

Kaiden must sense my conundrum because he doesn't wait for me to finish. "Just tell him to keep her body in the morgue for a few days, and we'll let him know what we decide."

"Can they stitch her up?" I whisper.

He nods.

31

Iris

"The usual, sir?" the flight attendant asks Kaiden.

"Yes, Natalie. Thank you," he responds from his seat across mine. Well, to be honest, the word seat doesn't do it justice because it resembles an armchair, the leather so soft I could very well be sitting on a cloud. I still can't wrap my head around the fact that Kaiden owns a freakin' plane.

Natalie smiles warmly at me. "And for you, ma'am?" I have to give it to her, for someone who has been woken up in the dead of night and had less than an hour to get ready, the woman doesn't have a hair out of place—unlike me. I look as though death punched me in the face. Not only are my eyes swollen and bloodshot from all the crying, but I'm so ghastly white I'm questioning whether I'll become translucent any second now.

It didn't take long for Kaiden to find the Drunken Owl, a bar located in New Orleans. He insisted I should at least try to rest before leaving, but I couldn't stay there anymore, so close to where she died. Sleep was definitely out of the question. Every time I close my eyes, I get a repeat of tonight's events. So, I told Kaiden we should leave as soon as possible. Still, I didn't expect him to have a private jet ready at the snap of his fingers.

I don't want to be rude, but no matter how much I try to force my muscles to reciprocate the smile, they won't listen. "Can I have a water, please?"

"Of course. Would you like me to prepare a plate of cold cuts, or maybe I can heat one of our gourmet meals for you?"

"No, thank you. Just the water."

Natalie nods before excusing herself.

Even if I still had my usual appetite, I'm too nervous to eat anything. I blow out an unsteady breath as I fasten my seatbelt.

"You okay?" Kaiden's gravelly voice pulls my attention to him. I swear, every time I take in his rugged beauty, it becomes harder to breathe. Those mesmerizing eyes, the curve of his granite jaw, and the soot black lashes fanning over angular cheekbones. He's the embodiment of all my darkest fantasies and the antithesis of what one would expect a successful businessman to look like. Though, if you told me he was a mafia kingpin, I would one hundred percent believe you with the way his Italian suits mold to his sculpted, tattooed body.

"Yeah. Just a little nervous about flying. Kind of funny I'm twenty-three and this is my first time on a plane, huh?" *At least that I remember.*

"Is it because of your panic attacks?"

I turn away from his intense gaze to look through the window. "Well, partly. I never knew how I would react, you know. You can always stop a car on the side of the road, but you can't exactly ask a pilot to land while you're thirty thousand feet in the air, can you?" Wringing my hands in my lap, I continue, "But if I'm being honest, it was mostly because my hellseeker duties trumped everything. In all the years I've worked for the Order, I never even took the few days of paid leave they give us. Sam invites me yearly on her tropical holidays, but I never go." A bitter laugh escapes me. "Now I feel stupid because of how much life I've missed. It would feel like heaven to be on a beach, sipping on a cocktail, sinking my toes in the hot sand. Taking a swim to cool down in azure waters."

When Natalie comes back with our drinks, I take it as my cue to shut up and not reveal any more parts of myself to Kaiden. Whenever he's near, it's easy to forget his betrayal. Ever since the umbra attack, I feel as though I've been thrust into the middle of a never-ending storm, and he has been my life raft. It would be so easy to lean on him again. Especially now that I'm capsizing under giant waves of equal parts guilt and grief. But I can't.

God, I'm so fucking tired. Not only physically and mentally, but it's the kind of exhaustion that burrows deep, dismantles beliefs, shakes the foundation, and causes avalanches. Maybe that's my answer right there: after I resign the Order and am ostracized from everyone I've ever known, I can travel the world or move into a small house on the beach. Hell, I might even entertain the idea of getting a dog (definitely not a Chihuahua, though).

Somehow, this doesn't feel right either. I know myself, and I would get bored eventually. I need a greater purpose. Something that drives me.

The pilot announcing we're going to take off in the next few minutes pulls me out of my thoughts. I squeeze my eyes so hard I'm sure wrinkles form at the corners with the pressure. My nails dig into the armrests as the plane taxis off the runway. There's a shuffling sound, then a warm hand envelops my trembling one. And just like that, my entire body comes alive. I don't know why I get this giddy at such a simple gesture, but it feels more intimate than him whispering absolute filth in my ear while fucking me as though there's no tomorrow.

"It's okay. You're safe," Kaiden murmurs, before kissing the side of my head. My pulse scatters.

Dammit. How am I supposed to push him away when he is so sweet?

I'm so lost in my body's reaction to Kaiden that I don't even notice we're already in the air until he tells me. I should pull back and sit elsewhere; there's plenty of space, but he starts tracing circles in my palm with his thumb. It feels so good that I have to bite my tongue not to let out a content sigh.

I mean, I've already let him comfort me tonight. What's another two hours of handholding until the flight ends, right? I'll lay down the rules once we land in New Orleans.

THE CITY PASSES in a blur through the Escalade's window. Of course, once we landed, the SUV was already waiting on the tarmac. This man thinks of everything. This is the first time in months I don't feel the usual panic crawling beneath my skin while in a moving vehicle, and I thank my lucky stars. Flying was also unexpectedly easy. I suspect the sexy-assin demon tethering me to reality with his touch had something to do with it. Or maybe what happened in the last few hours wreaked enough havoc on my mind that it has reached its limit for torment. It's kind of a fucked up take on looking at the bright side of things, but I'll gladly bask in any moment of peace I can get.

Leaning back on the rest, I glance at Kaiden. There's something so inherently sensual about the way he drives—with an air of arrogant confidence that makes me weak in the knees. Only a few hours in his presence, and my brain is already at the bottom of the gutter. I blink to get rid of the hedonistic thoughts.

Spoiler alert: it doesn't work.

"So, what's the plan?" I inquire, breaking the comfortable silence.

"Since the bar is closed, we'll rest at the hotel until we can leave tonight."

"'Kay. Don't get the wrong idea, though."

"About?" he drawls.

Steeling my spine, I ponder my next words. My tongue is laden as I voice them. "Us. While I'm grateful, the fact that I've let you hold and take care of me hasn't changed anything. I had a few moments of weakness, but I'm better now. Actually, after we find out what the prophecy says, we're *done*—for good this time. Promise me you'll leave me alone."

He draws in a sharp breath. "Angel—"

The car rolls to a stop, and a valet opens my door. I pour out of my seat as if the Devil himself is nipping at my heels. The sun hasn't even made its appearance yet, but the air is so muggy it sticks to my lungs like molasses. Still, it's a nice change from the charged atmosphere in the car.

I throw a hasty "thank you" over my shoulder to the valet before scurrying into the hotel, where my jaw hits the shiny marble floor. The lobby exudes luxury and sophistication in every meticulously crafted detail—from the vaulted glass ceiling to the gilded chandeliers. There's also a statue of Poseidon smack dab at its center. You would think combining all these elements would have a gaudy and nauseating result. However, they only scream at me that I'm poor in seven different languages because, of course, everything blends harmoniously.

The moment Kaiden walks in, a zing of electricity goes down my spine. His burning gaze slams into mine. His strides are determined— as though he's a predator cornering its next meal. When he stops in front of me, he mutters, "I wasn't done speaking."

"But I was," I snark.

He dips to rasp in my ear. "You being a brat just makes me want to bend you over my knee and spank that perky ass until it gets your cunt so wet you'll beg for my cock. Don't worry, angel, I'm keeping count. And when the time comes to collect, I'll tie you to my bed for a fucking month." Kaiden turns on his heel to stalk to the reception, leaving me in a puddle on the pristine floor.

It takes more than a few seconds to make my legs listen again so I can follow him. The attractive brunette behind the desk lights up like a Christmas tree when her eyes land on Kaiden. "Mr. Black, so good to have you back. I have already prepared the penthouse suite, as per your request. I will personally accompany you to your room," she gushes.

What? Did he fuck her or something?

Crescent moons form in my palms from how tight my fists are. *Nope, Iris, we are not getting possessive over a lying demon.* Besides, I have to get used to him being with other women. I told him it's over. Eventually, he will finally get the message and move on.

The thought is so devastating, it knocks the wind out of me.

As if having a direct line to my thoughts, Kaiden throws me a worried look. When he turns to the receptionist, his eyes turn to two glaciers. His tone is equally arctic as he says, "There's no need. Can I have my key card?"

She flushes beet red when she slides it over the top of the desk. "Of c-course."

I should probably feel bad for the woman, but I don't have it in me to care. In fact, I fight the urge to smile. "What about my key card?" I chime in.

"You're staying with me."

I scoff. "You must be on acid."

He levels me with a stony glare. "Iris, don't make me throw you over my shoulder and carry you to the room because you know I will. I'm not leaving you alone after what happened only hours ago."

If I thought the receptionist couldn't turn any redder, I was wrong. She looks as though she's about to burst into flames. He has a point, though. What if demons come for me again? "Fine," I bite back reluctantly.

The usual electricity between us is intensified a hundredfold by the elevator's small space. Then the doors finally slide open, and unlike Noah's touch, when Kaiden places his hand at the small of my back to guide me to the door, the gesture feels so natural it melts my insides.

The room is precisely the level of opulence one would expect after seeing that lobby. It has a four-poster bed with a seating area in front of it, a bathroom that rivals the one in Kaiden's penthouse, though not as big, and a separate living and dining room. If that wasn't enough, there's also a pool table. However, the best part is the terrace that overlooks the city, which right now gives a breathtaking view of the sun cresting the horizon on a fiery background.

"What would you like to eat?"

I peel my eyes off the window. "I'm not hungry."

His brows furrow as he drops the room-service menu on the table. "How come? You didn't want to eat on the plane, either. I thought you would be starving by now. When was the last time you ate?"

Yeah, old Iris would be. I don't tell him that, though. "I had dinner with Sam." Well, it was more watching her stuff her face while I pushed the food around the plate.

Concern deepens the lines around his mouth. "Did you?" His eyes sail over my body, but it's not in a sexual way. "When I held you in the shower, you were too light. I thought I imagined it, but you've lost weight. Have you been eating at all lately?"

"That's none of your concern."

His nostrils flare as he grabs the landline. "I'm ordering you some chocolate chip pancakes. Do you also want some strawberries? Fuck that. I'm getting the whole goddamn menu."

I fold my arms in front of my chest—a feeble attempt at putting some kind of barrier between us because him being so worried about me flays me open. "Can you please drop it? It's a fucking waste to order that much food if I'm not going to eat anything. I can't, okay?"

"I can't watch you hurt yourself."

"And whose fault do you think that is, huh? The day I left your penthouse with a hemorrhaging heart was the moment I lost my fucking appetite," I blurt out acidly.

Fuck.

I didn't mean to give him a glimpse into how much he's broken me. Kaiden looks like I could have stabbed him, and it would have hurt less. I whirl around to open the terrace door and step out. I'm on the verge of tears, and I don't want to cry in front of him again. Plus, Kaiden's emotions are so volatile, they sink into my pores as if they're my own. It's weird and suffocating.

32

Iris

Kaiden's hand caresses my naked back, from nape to tailbone, pressing my cheek and breasts further against the velvet material of the pool table. Fireworks go off at every single point of contact. The coldness of his silver rings biting into my feverish skin only stokes what was, until now, a low-burning fire to a chemical one.

"Fuck, angel. I wish you could see yourself. You're a goddamn vision, all tied up and at my mercy." Silky rope is not only twisted around my torso, continuing along my middle and pinning my forearms flat against my back, but it also ties my ankles to each of the pool table's legs. I'm spread open for Kaiden's viewing pleasure. Just the thought of him having complete control over my body is incredibly arousing. So much so that I've already made a mess out of the fabric beneath me.

He teases me by dragging his thumb over my throbbing clit. "You're dripping for me, angel." He pours the amber liquid from his lowball glass in between my ass cheeks before bending to lap at it in long, languid strokes. Stars burst beneath my eyelids when he groans, then plunges his tongue into my pussy. Once. Twice. He stands, placing the empty glass near my head. "Mmm, so fucking delicious. I think this is how I'm going to savor my rum from now on – from your greedy little cunt that was made just for me."

"P-please," I whimper as I seek friction on the rubbery end of the table. However, the rope restricts the movement.

"Is this what you're begging so beautifully for, hmm?" He thrusts two fingers inside me and pumps them in a mind-numbing rhythm that makes me feral.

"Kaiden! Pleaseee," I cry in frustration when he takes them out after only a few seconds.

"What do you need, Iris?" he asks as he spreads a thick layer of lube on my back hole.

"Your cock. Please! I need you to fuck me."

"Mmm, impatient are we, love? Be a good girl and warm this up for me and maybe I'll consider it." He presses something cold and made of metal against my lips. It's in the shape of a teardrop with a bulbous head. "Suck on it," he commands.

I do. I have an idea what that's for, but I'm still not prepared for the sensation of fullness when he slides it out of my mouth to carefully insert it in my ass. Then the velvety crown of his cock is at my entrance. Oh, YES! That's the only warning I get before Kaiden slams into me to the hilt. The sudden movement causes my hard, aching nipples to rub onto the felt, setting me ablaze.

Kaiden swears under his breath before he starts dragging his length along every single nerve ending as if he wants to thoroughly savor this moment. At the same time, he's in so deep that I feel him everywhere. It's an exquisite torture that has my eyes rolling into the back of my head.

"Your body was made for me." Thrust. "Your tight cunt takes me so well." Thrust. "You might be the one tied up, but you have all the control." Thrust.

"*Because you own me.*" Thrust.

The sound of our bodies slapping together is a carnal melody. It bounces off the walls in waves to combine with my loud moans. Surely, the entire floor of the hotel can hear us, but I don't care — I'm too drunk on rapture. He adjusts the angle in a way that has his piercing hitting my G-spot.

"*Kaiden! Ahhh. Sooo g-good. I'm gonna — *"

I soar higher and higher until I touch the stars.

Then I fall and break into a million pieces with Kaiden's name on my lips like a prayer.

I jackknife into a sitting position, chest heaving. A fine sheen of perspiration covers my entire body. But that's not sweat between my thighs. I orgasmed in real life, too, and I have the wet sheets beneath me to prove it. *Wait.* Why am I in bed? The last thing I remember is reading a book on the couch while Kaiden worked on his laptop at the table. I must have fallen asleep, and he carried me to bed. He also removed my leggings because he knows I dislike sleeping in clothes, but he left my tee on.

"Good dream?"

Fuck.

There's no way he didn't hear me. I slam my eyes shut, then open them to find Kaiden leaning casually on the bathroom door frame, a towel wrapped around his waist. With the erotic dream still clinging to every neuron and synapse, I can't turn my gaze away from the expanse of bronzed, inked skin in front of me. It brings me back to the first time I saw him at his penthouse. He still looks like the fallen angel who would steal you under the moonlight and have his wicked way with you. The roguish grin he gives me makes my bones melt.

I swallow the barbed rebuke I was about to throw at him when my eyes zero in on his chest. The only spot previously untouched by the needle — the one right above his heart — is now filled by an exact replica of the iris in my sketchbook. It fits perfectly among the other designs but stands out because it's the only colored one.

He tattooed me over his heart.

He tattooed *me* over his heart.

He tattooed me over his heart.

I fist the sheets to hide the trembling in my hands as emotion grips me by the throat with an iron fist. Blinking rapidly because I don't want him to see how affected I am by this, I turn toward the window. Still, a tear jostles free from my eyelashes. I quickly wipe it away. God, I'm so pathetic it's not even funny anymore. I clear my throat. "It was a nightmare."

"Ah, I see," he drawls. "Yeah, the entire hotel heard how terrified you were when you announced you were about to come, then screamed my name."

Heat scorches the shells of my ears. "Whatever," I mutter. "Did you finish in the bathroom?"

"With those little desperate whimpers you were letting out and the heady smell of your arousal, I did…twice, actually."

No. Did he? Holy shit! Heat spreads between my thighs while I get impossibly wet again. The air between us pulls taut, fraught with friction. Kaiden's muscles are coiled as if he's teetering on the edge of pouncing on me. I don't dare move. Breathe. Because I'm afraid I'll voice the desire coursing through me like liquid fire, and I can't allow that to happen again.

His swallow is audible. "We're leaving in an hour," he grits out before turning on his heel and striding out of the room.

PHONE IN HAND, I pick up Kaiden's note from the table saying he's waiting outside, then resume scrolling through the million texts Sam sent me in the last few hours. A new one pops on the screen, but it doesn't make any noise. Kaiden must have put it on silent while I was sleeping.

> **Sam: Why the fuck is your phone location telling me YOU'RE IN NEW ORLEANS?!?!?!**

> **Me: Something happened last night, and trust me, that's not a conversation for texts...then I fell asleep and I had to get ready to leave.**

In the next second, the screen lights up with an incoming video call from Sam. Her emerald eyes are all hail and thunder as they fixate on me. "I tried reaching you all fucking day. I was so worried."

"Sorry."

"So, will you tell me what happened?" she snaps.

I heave out a weighted sigh before bringing her up to speed. She stares into space for a few seconds as she absorbs everything, eyes wide and lips pressed in a thin line. "Holy Hecate! I don't know what to say."

"Yeah. It's been hours, and I still feel shell-shocked."

"That shriveled old prune was full of surprises."

I gasp. "Sam, what the fuck?"

She rolls her eyes. "Oh, c'mon, she called me a prostitute more than once. But you know I loved her bitchiness."

"I don't think that's the term she used; she said harlot, if I remember correctly."

"Well, that's the same thing. Remember when she told the entire building you were hosting orgies in your apartment?"

I snort a very unladylike laugh. "How could I forget? Ms. Smith from the second floor was reciting Bible verses as though she was going to burst into flames by simply passing by me on the stairwell. God, I'm going to miss her cranky ass."

"I know...I'm sorry she died in such a horrible way."

"Yeah. Me too."

"How are you aside from that? I know it must be hard being near K—him again."

"It's okay, Sam, you can say his name. Yeah, it's fucking torture, but I have to see this through, and then we'll part ways when we know what the prophecy says."

"Be careful, okay? I don't want you to fall into the same pit you barely crawled back from."

"I am."

"You'll call me after you speak to that guy?"

"If we find him. 'Kay, I gotta go. Kaiden's waiting for me downstairs. Love you."

"Love you too."

I pocket the phone and mentally prepare myself to face Kaiden again after that insane wet dream while riding the elevator. As soon as I exit the hotel, the humid air slaps me in the face and sticks to my skin. I can't believe I complained about the heat wave in Ashville when this is a hundred times worse.

"Where's the car?" I ask as I take in the sleek, black motorcycle Kaiden is standing next to, a lit cigarette between his full lips.

He hikes a shoulder. "I thought it'd be a nice change. We can experience the city better this way."

"We're not here on vacation, Kaiden. We have work to do," I clip out.

"Relax, angel. It's only a means of transportation. The car is also too big to find a parking spot near Bourbon District."

I fold my arms in front of my chest, even though I'm thrilled he somehow got a bike for us. I missed the freedom of riding with him more than I would like to admit. "I'm starting to think you're hard of hearing. I told you multiple times to stop calling me *that*. I'm not your angel anymore. Better yet, I never was."

He cocks an eyebrow in my direction as he stubs the blazing cherry on the side of the trash can before flicking the butt inside. "That so? I don't think your body or mind got the memo, given how you were begging for my cock in your sleep. I wish I recorded you. It would have made the perfect ringtone." His eyebrows drop. "Actually, no, that sound is for my ears only."

Dammit. I'll never live this down.

The woman passing behind us on the sidewalk trips all over her legs, gawking at Kaiden. *Yeah, me and you both, lady.* I don't have to look in a mirror to know my face is as red as a tomato. "Keep your voice down," I hiss, throwing him a murderous look.

He winks. "You know you love my dirty mouth."

"I *don't* love anything about you." I snatch the helmet from his outstretched hand, failing to still my racing pulse because broody Kaiden I can take, but playful Kaiden—the side of him that only comes out when we're together—is too much to handle.

He mounts the bike and waits for me to slide behind him before revving the engine and gliding into the evening traffic. Maybe riding with Kaiden wasn't such a good idea after all. The proximity to his glorious body in the wake of that wet dream is frazzling me. As much as I try to concentrate on our surroundings, all I can focus on is the way his taut muscles flex under my fingertips. The vibration of the engine between my thighs and his heavenly scent that wraps around me in drugging waves don't help either. And then there's that new tattoo. He's wearing me on his skin and over his heart. I have him tattooed, too, only it goes deeper than the skin surface.

Kaiden eases off the gas as we drive into a new neighborhood where towering oak trees line the picturesque streets. Bougainvillea crawls on the walls and fences of the colonial-style houses in varying colors. I think we're in the Garden District. I wish I hadn't slept the day away, but it would have been too hot to walk around anyway. Even now, after dusk has settled around us, it feels as though we stepped into a sauna after being in an air-conditioned room all day.

When he stops in front of a restaurant, we dismount. "Are we walking from here?" I ask after handing him my helmet.

"No, we're grabbing dinner."

My nostrils flare. "No."

"Well, the bars on Bourbon Street don't open for another hour. We have some time to kill."

"What?" I shriek.

"C'mon, we have a reservation," he says as he takes two steps toward the entrance.

I scoff, flapping my hands in indignation. "I can't believe you've tricked me into a date."

"I haven't tricked you. I didn't tell you about it. Plus, it's dinner, not a date." His sinful lips tilt upward into that sexy smirk that makes me crazy. "Unless you want it to be."

"Same fucking thing. First, I'm wearing my gear, which is clearly not appropriate to go out in. And second, I'm not hungry."

A muscle feathers along his stubbled jaw. "Iris, you haven't eaten in over twenty-four hours. You can't keep going like that. You might faint.

The way I see it, you have two options: you either walk in there of your own free will, or I will hogtie you and bring you in, then spoon-feed you everything they have on the menu. What's it going to be?"

I choke on my saliva at the mention of Kaiden hogtying me like in the wet dream.

"You okay?" he asks. A rakish grin pulls at his mouth as if he knows *exactly* what got my cheeks blazing. "Do you need water?"

Jesus. Did I mention the ropes, too, while talking in my sleep? Judging by Kaiden's knowing glint, I sure did.

Kill me now.

"Yes, I mean, no, I don't need water. I'm fine." *Wow. Real smooth, dumbass.* He's right; I need to take better care of my body. I've already lost some muscle mass, and that's a big no when fighting demons. Or having curveballs constantly thrown at you because you have a bounty on your head. "Fine, but can we grab something to go while we walk around the neighborhood?"

He softens at that. "Of course."

Twenty minutes later, we each have a takeout bag in one hand and a drink in the other. I sip on my iced coke as we walk in comfortable silence. The architecture on these streets is spectacular. Sam would love the lush gardens.

"How's Emily?" I inquire.

"She's good. To everyone's surprise, she gained consciousness that same night you broke her out. I made arrangements for her to be airlifted the next morning and brought to the Iron Claw pack territory a few states over. She's staying with Hailey, her girlfriend—actually, fiancée. Logan let us know she proposed the second they saw each other. Logan and Ava are staying with her for a week to make sure she heals properly."

Needles stab the back of my eyes. "That's good. I'm really happy for her." And I mean it. Even if I just met her and Ava, these women have a special place in my heart.

"Do you want to sit there so we can eat?" Kaiden asks, pointing his chin at the bench beneath a gargantuan oak tree.

"Sure."

I finish my burger in record time. Turns out, I was hungry after all. Kaiden's eyes burn a hole through the side of my face as I use a napkin to dab at my mouth. "What, do I have something—" My words die off when I see the pain blazing in his tumultuous obsidian void.

"It killed me seeing you with him, you know." His head drops between his shoulders as he leans forward to rest his elbows on his knees. "There is nothing more I wish for than to take you out on dates, to freely hold your hand on the street, to kiss you without having to look over our shoulders every goddamn second as if what we had— have—is something dirty. Are you…is he…" He runs a trembling hand over his face. "Fuck." His fingers curl into tight fists. "Are you together? Do you…do you love him?"

Those broken pieces I keep together by the skin of my teeth are once again blown apart. It feels like acid being poured over an open wound, then someone rubbing salt on it for good measure. As much as I want to pretend I'm moving on with Noah, I can't do that to Kaiden.

"No. We're not together. I only agreed to the date because it was one of his conditions to help me, that's all. And while I was in love with him once, or better said what I perceived as love as a teenager, what Noah and I had is in the past."

"Good, because if I see you two together again, I'm going to fucking kill him. I wanted to, after the restaurant. If it weren't for Malik and Dominic talking me off the ledge…" I'm afraid the vein pulsing at his temple is going to burst any second now. "The way he looks at you—he wants you. You said one of the conditions. What are the others?"

Kaiden's confession stumps me because instead of being horrified—

like a normal person would—warmth spreads through me at his possessiveness. I should be concerned about him threatening to kill Noah, right? I don't know why I can't find it in me to care all that much, though. There's no point in mentioning the fact that he asked me not to lie to him anymore, so I say instead, "Just one. Another date, but at a charity event."

Kaiden's knuckles turn white under the pressure. "Then you're done with him?"

"I'm done with him anyway, because I decided not to go to the gala." Even though Noah might retaliate and rat me out for killing Cain, I stand by my decision. Not only because of his sleaziness but also because he represents everything I moved on from.

A flicker of relief sparks in his eyes, and the tension threading his shoulders seems to loosen a bit before he stands. "C'mon. The bar opens soon."

33

Iris

Jazz music spills all over Bourbon Street as we weave our way through the crowd. Honestly, I was expecting it to be busier — just like Raven district in the summer — but here, the heat is oppressive, and the air so dense it's borderline unbreathable. So, I guess this time of year is not too appealing for tourists.

The onyx stone in the choker around my neck warms up, and my muscles tense as I scan the perimeter for danger. The *ethereal sight* lets me know there are three possessed humans across the street, their tainted auras pulsing around their bodies. I exhale in relief, but my hands still itch with the need to free them of the possession. However, we don't have time for that. Maybe later, after we hopefully find Rhett. The only consolation I have is that they're possessed by lesser demons.

"Sorry," I mumble as I try to sidestep a woman who seems to almost be floating rather than walking. It's futile. She passes right through me. *Gah.* I shiver. I'll never get used to that.

Kaiden throws me a confused look. "Did you say something?"

"I wasn't talking to you. A ghost passed through me."

"Oh."

"Yeah." Well, this isn't awkward at all. After our talk on the bench, neither of us has said much.

Nestled between two neon signs, right on the corner, is the Drunken Owl. I stop in front of the door. Kaiden, however, keeps walking until he notices I'm not next to him anymore. He turns around. "What are you doing?"

"What are *you* doing? The bar is right here."

His eyebrows furrow. "I see nothing aside from a rundown building."

"But...I don't understand," I mumble as I take in the large green wooden door, the bar's name painted over it in black letters. I glance through the window at the people inside while nibbling on my lower lip in thought. There's no way only one of us can see it unless..."Wait. Do you think it's somehow concealed by magic?"

Kaiden closes the space between us. "Maybe it's the tarot card. You have it on you, right?"

I pull it out of my pocket. I asked Kaiden to look for it in the nightstand drawer before we left for the airport, because I couldn't go inside the apartment. It's the *Wheel of Fortune*, which depicts a wheel covered in esoteric symbols and surrounded by four different winged creatures: an angel, an eagle, a bull, and a lion—each in a corner. There's also a sphinx that sits at the top and a devil at the bottom. In my quick online research, I read it represents the turn of time, made of good and bad moments, which you have no control over. It seems strangely fitting to everything that has happened to me since the umbra attack. Of course, there could be infinite interpretations of the card.

"Here." The second I hand it to Kaiden, the bar disappears, and a ramshackle building with boarded-up windows takes its place.

"Give me your hand." Tingles bloom at the touch as I slide my hand into Kaiden's. "Can you see it again?"

"Yeah," I murmur.

The second he opens the door and pulls me inside, every head turns in our direction. Conversations and raucous laughter halt. You can hear a pin drop. We look at each other, and I shrug before tilting my head toward the bar. About thirty eyes follow us as we stride toward it, the sound of our soles hitting the floor like a shooting gun in the deafening silence. As we pass the patrons, their pointy ears catch my attention. They're all fae.

The lanky bartender, who can't be older than sixteen, studies us with a deer-in-the-headlights expression. I take back the tarot card before dropping Kaiden's hand to lean on the bar, immediately missing his warmth. "Hi. Can we get something to drink?" I ask casually, even though the eyes drilling holes in the back of my head make all my hairs stand on end.

His voice shakes as he says, "You need to leave."

I raise an eyebrow. "Well, that's not very welcoming, is it? Listen, we're looking—"

I'm interrupted by the man rounding the corner holding a crate full of whiskey bottles. "What's with the sile—" His shrewd, peridot eyes cut to me and Kaiden. He bends to place the crate on the floor, and I don't miss the stiffness in his shoulders when he straightens. "You don't belong here," he grits out through clenched teeth.

"We're looking for Rhett." I raise the tarot card but don't get the chance to slide it on the mahogany bar top because the man snatches my wrist in a punishing grip.

His nostrils flare. "Where did you get this?"

Kaiden disappears from his spot next to me and appears on the other side of the bar, holding the man in a chokehold. "Drop her hand. Now. Or I'll snap your fucking neck," he growls. Collective gasps fill the air, followed by panicked shrieks. The lanky bartender scurries away.

Face red and eyes bulging out of his head, the man releases me. Kaiden follows suit but levels him with a razor-sharp glare that could easily slash through skin and bone. "If you as much as blink wrongly at her, I'm going to pull out your organs one by one and make you watch as I feed them to hellhounds."

"If you would have given me the chance to answer, I would have told you Adrianna gave me the tarot card. She also told me to come here and ask for Rhett at the bar. There's no need for you to be so aggressive," I say.

"She would never do something like that. She doesn't like people."

"Trust me, I know. She was my neighbor. Now, can we speak to Rhett?"

He rakes a hand through the mop of cinnamon hair. "I'm Rhett." As if only now registering my words, his face pales. "What do you mean by *was*?"

"Can we talk somewhere private?"

"Why would I want to talk to a hellseeker—assuming you are one—strapped to their teeth in weapons?" He points his chin at Kaiden. "And...whatever you are. I don't trust you."

"Yeah, well, we don't trust you either. But we need your help."

"For?"

"This is a matter we should discuss in private," I repeat. This guy is starting to grate on my nerves.

"I don't deal with strangers. Who are you?"

"I'm Iris Harper, and yes, I'm a hellseeker." Well, not anymore, but I'm not going to start explaining the craziness that has become my life to a complete stranger, so this will do. "And he's Kaiden Black."

"Why the fuck isn't your hair blond?"

I lower my voice when I answer. "I'm a half-blood." I'm not even sure this is true anymore since I don't know what I am exactly, but I need him to trust us, and we already started on the wrong foot.

He whips his head at Kaiden so fast he must have gotten whiplash. "Wait, you said Kaiden Black? You're the head of the Obsidian Conclave?"

Kaiden folds his arms in front of his chest, making his biceps bulge. "Yeah."

Pure, unadulterated hatred bounces in the confines of Rhett's irises. "Your organization has treated my kind like nothing more than blood sacks for centuries. Get the fuck out of my bar, or I'll make you." A menacing gust of air that seems to come out of nowhere ruffles my hair and sends the stack of napkins from the bar top to the floor.

"That was Mammon," Kaiden fires back.

"I don't give a flying fuck. You're just another power-hungry demon in my eyes."

"That's not true," I snap. "He not only dismantled the human and dark creature trafficking, but he's doing everything he can to save the fae from the clutches of vampires who've started their own trafficking ring."

"I could have some of the fae women we rescued talk to you, if that's what it takes for you to help," Kaiden says reluctantly.

"I've heard some stories…but I never believed them." Rhett works his jaw as he ponders his decision. Then, he mutters, "Take a seat wherever you want. Everyone left anyway."

When I glance over my shoulder, I realize he's right. Aside from the blond, lanky bartender who looks as though he's about to bolt any second now, the pub is empty.

"Alaric, lock the door before clearing the tables, please," Rhett tells him.

Kaiden appears at my side to guide me to the closest table. He pulls my chair so I can sit, and I refuse to admit how I melt on the inside at the simple gesture. Unbuckling my sword strap, I lay it on the table before plopping down.

"What's your poison?" Rhett asks, busying himself taking out some bottles from the mirrored shelf behind. He flicks his gaze to Kaiden. "Lemme guess, whiskey or rum, top shelf." At Kaiden's nod, he turns to me. "And you...vodka."

A disgusted shudder passes through me. I haven't had vodka since that night I got smashed, and Noah appeared at my door. God, it seems like that happened a lifetime ago. "A beer is fine."

After a few minutes, Rhett strides toward us, bearing a tray with our drinks. He slides them in front of us before sitting down. He raises an eyebrow. "So, how come a hellseeker is working with a demon? Aren't you supposed to hate each other's guts?"

"We're looking for an oracle, and Adrianna told me you know where we can find one," I answer.

"And why didn't she come too?"

Cinder blocks pile one by one on top of my chest when I mumble, "Because she's dead."

Rhett curses before he stands abruptly, causing his chair to topple over. He throws the beer bottle into the wall, and the sound of the glass shattering slices through the weighted silence. "How?"

"She saved my life from a demon attack. She, um, she was my mother's friend. I wasn't even aware of this until yesterday. I thought she was just my elderly neighbor. But then she saved me, and with her last breath, she told me to find you."

He pinches the bridge of his nose, lifts the chair, and slumps back on it. "Where's her body?"

"It's at the morgue in Ashville. I didn't know if there are special customs for her burial and—"

"There are. She was from a fishing village near the Azrov Sea in the Seelie court. They don't believe in ground burials. Her body needs to be returned to the sea so her soul can find peace." He's silent a moment.

"I can't believe she's…dead. When I crossed with the last group a few days ago, I called to let her know there were rumors of an oracle hiding in the Wasting Woods. We've been searching for years."

"Wasting Woods? Is that in Faerie?" Kaiden inquires.

"Yeah."

"What do you mean by crossed? You bring people here?" I chime in.

"I do. Fifty years ago, a bloody war started between the Seelie and Unseelie courts. The gods have forsaken us because of it, and the lands are dying. There's barely any food left, but the kings don't care. They're too preoccupied measuring their dicks to see that people are starving. There will come a day when they won't have anything left but corpses to rule over," he spits out the bitter words. "So people are fleeing. A friend helped me find a portal at the cost of their life many years ago. I promised I would do everything in my power to return the favor by helping those in need once I got settled. I'm doing my best to find them shelter and a semblance of normal life."

Kaiden runs a hand over his stubbled jaw in thought. "Is there any way you can bring the oracle here?"

"I haven't met her. As I said, there are only rumors. King Orion, who rules the Seelie court, had all oracles executed because he didn't like their war predictions. If she does exist, I can't guarantee the knights haven't already killed her. Everyone in Faerie could have heard the same rumor I did, and the fae are in desperate times." Rhett leans back, folding his arms in front of his chest. "Besides, I can't force someone to cross into this world, especially given the constant threat presented by vampires."

Kaiden and I share a loaded look. "So, if we want to speak to her, we have to go to Faerie?" I ask.

"Pretty much, yeah."

Kaiden sucks on his teeth. "Can you help us find her?"

"The Wasting Woods is not a place I want to go anytime soon. She's hiding there for a good reason, and it's not because it's cozy, trust me."

"Well, if life has taught me one thing, it's that everyone has a price. What do you want in exchange for your guidance?"

Rhett sits for a few moments with Kaiden's words. "I want in on whatever you're doing to save the fae from those bloodsuckers."

"I'll do you one better. How about a seat at the Obsidian Conclave's table, too?"

Shock ripples through Rhett's features. "You would do that? Why?"

I'm equally surprised by Kaiden's offer, though I shouldn't be. His work within the Conclave is nothing short of amazing. If only the Celestial Treaty wouldn't be such a fucking joke when it comes to dark creatures, he would have a fair chance at fighting for their rights.

"Because I'm not Mammon, and I don't rule by myself. Every other dark creature already has a representative to speak for them. It's time the fae got one, too."

"No, thank you," Rhett snaps, his upper lip curling in disgust. "I would rather shit in my palms and clap than sit at the same table as a vampire."

"That vampire you're talking about is the one risking his life every single day to save the fae. So, if you want in, you're going to have to work with him," Kaiden counters acidly.

"Not if I have to breathe the same air as that leech."

I snort an incredulous laugh. "You're telling me you have the chance to make a change for the better for your people, and you won't take it? Because of fucking pride? Cause how I see it, you're hiding. Living in fear. Wouldn't it be easier if you were under the protection of the Conclave? You have such disdain for your kings, but how are you any better when you can't move past your ego?"

Rhett's cheeks take a reddish hue. "I'll think about it."

"Well, don't take too long. We need the oracle," Kaiden tells him.

"Do you think portals grow on trees? It sometimes takes me months to make a trip to Faerie. I don't exactly have the funds to travel all over the world when one opens, so we'd have to wait for one that's close."

I tilt my head. "Really? Are mushroom rings that hard to find?"

"Mushroom rings are not portals. That's a myth. Dragons created portals thousands of years ago to travel between worlds. They appear like rings of fire in the sky. Humans think they're fallstreak holes happening simultaneously as circumhorizontal arcs — an optical illusion caused by the sunlight refracting through ice crystals in the clouds. You wouldn't believe how many planes simply vanish through them and end up crashing in Faerie. The altitude, too, makes them difficult to access, but some open on mountain peaks, which is how we can travel through them without dragons."

"I have a plane, so you only have to worry about finding a portal."

Rhett reels back at Kaiden's words. "You have a fucking plane?"

He smirks. "Being the head of the Obsidian Conclave has its perks."

34

Iris

"We're really going somewhere where there are giant, fire-breathing dragons?" Sam asks Rhett in a high-pitched squeal when he finishes explaining how the portals to Faerie work. We landed in Ashville about half an hour ago, and we're on the tarmac stretching our legs while waiting for Malik to arrive. I didn't want to put anyone else in danger, but Kaiden made a good point in saying that Malik is our best shot at surviving if we're attacked along the way. And then Sam went ballistic on my ass when I told her she couldn't come.

"Dragons are extinct. No one has seen one in hundreds of years, so you don't have to worry about them. But trust me, there are many other creatures that can kill you. Especially in the Wasting Woods," Rhett answers.

She throws me a sidelong glance, laying on the sarcasm thickly when she mutters, "Great. This trip is going to be so fun."

"You didn't have to come, Sam. I still think it's a bad idea."

"Ha, like I would let you travel to another realm by yourself."

Kaiden huffs. "What am I, chopped liver?"

"What you are is number one on my shit list, demon boy," she bristles.

"I know. You made it pretty clear when you defiled all twenty-five of my cars," he drawls, arching an eyebrow.

She gives Kaiden a saccharine smile. "That's because you hurt my bestie. What about your pristine floors? Are you still scrubbing glitter off them?"

He only grunts in response, but his twitching eye tells me he's on the verge of throttling her. My eyebrows draw together. "What are you talking about?"

"Your best friend thought it would be funny to send me a package containing a glitter bomb. It exploded right in my face," Kaiden grits out as a black SUV approaches us.

Rhett whistles. "Remind me not to get on her bad side on this trip."

No, she *didn't*. The laughter bubbling up my throat morphs into a hearty howl. Sam joins in, and we both struggle to breathe at the mental image of Kaiden covered in glitter and still finding specks on the floors days later. My best friend is a freakin' menace.

"That's what I call a welcoming party. What's so funny? I want in on the joke," Malik says, getting out of the car and sauntering toward us.

All the levity in the air is shot to pieces, as a crestfallen look takes over Sam's features. Their gazes clash—both flashing with pure shock. There's a wheezing sound as if someone punched Sam in the gut before she bellows a heart-wrenching scream. She lifts her palms. A blinding green light hits Malik square in the chest. But the look of equal parts resignation and sorrow on his face as he takes the blow is the most confusing part. He flies back a few feet, narrowly missing the car and landing with a sickening *thud* on the asphalt.

"YOU MOTHERFUCKER! Where is it?" Sam screeches, spittle flying out of her mouth. Her legs eat the distance between her and Malik faster than I thought possible. She looks possessed as the same green light from before encompasses her body. Thick, leafy vines sprout from the ground, cracking the concrete before lifting Malik upright and immobilizing his limbs.

"Whoa, Sam! What the fuck? This is Malik. What are you doing?" My question falls on deaf ears. I throw a confused look at Kaiden, but he shakes his head as if he has no idea what's going on, either.

"I said, where the fuck is my family's grimoire, you filthy, lying, murderous thief?" Sam seethes.

"Nice to see you too, freckles." Malik flashes her a grin, but it's a poor imitation of his usual rakish smile. He flicks his gaze to Kaiden, nostrils flaring. "You didn't tell me anyone else was joining us."

"Answer. My. Question." When Sam flexes her fingers, the vines climb upward to squeeze Malik's throat. Still, he sits there and takes it, even though I know he is strong enough to counter Sam's attack with dark magic. Or simply shift into a panther.

"Sam, this is Malik, Kaiden's friend. He's here to help us. What are you doing?" I try again, this time placing a hand on her shoulder. As if sticking a wire into an electrical socket, the second I touch Sam, I'm thrown back by an invisible force.

Kaiden catches me before I fall. "You okay?"

"Yeah," I mumble.

A bitter laugh leaves Sam. "So, is that your real name? And here I thought I was speaking to Ian," she spits the words out as if they're poisonous. "This is the last time I'm asking. Where the fuck is my family's grimoire?"

Ian?

"It's gone, okay? I absorbed its power," Malik wheezes out.

Sam stumbles back at Malik's response. "What? That's why you stole it? I don't understand—how?"

"I don't either, okay? I don't know *how* I did it. It just happened. And I didn't steal it. My coven did."

"Oh yeah, and you weren't a part of it, right? Manipulating the foolish Ambrose witch into falling in love with you so your coven could break in and steal my family's most prized possession."

Malik's taupe skin takes a blueish hue. He's clearly suffocating. "Enough!" Kaiden bellows as he lets me go. Hellfire envelops the vines, turning them to ashes in mere seconds without even touching Malik. He pops off to appear next to Malik, who hits his knees, chest heaving. "I don't know what the fuck happened between you two, but I don't care. You need to calm the fuck down," he clips out to Sam.

"You seem very fond of your friend here, Kaiden. Tell me, did you also know that he's a murderer? Or is that not something you like to share with your friends, Ian?" Her upper lip curls in disgust. "Sorry. Malik."

Kaiden's jaw ticks. "Malik, what is she talking about?"

Malik pushes up. Anguish pinches the planes of his face. "They were supposed to steal the grimoire. That's it. I swear I didn't do anything to her father."

"Then why did you disappear after, huh? Why did you put me under a sleeping spell the same night he was killed? Why did you erase every trace of us meeting if you are so innocent?" Sam fires back.

Malik's only response is to cast his gaze to the ground. His throat rolls on a hard swallow.

"Yeah, that's what I thought. You might not have pulled the trigger, but your hands are bloody all the same." She turns on her heel to me. "Did you know he's Ian?"

"Of course not," I tell her.

"'Kay then, let's go." Instead of striding toward her car like I was expecting her to, she stomps in the direction of the airstairs. "I can't believe he's still wearing that stupid trench coat," she mumbles under her breath.

I hurry my pace to catch up with her. "Sam, what are you doing? We're not traveling to Faerie anymore." Malik and Kaiden are sharing some sharp words behind us, but Malik must have put up a sound shield because, aside from their body language, I can't make out what they're saying.

"What? Why?"

I throw her an incredulous look. "Are you kidding me? Because of what just happened."

"I'm fine," she sniffs.

I scoff. "You clearly aren't."

"Iris, we need to know what that prophecy says, so we're going. I'm not sitting around and waiting for you to be attacked again by demons. Plus, Rhett said that the oracle is in danger of being found by the king's knights. We can't waste any time if that's the case."

I saw my lower lip between my teeth in thought. She's right. But I can't do this to her. "No. I'm going to ask for our bags, and we'll go home, okay?"

She levels me with a stony glare. "No, we're not."

"Fine, then Malik's not coming."

Sam tilts her head skyward and sucks in a lungful of air before blowing it out as if trying to gather all the patience in the universe. "As much as it pains me to say this, I don't even come close to his healing abilities without my family's grimoire — I bet the bastard is so powerful because he absorbed its magic. The potions I packed for the trip are not going to help if something really bad happens. He should come. Besides, he has already saved your life and healed you more than once. That's the only reason why I'm even considering this."

I shuffle on my feet. "Are you sure?"

She nods. "But if he as much as breathes in my direction, I'll make him regret the day he was born." She stomps up the stairs as if they personally offended her. Rhett, who has been watching everything unfold from a quiet corner, follows her with a *what the fuck did I get myself into?* expression painting his face.

"Is she okay?" Kaiden asks as he steps next to me.

"No, I—fuck. I wasn't expecting this. Did you know about any of this? That she and Malik knew each other?"

"The only thing I was aware of is that Malik got into some bad shit in California when he joined a coven of dark witches. When I found him, he was barely alive. He never opened up about that part of his life much, and I didn't push his boundaries. I figured he would share if he ever wanted to."

"But he must have known Sam is my best friend. There are photos of us scattered all over my apartment. You said he was there when he put up the wards."

He runs a hand over his stubbled jaw. "Yeah, but he didn't say anything about it. And I didn't tell him she was coming." There's a weighted pause. "He's waiting for our decision."

I cast a glance at Malik, who's leaning on the SUV, looking like someone kicked his puppy. Or like he kicked someone's puppy.

"Sam said he should come because of his healing abilities," I say.

"Maybe she should go home, then. It's dangerous anyway."

"Trust me, once Sam sets her mind on something, there's no deterring her."

A soft smile pulls at his mouth. "Sounds like someone else I know." He tied his hair at the nape today, accentuating the sharp planes of his gorgeous face while creating a stark contrast with the softness of his lips. God, he's beautiful in an otherworldly yet terrifying way. Not only does every cell in my body yearn for him, but my soul does, too. And as if his devastating beauty wasn't enough, he's also charming on top of it.

I brush his comment off my shoulders. It's going to be nothing short of a miracle if Sam doesn't end up killing Malik.

Icy Iceland wind cracks across my face like a whip. As if sensing the guilt and sorrow blazing through me, the ocean roars, crashing against the onyx rocks. Droplets of salty water rain down on us to mix with the tears carving a fresh path on my cheeks. Sam intertwines our fingers and squeezes my hand in a silent show of support while Kaiden flanks my other side.

"I wish you would have given me — *us* — a chance," Rhett whispers, bending at the waist to place a soft kiss on Adrianna's forehead, whose lifeless body is laid inside a small wooden boat. I don't want to intrude more than I already have on their moment, so I concentrate on the ocean's rage as he murmurs something else in her ear.

When he straightens, shoulders sagged as if weighing a thousand pounds, he gives a curt nod to Kaiden. He, Malik, and Kaiden push the boat into the tide. Malik uses magic to make it float atop the swell. Rhett picks up the wooden bow and arrow from the coal-black sand at his feet, then widens his stance, nocks the arrow, and draws back the string. With a touch of his fingers, Kaiden sets the gasoline-soaked cloth wrapped around the tip ablaze before Rhett releases it. The arrow streaks across the sky until it lands inside the boat. In less than a minute, hellfire envelops the wood.

We all watch the flames kiss the gunmetal clouds in heavy silence. I inhale a shuddering, briny breath. *I'm so sorry, Ms. Robbins. Say hi to*

Mom, will you? Tell her I miss her.

One by one, we make our way to the chopper Kaiden rented once we landed in Iceland, giving Rhett a few moments to say his last goodbyes.

The tension between Sam and Malik is so fraught in the cramped space that it makes my skin itch. It wasn't much better on the flight here, but at least the plane also had a bedroom where Sam and I hid for the entirety of the seven-hour flight.

Every few seconds, Malik's dejected gaze finds Sam as if he's starved of her and can't get his fill. She, of course, pretends he doesn't even exist. But if the muscles around her spine get any stiffer, I'm afraid she's going to snap in two. I still can't wrap my head around the fact that Malik is Ian, the same boy who shattered Sam's heart to smithereens — the reason why she's not able to trust men anymore and throws herself into meaningless hookups instead. I mean, what were the chances?

The air currents aren't strong enough to hinder our journey, but they make for a bumpy ride, which combined with the small space must trick my brain into believing I'm in a jostling car. I fist my sweat-slicked fingers to stop their tremor.

"You okay?" Kaiden rumbles, his gravelly voice filling my headset over the loud sound of the propellers. The second he tries to place his hand on my knee, Sam slaps it away while throwing him a withering glare.

"I got her," she snaps.

A muscle feathers along his taut jaw, but he doesn't respond.

"Iris, close your eyes. Imagine you're somewhere open. Safe." She laces our fingers, using her light magic to send calming waves through my body.

It works. For the rest of our twenty-minute ride to the Vatnajökull National Park, I keep my eyes closed. The pilot lands the helicopter with expert maneuvers right next to the highest peak, where — if Rhett's calculations are correct — the portal to Faerie should open in the next ten minutes. Snow crunches under our boots as we hop off, then slide on our hiking backpacks. The cold is jarring after Louisiana's torrid heat.

"Any minute now," Rhett says while taking out an unusual compass, his breath fogging in front of his face. "Remember, we never know where the portal might send us. I can only approximate its location near the forest, but a different magic imbues the lands of Faerie than the human realm. It's sentient. We call it Mother Draia. Sometimes, she can be fickle...or even volatile. I don't know how she's going to react to strangers, so be prepared for anything."

As the needles in the compass start spinning, a perfect, fiery circle appears out of nowhere in front of us — as if someone took a flaming dagger to the immaterial air. Aside from Rhett, we all stare at it, slack-jawed.

"Okay. Don't forget to count to twenty after the person in front of you crosses," he instructs.

Malik is first, followed by Kaiden. The moment I step through, the world whirls around me at a dizzying speed.

35

Iris

I'm falling.

FUCK.

My ears pop and ring back to life as tree branches snap under my plummeting weight one by one. At least they somewhat slow down my descent. There's only one thing I can do: mentally prepare myself for impact. Grinding my teeth, I wait for the sickening moment my organs will be rearranged, but at the last second, something akin to a gentle breeze catches me, then releases me slowly until my feet touch the ground.

Kaiden and Malik zip through the trees before skidding to a halt. They're inhaling labored breaths as if they just ran a marathon. "You all right?" Kaiden asks, alarmed, while his obsidian eyes scan every inch of me.

"Yeah. Thanks for catching me," I tell Malik, who's bent at the waist, a hand on one of the gargantuan tree trunks.

"That wasn't me," he wheezes out.

"I did that," Rhett chimes in as he floats to the ground from the same direction I came. "I'm an air wielder."

"Oh. Thanks. Wait. Weren't you the last one? Where's Sam?"

A shrill cry cuts through the eerie silence. Our heads jerk in its direction. Sam is plunging from the sky straight toward the startling turquoise lake below. Before I can even move, Malik is already zipping toward her. We all follow, and I try to tap into the unearthly speed, but it's as if I'm hitting a wall. Despite countless attempts, my legs refuse to move faster. I wrestle off my heavy backpack and throw it to the ground. However, that doesn't help. Rhett lifts his hands and uses a gust of air to slow her down.

"Can you hold her weight?" I ask him through heavy pants as I pump my arms.

"Only for a few seconds."

Shitshitshitshitshitshit.

"Iris!" she bellows.

"I'm coming!" I shout back. Then terror sinks its sharp claws into me when she drops into the water with a plop. "She doesn't know how to swim," I scream to the others. "Kaiden! Do your Houdini thing!"

"I can't."

"What do you mean you can't?!?"

"I already tried when I saw you falling. I can't."

Malik dives. Sweat drips down my face, and a coppery tang coats my tongue when I finally reach the rocky shore, soles on fire. Water splashes around me as I dart through it. I only get in to my thighs when Malik pops to the surface, holding an unconscious Sam. He ignores my attempt to take her and lays Sam on the beach, tilting her head back before fusing their mouths to blow life back into her.

Why the fuck isn't he using magic?

I drop to my knees and hold on to her pale hand like to a lifeline. "Sam, you better not die! You hear me?"

Malik laces his fingers and begins applying chest compressions at the perfect rhythm. Each passing second blisters my skin with dread. Then, there's a wet gurgling sound. Her eyes fly open. She throws up water, then coughs as though she's going to hack up a lung. The next breath she takes feels like my first one, and I almost faint from relief. Malik turns her to the side. I want to hug her so badly my whole body is shaking, but I should wait for her to fully regain consciousness.

Malik's fingers tremble as he brushes the drenched copper strands out of her face while murmuring, "It's okay. You're okay." However, it seems he's trying to reassure himself rather than Sam, who's still out of it.

After a few moments, the hazy fog covering her emerald eyes dissipates. She leans into his touch for a fraction of a second, then, as if finally realizing her mistake, she bats his hand away. "Don't fucking touch me," she hisses.

Hurt ripples through Malik's features before he pushes to stand next to Kaiden and Rhett.

Thanking every deity in the universe, I pull Sam to my chest, careful not to restrict her breathing. "Fuck. Don't you scare me like that ever again."

She snorts. "Welcome to the club. Hecate knows how many times I wanted you to understand what it's like to almost lose your best friend." Her nose wrinkles. "But this is not exactly what I had in mind."

Now that the adrenaline is wearing off, I'm cooking from the inside out in the light winter jacket. I unzip it before shrugging it off and throwing it over the pile where the others left theirs. When I try to help Sam take off hers, she doesn't allow me. "Wait, let me dry myself first." She waves a hand in front of her body. Nothing. She tries again. And again. "Why is this not working?" she mutters in pure frustration.

"I think we can't access our powers," Kaiden cuts in. "I can't pop around at whim anymore."

"And when I tried to magically resuscitate you earlier, it didn't work," Malik adds as he wrings the water out of his long, silver hair.

Rhett presses his lips in a tight line. "I was afraid this might happen."

"And why didn't you say anything?" I inquire, annoyance dripping from my tone when I remember trying to tap into my enhanced speed and failing.

"I did." He shrugs. "I warned you that I didn't know how Mother Draia would react to strangers. I've never brought someone from the human realm to Faerie before; I'm always getting people out, not in. Even when I first crossed into your world, it took months before I could wield air again. I can only assume Mother Draia was furious I dared to leave Faerie. She's probably blocking your abilities, now. Or she's just playing a cruel joke. You never know."

"Great," I mutter, then look up at Kaiden. Worry is etched in the lines around his eyes and mouth. I'm sure they mirror my own. "What about your helltire?"

"I can try." Concentration creases his forehead as he flexes his fingers. His sheer effort is evident in the protruding veins over the thick ropes of muscle while sweat dots his forehead. We wait with bated breath, but nothing happens.

"We should get going," Rhett tells us.

I offer Sam a hand and pull her up. She huffs out a frustrated exhale as she stands on wobbly feet. "Shit. My backpack. It's at the bottom of the lake, with all my stuff."

"I can give you my spare change of clothes," I tell her.

"I might be able to help dry you," Rhett chimes in, lifting his hand. When he turns it, something resembling a small tornado envelops Sam.

Her hair whips around her in a copper blur. The tornado moves to Malik, then to me. It's like being caught in a wind tunnel.

We mumble a "thank you" before making quick work of gathering our belongings. Rhett leads the way.

As we pass the knobby driftwood, I'm finally able to take in my surroundings. I've never seen trees as big as these, resembling sleepy giants that rise from the earth to brush the cloudless sky. Their bark is a vivid reddish-brown, and thick crimson vines climb along their length. The closest thing I can compare them to are sequoia trees. Still, these are much taller and bulkier at the bottom.

They make me feel small. Inconsequential. More so now that I can't access my abilities. It's as if someone took away my crutches, and I have to learn how to walk again. It's unsettling. The only time I remember feeling this way was right after I woke up in the hospital after the car accident. For years, I thought it was because of losing my memories… but now I know it's because of the barrier in my head.

It's only here, now, smelling wet mud, rotting wood, and something sweet that reminds me of honeysuckle, that I make the connection implied in my mother's journal. I might be half fae. This could have very well been my home, in another life. My mother's home, too, in that alternate universe. I have no idea what it all means.

Upon our arrival, everything quiets — the foreign birdsong, the small animals moving in the underbrush, even the wind rustling through the branches. It's as if the forest itself is holding its breath. The only sound is that of loose pebbles and fallen foliage crunching under our boots.

"So, where are we?" Kaiden asks Rhett. He's walking behind us with Malik, surely to watch our back in case something happens.

He turns to look at us over his shoulder. "The portal dropped us on Seelie lands. The Wasting Woods forms the barrier between the Seelie and Unseelie courts, so we should enter it in about two or three days."

"You said time flows differently here," I chime in as I rearrange the straps of my backpack. The farther we venture into the woods, the more the sensation of being watched prickles the back of my neck.

"It does. But it's unpredictable. Sometimes, when I cross back to the human world, the months I spent in Faerie are mere days, and then other times, the weeks here turn into months there."

"I hope time will work in our favor because my flower shop can't run itself. Trish is going to kill me if I'm gone more than a few days," Sam mumbles from beside me.

Rhett prattles on about the enormous plants resembling ferns as I throw Sam a worried look. "Hey, you okay?"

She nods and offers what should be a reassuring smile, but it's brittle—devoid of the usual confidence she wears like armor. Sam is terrified of water in the same way I'm afraid of being in a moving car. Her mother suffered from severe post-partum psychosis, which resulted in delusions and mania. She tried to drown Sam in their backyard pool when she was eight months old. Even though she can't remember it because she was just a baby, the scars are still there. And they're bleeding. I recognize those haunted shadows in her eyes; they're what I see in the mirror every time I wake up from a night terror.

"Are you sure?" I insist.

She puffs out a breath before lowering her voice to a whisper. "No. Between Ian—Malik—being back and almost drowning, I feel as though my life is spinning off its axis. And my magic has been a part of me since the moment I was born. It's like someone cut out a big chunk of my soul and misplaced it. I keep wanting to draw from it, but I can't. There's only an empty well...I don't like it one bit. This place gives me the heebie-jeebies."

"It is kinda creepy, right? I can't shake the feeling that we're being watched."

Sam swivels her head left and right. "Yeah, me neither." A few more minutes go by before she asks, "What are you going to do about the Order if weeks or months pass in the human world while we're here?"

Shrugging, I say, "I don't know. I was going to tell Grayson I quit yesterday, but everything happened, and yeah…now we're here. I guess it doesn't matter anymore. He surely is aware I missed my shift last night, since we're still supposed to work in pairs. He probably already fired me."

I didn't even tell Aunt Josephine I was leaving Ashville for a few days. I am bitterly disappointed in her because she stayed silent about Emily. Her only concern was the non-existent repercussions that might follow a violation in the Treaty.

Sam shakes her head incredulously at my indifference. "Who the fuck are you, and what have you done with my workaholic bestie? I'm proud of you, Iris. I know what being a hellseeker meant to you. It takes guts to do what you did." She smiles. "I love you to pieces, but you were a little brainwashed."

I huff a laugh. "Love you too. Good thing I finally woke up, huh?"

We continue our trek through overgrown berry bushes, crisscrossing giant tree roots that are a bitch to climb over, and mossy rocks. With each step toward the Wasting Woods, this weird feeling filtering through me only intensifies — as if something is calling out to a part of me from beyond the dead forest. But when I try to decipher it…I can't. It feels as though I'm underwater and can't break the surface. It's unsettling. More so because I can't help but wonder if it's because my mother was fae.

With the dipping sun, the temperature also drops, cooling the fine sheen of perspiration on my exposed skin. Even if I'm used to prolonged effort, my legs are starting to tire. Sam hasn't complained much, but she too must be exhausted since she abhors any form of physical exercise.

Rhett stops when we encounter a small clearing on our left. "We're going to camp here for the night."

"Oh, thank Hecate," Sam huffs quietly as we jump over a small creek.

I down what's left of my electrolyte drink, shell out my weapons, then let out a tired sigh as I slide off the heavy backpack. Kaiden, Malik, and Rhett do the same while I rummage for my tent. When I get all the parts out, both Sam and I stare at them with pursed lips.

"Don't look at me. I've never been camping. If I still had magic, all I'd have to do is snap my fingers, and it would already be pitched." She wrinkles her nose. "I swear this is the first and last time I'm trading my stilettos for hiking boots."

I scratch my head as I pick up the poles. "I think these go through the holes, right?"

"I don't know, but um, nature calls."

"Don't go far."

"'Kay, Mom."

"Need help?" comes the deep cadence of Kaiden's voice. With Sam guarding me like a Pit Bull and everything unfolding between her and Malik, we haven't said much to each other since we left Ashville. I turn on my heel to look at him. The stubble on his cheeks is longer than usual. I lock my muscles so I don't cave into the urge to rub my palm against it.

"Um, yeah," I respond.

He bends to place a rolled-up sleeping bag on the ground. "It's Malik's. He wanted Sam to have it."

"Oh, that's nice of him." I look over my shoulder at Malik and Rhett, who are busy making a fire pit.

"I don't think it's a good idea to tell her it's his, though."

I grimace. "You're right. She would probably prefer sleeping on a bed of snakes than accepting anything from him."

He crouches to clear the ground of twigs and rocks. When he stands, he's so close we're practically sharing the same breath. "I'm going to need these." Kaiden's hands linger on mine as his fingers wrap around the poles. Electricity sparks in the air between us. I let out a shaky exhale. His eyes are obsidian fire as they drop to my parted lips. "Fuck me. That little freckle above your lips is driving me crazy. I *dream* about it. I'm so desperate to taste it."

"I might not have magic, but I swear to Hecate, if you don't back off, demon boy, I'll throw rocks at you," Sam clips out from behind me.

Her words are the equivalent of being pushed into a pool of ice-cold water. I step away, barely keeping my balance because my legs have turned to mush. Jesus, it's like we're two magnets on a collision course. No matter how many times I try to remind myself of his betrayal, I still can't escape this insane attraction we share.

Kaiden glowers at Sam over my shoulder. Heaving out a heavy exhale, he starts putting together our tent. Soon enough, we're all gathered around the fire, sharing beef jerky and the freeze-dried meals Rhett had already prepared for his next trip to Faerie. As much as I hate to acknowledge it, since being in Kaiden's presence again, my appetite has somewhat returned.

"I was expecting to see more destruction, to be honest," I say to break through the awkwardness blanketing the air. I have to admit, Rhett is an attractive man. His looks are not as striking as Kaiden's or as unique as Malik's, with his lively silver hair and feline eyes, but you can definitely tell he's not human. His features seem to have become sharper since we crossed through the portal. More startling.

The flames reflecting in the peridot of his irises only enhance that otherworldliness. "That's because there are no villages or cities this close to the Wasting Woods. It's dangerous to settle around here," he says.

"How was growing up in Faerie?" I ask not only because I'm curious, but because I want to know what my mother's life would have looked like. She mentioned in her journal how she always longed for another existence. I wonder if she would have been happier here in Faerie, or if she ever came to terms with what my grandparents—if I can even call them that—did to her.

"Well, obviously, there's no technology, so it was pretty different from what you experienced. But...I had a good childhood. My father was a swordsmith, and my mother owned a bookshop." A wistful expression softens his features. "There were only two years between my brother and I, and we would always get into trouble. Fighting the neighbors' kids, pulling stupid pranks, you name it. Once, we almost burned down the house. Mom was furious. We never had much, but it was enough to keep us happy and well fed. Until the war came."

He doesn't have to continue for us to deduce that his family is gone—the pain is written all over his face—so I decide to change the subject. "Did Adrianna ever mention my mother? Her name was Eliana Harper."

"I'm sorry, no. She also never said why she was looking for an oracle. But she wasn't the type to share too much anyway. That woman was harder to crack than a safe."

"How does magic work here exactly aside from it being sentient? Do all fae wield the elements like you and Adrianna?" Sam chimes in. Her back is almost fully turned to Malik. Ever since she fell into that lake, he has been orbiting around her like a hawk. It's as if he's afraid she'll vanish into thin air if she's farther than three feet away.

"Mother Draia bestows her gift upon chosen fae. Those who receive her blessing are born with it. Most times you're not even aware you can wield magic until it awakens. However, it's rumored that all fae born after the war are powerless. Even the royal children, which is unheard of because the royal bloodline is sacred—the closest to our gods. They are said to have the most aether coursing through their veins, which all fae inherit from the gods." He takes a swig of water. "It's the reason vampires hunt us; aether makes the blood addicting and allows us to live for hundreds of years. But the war angered the gods and Mother

Draia, and she has turned her back on us. Not only are the lands dying, but magic is dwindling too. That's why King Orion forced all fae who can wield the elements to join his army by royal decree. The most powerful form his personal guard."

"And if you refuse, what happens?" Malik inquires.

Rhett arches a brow. "Guess."

I can't resist my next question. "Have you seen or heard about fae with the ability to wield shadows?"

Kaiden's eyes are two blazing coals that brand the side of my face as soon as the words leave my mouth, but I don't meet them.

"I've only heard of it. The only fae who can wield shadows are those in the royal family of the Unseelie court."

Sam holds my gaze for a few weighted seconds. That moment when the vampire bit me in the cathedral's crypt pushes to the forefront of my mind. He said that my blood smelled sweeter than any of the fae he ever drank from. I know it's a crazy jump, but what if my mother was from the royal Unseelie bloodline? Or are my powers a result of the experiments my grandparents did on her?

No matter how hard I try, though, instead of getting answers, I only end up with more questions. It's frustrating. I feel as though my whole life has been blown to smithereens and no matter how hard I try to put the broken pieces back together, they don't fit. *I* don't fit. Leaving the Order was the best decision I ever made—I know that. But at the same time, I feel I've lost my place in this world. I hoped maybe I could find it here...but here doesn't feel right either. I'm starting to think I'll never find it, even after that wall in my head is torn down.

Sam yawns from beside me, pulling me out of my thoughts. "I'm beat. See you guys in the morning," she says while stretching and disappearing into the tent.

I follow quickly after, leaving Kaiden, Malik, and Rhett talking about the Conclave and the progress they've made so far in finding the kidnapped fae. But even though I'm tired as fuck, I can't doze off because I keep staring at Sam, sleeping like a rock, to make sure her chest still rises and falls, rises and falls. As quietly as I can, I slide out of the sleeping bag, grab my jacket, and exit the tent.

Rhett said he was going to keep watch for tonight, but instead I find Malik. He's staring into the fire with a forlorn expression and turns at the sound of leaves crunching under my boots. "Hey, sweets."

"Mind if I sit?"

"Go ahead. But if you're going to punch me, please do it here." He taps his right cheek. "The left is my good side. Gotta keep looking handsome for the ladies. Or men. I don't discriminate." The smile he gives me doesn't reach his eyes, though.

I plop down next to him. "I'm not here to hit you. Though you deserve it."

"Oh. Couldn't sleep?"

"Yeah."

"Me neither."

"I, um, I keep seeing Sam after you pulled her out of that lake. Not breathing." A shudder passes through me. "That was close. Too close."

"I know what you mean." There's a pause filled only by the crackling wood. When he speaks, it's barely above a whisper. "How is she?"

"Physically, I think she's okay. Emotionally...not so much." I let out a sigh. "Listen, there's this big part of me that wants to wring your neck, but no matter how much I want to hate you for everything you put her through, I can't. Maybe that makes me a shitty friend because I don't truly *know* you. And let's just say I've come to the bitter realization that my judgment is not the best when people are involved, but you always gave me the impression that you're a good person. And I already know Sam's side of things. I was wondering if you would like to share yours too. If you want, of course," I blurt out the last part.

We sit in silence once again while Malik ponders my words. "I don't talk about that part of my life — it's too painful. I haven't even told Kaiden aside from some bits and pieces. But I swear I never wanted to hurt her. You have to understand…back then, before Kaiden took over the Conclave, things were different between dark and light witches. Mammon didn't give a shit if we killed each other. And nothing makes you more ruthless than the thirst for power." He lets out a bitter laugh. "I just couldn't see it because I was nothing more than a stupid kid ready to do anything for his mother's approval. Not that it makes me any less guilty because, at the end of the day, I did everything she wanted without coercion. But my little sister — fuck — she was so sick," his voice breaks as he blinks rapidly to clear the brimming tears.

"There's a steep price to pay for wielding dark magic. Your body either gets accustomed to it, or it doesn't. Few make it. And that grimoire was the one thing that could make my sister better. At least that's what my mother told me, and I believed her because why would she lie, right? What kind of mother doesn't want to save her child? They were supposed to break into the house, steal the grimoire, and leave… but they did so much more."

Brows drawn, I stare at my feet for a few moments, speechless. "I don't know what to say. While I'm not sure she'll ever be able to forgive you, I think you should at least try explaining everything to Sam."

He huffs. "She would rather jump off a cliff than talk to me, and I don't blame her."

"That's because she and her father shared a very special bond. And trust me 'cause I'm speaking from personal experience; even if you can't remember your relationship with your parent, their death is not something you can easily get over. And Sam…she idolized her father. But I still think you should try." I let out a weighted sigh. "Can I ask you something else?"

He hikes a shoulder. "Go ahead."

"After you healed me and Emily in the cemetery, why did you refuse to pull more power from Kaiden so you could heal yourself?"

"Because someone like me doesn't deserve redemption or absolution." His words are whispered.

I don't want to poke old wounds further, so I stand.

"Can you please keep everything we talked about between us?"

"Of course," I say as I turn away.

Malik circles my wrist to stop me. "I don't think you're a poor judge of character. Kaiden is the best man I know and the closest thing I have to a brother. You weren't wrong about that. If someone deserves a second chance, it's him."

"He took away the first fifteen years of my life. And then he lied to me — by omission, but he still did."

"Sometimes, you do desperate things to save the people you love. And he does love you. Fiercely." He lets me go.

I trudge back to the tent with my heart lodged in my throat and another dent in my armor.

36

Iris

I mumble a curse under my breath as I trip for the umpteenth time on yet another tree root. Not only do I miss my enhanced vision that allowed me to see in the dark, but my legs feel as heavy as cinder blocks from trekking through the woods for three entire days. I know it's crazy, but it's as though these roots have free will and they're playing tricks on me because I could have sworn there weren't this many on my way out to pee. I knew it was a bad idea to drink so much water before going to sleep. Especially since the flashlights we brought from home have already died. Rhett said things from the human realm rarely function here for long or at all.

While my eyes are glued to the ground, a gnarled branch smacks me across the face. It splits my cheek open like a serrated blade.

Motherfucker. Blood trickles down from the cut, and I wipe it gingerly with my fingers. Once we started approaching the Wasting Woods, the trees became slimmer but denser and apparently deadlier, too.

I whirl my head at a twig *snap* behind me. Goosebumps break over my entire body as I tighten my grip on the dagger's hilt. I might not have my abilities, but I still know how to fight. However, I will not wait here and be an easy target.

Hurring my pace, I spill into the clearing we're using as campsite and freeze at the sound of muffled giggles. Malik is fast asleep on the dead grass while four glowing dragonflies buzz above his head. I have to do a double take at the image before me because the bag filled with all our food — the one we hung in a tree earlier — starts floating away.

What the?

"Malik. Wake up!" I shout while breaking into a run.

A collective gasp resounds before I'm swarmed by about a dozen angry dragonflies. Once they're close enough, I realize they're not bugs but tiny, winged elfish creatures. They let out a collective high-pitched battle cry as they attack me, pulling at me from all directions and halting my momentum. As I swing my dagger into the air, one of them pokes me in the eye while another sinks its unnaturally sharp teeth into the meaty part of my hand. Disproportionately blinding pain shoots up my arm.

There's the distinct hiss of zippers being opened. "What the fuck?" Sam shrieks.

A gust of air blasts the little creatures. They screech as they disappear into the forest with freakishly rapid wingbeats along with our food.

Next thing I know, I'm being pulled into a warm chest. "You're hurt," Kaiden rumbles as he places a finger under my chin to tilt it upward. Butterflies awaken and start rioting in the confined space of my ribcage.

"I'm okay." Cringing, I add, "But really fucking embarrassed."

"What the hell was that?" Sam asks from behind us on a hearty laugh. "Dude, you should have seen yourself. I wish my phone worked so I could film you."

"Pixies. They're small but can be vicious. Especially when they're hungry," a sleep-rumpled Rhett says while approaching Malik and dumping water on his face.

He gasps, then shoots upright into a sitting position. "Those little—"

"I told you it wasn't a good idea to keep watch so soon after your first night," Kaiden tells Malik.

"I wasn't sleeping. They blew some shimmering dust in my face and—"

"You're bleeding," Rhett interrupts as his gaze cuts to me. All color drains from his face.

I reluctantly step back from Kaiden. "Yeah. A branch hit me in the face earlier, and one of those damn pixies bit me."

"Shit."

As soon as he finishes saying that, a low growl vibrates the ground beneath our feet. About ten wolves step out of the tree line. We're surrounded.

There's something wrong with them, though. They're so emaciated, their bones are sticking out through paper-thin skin. And there's no spark in their eyes. Somehow, I know it's because there's a void where their souls should be.

"Can you shift?" Kaiden asks Malik in a strained voice.

"No," he grits out.

"Grab your weapons," Rhett bellows as the wolves pounce. He lifts his hands, and the beasts ricochet a few feet back when they smack into what I assume is an air barrier.

"Stay close to me," I tell Sam, dashing toward our tent. Kaiden and Malik zip for theirs, too. "Here." I shove the dagger at her before grabbing my whip and sword.

"I don't know how to use this," she blurts out, voice steeped in panic.

"You're not going to need it, okay? Stay behind me."

"I can't hold them much longer." Rhett's T-shirt is drenched in sweat, and his knees wobble as the creatures continue throwing themselves at the invisible wall.

We sprint back to Rhett at the same time as Malik and Kaiden, who's holding two swords. The second must be Rhett's. We turn so we're back to back, forming a protective circle around Sam. The wolves rush at us—all snapping teeth and deadly claws.

Chaos ensues.

I flick my wrist, sending the whip cracking through the air. It slices through the wolf's chest. I expect blood to gush out of the deep wound, or at least a howl. But there's no reaction. The only noticeable thing is the horrid stench of rotting flesh as the creature forges forward. There's no explanation other than—"They're dead!" I yell. "Try cutting off their heads."

In the corner of my eye, Kaiden is wielding the sword as though it's an extension of his body—which equally shocks me and ignites my blood. Malik and Rhett aren't as graceful, but they're holding their own. I retract the whip, then crack it back. It wraps around the beast's throat. However, when I try to pull it toward me, the movement lacks my usual strength, so when it thrashes, I lose my balance. A second wolf takes advantage of the situation and charges. Inhaling deeply, I let muscle memory take over. Tracing a perfect arc, I sever its head clean off with my sword. It slaps the ground before rolling backward.

Sam gags at the foul smell emanating from the twitching corpse. This time, I throw every ounce of energy I possess into yanking the whip to drag the wolf toward me and bring down my sword on its neck. By the time I'm done beheading another, I'm panting as if I fought a horde of demons on my own. A bead of sweat gets stuck in my eyelashes. I blink to jostle it free as I take in our campsite. Headless corpses are scattered all over, while two of the tents are destroyed.

"Good idea for everyone to have weapons," I say to Rhett, who's breathing as hard as I am. I spin to look at Sam. "You all right?"

She nods, but she's getting greener by the second until she jerks forward, bends at the waist, and starts projectile vomiting. I don't blame her because the odor is downright fetid, though not much different from that of demons. It just lacks the strong sulfur.

The need to make sure Kaiden's not injured is all-consuming. However, I'm not prepared for my eyes to slam into the wall of glistening, rock-hard muscles on his chiseled chest and abs as he lifts his tee to wipe the top of his eyebrows. Dammit. He winks, and I damn nearly combust.

"We should do something about your cuts before we go. Otherwise, these wolves won't be our only problem," Rhett says, snapping me out of it.

"Do you still have the salve I gave you on the plane?" Sam chimes in, her eyebrow raised in a manner that tells me she caught the way I was ogling Kaiden.

"Oh yeah, I completely forgot about it."

She pushes past me as if her ass is on fire to rummage through my backpack in our tent, which has been spared. I join her while Malik, Kaiden, and Rhett gather what's left of their stuff.

Her eyes widen as she inspects the wound on my cheek. "You got this by smacking into a branch?"

"To be honest, it felt more like the tree whacked me."

"This place is really trying its hardest to kill us," she mutters as she pours water from a bottle into my awaiting palms. She uses the rest to rinse her mouth while I wash my face. I hiss when she applies a thick layer of the minty salve to the throbbing gash on my cheek.

Kaiden strides toward us. He showed me how to put up and break down a tent, but he's still taken it upon himself to do it for us every day, so I guess he's here to help.

"I wasn't expecting you to be so good at wielding a sword," I say as I roll up our sleeping bags.

He drops to his haunches next to me. A small smile tugs at his lips. "I had an excellent teacher, who, even though I was a little shit and complained endlessly, instilled in me the fact that my power might fail me one day and I would be defenseless. It is one of the best pieces of advice I ever received. To this day, I train with it in mind."

"And Malik? Where did he learn?"

"Well, I needed a partner, so I made him train with me. He usually asks for crazy shit in return, just to grate on my nerves, but I know he secretly loves it."

WE EACH TAKE turns bathing in the stream's icy water while vermillion and pink streaks clash in the sky with the approaching dawn. Though, by the time we finish, a thick fog envelops the forest in a misty blanket that even the sun can't penetrate.

The silence is oppressive — the type that belongs in a cemetery. Spiny bushes scratch at our legs while spindly boughs resembling claws seem to reach for us as we trek through the thicket of rotten trees. Scavengers have long since picked apart the animal carcasses scattered across the cracked ground.

Everything here screams *death*.

"Holy Hecate! That's big," Sam says in a low voice as she stares at the skull the size of a truck peeking out the top of the steep canyon on our right. The haze covers the rest of the skeleton.

"That's what she said," Malik shoots back.

Kaiden shakes his head while Sam's lips twitch slightly before she schools her expression into a scowl.

"Is that what I think it is?" I ask in awe. We're all whispering as a precaution.

"Yeah. That was once a dragon," Rhett replies.

I have the sudden urge to pinch myself. Never in my life had I imagined seeing a dragon's skeleton. "If the head is this big, its body must have been over two hundred feet."

"Well, that canyon probably formed when it fell, so that sounds about right." He fishes the intricate compass from his pocket. "By my calculations, we should reach the oracle soon."

"How does the compass work, exactly?" Kaiden inquires.

"By magic. It was created to find portals but can also point you to the thing you want to reach even if you don't know its exact location. However, it doesn't work that well for locating people—that's why I couldn't find the oracle sooner. But once I heard the rumor about the Wasting Woods, I could give the compass something to work with." He pauses. "My mother received it as payment from a mage for some of the rarest books she had. We were all supposed to use it to escape to the human world, but our city got attacked the night before. Only I made it out."

Kaiden sounds genuinely sympathetic as he says, "I'm sorry."

We continue our journey in silence for the next few hours. When my muscles scream in protest because we haven't stopped even for one second, a tiny wooden cottage squatting in a clearing takes shape through the dense murk.

"It's hard to believe someone lives here," I muse, taking in its crooked lines and the huge claw marks scoured into the decaying wood planks. "It's too quiet. Do you think the king's knights got here before us?" I ask Rhett.

He doesn't get to answer because the door screeches as it opens, barely holding onto the rusty hinges. A small body flies at us.

"Hello," I say to the girl, who can't be older than eight, when she stops right in front of me. "We're here—"

"I've been waiting for *you*." She tucks a white strand as pure as snow behind her pointy ear as she regards me through thick lashes of the same color. Her dusty blue dress hangs at least three sizes too big on her, and the way her collarbones stick out is gut-wrenching. No child should look so malnourished.

"Thalia! Come back inside right this second!" A woman yells before appearing in the doorway, anguish marring her features. She blanches as her gaze finds us.

Thalia points at me. "She's the girl from my dreams."

We all share a *look*.

"Thalia, inside. Now," the woman scolds again, then to us, "Who are you?" While there is some resemblance to Thalia, she has thick, chestnut hair braided like a halo around her head and shrewd hazel eyes that glare at us with suspicion.

"You should listen to your mother," Sam murmurs to the girl.

"She's not my mother," Thalia huffs in a way that would make a teenager proud before trudging back toward the cottage.

"They're with me," Rhett answers. "We're here to speak to the oracle."

The woman's tone could freeze over an ocean as she says, "There's no oracle here. Now leave before the sun sets, and the dead come."

"I'm a traveler. Maybe you've heard of us before. We help those who want to escape the war. These people are from the human world."

She arches an eyebrow at Rhett as she ushers Thalia inside the dilapidated cottage. "I can tell. I have eyes, you know."

"We mean no harm. Please, we only need a few minutes of the oracle's time, and then we'll be on our way," I intervene, trying to placate her.

She ignores me. "You really bring fae to the human world?"

Rhett nods.

She nibbles on her lower lip. "What about the vampires?"

"They still pose a threat. But we've found ways to hide. It's much better than living here amongst death and war."

A stifling silence settles over us as the woman ponders her decision. "If I let you speak to the oracle, will you take us back with you?"

Rhett's answer is immediate. "Yes. Even if you don't help us, I will still take you."

She crosses her arms over her chest. "Fine, but only one of you can come in." She points her chin at me. "You."

"I'm not letting her go alone," Kaiden says, stepping up next to me.

I turn to look at him. "It's okay. There's a child inside. What do you think could happen? They're spooked enough as is without adding a scary, six-foot-four tattooed demon to the equation."

His nostrils flare, but he nods stiffly.

"Leave your weapons," she clips out.

I slide off my backpack, then make quick work of removing all my weapons and handing them to Sam. An ominous feeling thrashes beneath my skin with every step toward the cottage. The rickety porch stairs creak under my weight as I ascend. The woman lets me pass through the warped doorframe, a glint of interest shining in her eyes as they rove over my hellseeker gear.

"I'm Iris," I tell her. She's as skinny as Thalia and much younger than I first thought. She might seem fragile, but the way she carries herself and the look in her eyes—the kind you only get after a life of hardship—tells me she's wise beyond her years.

"Yana. I'm Thalia's sister."

The cabin has only one room. The pallet pushed against the farthest wall and covered in rags must be their bed. Still, even though it's cramped, it's clean. I expected another person to be here, maybe an old woman, but there's only Thalia. She's hunched over on the floor while playing with a doll made of sticks.

Something boils in the pot above the fire crackling in the hearth, the smell of food making my belly grumble loudly. Last night, exhaustion kept me from eating what we had left after the pixies' theft. And after trekking through these woods on an empty stomach, it feels like my organs are sticking together.

Yana's lips thin. "We're not sharing our food."

I would have considered it rude coming from anyone else, but who knows what she had to do to procure it. "I wasn't going to ask you to." My eyes snag on the engraved onyx plaque hanging from a rusty hook beside the oil lantern.

"The stone is spelled. It's the only way to keep the dead animals from entering. They come at night, claw at the walls." She shudders before clearing her throat. "Go ahead."

I had an inkling Thalia might be the oracle, but it's still unbelievable that a child could possess such power. I drop to my haunches next to her. "Thalia, my name is Iris. I came all the way from the human world so I could speak to you about a prophecy."

She stops playing and glances at me. Up close and personal, the subtle pink in her light aqua eyes is noticeable. "A prophecy cannot be given freely."

"What do you want in return?"

"The Fates decide, not me. I have to touch you if you want to find out the price."

"That's fine."

The second her wispy fingers meet my temples, her eyes roll to the back of her head. A flash of white. Then, I'm no longer in the cabin, but in a sunlit clearing.

Three women stand in front of me. "The price has been decided. Are you ready to pay, Iris Harper?" they ask in a solemn voice at the same time.

"What is it?"

"A happy memory."

Their words are bone-crushing because the memories — good or bad — I've made after the car accident are all I have. But I nod. Everything we've gone through can't be for nothing.

Two women grab my shoulders, while the third places her palm on my forehead, and I'm thrown into the past.

"Hi, angel."

"Of course, you're a morning person," I grumble as I shuffle into the kitchen on autopilot.

Kaiden arches an eyebrow before he lets his heated gaze rake lazily over my body. Like fingers dancing across my skin, I feel it everywhere. "It's past noon," he says, extending a large cup of coffee toward me.

Fuck me. He's dressed in a pair of basketball shorts and a sleeveless shirt that puts all his bulging muscles and tattoos on display. I want to kick myself for not even looking in the mirror before getting out of my bedroom. But I'm not used yet to having a demon live with me. And this is the first day. To be honest, it all seemed like a fever dream — him announcing he's moving in with me over dinner. Glancing down, I notice I forgot to put pants on and am only wearing the T-shirt I slept in, which barely covers my ass. Shit. "Potato, potahto. Noon is morning for me."

Our fingers brush as Kaiden passes me the cup. I take a sip. The coffee is perfect — just like the last time he made me one after I woke up in his penthouse after the umbra attack. "Man, this is so good, I could kiss you right now," the words slip out before I realize my mistake.

"Careful, angel. Or you might find yourself on top of the counters with my head between your thighs and my tongue inside you. I haven't forgotten how you made yourself come while screaming my name."

I almost spit out the coffee as heat scorches the tips of my ears. Kaiden throws me a rakish smile that makes my bones melt. He shakes his head. "I love how easy it is to make you blush." He closes the space between us and brushes a wayward coal-black strand behind my ear. My pulse skyrockets as our eyes lock. "You're devastatingly beautiful when you're sleep-rumpled. C'mon, I'm making breakfast and then we can go for a run." His big hand engulfs mine before he pulls me to the table.

We spend the rest of the day doing mundane things, and while it seems silly, this is one of the happiest days of my life. Because of its simplicity. Because moments like these are the ones that brand your soul and burrow deep. Because I didn't even realize how barren my life was before Kaiden barged in.

I hold onto this memory by the skin of my teeth, but it's futile because in the next breath, it's gone. It dissipates like smoke in the wind. The only thing that's left is a hollow in the space between my ribs where that spark of happiness once resided. With another flash of white, I'm transported somewhere else as the Fates' warped voices ring in my ears on a loop.

"When the blood moon hangs from the sky,

and the clock strikes midnight,

The sacrifice will come forth.

At the twenty-third circle of life,

The Daughter of Starlight and Shadows,

will open the gates and raise the black death,

bathing the world in blood and despair.

When all virtue is lost,

a soul will be taken.

Ravens will circle the skies,

their master awaken.

A choice will be made,
One will be dead.
Time will sit still in the night
And the world of the living
will meld with the beyond."

Images of the ground cracking wide open while bubbling lava rises to the surface and hellfire, scorching through flesh and bone, assault my brain as the chant continues like terrifying echo chamber. Thousands of demons flying freely, crawling on the streets, feasting on the innocent, leaving gory destruction in their wake, a thick river of blood overflowing, coursing through the mass of cadavers lined streets, people wailing in horror.

When I come back to reality, it's to screams. At first, I think I'm still hearing the gory reverb, but then I realize it's Yana. The planes of her face contort in abject terror as she shakes Thalia—who is still catatonic—her eyes encased in white. Dread sinks its icy hooks beneath every layer of skin.

Tears stream down Yana's cheeks. "Thalia! They're here! We need to run."

The unmistakable clash of metal as two swords meet slices through the air. I don't waste another second.

I jump up and barrel out the door.

37

Iris

I almost eat shit as I narrowly avoid the swinging blade coming straight for my throat. Dropping low, I swipe the blond fae's legs from under him. A loud *crack* resounds as the wooden stairs give out under his weight. That shiny armor he's wearing must be heavy as fuck.

With a quick sweep of my eyes, I assess the situation: Kaiden and Malik are each sword fighting a golden-clad soldier while Rhett uses air against a fire-wielding one. Sam is nowhere in sight.

Fuck.

"Kaiden!" I shout when another fae sneaks up on him. He expertly parries the attack. However, Malik isn't as nimble. The blade slashes through the skin on his shoulder, and blood gushes from the wound in streams.

I don't have time to dwell on it. I snatch the sword the fae dropped when he fell. But I'm not prepared for him to be so inhumanely fast. When I straighten, I'm met with a stunning blow to my temple. White-hot pain erupts in every single nerve ending. Ears ringing, I fall back against the open door. I lose consciousness for a few seconds, only to be brought back when he stomps on the hand I have wrapped around the hilt of his blade. *Snap. Snap. Snap.* My bones crunch. I bite my tongue until I taste copper to stop from screaming.

He grabs me in a chokehold and lifts me. The sword clatters against the wood as my lungs scream for air. He keeps me just far enough that I can't gouge his eyes out with my swinging hands. "You dirty rat," he seethes, nostrils flaring as though he's an angry bull. "You have no right to touch something so sacred."

I hack a glob of spit and blood at his face before I put every ounce of energy I possess into sending my sole right at his crotch. He lets out a sharp curse, then drops me like a sack of potatoes. My teeth gnash as my knees meet the wooden planks. This time, when he charges, I'm prepared—my uninjured hand grabs the sword's hilt before I spring upward. With an agile whirl, I'm behind him. However, I'm not used to the sword's hefty weight, so my movement is jerky as I thrust it to slice through the tendons at the back of his knees. His howl is music to my ears when he crumbles behind me.

"How's that for a dirty rat?" I say, turning. I whack him on the back of his head with my hilt. Hard. There's a loud *thud* when he falls.

Sam screams. I forget all about my aching muscles as I sprint toward the sound with everything I've got. I skid to a halt when a behemoth of a fae comes out of the tree line, an elbow crooked around Sam's throat while she struggles like a fish out of water, her feet in the air. Blood is trickling down her nose, and her left eye is swollen shut.

The blazing heat of a thousand suns kindles a firestorm in my veins. "Let her go!"

He raises an unimpressed eyebrow, as if I'm nothing more than an annoying insect. "Drop your weapons now, or I will kill her," he says in a bored tone.

"Don't!" Sam wheezes out.

A slow, feline smile spreads across his face as he unsheathes his sword, pressing the tip of the blade at Sam's carotid. Blood seeps out from the superficial cut. She freezes.

"You motherfucker," Malik snaps. If looks could kill, the fae man would already be a pile of bones on the ground. Kaiden, Malik, and I drop our swords while Rhett lets his arms fall limply at the sides of his body.

The fae man narrows his eyes at Malik before glowering at the other fae knights in blatant disgust. Judging by the lion head on his golden chest plate and the ornate armor he's wearing, he must be their commander. "Bested by human rats." He spits on the ground. "You're all a disgrace, not worthy of serving the crown. You're to clean the latrines for the next six months."

"Yes, sir," the soldiers collectively murmur, their shoulders slumped.

He tilts his chin toward the cottage. "Bring me the oracle," he orders. While six more soldiers march our way from the forest, I chance a quick look at Kaiden. Aside from a few cuts and the giant bruise already forming on his jaw, he seems okay.

The relief is short-lived, though. "No! Please! Stop! She's only a child," Yana howls as she's dragged out of the cottage by the hair.

Then a shaking Thalia is pushed out with the tip of a sword between her bony shoulder blades. Despite the silent tears streaming down her face, she holds her chin high. She suddenly looks ten years older. And braver than us all.

My trembling fingers unconsciously reach for one of the daggers I normally carry at my belt. *One, two, three, four,* I count in order to stop myself from running toward them and pummeling the asshole behind her until he's six feet under.

The fae commander's arctic gaze finds Thalia. There's no trace of sympathy in his eyes — only a thick sheet of ice. "You are charged with high treason against the Imperial Court of Seelie. You're to be executed in front of the king and his loyal servants, the Seelie fae."

"No! Please!" Yana begs, crawling toward Thalia. She lets out an *oomph* when a soldier plants a boot in the middle of her back, flattening her to the ground.

"Kill the big-mouthed one. She's becoming a nuisance," the commander snaps.

Before I can blink, the soldier has already thrust his blade through the center of Yana's chest.

"I love you," are her last gurgled words to Thalia. Blood paints the ground in crimson streaks of violence. I can feel her soul — a ball of blinding light — clinging desperately to her body. It's useless, though, because her strained breaths fade with brutal finality.

"Yana!" Thalia launches herself at her sister's lifeless body. The soldier grabs the back of her dress, halting her momentum.

I'm grinding my teeth so hard, I'm surprised they haven't turned to dust. The only thing stopping me from moving is the fear that Sam will meet the same fate at their callous hands. And I can't have that, however painful it is to hear Thalia's whimpers. Somehow, they slash deeper than the most deafening wails ever could. I might not be able to do anything right now, but I make Thalia a silent promise that I will find a way to avenge her sister's death.

"Should we kill the humans and the traitor, too?" one of the soldiers asks. I'm assuming the traitor is Rhett for aligning himself with us.

Tilting his head, the commander contemplates his decision. "No. We haven't had a good spectacle in months, so we will execute them all in the square as an example. Bring the chains."

"And Evander?"

The commander's upper lip curls in revulsion as he casts a withering glance at the fae I knocked out earlier. "Weaklings have no place serving the Seelie court. Leave him here for the beasts to feast."

38

Iris

The carriage—or better said, the prison on wheels—rattles as it hurtles over another pothole. I grunt when the metal bars dig into my lower back. It feels as if the rapid *clip-clop* of the horse's hooves is stomping on my brain rather than the grass. I don't know if it's because of what has now become normal migraines or because of the blow I received to the temple.

To top it all off, I don't remember ever being so tired in my entire life. It goes further than bone deep. The chains they shackled us with are not only spelled to tighten at the slightest attempt of removal, but they also suck the energy out of you. And it's all made worse by the way my stomach is sticking to my spine. They only gave us small portions of water—enough to keep us alive but not to satiate the thirst in this sweltering heat. And why would they feed us? We're going to be executed like the human rats they think we are, anyway.

They can all go fuck themselves.

Especially their commander.

"If we somehow manage to escape, and I ever tell you again that I'm going on a diet, you have my permission to stab me. Multiple times," Sam half mumbles–half whispers from beside me because Thalia is finally asleep, curled up between us, her head resting in Sam's lap. She has been in a state of shock since they shoved us in here three days ago and hasn't said a word or slept. Understandably so.

"How's the eye?" I ask in the same low tone while I squint against the glare of the broiling sun to scan her face. At least she can open it a smidge. But the area around it, aside from being an angry deep purple, is still swollen.

Fuck me. I'm regretting the decision to wear my hellseeker gear after we bathed in that creek. It feels as though I'm cooking from the inside out on high heat.

"Not much different since you last asked twenty minutes ago. Seriously, I'm okay. Stop worrying about me." She blows out a weak, frustrated breath. "Your hand?"

"Eh, I've had worse. But it still hurts like a bitch." Those accelerated healing abilities would come in real handy right now. Being reduced to nothing more than a human sucks ass. I guess I never realized how good I had it before because my injuries would never last this long. The gash on my cheek is starting to scab, and the itchiness is driving me up the wall. It's incredible how something so small can be this annoying.

Raising both of her shackled hands so she can wipe the perspiration beading her forehead, she adds, "Gah, I would kill for an extra-large pepperoni pizza right now."

"Or some shrimp tacos from *Tu Tia Loca*," I retort.

Malik lets out a painful, muted groan. He's seated across from us between Kaiden and Rhett. "Or a burger and a cold beer."

"Or a juicy steak and a salad," Kaiden chimes in. They all look as exhausted as I feel, with cuts and various bruises marring their faces and bodies. Every time Kaiden glances at the side of my face, where that asshole punched me, his jaw — which is still swollen — turns into an iron bar of tension.

"A salad? Dude," Sam scoffs. "Salad as a comfort food is a fucking crime against humanity."

"Throw some mac and cheese at me, and I'll be a happy camper." We all turn toward Rhett, who did a piss-poor attempt at a Southern accent. A good chunk of his left eyebrow and the lower half of his shirt have been burned off in the fight. At least he still has eyelashes.

I huff a laugh. "How very American of you."

"Are you going to finally tell us what that prophecy said?" Kaiden inquires, his tone losing all traces of humor.

I flick my gaze to the two soldiers guarding our wheeled cell at the rear of the small convoy. They're on the verge of nodding off in their saddles, so I don't think they're listening. Glancing down at Thalia, I observe the steady rise and fall of her chest. I've been worried that talking about the prophecy would agitate her, given everything that happened after...But if I'm being completely honest, that is just an excuse. I don't want to talk about the prophecy because the implications are a bitter pill to swallow — scratch that, they're more a boulder the size of China.

Swallowing thickly, I finally say, "Yeah."

I recite the prophecy for them. I've repeated it so many times in my head these past days, trying to decipher its meaning, that I know it by heart.

"Daughter of Starlight and Shadows...where have I heard that before?" Sam asks when I finish.

"It's from the book about ancient demons Iris bargained for with a dark witch," Kaiden cuts in. I can almost feel the wheels spinning in his head at the speed of light while his brows furrow.

"Oh yeah. What did it say again?"

Kaiden recites it before I can:

"'Beware of the shadow that lurks in the dead of the night. It whispers of forgotten souls and eclipses the light of life.

"'Beware of the nocturnal wind that carries the mournful wails of those denied peaceful rest.

"'Beware the dying breath, for the umbra seeks to ensnare those who linger between worlds, compelling them to a never-ending, soul-stealing twilight.

"'No escape shall be granted, for the umbra's grip tightens, and the stolen souls become eternally entwined in the ominous dance of celestial thievery.

"'A cosmic cataclysm, foretold in the shadows and unleashed at the hands of the Harbinger of Death, the Daughter of Starlight and Shadows.'"

"The twenty-third circle of life," Sam muses, quoting Thalia's prophecy. The color in her cheeks drains in slow increments. "Wait... you're twenty-three. The umbra came through the Hell portal right on the night of your birthday. And when Erik attacked you at Sin, you said shadows started emanating from your body."

I nod, my lips pressed into a tight line.

"I don't like where this is going," she continues, worry etched in the lines around her mouth. "But, Iris, what if *you* are the Daughter of Starlight and Shadows?"

"The night Adrianna saved me, while I blacked out, I had another memory flashback. I was unintentionally eavesdropping on a conversation she and my mother were having when I was a kid. They were looking for an oracle because a seraph warned Mom about the prophecy...and she was desperate, I could tell. She said it was already difficult keeping me hidden because of my rising power."

Kaiden's accusing gaze grates on my skin like sandpaper. "You didn't say anything."

I huff. "And why should I? Because I trust you wholeheartedly?" I tilt my chin and raise an eyebrow at the way his nostrils flare. But his anger is only a thinly veiled mask because, behind it, there's something else—pure, unadulterated fear.

So, he figured it out. At least, now I know he didn't lie about this, too, because there's also shock there. But what if he—

"When I first sent you the translation of the Enochian text, you said you weren't sure what it meant. Did you suspect it had something to do with me?" I blurt out.

He sucks on his teeth but doesn't say a word.

"That's what I thought. Another lie to add to the list," I snark. And once again, I'm bleeding.

"I didn't lie," he counters.

"Oh no, you didn't. You were purposely vague. Bravo, you're a true champion at skirting the truth." I applaud mockingly. But my shackles hinder my movement, so it doesn't have the effect I wanted.

"The prophecy is talking about the Hell gates, isn't it?" Malik says grimly, cutting the suffocating tension. "And the Daughter of Starlight and Shadows is the key to opening them."

"But that would jumpstart the Apocalypse," Sam squeaks. The shock must have made her forget she replied to something Malik had said.

"'A cosmic cataclysm, foretold in the shadows and unleashed at the hands of the Harbinger of Death, the Daughter of Starlight and Shadows,'" I repeat the last part of the text about the umbra demons. "Or the black death, according to the prophecy."

What I don't tell them is that among the bloodbath the Fates allowed me to see, I was at the epicenter, commanding the umbra demons to steal souls.

The silence is loaded — as if one of us stepped on a landmine.

Kind of funny that I've been struggling to find my place in the world when fate had already decided it for me hundreds of years ago — as a weapon of mass destruction. I'm nothing more than a means to an end. A pawn. The Universe's punchline. I might seem apathetic on the outside, but I want to grab destiny by the throat and scream in its face.

It's not fair.

It's *not* fair.

It's not fucking fair.

I would give away all my powers and live as a human for the rest of my life if it meant I wouldn't be the Daughter of Starlight and Shadows anymore.

Malik pops a shoulder. "Hey, at least look at the bright side. You can't exactly jumpstart the Apocalypse if you're executed."

I snort while Sam glowers at him.

"Shut the fuck up, or you won't make it to the gallows," Kaiden bites back, the vein on his temple pulsing as though it's about to burst any second now.

Whoa. Way to make it awkward, Kaiden.

"It was just a joke, man. Calm down." Malik turns to me, a sheepish smile pulling at his lips. "Sorry."

"It's okay. I thought it was funny."

Determination steels Sam's tone. "Well, I didn't because I'm not accepting this as fate. We will somehow make it out of here. And the first blood moon in centuries will fall on New Year's Eve, so we have a few months to figure out how to stop it."

"The blood moon forces the veil between Hell and Earth to thin, right?" Rhett inquires, a stricken look on his face. This is quite a lot to take in, so no wonder he has stayed silent until now.

"Yeah, it's wrongly believed that it happens every year on Samhain. While that's true in Faerie's case, if that happened with Hell, a lot more demons would breach through, causing massacres each year," I answer.

"Correct me if I'm wrong, but according to the Celestial Treaty, if anything disrupts the balance like, say, opening the gates of Hell, the archangels and seraphim would wipe out Earth and close Heaven," Rhett says.

I shudder. "Exactly. If all demons escape topside, they will consume souls by mass possession and slaughter all humans to feast on their flesh. Then, if by any chance you escape the beasts, the Archangels will come down to wipe the scraps and blast the demons with their *illum*. I don't know which is worse, being the main course meal or burning alive."

"Kaiden, you told Iris that the uprisings in Hell are getting worse by the day, right?" Sam interrupts.

He nods stiffly.

"So that's why there's a bounty on you," she tells me. "They somehow found out about the prophecy, and they want to use you to open the gates." This is the same conclusion I came to three days ago. It's made pretty clear by their matching frowns that Kaiden and Malik realized this, too. "Okay, so we search for a way to stop the prophecy. There must be a book or a spell or something. Or we could try finding who's behind the mutinies in Hell and kill them, so the demons would stop coming for you, at least while we figure it out."

Malik arches an eyebrow. "Seriously, freckles, you want to counter a prophecy with a spell? And we've been trying for years to find out who's behind the resistance. Not even Lucifer could, that's why he's in hiding."

"I wasn't talking to you," she snaps, then narrows her eyes. "Call me freckles one more time."

"Let's not get ahead of ourselves. We first have to escape this place. Any ideas on how we could do that?" I intervene because a hungry and tired Sam is never a good combination. She's about to bite off his head any second now.

"We would need a portal for that. And I'm pretty confident we're going straight toward one," Rhett whispers, while sneaking a look at the guards to make sure they're not paying attention. Then, slowly and awkwardly, because of the shackles gluing his wrists, he slides out a small portion of the compass from his pocket before shoving it back in.

"Whoa. You still have it?" After they chained us, they patted us carefully for any weapons and threw all our things on a bonfire before we left that clearing, so to say I'm flabbergasted doesn't even cover it. I'm still furious they burned my whip.

The corner of his lips tilts upward. It's the first time Rhett has shown something akin to a smile since I met him in New Orleans. "The best part about magical objects is that you can make them disappear and appear at whim if you know the right words." He tilts his chin to point behind us. "We're about two hours away from Aurelis — the capital. The sunset is approaching, so they will most likely hold the execution tomorrow and move us to a cell in the meantime. We can talk more about this later."

We all turn. The blinding light bouncing off the approaching gargantuan castle sears my retinas. I have to blink a few times to adjust my vision. In blatant contradiction to the plundered villages — reeking of sadness and death — the capital's fortified walls stand proud, and the castle looms from the highest point on the hill with gleaming spires reaching for the cloudless sky.

"Fuck. I think I just gave my eyes third-degree burns. What is that, real gold?" Malik asks, a grimace pinching the planes of his face.

Rhett lets out a mirthless chuckle. "Yeah, in fact, it is."

BRINY AIR TINGLES my nose as the convoy passes over the wooden drawbridge on a background of clattering hooves. Malik whistles when he takes in the moat that must be deeper than forty feet. We stop in front of the portcullis, flanked by two giant statues of gilded lions. A loud screech erupts from its mechanism as it's lifted by the two helmeted soldiers manning the gate. However, we don't move. My ears ring at the loud horn announcing our arrival.

The commander — who's carrying a flag — and the rest of the Seelie soldiers lead their horses at a strutting pace in front of the carriage with an air of importance. One might assume we are the most dangerous war criminals, given how they puff out their chests. What a joke. Especially since the swarm of people crowding the cobblestone streets, windows, and open doors stare at us from gaunt faces. Dejection clings to their gazes. Some show a spark of interest when they notice our ears. It fizzles the second their eyes drop to a now-awake Thalia, though. That spark turns to anger, but it's overtaken by resigned lethargy.

Thalia has crumbled far within herself — as if she's trying to disappear into thin air. I squeeze her small, trembling hand in mine and offer what I hope is a reassuring smile, but she doesn't reciprocate and only hides further under the curtain of snow-white hair.

The houses are made of the same gilded stone as the stronghold's walls. However, most of them are crumbling under neglect. A few even have broken windows that are boarded up. In comparison, the sparkling walls of the castle reflect the fiery horizon like a burnished mirror, casting everything in a golden glow. Instead of creating beauty, it only serves to enhance the disparity.

"Grammie always read stories to me of the fae folk at bedtime when I was little. She used to tell me how they're beautiful beyond reason, and the riches found in their cities is a sight to behold. But these people, they're…"

"Emaciated?" I offer.

"Yeah, and just…sad. I mean, they're beautiful, sure, but —"

Rhett's tone is bitter as he cuts Sam off. "That's what war does. For fifty years, King Orion has drained all the land's resources for his army while his people starve. Yet he feasts at the palace alongside his noblemen. Why do you think so many of us cross back to the human world, even though we're still viciously hunted by vampires?"

We advance further into the portion of the city that reminds me of the slums at the edge of Ashville. The cloying smell of urine and garbage stabs at the back of my eyes and burns a trail straight to my brain. If I thought the houses looked bad before, these are in a state of ruin, while fae that resemble wraiths wander the streets blank-faced or curled up in shaded corners. I wonder what's in those bottles they cling to with desperate hands. It must be something to numb their suffering.

Narrow, barred windows line the portion of the stronghold's wall we are approaching. We enter through another portcullis — this time smaller — but heavily guarded. The carriage comes to a jarring stop. As one soldier dismounts, I notice half of the convoy is gone. They probably separated at some point, and the douchebag commander is not among them anymore.

When the soldier ambles toward us and unlocks the fortified door at the rear of the carriage, my eyes snap to the other set of keys dangling from his belt. I elbow Sam before tilting my head subtly toward them. The movement doesn't go unnoticed by Kaiden, Malik, or Rhett. We push up one by one at the speed of snails. My head swims with the movement while pins and needles follow in the wake of blood circulating again in my extremities.

"Make haste," the soldier snaps.

Sam and Thalia are the first to get out. Malik and I follow. The second he steps next to me, I push him as hard as I can into the soldier, catching him by surprise. "You fucking, bastard," I bellow.

"Whoa. What the fuck, Iris?" he plays into it. At our back, Kaiden and Rhett have gotten into their own fight, hurling insults at each other. The rest of the soldiers dismount in a frenzy, running toward us.

I rush at Malik. "Do you think I'm stupid? I saw how much water you drank. You think you're better than all of us, huh?"

Kaiden and Rhett are tackled to the ground with matching grunts. Malik takes advantage of the momentary chaos to snatch the keys and let them fall to the pavement. He kicks them toward Sam. At the same time, the guard unsheathes his sword and points it at me. I halt, millimeters away from the tip. In the corner of my eye, Sam is bending while pretending to tie her shoelaces. She palms the keys she hid under her sole before slipping them into her hiking boot.

"Kneel!" the soldier bellows, spittle flying out of his mouth. His face is the color of a pickled beet while his eyes bulge out of his head.

I can't stop myself from throwing him a defiant glare. Before I can move, a heavy boot collides with the back of my left knee. The impact is teeth rattling as I land on my palms and knees. White-hot pain pulses from my injured hand all the way to my shoulder.

"You filthy bitch," he spews, elbowing Malik out of the way before closing the space between us and fisting my hair. Strands snap from the root as he forces my head backward. He punches me so hard, my head flies to the side. Skin splits. Blood gushes out. I swallow the scream bubbling up my throat. The dipshit hit me right in the same place as the fae I fought back in that clearing.

"Motherfucking piece of shit," Kaiden growls. I can hear him thrashing while spewing more profanities.

Anger prickles the back of my neck. It trickles down until it ignites every cell, but I can't risk putting us in more danger right now. So I clench my aching jaw and breathe through it until the trembling in my limbs subsides.

"Stand, bitch! And if I have to wait one more second, I'll shove my sword down your throat."

The effort of the fight has completely drained me. Not only that, but the world is whirling around me in fuzzy circles, so when I try to get up, my body careens to the side. Malik is quick to catch me by the elbow and stabilize me.

One of the other soldiers shoves us toward the open metal door. "Fucking move already."

I glance over my shoulder as I advance alongside Malik. Kaiden now has a shiner to match Sam's. "You okay?" he mouths, wrath stiffening his spine as he catalogs every single injury of mine in his head and obviously makes a hit list.

I nod, then turn my head back when the soldier snaps again that we're being too slow. We're led through a narrow corridor that smells of mildew and despair. At least it offers a bit of reprieve from the blistering heat. At the end, we descend a set of spiraling stairs. The low-lit sconces throw creepy shadows over the grimy stone walls of the empty cells. They separate us, locking me, Sam, and Thalia in one cell and Kaiden, Malik, and Rhett in the other across the hall. The soldier's disappearing footsteps echo in the cavernous space.

"You got them?" Rhett asks after waiting a few minutes to make sure no one can hear us.

"Yeah," Sam replies. She retrieves the keys from her boot, straightens, and frees Thalia from her shackles, then moves to me.

When the chains are finally off, I take my first full breath in days. The rush of energy flooding me is better than a shot of adrenaline.

"If I had my magic, that bastard would be nothing more than a cockroach that I would stomp over and over again," she clips out. She turns to me then, and regret shines in her emerald gaze. "I'm sorry I didn't do or say anything. But I was afraid something would happen to Thalia since she was right next to me —"

"Sam, it's okay," I cut her off as I take the keys and unlock her restraints, then pull her into a hug.

"Holy shit. It's like I drank ten energy drinks and a bucket of coffee." She gags a bit before stepping back. "I don't know who stinks worse. You or me."

A hearty laugh leaves me because she's right.

"As heartwarming as this is, we're wilting here," Malik drawls with a crooked smile.

I throw him the keys, and they get rid of their chains.

"We need to put them back when they start rotations, though," Rhett says.

"What now?" I ask while massaging the deep stiffness from my wrists.

"Now, we make a plan."

39

Iris

Six ropes flutter in the slight breeze from the gallows placed at the center of the town square. The commander leads the convoy while his soldiers make a path through the throng of people who regard our wheeled cage with the same apathetic gazes as yesterday. They seem as happy to be here as we are. When I look up, the light that bounces off the king's bejeweled crown stabs me in the eye. About thirty knights guard the dais to the right of the gallows, where he's sitting atop an ornate chair that could rival a throne.

In stark contrast to the fae people gathered in masses to watch the spectacle, the king is a stout, bearded man, his giant belly spilling over his belt. What I assume is the queen and their children are occupying the other four chairs. All of them have gold-spun hair and wear fine embroidered silks. It's sickening how healthy and well-fed they look.

The carriage jerks to a stop. If we don't succeed, we're fucked.

"Ready?" Kaiden whispers.

We all nod—even Thalia.

I square my shoulders and inhale a lungful of calming air.

Dismounting with feline ease, the commander strides toward us while one of the soldiers unlocks the fortified door. I didn't realize last night that the douchebag would be personally escorting us.

I push Kaiden out of the way to get to the door. He gives me a *what the fuck* look because I'm deviating from the plan. I mumble under my breath, "He's mine."

Kaiden's anger is palpable, but before he can say or do anything, I jump out. He follows, then Malik and Rhett, while Sam and Thalia stay behind. The commander glares at me over his hawkish nose. "Move!" he bellows as he reaches to grab my arm.

He doesn't get far enough, though, because I snap out of the chains shackling my wrists. The rush of energy hits me like a tidal wave—somehow a hundred times stronger than yesterday. I swipe his sword from its holster in a fluid move. "Surprise, motherfucker." I smirk as I drive the blade straight through his throat. "This is for Yana and for laying your dirty hands on my best friend."

The planes of his face contort in equal parts shock and anger. Disbelief follows. Blood sprays all over me when I pull out the blade. He resembles a gaping fish as his mouth opens and closes before crumbling to the ground. He falls face first while his dirty soul slips away, armor clattering against the pavement.

Silence engulfs the square.

Then, the crowd erupts into chaos.

Half of the knights guarding the dais sprint toward us. What I'm not prepared for is the people to shove them back and start a riot, forming a protective wall between us. However, the ten soldiers who were part of the convoy dismount in a frenzy and charge. I whirl just in time to parry a sword coming at me strong enough that the force of the blow reverberates through my entire body. The "Death to the tyrant king!" chants coming from the angry mob stifle the loud metallic *clang*. It's like they were sitting on a barrel full of gunpowder, and we were the spark that made it explode.

Ignoring the pulsing pain in my right hand, I tighten my grip on the hilt. I might be dehydrated, malnourished, and powerless, but adrenaline and pure rage fuel my attack. Years of training and muscle memory take over. I shift effortlessly through low and high guards in a graceful dance. Then I see it—the hesitation. It's all I need to thrust my blade through his side where there's a gap in the armor plates. Blood gushes out as he shrieks. I put him to sleep with a blow to his temple.

I turn just as Kaiden kicks the asshole who punched me yesterday square in the chest, sending him sprawling backward. He disarms him with ease and snatches the sword from the air. Tracing a wide arc, Kaiden decapitates him in one clean move.

The furious crowd swallows the rest of the soldiers from the convoy. However, they start fighting back with magic. One of them is using water as a cannon and another is setting the civilians on fire.

Horns of distress resound over the plaza.

Even more soldiers are going to swarm this place, and it's about to turn into a bloody massacre. We need to go.

Now.

Rhett has already taken his place at the carriage's driver seat behind the horse, and Malik hops inside to join Sam and Thalia. I dash toward them at the same time as Kaiden, and I finally have hope that we're going to get home in one piece.

In the next second, though, we're all forced to our knees by a high-pitch sound I've never heard before. It pierces my brain like an icepick. The ground beneath us shakes and cracks as if we're experiencing a magnitude seven earthquake. I slap my palms over my ears, but that does nothing to muffle the horrible noise that could only be described as nails on a chalkboard intensified by a millionfold. My eardrums bleed.

Forcing my neck to turn, I look back toward the source: the king. He's standing on the dais with an open mouth like he's screaming. A few fae start convulsing right in front of me while foaming at the mouth. This is how we die.

No! I can't let that happen.

That's when something prickles at the nape of my neck. The weird sensation continues to flow through me until it saturates every cell, picking up strength by the second. Without preamble, it ruptures. Explodes from my very nucleus outward like an atomic bomb.

The world turns black.

I am no longer Iris. I am no more than an absence of light seeking the poisoned core that resides inside the king's chest.

My shadows form a claw that tears through skin, muscle, and bone. I yank the fetid ball of energy and snuff out its remaining light. I have no need for something so rotten. The vibrations stop.

But there are so many other souls here. Ripe for the taking. It would be so easy to reach over and —

"*Iris! Snap out of it!*" Someone pounds desperately at the fortified door of my mind. No. Not someone — *him*. The one we love, our *home*.

In the next blink, I'm pushed back in the driver's seat of my mind. For a moment, I think I've blacked out because I see nothing, no light. But then I realize it's *me* — I'm the epicenter of the darkness. The inky blanket that enveloped the square is emanating from my body.

Then, the dais bursts into deep scarlet flames, illuminating the king's cadaver. Someone screams bloody murder over the ringing in my ears.

Akin to a cord pulled too tight, the shadows snap before retreating. I double over and start heaving from the influx of overwhelming power blistering me from the inside out as it all flows back into me.

Holy fuck.

I killed the king.

I ripped his soul right out of his body.

That must be what I did to Erik—I rotted him by snatching his soul. But it still doesn't explain the state of those demons at Adrianna's apartment because demons are soulless.

I'm pulled to my feet by Kaiden, whose irises are a deep crimson over an obsidian background. His lips move. My discombobulated mind can't comprehend a single word, though. I grit my teeth and push through the debilitating pain as we run toward the barred carriage, then jump inside.

The soldiers elbowing through the masses in a frenzy to get to the burning dais don't pay us any more attention. Rhett grabs hold of the reins, spurring the horse into a gallop. We fly over cobblestones at warp speed as Malik murmurs something under his breath. He's surely using magic to make the horse run faster. The carriage whines and trembles as if it's going to snap in two.

"Was that you, Iris?" Sam asks, eyebrows raised to her hairline as she holds on to the metal bars for dear life with one hand, the other wrapped around a stoic-faced Thalia. "Your eyes—they're violet again."

I can't respond. I hit my knees as the nausea and violent heaves come back with a vengeance. Nothing but bile comes out. Blood is coursing down my nose in rivulets while the sensation of being stabbed directly in the brain by a fiery dagger completely overtakes me. Everything spins.

"Why is she bleeding?" She inhales sharply before shrieking, "The barrier!"

"Malik!" Kaiden bellows.

"I'm here," he says and I feel his hands at my temples. I sway as if

I'm on a ship navigating treacherous waters but a strong arm banded across my middle is keeping me steady.

"The cracks have widened," Malik says. "I can only put a Band-Aid over them and hope for the best."

"Do it."

After only a few moments that feel like lifetimes, the world comes back into focus and the fog of black magic retreats.

"Welcome back, angel," Kaiden murmurs as he places a soft kiss on my forehead. I almost melt into it, then I remember he spoke to me in my mind, back in the square. No, that's crazy. It was only a hallucination, right? It had to be. Surely it was my conscience trying to reach me in any way possible.

"Was I out long?" I croak.

"Only a minute or two," he answers, then shouts to Rhett, "How much time do we have left until the portal opens?"

Rhett takes out his compass. "Less than ten minutes."

The gargantuan castle looms over us in all its garish glory. We're so close. As we take a sharp left turn, soldiers on top of horses start pouring from the other end of the street. They rush at us—swords at the ready.

Rhett sends a blast of air, stopping their momentum while Malik kicks the door open and jumps. He shifts mid-air. A majestic nine-foot panther lands into a nimble crouch in his place.

Sam's jaw is on the floor. "Holy Hecate!"

Malik jumps over the carriage to meet them. He roars. The horses throw off their riders and scatter. More than half of the soldiers take their lead, and the remaining ones form a wall, but they shake so violently that they resemble leaves in the wind. Whatever spell Malik cast still affects our horse, which remains oblivious to its surroundings. He only forges forward.

It seems Mother Draia has finally approved of our business here in Faerie.

Sam lifts her hands. Leafy vines shoot from the ground, parting the soldiers like Moses did the Red Sea while immobilizing their bodies and pinning them flat to the houses on each side. Malik continues to run in front of the carriage in panther form.

The iron gates of the castle come into view. Archers shoot at us from their outposts, but Kaiden turns the arrows to mere ashes before they can reach us. Rhett blows the gate open with a tornado, so we zip through the courtyard as Sam puts up hedge walls between us and the incoming soldiers. When we reach the stairs, Kaiden helps me down, then does the same for Thalia and Sam.

"You trust me?" He crouches before Thalia, locking their gazes.

She nibbles on her lower lip before nodding.

"Good, we're getting you out of here, kiddo. I know this is scary, but I promise you I will do everything in my power to keep you safe."

I never even considered having kids until this moment. But seeing how gentle Kaiden is with Thalia has me yearning for a future I know is out of the realm of possibility for me — us.

I take a fraction of a second to mourn that unattainable future, then shove it down alongside all my shattered hopes. He picks up Thalia and we all dash toward the stairs as Rhett joins us from the front of the carriage. Malik is already waiting in front of the gargantuan door.

Sam flicks her wrist to open it. A human woman holding a broom pales at the sight of us spilling over the threshold.

"Where is the entrance to the towers?" I ask.

She points a trembling hand to her right before scurrying away. Our hurried footsteps echo loudly against the ornate plastered walls. The corridor goes on and on and on. Sam is panting; she's doing everything she can to keep up, but she's running behind.

"Malik!" I shout. He slows down. "Can you give Sam a ride?"

He offers what resembles a human nod, then stops and bends his knees.

"Are you out of your fucking mind?!? I'm not doing that!" Sam spews, throwing daggers at me with her eyes.

"It's either that or I give you a piggyback ride," I snap.

"Three minutes," Rhett cuts in.

She sucks on her teeth. Snaps her eyes closed. Opens them. "Fine." She hops onto Malik's back and circles her arms around his neck. She lets out a surprised squeak as Malik bolts. A wooden door greets us at the end of the corridor. Rhett kicks it open before we ascend the spiraling stairs of the tower. Heavy footfalls resound behind us, and Sam puts up another green wall at our back.

Despite having my enhanced strength and speed back, I'm about to hack out my lungs from the effort when we finally reach the top of the tower. I welcome the powerful gust of wind that cools my overheated cheeks and makes the strands of hair that escaped my braid flail about.

Malik lowers his body for Sam to jump off before shifting back. We all bend over the stone banister to look at the ring of fire that punched through the cloud right below us. The soldiers still using their swords to hack through the hedge walls Sam erected earlier resemble ants from this height.

"I'm going last and I will use air to push you toward the portal like we discussed, okay?" Rhett says.

There's a collective murmur of approval.

Malik is the first to jump. He makes it through without a hitch.

Kaiden passes Thalia to me so he can climb over to the other side of the banister. His eyes lock with mine as he takes her back, and the softness in his gaze pulls at my heartstrings. Is he having the same thoughts I did earlier?

"Ready?" he asks her.

Her "yes" is nothing more than a whisper.

I hold my breath as I watch them dive, but they make it as easily as Malik.

Rhett looks at the compass again. "You need to hurry. The portal is going to close soon."

I help Sam over the rail.

Hand in hand, we leap.

Air rushes around me as gravity pulls us down. Then the world whirls.

40

Iris

The portal spits us out somewhere green. That's all I can make out through the blur. Sam's elbow stabs me between the ribs viciously as we roll in a flurry of tangled limbs on the ground at lightning speed. We bounce against something soft that stops our momentum, and it takes me a few moments to discern which way is up or down. I wait until my vision clears somewhat before disentangling myself from Sam and pushing up into a seated position, but the horizon is still doing pirouettes. I press the heels of my palms into my eyes.

"Fuck, I think you gave me another black eye," Sam mumbles from beside me.

"And your freakishly sharp elbow almost pierced my lung," I retort.

"You all right?" I startle slightly when Kaiden materializes in front of us.

He offers a hand to pull me up.

"A little crumpled, but it's better than falling from the sky," I respond as I find my footing.

"Or drowning to death," Sam adds dryly, waving her hand to retract the bed of moss she created for us to land on.

The humid air is thick with the smell of mud, something flowery, and rotting vegetation. Thankfully, it's far from the scent of rot we encountered in the Wasting Woods, which seemed to permeate to the depths of your soul akin to an insidious shadow.

The lush canopy of gleaming leaves above us rustles. We all look up when Rhett floats through them on his way down as if carried by a gentle breeze until his feet touch the ground. "Everyone got here in one piece?" he inquires.

"Yeah," Malik says while pushing away a giant fern so Thalia can pass.

"Good thing you guys got your powers back just in time, or our plan would have gone to shi—shasta." Rhett cringes as his eyes land on Thalia.

She scoffs while rolling her eyes. "You've said far worse in my presence."

We all gasp because this is the first time she's let out more than a word in days, and she sounded so much like her sister.

"We were reckless thinking we could make it out without them, huh?" I say because I don't want her to retreat into her shell again, and her cheeks are already turning cherry-red from being the center of attention. "Why do you think Mother Draia gave us our abilities back?"

"I'm not sure. Maybe it had something to do with us starting a riot and finally waking up the Seelie fae to stand tall against their oppressor."

Malik wrinkles his nose. "So where do you guys think we are because if I don't take a shower soon, I'm going to lose my sense of smell forever."

"It's clearly a rainforest," I muse as I turn to take in my surroundings. Ropy vines are snaking down tall trees, while the sounds of beating wings, buzzing insects, and what I'm pretty sure are monkeys howling surround us.

"Well, judging by those heliconias and the emerald green epiphytes right there, we're in South America — Costa Rica, more precisely," Sam tells us while rocking on her feet to stand after refusing Kaiden's help with a scowl. Guess he's back on the shit list. She already looks better, and I assume it's because of the abundant vegetation surrounding us, not to mention her magic being back.

"Malik, can you do a location spell so we can find our way back to civilization?" Kaiden asks.

SILVERY STRANDS OF light entangle in a dance on the ceiling I've been staring at forever. Even though the mattress is as soft as a cloud beneath me, and my body is screaming in protest that I should sleep, I can't. The prophecy's weight is heavier and far more crippling than the chains they used to shackle us in Faerie.

Not only that, but I stripped someone of their soul with my shadows. The fact that I can do that is mind-boggling. I don't feel bad for killing the Seelie king because the bastard deserved it. Akin to a fetid, festering wound, his soul was poisoning everything in its path. But what followed is what wraps around my throat like an iron vise until terror saturates my lungs. The way I wanted to reach over and take…

Fuck.

I squeeze my eyes shut, but it doesn't help quench the brewing anxiety. Needing a distraction, I look to my right, where Thalia is curled up in a little ball — as if she's trying to keep the world away even in slumber. Malik spelled her ears to appear rounded until Rhett can take her to get a magically infused tattoo that resembles a birthmark so she can hide her true identity. He will also try to find her a good fae family after they arrive in New Orleans.

Sam is occupying the other side of the bed, a forearm thrown over her forehead while her breath wheezes through her parted lips. The bruise surrounding her eye is now a yellow-green. She vehemently refused to let Malik touch her, let alone use the magic he absorbed from her family's grimoire to heal her after he finished with everyone else.

We didn't want to leave Thalia alone tonight, so we chose to sleep together even though the beach house Kaiden rented is spacious enough. Because of Malik's tracking spell, we found a mountain road in only two hours. Luckily, someone driving a truck picked us up. We rode in the bed until we reached the nearest village. From there, it was easy to find a phone and for Kaiden to make lodging arrangements while his private jet flies toward us. The week we spent in Faerie accounted for a month here. It's the middle of August now, which means I have a little over four months to stop the prophecy.

Tomorrow we're heading back to Ashville, but I can't stay there. I can't put everyone I love or innocent lives in danger. Not because I'm hunted by demons, but because my newfound power terrifies me. I am the threat—the monster lurking beneath the shadows. Every second that passes tightens the noose around my throat.

What if I had taken their souls? The thought invades my mind. *What if I had killed everyone?*

Letting out a frustrated huff, I push up and almost break my neck as I narrowly avoid stepping on a gecko scurrying on the floor. I would laugh if the walls weren't closing in on me. When I reach the sliding glass door, I open it with trembling fingers and step outside. However, the salty breeze does nothing to calm my heaving chest.

I break into a run, and the sand turns to shards of glass beneath my soles, the palm trees nothing more than a green blur. I halt when my eyes land on Kaiden, who resembles a Greek god bathed in moonlight while emerging from the water in only a pair of swim trunks. He senses my presence and looks my way. Worry pinches his brows, but electricity sizzles in the air between us all the same. An inferno of longing replaces the anguish I'm crumbling under. This is what I need—a distraction. It doesn't have to mean anything. We can just use each other. At least, that's the lie I tell myself as I launch toward him.

He catches me, sliding his big hands beneath my ass cheeks while I hook my ankles around his back. Water laps at our joined hips. "Angel? Talk to me."

"I need you," I say, voice steeped in desperation.

"What happened?"

"No talking," I mumble, wrestling out of my T-shirt before balling it and throwing it back on the wet sand to press my naked chest to his. I get impossibly wet at the contact while his intoxicating smell, mixed with that of salt water, puts me in a dizzying spell.

"Fuck, you feel so good against me," he rumbles. "Tell me what my girl needs."

"I need you to fuck me," I breathe, my right hand coasting down to palm his growing erection while the left is already pulling at his wet strands.

His groan vibrates through me as he bends to suck my nipple into his greedy mouth. "Mmm. Slow? Hard?"

"Hard, please. I want to forget everything."

He straightens, searching my eyes with intensity. Fuck. He's looking at me again as if I'm the answer to all his prayers, and I don't want that. When he dips to press his lips to mine, I pull back.

"No kissing. This is nothing more than sex," I tell him.

The hurt rippling through his features wraps barbed wire around my lungs. Nostrils flaring, he clips out, "No." Then he drops me into the water unceremoniously and stalks out.

"Are you for fucking real right now? What do you mean, no?" I sputter in disbelief as I balance myself.

He turns to face me, his hands balled into tight fists at his side. "You really don't get it, do you? I don't just want your body, Iris. I want your heart. I want all of you like you have all of *me*."

"What happened to I will take everything you're willing to give me, huh?" I retort acidly.

"Well, I changed my mind," he bellows. "I won't let you reduce us to something so meaningless. You're everything to me. My North Star and my sun. My goddamn religion where I worship on my knees. Saying I love you is a blasphemy because it will never encompass what I truly feel for you. Those words are not enough and will never be."

I'm ripped in two. What I thought were carefully placed stitches over my heart fly at the seams, bleeding me dry. I'm not able to do anything but stare back at him as my lips part. It's too much. I can't fucking breathe. Steeling my spine, I stomp to where my now wet T-shirt is and pull it over my head.

But when I push past him, he stops me by circling my wrist. "I flayed myself open, and you're not going to say anything?" His voice comes out in a gravelly whisper.

I look over my shoulder at him. "You want my heart?" A brittle laugh slips free. My next words are sharper than a million razor blades, slashing my throat and tongue as I voice them. "Kaiden, you already held it in the palms of your hands, and you crushed it to smithereens. We've heard the prophecy, now I have nothing left to give you. You'll learn to come to terms with it. I'm sure you'll forget about me in no time."

He winces, but determination steels his jaw. "That's impossible. You're my forever."

My retort is bitter. "Haven't you heard? There's no such thing as forever anymore. The world is ending."

"Do you really think death can keep us apart? I will find you in every world, every universe, even if I have to crawl back to you. Now tell me the real reason you came running out of your room."

"Let me go," I mutter, but he only tightens his grip.

"Not until you tell me why you're acting like this."

"You want to know? Fine. I stripped King Orion's soul from his body. With half a thought. And there was a moment right after when I wanted to take more. There's an insatiable hunger inside me, and I'm afraid I won't be able to stop the next time." I expect to at least see a flicker of bewilderment on his face, but there's...nothing. I narrow my eyes. "Wait, why are you not surprised?" My face falls as it hits me. "The voice. It really was you, wasn't it? How did you speak in my mind?"

There's only silence.

This time, I put enough force into freeing my hand that I can fully face him. "Kaiden, I'm going to ask this again, and you better answer; how the fuck did you speak in my mind?"

His Adam's apple bobs on a hard swallow. "We're bonded."

"I don't understand. Bonded how?"

"Have you ever heard of fated mates? It's something...similar."

Shock waves ripple through me. "What? I thought those were stories—make-believe." My first instinct is to reject this as a possibility because it's too crazy to be true. I don't know much about fated mates. But if I truly look inward, his word choice—*bonded*—is exactly how I feel because there's this thread that perpetually pulls me to him. Hell, my subconscious already knew he was here on the beach. That's why I came running out of my room—I needed him. And there were so many moments when I was drowning in *his* emotions. "What does that even mean?"

"I can't tell you anything more than that."

"For how — ?" I suck in a jagged breath. "For how long have you known?"

"Since the bond snapped into place the first time we had sex."

I stumble back as if he stabbed me, and in all honesty, it would have hurt less. "God, Kaiden, do you even hear yourself? You profess your love to me one second, then I find yet another life-altering secret you kept from me in the next. It's never-ending, and I'm so fucking tired of getting whiplash."

"Do you think this is easy for me? That I want *this*? Every single second of every goddamn day, I'm crushed under the weight of my secrets. However, I'll take that over you being hurt because if something ever happens to you, I will never be able to forgive myself. You have no idea how much I wanted to tell you, but my answers will never be enough, and if I accidentally slip up and say something that triggers the wall — "

"So what, were you waiting for me to miraculously get my memories back? Was that it?"

"Fuck." He scrubs a hand over his face. "I don't know."

"Well, this doesn't change anything about us. Stay out of my life," I grit out, then storm off on laden legs. I don't look back, even though what is left of my hemorrhaging heart stays with him.

41

Iris

Sam: U hungry? Wanna grab dinner—my place?

Changed my mind.

I'll come by because demons are hunting your ass down, and your apartment has stronger wards.

Do you want sushi? I've been stuffing my face with only pizza since we got back.If I see another pepperoni slice, I swear I'm going to puke.

Sam: Can't come over after all. I'm buried in flower arrangements. I had to give Trish some time off since she managed the events and flower shop all by herself for a freakin' month. Ugh. I'm gonna be stuck here all night. 😫 Peel me off the shop's floor tomorrow morning? We can get donuts—my treat. 🍩

Sam: Did your phone fall into the toilet or smth? Why aren't you picking up? 😕

Sam: Dude, I've called like ten times. Hello?????

Sam: You better answer me, ho-bag. 😠

Sam: We need to come up with a plan to stop that prophecy.

Sam: Are you fucking kidding me, Iris? It's been three days. 😡😡😡

Sam: You do know I can see you're at home, right? 😒 You're still sharing your location with me.

Sam: You're lucky I'm so busy with the flower arrangements for this event, but Hecate help you when I have a little free time because I'm gonna hex your flat ass.

> **Sam:** Can you at least give me a sign, a smoke signal...something to let me know you're alive???

> **Me:** I'm alive. Just busy.

The text feels just as guilty as it sounds. I've been ignoring her for the past five days since we've been back. But just the thought of being alone with her spikes my anxiety through the roof. What if I somehow hurt her? Snatch her soul.

> **Sam:** Doing what exactly?
>
> Hiding?
>
> Planning something?
>
> You know you're not getting rid of me, right? I'm worse than scabies, bitch.

Heaving out a weighted sigh, I slide the phone into my back pocket without replying, yet again. I'll turn off the location sharing when I leave tomorrow. She's going to hate me when she realizes I left without a word. But it's better this way. Safer.

I massage my temples. Since coming back from Faerie, the migraines have increased in intensity by a hundredfold. There's a constant fiery throb in the back of my head.

On my bed lies a pile of clothes and the two remaining sets of hellseeker gear I had left in my closet. All I need is my weapons, toiletries, and I'm all set. I don't have a plan yet, but I need to get out of Ashville. Then I'll figure everything out. I don't know how long those bandages Malik slapped on the cracks in my mind barrier are going to hold, but I can't risk staying here any longer. Maybe in the absence of the crushing feeling that I'm a ticking time bomb, I will gain some clarity.

Sadly, my mother's journal is still at the compound. I left it there when I got Emily out. It cuts me deep that I can't take with me the only thing that belonged to her, but I can't show my face at the compound. I also can't ask my aunt to get it from my locker. I haven't yet read through the hundreds of messages from Noah and Aunt Josephine. Or called Grayson back. As far as they know, I suddenly disappeared for a month. I wonder if they think it's linked to the umbra demons or if I had something to do with Cain's or Erik's disappearance and fled like the little lightborn murderer I am. It's better they all think I vanished. If the Aureal Knights are looking for me to make an arrest, it gives me a head start.

However, I do have to sneak into my aunt's house before leaving. Those books in my grandmother's office, filled with medical jargon about fae, were a study into their anatomy. I ignored them at the time because I was looking for an oracle, but I have to go through them again and search for some clues about my mother and what they did to her. Maybe I can make sense of what I truly am and the full extent of my powers, especially how to control them. Unfortunately, when my grandparents died in that lab explosion, so did their research. But there's a safe in that room, hidden beneath a painting—my mother mentioned it in her journal. Maybe my grandmother kept some research documents inside. It's worth a shot, even though I have no idea what the combination is.

I kneel and bend forward, resting my weight on my elbows to pull out the suitcase from under the bed. Damn it. Why the fuck did I push it so far back? Huffing in frustration, I crawl until I reach the side handle, ass in the air. Something pulls taut beneath my solar plexus.

"Need a hand?" Hearing Kaiden's gravelly voice in my mind startles me, and I hit the top of my head on the bed frame.

Ow! Motherfucking fuck. I swallow the rest of the profanities as I scoot backward.

"Don't stop on my account. The view is fantastic," he drawls as I look at him over my shoulder. He's leaning on the doorframe, tattooed arms folded over his chest. Of course, that infuriating, sexy smirk is pulling at his full lips.

Why must I always make a fool of myself in Kaiden's presence? "What do you want?"

He arches an eyebrow after taking in the spread on my bed. "Going somewhere?"

"That's none of your concern," I snap.

As soon as I finish saying that, the sound of the front door slamming shut reverberates through the apartment, followed by Sam's angry voice. "I swear to Hecate, Iris Harper, I'm going to shove that fucking phone up your ass."

I scramble to gather all the clothes and shove everything in the closet before flinging shut the door. Kaiden's eyebrows draw, but thankfully, he says nothing as my best friend comes into view.

Wrath-filled emeralds land on Kaiden and she quips, "What the fuck are you doing here?" before shoving past him to stomp into my bedroom.

"Hello to you, too," Kaiden says, sarcasm dripping from his tone. "I popped in to let Iris know she's my date to a charity gala tomorrow."

I snort a surprised, unladylike laugh. "Yeah, sure. Dream on, buddy."

"Call me buddy one more time, angel. I dare you. But if you think I care that we have an audience, you're sorely mistaken. I'll bend you over my knee and have my belt bite into that perky ass faster than you can blink," he tells me through our mental bond.

Heat crawls on the back of my neck, blazing in my cheeks, which earns me a side-eye from Sam.

"There are rumors that Lucifer is back, and he's allowed passage topside to Belial—one of the nine kings of Hell," Kaiden says, out loud this time. "He's going to make his first appearance at the gala."

I scoff. "Why would a demon attend a charity event?"

"How come Lucifer is back? Wasn't he in hiding because of the uprisings? Did anything change?" Sam juts in.

"Because the most influential people in Ashville will be present," he answers me. "Belial is the king of fraud, opportunity, and lies. Think of him as the slimy politician, whose honeyed tongue traps flies before they can realize it was venomous all along. Lesser demons will consume your soul by possession, but Elite demons or kings of Hell don't dirty their hands. They will persuade you to sell it for a price. Besides, secrets are the highest form of currency in our world. You wouldn't believe what information people would sell their souls for." Kaiden turns his head toward Sam. "And I don't know what changed or why Lucifer is back."

"How did you get that information?" I ask.

"A demon working at Lucifer's palace sold it to me. He's been working for me for a few years now. He was also the one who let me know Adramelech would be at the succubus party."

Sam purses her lips. "What if it's a trap, and Belial asked to come topside just so he could get his hands on Iris?"

Kaiden hikes a shoulder. "If that's the case, then we kill him. However, I doubt Belial is the one behind the uprisings, since he has always been the most loyal to Lucifer. But you never know with demons. They all crave power above all else. It could have been a long ploy to overturn Lucifer."

"So what, we're going to off a king of Hell in the middle of dessert?" I chuckle out.

"We're not killing him unless we have to. But it's an opportunity to ask some questions. In Hell, you have to wait months to be granted the audience of a king. And even then, you can't expect demons, especially kings, to be straightforward with their answers. They're experts at manipulation and deceit. So, we'll trap him in the Seal of Solomon while we interrogate him, then Malik will erase his memory."

"Is this the same gala taking place at the mayor's house? The one raising money for human trafficking victims?" Sam chimes in.

Kaiden nods. "Yeah, that's right. How did you know?"

"They hired me to do their flower arrangements. I decided not to charge them when I heard about the cause, so they invited me. I can sneak into one of the rooms on the second floor tomorrow morning when my team is arranging everything in the ballroom and draw the seal. Then you could lure him there, and Malik could perform the spell to trap him."

"Sounds like a plan," Kaiden says, then gives me a roguish grin that steals my breath. "I'm picking you up at seven." He pops off before I get the chance to protest.

Sam sucks on her teeth as she turns toward me. "I don't know what the fuck has gotten into you since we came back from Faerie, but I'm not letting you pull a Noah on me. You're not allowed to ghost me."

God, I'm going to miss you so fucking much.

The hurt shining in her eyes blisters my insides. But I have to protect her.

Shit. I sound exactly like Kaiden. Is this how he feels whenever he can't share anything about my past? Maybe I've been too harsh because it's a horrible position to be put in. I feel like I'm being ripped in two.

"Uh-oh. What's that look?"

"What look?"

"You're looking at me funny."

I swallow through the lump in my throat. "I just love you."

"I love you too, ho-bag," Sam says before rummaging for something in her designer tote. She extends a book toward me. "Here, I came by to give you this. It's about fated mates. Grammie said you might find it useful."

"Thanks." I offer a tight-lipped smile and wrap my fingers around the spine.

"Of course. I gotta go. The traffic is brutal, and I have to prepare everything for tomorrow. I won't have time to doll you up, though, before the event. That mansion is ginormous. It's going to take us the whole day to put up the flower arrangements. I even think I will have to bring my dress and change there."

The relief her words bring me almost makes my knees buckle. "'Kay. No worries."

I step back when she approaches to pull me in a hug. Her eyebrows scrunch, then she huffs a "whatever" under her breath before storming off.

I spend the next two hours packing while cinder blocks pile on top of my chest because even though I know it's the right thing to do, leaving everything behind is proving far more difficult than I thought.

I just have to delay my departure for one day. Hopefully, tomorrow will bring some answers.

42

Iris

"You're breathtaking, angel." Kaiden's voice wraps around me in pure liquid silk. He's waiting in front of his Escalade, posture relaxed. I can't help but drink him in. The way that black suit molds to his tattooed body should be illegal.

"Thank you," I breathe, stopping in front of him. I didn't recognize myself when I looked in the mirror earlier. Retro Hollywood waves cascade down my back while my face is painted to perfection. Kaiden sent an entire team to my apartment: a makeup artist, a hair stylist, a nail tech, and a masseuse. I've never been more pampered in my entire life. The makeup artist paired a classy eyeliner with crimson lips—the exact shade of the floor-length silk dress I found waiting for me on top of my bed when I got out of the shower.

A gust of wind parts the generous side slit, giving Kaiden a full view of the three daggers I have strapped to my upper thigh. *"As devastatingly beautiful as you look in red, I think I prefer you in purple,"* he says through our mental link as he opens the passenger door for me to slide in. He rounds the car to settle behind the wheel, then glides into the evening traffic effortlessly.

What is he talking about?

Wait.

The lacy thong I wore to bed last night was a deep purple.

"Have you been watching me sleep again?" I sputter, then realize I spoke back to him in my head. This is so freakin' weird.

"Bold of you to assume I ever stopped. It's been the highlight of my day for years."

I open the window, letting the fresh air blast my face. Last night, I had another explosive sex dream. We were back at the succubus party, using one of the rooms. I came so hard I had to take a shower after.

"Don't worry, I fully enjoyed you moaning my name for hours on end," he rumbles as if reading my thoughts.

"I thought I told you to stay out of my life," I snap while pressing the button to close the window because I don't want to ruin my hair.

"And I thought we already established that's never going to happen," he counters. "I haven't forgotten about you packing a bag. I'll follow you to the depths of Hell and beyond if I have to."

I only huff in response, and we don't talk for the rest of the drive. He slows down when we enter a gravel road leading to a gargantuan two-story mansion on a sprawling estate bigger than the compound's. Soon, this place will be brimming with people—whose souls I could steal before drawing my next breath.

I take in the front façade, made of red bricks and punctuated by a limestone portico supported by Ionic columns. However, I'm distracted by the weird buzz beneath my skin that gets louder as we get closer. I recognize it as the same sensation I had in the cemetery because soon enough, my brain screams at me that there are two hundred seventy-eight dead people buried on this property.

Just my luck. They must have built this place over a burial ground or something.

After Kaiden stops the car in front of the stairs, the valet opens my door. But my legs have turned into cement blocks. When Kaiden hurries to round the car and extends a hand my way, I don't take it — not because I don't want to, but because I'm paralyzed at the thought that I might harm someone innocent. My pulse thunders in my ears while my vision goes fuzzy at the edges.

Kaiden, cradling my face in his big palms, snaps me out of it. I lean into his touch because it's the only thing grounding me while I capsize under waves of dread. Concern mars his forehead. "I won't let anyone hurt you."

My gaze crashes into the obsidian sea. I inhale a shuddering breath. *"I'm not worried about me. I'm worried about the danger I represent,"* I send him through our bond, barely above a whisper.

The moment my words land, his eyes soften. "Do you want to leave? Just say the word and we'll go."

I clear my throat as a car honks. Glancing over my shoulder, I realize there's a long line behind us. And Belial could be in that mansion. "No, it's okay. I'm okay. Let's go."

"You sure?" he insists.

"Yeah," I breathe. This time, when Kaiden offers me his hand, I take it.

We pass candles in tall glass cylinders and flower ornaments lining the ruby carpet flowing down the stairs. My high-heeled sandals make sharp *clicks* against the foyer's shiny marble floor. The sounds fade into classical music, the murmur of overlapping conversations, and laughter spilling from the open ballroom in front of us. The white floral arch where guests are lined up to take photos blends perfectly with the elegance of the vaulted ceiling and the embellished high walls. I make a mental note to let Sam know she's incredible. Not like she isn't aware, but my admiration for my best friend's talent knows no bounds.

When Kaiden pulls me toward the arch, I hiss, "What are you doing?"

"I want a reminder of having the most gorgeous woman on my arm."

I roll my eyes at his cheesiness. *"You know this is not a date, right?"* I scoff. *"I'm here because we need to trap Belial."*

"Doesn't matter. It's still one of the best nights of my life." He wraps his hand around my middle to pull me closer for the photo.

We stride into the ballroom. I let my gaze sweep over the mass of people and servers balancing trays of canapés and sparkling glasses of champagne to search for Sam and Malik. The warlock is engaged in a conversation with about five people across the dance floor, near the open French doors leading to the garden. When he notices us, he lifts his chin before excusing himself to amble toward us.

Malik beams at me. "Whoa, sweets. You clean up good."

"It's a far cry from Faerie, huh? You look pretty good yourself," I say, reciprocating the smile, and I mean it. The deep navy suit hugging his slender yet muscular frame enhances the speckles of blue in his hazel eyes, while his lively silver hair is tied at the nape.

"Any sign of Belial?" Kaiden asks him.

Malik isn't paying attention, though, because he's busy staring—mouth agape—at a sashaying Sam on her way to us. Men and women's heads equally snap in her direction. For good reason, because my best friend is the embodiment of a goddess in a halter-style olive dress that has an open back and a slit to match mine.

Malik's throat bobs on a hard swallow when she steps next to me. "Damn, freckles, you're...that dress...I mean..."

She gives him an unimpressed once-over. "Are you having a stroke?"

Ouch.

371

"I think he means you look incredible," I chime in because I feel bad for him. "Not only that, but you overdid yourself with the flower arrangements."

She winks at me. "I know. So, did the king make an appearance yet?"

"I don't think so. My onyx choker would have alerted me by now," I reply.

Sam lowers her voice as she tells us, "I drew the Sigil beneath a rug in the office on the second floor. It's the third door on the right." She opens her clutch, fishes something out, then passes Kaiden a key. "Here, I snagged it earlier."

"Thanks," he says before sliding it into his breast pocket.

"What now?" Sam inquires.

I pop a shoulder. "I guess we just have to wait."

"Would you like something to drink?" Malik asks.

"Yes, please, a glass of white wine," I say.

"Rum. Neat," Kaiden adds.

Sam flicks her piercing emeralds to me. "Can you please text me when Belial shows his face? I have to get back to my date."

My eyebrows raise. Sam never dates. "Um, sure. You brought someone?"

"Not really, but I met this guy here. He's got a panty-dropping smile, and I bet he's a beast in bed."

I don't miss the way Malik's hands ball into tight fists at his sides. "I'll fetch our drinks," he grits out as he stalks toward the bar, spine stiffer than a steel rod.

"See you later," Sam tells me before disappearing through the double French doors at the back.

It doesn't take long until Malik follows her.

"Guess no drinks for us," I say on a chuckle. The dreamy notes of a new melody played by the classical orchestra bounce off the walls. They not only pull at my heartstrings but also move through me like an earthquake. There's *something* about this song. I'm not sure how I know this, but it's a rendition of "Love" by Lana del Rey. I blink, and for a fraction of a second, I'm transported somewhere else.

"Will you save your first kiss for me?"

"I'll save you all my kisses, angel."

It's as if a ghost from the past whispered the words in my ear. Is this a memory? I hold on to it with desperate hands. But it's as though I'm trying to grasp air — as soon as I have it within my reach, it slips right through my fingers. The bitter pang of disappointment tastes acidic in my mouth.

"Dance with me, angel," Kaiden rasps, bringing me back into the present.

The equal parts vulnerability and yearning in his voice thaw what's left of the ice wall I'm trying — but failing — to keep between us. One last dance can't hurt, right? I'm leaving tomorrow, after all. However, the distance between us won't matter because our souls are entwined for all eternity… if the things I've read so far in the book Sam brought over are true.

I offer a nod.

He leads me to the dance floor while splaying a hand on my lower back. Kaiden presses our bodies close before swaying to the slow song under the massive, tiered crystal chandelier. Warmth pools between my legs at the electric contact. I can't help but compare this moment with the one we shared at the succubus party — when he kissed me for the first time. In his steadfast arms, everything fades: the murmured conversations, the clinking of glasses, and the raucous laughter. We are the only two people in the universe.

"I think I remembered something…about us," I whisper, then repeat the words, "Will you save your first kiss for me?"

Kaiden sucks in an unsteady breath. His steps falter. We stop moving, but I don't care. The obsidian sea of his irises turns into liquid fire and his voice is a thick timbre as he replies, "I'll save you all my kisses, angel."

He dips.

One heartbeat passes.

But before his lips can meet mine, someone snaps from behind, "Get your dirty hands off her!"

Not someone — Noah.

43

Iris

I turn. Before Noah can grab me, Kaiden's fist meets his jaw in a vicious uppercut that sends him skidding back. Gasps resound around us. Who the hell would have thought this was the same charity gala Noah had invited me to? I mean, what were the chances? He never mentioned a date or the cause they were raising money for.

"You're lucky there are so many people here. Mark my words, demon, this is not over," Noah spews, wiping off the blood trickling down his chin from his split lip. "Iris, come here. That's Kaiden Black you're so cozy with—the head of the fucking Obsidian Conclave." Vitriol laces his words as he cuts a death stare toward Kaiden. His hate is more than the usual lightborn repugnance toward demons. It goes further than loathing or abhorrence.

I scoff. Who the fuck does he think he is to order me like that? I'm not his lapdog. "I'm not coming anywhere near you."

"You heard her. Fuck off before you make an even bigger fool of yourself," Kaiden clips out in a glacier tone.

There's newfound scrutiny in Noah's mercurial gaze as it jumps from me to Kaiden. His mouth opens. Closes. Undisguised rage contorts the planes of his face when realization dawns. He shakes his head in disbelief. "You—you know each other. Are you fucking kidding me?" A manic laugh belts out of him. "This is him, right, the Kaiden from that voice message? He's also the one who was watching you in that video. I was sick with worry because you disappeared for a month. A. Month. I've been looking everywhere for you. I'm so stupid. How did I not see this? You whored yourself to a fucking Elite demon? You ruined everything, you dumb bitch." The words are venomous.

And just like that, the mask he's been wearing since he came back is off. This is the *real* Noah.

His true colors remind me that I don't have to be worried about being seen in public, by the Order, on Kaiden's arm. Because I'm not one of them, and they can't control me anymore.

Kaiden's fury flows through me with the scorching power of a thousand suns. "Watch your fucking mouth," he growls. The lights flicker for a fraction of a second.

Considering we've become the center of attention, I place a hand on his chest to stop him from charging at Noah. Suddenly, it's hard to breathe—as if something is sucking out all the oxygen around us. The onyx stone is a hot poker against my skin. "Something is wro—"

Noah cuts me off. "Or what? What are you going to do, demon? Kill me like you killed—"

"What is that?" a woman screams.

We jerk our heads collectively to look behind Noah. There's a jagged, onyx line cutting through the air, right in the middle of the dance floor. It expands at the speed of light, transforming into an abysmal hole.

Kaiden swears sharply under his breath. "A Hell portal."

"Sam and Malik. We need to warn them," I say, then shout, "Everybody, RUN!"

Kaiden clasps my hand in his big one. We dash toward the French doors, Noah hot on our heels, then fly down the marble steps and take one of the pebbled paths that lead into the sprawling garden.

A blood-curdling shriek slices through the air.

"What is happening?" Sam asks, out of breath, while sprinting toward us. Malik is close behind.

Glass explodes.

Over fifty draconic ravengers crash through the windows to reach us.

They pound over the gravel, their horned heads and leathery reptilian skin on bodies that look like a cross between a hellhound and a panther, muscular limbs and deadly claws. The ground shakes under their stomping, as if we're in the middle of an earthquake. I unsheathe the three daggers strapped to my thigh, darting to take a defensive stance in front of Sam. But Malik has already beaten me to it.

Power detonates from Kaiden.

Hellfire engulfs the demons. They crumble to ashes before I can blink. The disgusting smell of charred sulfurous meat spreads like a deadly mist that burns holes in my nose and brain. Shrieking men and women spill from the open doors and bolt toward the parking lot. Some even leap through the shattered windows to escape what I presume are more demons. I can't be sure because an inky haze has taken over the ballroom. However, in the next second, we catch glimpses of draconic ravengers and voidstalkers feasting on human flesh while ghouls suck their souls out of their twitching bodies, which are lying in pools of blood.

"Holy Hecate!" Sam mutters under her breath, then gags.

"C'mon, we have to go!" Kaiden tells me as he grabs my hand and pulls.

I dig my heels in. "What?!? No! We can't let those demons get into the city. Who knows how many more will come through the portal? And we need to save these people. Give them a chance to flee."

A muscle jumps in his granite jaw. "I don't give a flying fuck about them. Your safety is my only concern."

"Well, I do. You can go if you want, but I'm staying," I retort as I throw off my high-heeled sandals.

Kaiden sucks on his teeth. "Fine," he snaps, popping off.

Shit. I didn't think he would actually leave.

I whirl toward a slack-jawed Noah. Kaiden's disappearance must have rattled him. "Call this in to the Order."

He levels me with a stony glare.

"Seriously? Can you push your fucking ego aside until we make it out?" I bark.

He puffs out a breath through flared nostrils but nods, fishing out his phone from his suit jacket. I almost jump out of my skin when Kaiden materializes back, holding a few of the weapons I already packed. I take the whip and sword from his outstretched hand. Then, surprisingly, he throws my spare sword to Noah. He catches it in mid-air while giving Grayson a quick rundown of the situation.

It takes me a few seconds to remember that demons, Elite or not, shouldn't be able to touch blessed weapons. I shove this information in a corner of my mind to pull out later.

"What did Grayson say?" I ask Noah.

"Thirty minutes," he responds.

"All right. We just need to hold the demons back until the hellseekers get here."

Kaiden flicks his gaze to Malik. "Can you shut down the portal?"

"I don't know. I would need to get close to it."

"Then we'll clear a path for you," I say. Sheathing back the daggers, I tilt my chin in Sam's direction. "We need to find your car first."

"What? Why?"

"Because you're leaving."

She huffs. "No, I'm not. I'm staying to help."

"In a demon fight? Are you crazy?"

"I can hold my own. I'm a witch, remember?" She punctuates her words by waving a hand when two voidstalkers rush at us, all snapping teeth and gaping maws. A huge Venus flytrap sprouts from the ground. It swallows them whole. "See?"

"Okay. But don't you dare leave my side," I grit out. We don't have time to argue, and Sam's as stubborn as a mule. "Let's—"

Souldrakes—too many to count—fly at us at warp speed from all available exits.

Fuck.

"Kaiden!" Malik bellows.

Kaiden hesitates for exactly two heartbeats, then declares "On it."

The ground starts shaking again. Clouds roll in. Burnished gold floods Kaiden's crimson irises while his black-as-night scleras turn white. Obsidian wings explode from his back. He launches into the sky with swift flaps to meet the spiked, vulture-like demons. When he lifts his hands, bolts of blinding light strike down in a downpour over the horde. The souldrakes screech as they burst into blueish, almost transparent flames that are too bright to watch.

Is that *illum*?

I'm equally as dumbstruck as Noah and Sam while gawking at the unfolding scene. Given the color of his blood and how the national park looked in the aftermath of the umbra attack, I should have expected this, but it seemed impossible an Elite demon could wield divine light. It's unheard of. I *knew* I saw his wings that night he saved me, but the excruciating pain had me thinking it was nothing more than a hallucination. He must have angel blood. There's no other explanation.

The outside wall of the mansion collapses under Kaiden's power. A thick plume of dust joins the blanket of ashes akin to sooty snow flurries that start falling from the sky. If I thought hellfire was destructive, the *illum* is that times infinity. It pulverizes the crimson-winged creatures in milliseconds.

Fuck me. He's spectacular.

But no matter how many souldrakes Kaiden kills, others replace them in the blink of an eye. They keep coming. And coming. Ravengers and voidstalkers soon join them on the ground, charging at us.

"Heads up! Kaiden can't strike down here because he'll incinerate us," Malik bellows over the shrill cries. He opens his palms wide to send a blast of dark magic that takes the form of a giant, atramentous boomerang. More than half of their beastly heads fall.

Sam glows a bright green from beside me. A hedge wall shoots up at the flick of her fingers. The remaining demons tear through it one by one. Still, it served its purpose of slowing their momentum. My head swivels from Sam to the incoming beasts. I feel as though I'm trapped between a rock and a hard place because I don't want to leave her side, but I can't let the demons get closer, either.

"I got her," Malik tells me, stepping in front of Sam.

I nod. Noah and I throw ourselves into the fray, our moves mirroring each other's as if we're dancing to the same tune.

"I don't need your protection," she snaps at him as she shackles ten voidstalkers with stocky vines that are full of thorns.

"You're using a lot of power. How much longer until you run out?" I ask Kaiden through our mental link as I whirl on the balls of my feet to slice the horned head of the ravenger I trapped in my whip.

"Worried about me, angel?"

I careen to the side, avoiding the spray of ichor, then trace a wide arc to decapitate another. *"Answer the damn question!"*

"To your right!" Kaiden booms, voice steeped in panic.

I feint just in time to dodge a voidstalker's poisonous scorpion tail aimed at my chest. Its hideous heads, made of two gaping maws lined by razor-sharp teeth, smack the ground after I thrust my blade through the beast's necks. *"Thanks,"* I shoot back.

"Concentrate on the fight!" He pushes me out of our connection.

"How much longer until Kaiden runs out of power?" I yell at Malik, since I didn't get an answer from Kaiden.

"I'm not sure. But he's probably going to burn out soon," he answers.

Shit.

Even though we keep fighting with everything we've got, we've barely made a dent in their numbers. They obliterated every wall Sam put up while pushing us back. We're almost at the maze's entrance. I can't help but notice how differently these demons act compared to the ones that came for me the night Adrianna died. Sweat plasters my dress to my body as I slash and maim. I chance a glance up. Kaiden's strikes have become less and less frequent, but there's only a handful of souldrakes left. Hurried footfalls resound. Hellseekers have joined the fight. Thank God.

My relief is short-lived, though, because a sulking figure stalks out of the mansion.

Adramelech.

One hand's holding a crossbow, the other a chain. He points the crossbow skyward.

Nononononononononononononono.

"KAIDEN! DUCK!" I shout through our mental link.

He veers to the side. Too late. The arrow pierces his right wing. Adramelech shoots another. It impales the left wing. Kaiden yells, then starts freefalling.

My heart stops.

Time slows to a crawl.

I forge ahead, tapping into every ounce of speed I possess to get to him. In the next second, though, white-hot pain obliterates my nerve endings, making me double over—not mine, but Kaiden's. He crashes to the ground. Abject terror drags its icy claw down the ladder of my spine.

"KAIDEN!"

Nothing.

I try again and again.

There's only silence.

"Malik! Do something!" I scream.

"I fucking can't. I'm almost tapped out."

Adramelech wraps the chain around Kaiden's wrists and pulls him back toward the mansion. I demand the darkness inside me to take over and save him as I slash through the throng of demons. But I only hit a wall. At the same time, though, the buzz beneath my skin intensifies to a roar. Sound warps and muddles. On instinct, I hit my knees, then answer the call from beneath by slapping my palms against the grass. As if I'm a ghost magnet, orbs of light slam into me. I push the newfound energy into the earth in pulsing waves.

The ground trembles. Almost three hundred dead bodies claw their way out of the ichor-stained soil. They jump the demons, their efforts unrelenting while clearing a path for me. Not wasting a second, I bolt.

The edges of the portal shrink at the speed of light as Adramelech hauls an unconscious Kaiden through the void.

"Iris! NO!"

I ignore Sam's desperate plea. Copper coats my tongue, and broken glass impales my bare feet as they slap the marble floor of the ballroom. But I don't care. I push my screaming muscles further than I ever have.

Then jump.

I cannot express enough gratitude for every single reader who took a chance on my book.

Everything I write is for you.

If you enjoyed the story, please consider leaving a review on
↓ Amazon   *and*   Goodreads ↓

If you haven't already read "Fated Hearts", the Echoes of Darkness Prequel — Ava and Logan's story — you can find it here:

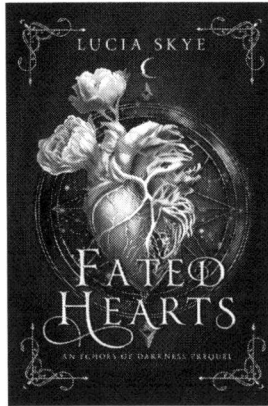

Ava

Waking up in the hospital with a harrowing diagnosis is a hard pill to swallow.

But it also opens my eyes to the truth.

Law school was never my dream. It was my mother's.

I've been living like a bird locked in a cage, and the bars are closing in on me, crushing me under

their weight.

I'm done letting others dictate my life.

The thing is…trying to cram a lifetime of experiences in a few months can lead you on a t

reacherous path.

I let myself live. But at what cost?

Looking back, it was all worth it because it led me to him.

Logan

Reality is overrated.

Especially when my fated mate's wolf appears in my dreams, and shouldering my Alpha

responsibilities becomes harder by the day.

And you know what they say about fate…

It's not only fickle. It also loves irony.

My life takes an unexpected turn when my eyes land on her.

A human.

She pollutes my mind. My dreams. My whole being.

I know I should stay away from Ava. My pack would never accept a human.

The question is, will I be able to resist temptation?

THANK YOU!

For some reason, I would rather write another book than have to write a blurb or a thank-you note. But here it goes.

What I will say is that writing this book wasn't easy. Not only due to the fact that I set a strict deadline to finish it—insert facepalm because I realized that I, in fact, don't work well under pressure—but also because I scattered jagged pieces of myself, and bled my feelings...my insecurities all over these pages.

I struggled with depression my whole life, and diving into those murky depths alongside Iris and Kaiden forced me to face the shadowy corners of my mind. To lock myself inside that cage and stare back at the reflection of all my ugly demons. Luckily, Iris was also there to lend me her sword. And while I haven't slain all my demons—I'm not sure I ever will—facing these parts of myself, even if it left me raw, it was also cathartic in a way.

I hope that joining Iris on this wild ride has offered you an escape. And if you are struggling, please don't forget that you are not alone. This world needs you—your glow. Don't be afraid to reach out. You can call or text 988 in the US and Canada for free, 24/7 confidential support from the Suicide & Crisis Lifeline. In the UK, you can contact Samaritans at 116 123 or email jo@samaritans.org.

Ayden, thank you for sticking with me and my characters from the very beginning! Your developmental commentary and line edits were invaluable.

To my amazing Beta readers, Becci, Kirsten, Arianna R., and Nicole, thank you for being willing to read my story in its early stages. I appreciate you more than you know.

And to my lovely ARC readers, your love and support means the world! A special mention of some special girlies: Karina, Hannah, Arianna L-C., Kim, JenJo, Sylvana, Ariel, Amanda (Hopmomma), Lindsey, Kelsey, Sara, Cassandra, and Ash.

And last but not least, Mel, you did an outstanding job proofreading this book.

About the author

Lucia Skye

Lover of beautifully written words, strong heroines, anti-heroes, steamy romance, and swoon-worthy, broody MMCs, Lucia spends most of her free time, you guessed it…reading. Or better said, devouring books until the early hours of the morning because the main characters *finally* kissed after an agonizing slow burn, and she needs to know what happens next.

When she's not glued to her laptop, writing, drawing character art for her stories while listening to true crime podcasts, or daydreaming about falling through a magical portal in a mystical realm, you can find Lucia on the couch with her two fur babies, watching *House of the Dragon*.

http://linktr.ee/LuciaSkye.Author

Find her on socials

Printed in Dunstable, United Kingdom

71350025R00224